# THE TEMPLARS QUEST TRILOGY

# THE LOST ARK

## BOOKS ONE – THREE
### OF THE TEMPLARS QUEST CHRONICLES
*A JACK GUNN ADVENTURE*

## Thomas H. Ward

THE TEMPLARS QUEST TRILOGY

THE LOST ARK

BOOKS 1-3 OF THE TEMPLARS QUEST CHRONICLES:

GHOST KILLER

THE ANCIENTS

LUCEM SANCTAM

ISBN-10: 0-9987576-8-3
ISBN-13: 978-0-9987576-8-1

Transcendent Publishing
PO Box 66202
St. Pete Beach, FL 33736
www.transcendentpublishing.com

Printed in the United States of America

# OTHER EXCITING BOOKS BY THOMAS H. WARD

# Follow Me On Facebook:

www.facebook.com/thomas.ward.71271466

There are two ways you can receive my next book for FREE:

1. **Email me at:**
   THOMASHWARDBOOKS@GMAIL.COM
   with your comments or suggestions and receive my next Kindle book in PDF FREE. Only notices about my new books or book giveaways will be sent to you. Your email address will be kept confidential.

2. **Answer the following questions:**
   How many men did Jack Gunn actually terminate by himself in The Finger Collector? How many fingers were actually collected? Email me the correct answers to both questions and receive my next book FREE in PDF.

If there is a certain book you would prefer to receive just let me know. I value your feedback and comments. Thank you for reading my stories.

*"In every truth there is non-truth;
in every fiction there is non-fiction."*

—Thomas H. Ward

# CONTENTS

# TEMPLARS QUEST
# GHOST KILLER

## BOOK ONE
### THE TEMPLARS QUEST CHRONICLES

# INTRODUCTION

Over the past two years we have been in continuous battles to protect our way of life on Tocabaga. We are living in a utopia compared to other poor souls who weren't so lucky. Maybe they didn't plan for the collapse like we did, or maybe they wanted the government to take care of them.

We dare not venture too far from Tocabaga because it's a mean cruel world out there. The furthest we have ever traveled is about 120 miles north of here, on a hunting trip to Bushnell countryside. That's where we met the Knights Templar for the first time. We had no idea that the Knights Templar still existed. I'll never forget the date because things changed forever after that day. It was August 3, 2025.

This is a strange story, but true. My small group of hunters happened to come upon the Knights Templar, at four in the morning, who were camped on the side of the road. An old man came up to me and asked if we could spare any food. I didn't know it at the time, but he was Jack de Molay, the Grand Master of the old Knights Templar.

We had never met before, but somehow he knew my name. Jack de Molay told me this bizarre story that God had sent me to protect his grandchildren, Adam and Emma. It was strange because my loyal guard dog, Adolf, was friendly to them and usually he does not take to strangers.

Old man Jack asked me to take care of the kids until they were older. He wanted them to have, as he called it, a more or less normal life. Jack went to rest in his car, telling me he would advise more details later, after a short nap.

Unfortunately he passed away in his sleep with my dog sitting next to him, who let out a howl noting his departure from this earth. We buried him on the roadside and the children ended up coming with me to Tocabaga, because according to Jack, it was God's will.

I had no choice but to follow his wish, and adopted twelve-year-old Adam and nine-year-old Emma. I'm a pushover when it comes to taking care of kids. I have already adopted six children. I took them off the streets of death and brought them to live with my family where they could grow up without fear. They would grow up like normal children with a caring family, and a community to help guide them. They'd never be hungry again. Without children there is no future for Tocabaga, or for the United States to survive.

Young Adam de Molay has now become the Grand Master of the modern Templar Warriors. A new adventure is beginning. We are preparing to proceed on the Templars Quest.

I can't explain it, but I was compelled, or for lack of

a better word, commanded to take up this journey, by a higher power.

My name is Jack Gunn and these are my chronicles.

The year is 2026 and we have survived over two years living on Tocabaga Island since the collapse of the government. I live here with my entire family. The real name of this island will not be disclosed, nor the location. Tocabaga is a clue as to our general location. It is a sanctuary where one can be safe from what is going on in the outside world. If you happen to come here, are of good character, and believe in Constitution, you are welcome to stay. The current population is 556 people. We help each other stay alive.

I was elected Vice President and Director of Security on Tocabaga because no one else wanted the job, or maybe because I have the most experience in security matters. I won't hesitate to terminate anyone who is a threat to our community.

I am the oldest of three Brothers. We grew up fighting bullies and gang members in a tough neighborhood in south Chicago. My Dad, one of the most honest men I have known, always stressed tell the truth, and help each other. Never ever be a bully, never steal, and try to protect those who cannot protect themselves. I have always stood up for the people who could not defend themselves. I hate liars and bullies.

Standing 6 feet tall at 180 pounds, I'm in great shape for my age and my body is honed by years of physical training. I keep in shape by lifting weights almost every day and running three miles, four times a week. I shave my head two times a week as it is cooler with no hair in the hot south. I sport a gray mustache and goatee that I keep well-trimmed and short. There is a two-inch scar on my forehead from a knife fight years ago.

I spent four years in the Army as a Military Policeman, and became an expert in the use of handguns, rifles, shotguns, and in hand-to-hand combat. My legs have skin grafts from burns due to an explosion when I worked for the DOD (Department of Defense) doing security work for seven years. I always carry my Glock 17, and Black Bear Cold Steel fighting knife, no matter where I go.

I love our country, freedom, my family, and friends. If anyone messes with my family, or friends, justice will be swift and painful. I have no use for anyone who breaks the law, cheats or steals. For the most part I follow the Ten Commandments, but also believe in The Code of Hammurabi, which is an eye for an eye. I fight to keep our Bill of Rights under the United States Constitution.

Now, I am fighting alongside the Templar Warriors to find the lost treasure. We are following the clues of a holy relic named the 'Sword of Jerusalem.' The Ark of the Covenant, designed by God, and made by man, is one of the holy items we are seeking. Whoever finds the treasure could very well control the destiny of the United States.

# REMENISCING

I'll never forget what happened on September 14, 2025. That's the day that Adam de Molay became the Grand Master of the new Templar Warriors. It's the day that either Adam, God, or an Angel killed Adam's uncle, Christian de Molay, using the Sword of Jerusalem. It was the weirdest and most supernatural event I have ever witnessed.

Adam de Molay is a descendent of a long line of Templar Knights. His bloodline dates back to Jacques de Molay, who was the last Grand Master of the Knights Templar. Rumor has it that Jacques hid the treasure taken from Jerusalem. In 1314 the King of France had him burned at the stake for not revealing where the treasure was hidden. The King coveted the long lost Templars Treasure and searched for it in vain, all over Europe.

As I was making final preparations for our long trip to search for the holy treasure, I thought back to that day. This is an account of what happened.

*On September 13, 2025, a man named Christian de*

*Molay showed up, out of nowhere, at our gate which secures the entrance to the Tocabaga Bridge. There was an entourage of twenty four men with him and they were well armed. He wanted custody of Adam and Emma claiming to be their uncle. If he was their uncle then he was entitled to lawful custody. However, he also wanted the Sword of Jerusalem.*

*After discussions with Adam, I believed Christian was a dangerous person who would do harm to Adam and use the holy sword to his advantage. I made a plan with my men, to terminate Christian the next day, if he wouldn't listen to reason.*

*Since Adam and Emma didn't really know their uncle, and had only seen a picture of him, he was a stranger. Both children wanted to stay with my family as their real grandfather had wanted them to do.*

*The next morning, September 14, 2025, I sat in the kitchen thinking about my plan to negotiate with Christian, or to terminate him, when Adam walked in and gave me a hug. "Grandpa, I don't want you to get killed protecting me."*

*"Adam, don't worry, I'm not gonna get killed. You're part of my family. On Tocabaga we're all family. The one thing I do know is how to protect my family. Besides, I think God is on our side."*

*"More than you may think, Grandpa."*

*My radio hissed. "Jack, you better come down to the gate. Christian de Molay is demanding to talk to you and Adam."*

*I checked my watch; it was only 10:30 am. "Ok, I'll be right there."*

Adam said, "Don't go."

I replied, "You stay here with Adolf, and I'll go talk to him." I left the dog with Adam so it wouldn't be a distraction during a possible gun battle.

Twenty minutes later, taking my time, I approached the fence. Christian yelled, "Where the hell is Adam?"

Peering through the wire mesh I said, "Calm down. Adam just woke up."

He grabbed the fence and shook it. "I told you, I'm not leaving here without Adam. We have to leave today!"

"It's not that easy. Adam and Emma don't wanna leave here. We discussed it last night."

"Bring Adam here, right now! I wanna talk to him."

Looking directly into his eyes, I softly told him, "My friend, that's not gonna happen."

Christian let out a yell and shook the fence like a mad man. Now I knew he was just another bully trying to get his way through intimidation.

"Jack, I'm warning you! I'll release fire and brimstone on you."

"Is that a threat?" I calmly asked, as I pulled out a smoke.

"It's a promise. If you don't bring Adam here in 15 minutes then we're going to have trouble."

"Look, I'm trying to reason with you. Your father wanted it this way. According to him, so did God. Besides, the kids are safe here."

Christian replied, "Here's what I suggest. You keep

*Emma, and Adam comes with me. Does that sound fair?"*

*I laughed in his face. "Christian, I know what you want. So cut the bullshit. If you think I'd let Adam and the sword go with you then you're crazy."*

*Christian grabbed the fence again and shook it like a crazed gorilla. "You're really pissing me off, Jack! If I get my hands on you, you're dead meat. Open the damn gate! Come out and fight me like a man. No weapons, just good old hand-to-hand combat."*

*Blowing a white cloud of smoke in his face, he backed away from the fence and coughed. I asked, "Why in the hell should I fight you?"*

*"You're a coward, a chicken shit. You know I could beat your ass."*

*"You just don't get it. This isn't about you and me. It's about the kids and perhaps the future of mankind."*

*Christian's men were gathering behind him. They had their weapons in low ready position. They could kill me and maybe some of my men before they died.*

*I was trying to buy some time until my men were all in position, at noon, to spring my trap. It was only 11:20 so I had to stall him as long as possible.*

*Christian asked, "What do you mean the future of mankind?"*

*"The way I see it, if you get hold of the treasure, then the future of mankind is at risk."*

*"How do you know about the treasure?"*

*"Adam told me everything, including the fact that you tried to steal the sword and kill your brother. That's*

*why you were outcast from the Knights Templar."*

*"That's a damn lie! He was killed by someone during a home break-in."*

*One of his men walked up and asked Christian, "Is that true?"*

*"Yeah, he was killed when someone broke into his house, so shut the hell up."*

*I replied to the solider, "That's not what Adam told me. Christian tried to steal the sword."*

*I heard a commotion behind me and turned to see Adam walking towards us wearing a white mantle with the crimson cross on it. The Sword of Jerusalem was strapped on his waist.*

*I asked Adam, "What are you doing?" He looked at me but didn't reply.*

*Adam walked up to the fence peering at Christian. "I'll give you the sword under the condition that Emma and I stay here."*

*Big Christian thought about it for a minute. "It's a deal, if you tell me what the sword says."*

*"Ok, I agree." Adam replied.*

*I said, "Adam, wait don't agree to that."*

*"I have to. Please open the gate."*

*I hesitated but nodded ok. Slowly I unlocked the gate and pushed it open. Adam stepped outside with me by his side. I flicked the safety off my M4 as we walked out into the danger zone. I was prepared to kill Christian on the spot.*

*Adam walked by Christian and stepped up onto a foot high rock next to him. Christian and his men were* watching his every move. Gazing at the Templar Warriors, he shouted in a firm voice, "My name is Adam de Molay! I'm the rightful heir to be the next Grand Master!"

In one swift movement, he pulled the sword out of its scabbard, kissed the golden handle, and pointed it at the sky. Holding the blade high in the air, Adam shouted, "This is the Sword of Jerusalem! It holds the secrets to God's Treasure!"

The blade was glowing in the bright sun. It reflected the sunlight like a mirror. Christian's soldiers all dropped to one knee. One warrior shouted, "Praise God!" They all repeated the words in unison and bowed their heads.

Christian saw his men all drop to one knee and so did he, right in front of Adam, a couple of feet away. With Christian's head slightly bowed I saw the sword reflect the sunlight over him.

Quickly and unexpectedly the sword flashed a white blinding light as if it was hit by a lightning bolt. A strong gust of wind blew up at the same time. The odd thing was, there was no noise. It was dead silent. I had to glance away and close my eyes from the intense flash of light. It was so strong; I could only see white spots for a second or two as I was blinded by the brilliant flash.

Opening my eyes, I looked up at Adam holding the sword high in the air. Blood was running down the blade. I realized what had just happened when I noticed Christian's head on the ground. His body, slumped over, was pumping blood out of his open neck.

Adam was still pointing the sword at the sky as

*crimson red ran down the shimmering blade, and he said, "Glory to God in the highest."*

*The soldiers keenly looked at Adam and all repeated, "Glory to God." Then they all stood and bowed to him.*

*I wondered what just happened. Was that an act of God? Did God move Adam's arm to behead Christian? Was God actually using the sword to protect his treasure? Did Adam plan this all along? Supernatural forces were at work for sure.*

*Adam kissed the handle, wiped the blood off on his white robe, and sheathed the blade. As Adam stepped down from the rock, he slumped to the ground. I jumped to help him back on his feet. He looked dazed and confused.*

*I kept an eye on Christian's men, not knowing what they would do. Then one man stepped forward towards Adam. Swiftly, I pointed my M4 at him.*

*Holding his hands up he stopped and said, "Have no fear. My name is Captain George Baldwin, leader of these new Templar Warriors. We're at your command, Adam de Molay. You have just proven that you're the real Grand Master. The law states: 'Whoever controls the sword shall be the Grand Master.' We vow to follow your orders."*

*The warriors were dressed in all black, SWAT type, combat gear. Baldwin himself was a compelling figure; standing at a little over six feet tall. You could tell he was in the best of shape by the way he moved and stood. One thing made him stand out which was an ugly scare that ran down the entire length of his left cheek.*

*Now I knew things would never be the same. Adam had become Grand Master by the Power of the Sword. Now he had his own warriors to do God's work.*

*Adam said, "Thank you Captain Baldwin. I'll need your help and support."*

*I stepped up and shook Baldwin's hand. "I'm Jack Gunn, Director of Security for Tocabaga."*

*"It's a pleasure to meet you," George replied.*

*I said, "Since Adam is under my protection, I need to know your intentions."*

*"I understand your concern. We're Templar Warriors who do God's work. It was clear to us that God terminated Christian by working his will through Adam. There is no doubt that Adam has the Power of the Sword and God is on his side.*

*"As for my men, we were all once Marines before becoming enlightened by God. Most of us saw combat in the middle-east fighting ISIS. After that we decided to do the Lord's work and became his warriors."*

*Knowing that Captain Baldwin was the commander of twenty-three combat hardened retired Marines made me feel more at ease.*

*"Captain, Jack Gunn is my guardian, and you will receive your orders from him and me," Adam advised.*

*Baldwin nodded his head. "I understand."*

*Tommy, my son, came running over and saw Christian's head on the ground. "Holy crap! What happened?" he asked.*

*I replied, "I don't know. Get some men over here and remove the body."*

*Tommy had a puzzled look on his face. He then signaled for a few men to remove the body. As they picked up the body Adam said, "May God bless his soul."*

*"Captain, please wait here with your men while I talk to Adam," I said.*

*I put my arm around Adam and we walked up the bridge. I asked, "What just happened?"*

*Adam stopped walking and faced me. "God told me in a dream to take Christian the sword. He told me how to hold it. God told me not to fear for my life because he would protect me. When the bright light hit the sword, I lost control of my body. I don't even know what happened."*

*"Adam, that's incredible. I've seen a lot of stuff in my life, but never anything like that."*

*"Yes, it was a miracle," Adam said.*

That's what happened on September 14, 2025 when young Adam de Molay became the new Knights Templar Grand Master.

THOMAS H. WARD

# THE SWORD OF JERUSALEM
## APRIL 20, 2026

There was a lot of work to do before leaving on the Quest. Using the ACWWW, the Army Command World Wide Web, I found out that the summer solstice would occur on June 21st which left us two months to find the correct location to be in, when the sun rose on that day. One of the clues on the sword stated; *at the head of the trail, leading into the fissure, look for the cross and the Solstice Sun will light the way.*

That meant we had to be at a certain location when the solstice occurred or we would miss the sun lighting the way. We would have to leave tomorrow, if possible. The twenty-four new Templar Warriors, Maggie, and I were working feverishly to make ready for our journey.

We had no idea where the treasure was actually hidden, but only the clues from the Sword of Jerusalem. Over the past six months I had studied the clues and had a general idea, or should I say a guess, of where the treasure could be located.

Now you're wondering: What is 'The Sword of Jerusalem'? Why is it so important?

I first found out about the sword on August 3, 2025. Adam's grandfather gave it to him before he died. I had no idea what the sword was really for or how important it was. I had no idea it was blessed by God and was a powerful weapon in the right hands. If it got into the wrong hands, no one knows what could happen. The following is the true story about the Sword of Jerusalem.

*On September 13, 2025, the day before the sword killed Christian, Adam took me to his bedroom to show me the secret sword. I had never seen it close up, out of its box. After walking in the room, he closed and locked the door. He said, "What I'm about to show you is the most amazing secret you'll ever see. Only a few people know about this."*

*I said, "Don't worry; your secret is safe with me."*

*Adam stood there next to his bed and took a deep breath. "Ok."*

*He reached under his mattress and pulled out a wooden box. Opening the box he took out the old broadsword. The scabbard looked old. The handle or grip was inlaid with gold and contained embedded rubies. The pummel had a golden cross on it. Holding the sword in both hands, he kissed the handle and then pulled the big blade out of its scabbard.*

*"This is the Sword of Jerusalem." Adam said.*

*It was a beautiful looking weapon. The long blade almost glowed as he held it up in the air. It was shiny and looked like new. I was amazed by what I saw. Adam gently laid the sword on the bed.*

*"Here, look at this," Adam said, while pointing at*

*the sword. "But don't touch the blade. The rubies in the handle are a symbol for the blood of Christ."*

*I bent over and closely observed the blade. Some kind of foreign writing was etched in the metal blade. "What does it say?" I asked.*

*Adam didn't reply. He turned the sword over, showing the opposite side. There was more writing and a map etched into the metal. Adam said, "This is why Christian really wants this sword."*

*The map was so tiny I couldn't make it out with my bad eyesight. I didn't know the language it was written in. "Ok, I give up. What does it mean?" I asked.*

*Adam turned the sword back over to show me the text. "This writing lists all the items in the Templar Treasure." Turning the blade back over, he pointed at the map. "This map shows the location of the treasure."*

*I asked, "Do you mean the treasure items taken from Jerusalem?"*

*"Yes. I told you before, these are holy items. These items were once in the Temple of Solomon. They prove there is a God and there was a Christ. Men have killed each other for a thousand years to find this treasure."*

*"Holy crap." That was all I could mutter while glaring at the magnificent sword.*

*It was amazing. Now I knew the treasure was real, according to the sword and Adam. I commented, "Let me get this straight. If you have this sword, then you can find the treasure."*

*"That's correct. This is why we can't let Christian obtain this sword. No evil man should be in control of God's Treasure. I fear my uncle would use it to gain*

17

*power and wealth."*

*"Why do you think he'd do that?"*

*"Well, Grandfather told me that Christian was outcast from the Knights Templar years ago because he tried to steal the sword. Grandfather also believed that Christian killed my father so he could become the next Grand Master in order to obtain the sword."*

*I nodded my head and thought, this thing has turned into a very big and dangerous mess.*

*I said, "If that's true then we certainly can't let your uncle take custody of you."*

*"It's true, alright. Grandpa would never let Christian near us."*

*"Didn't you tell me you saw the treasure once?"*

*"Actually, I've never seen it, but I know it's real because of this sword."*

*I pointed at the sword. "Can you read this writing?"*

*"Yes, I know exactly what it says. Grandpa taught me. He could read the ancient Latin writing."*

*A light went off in my head. "Now I get it. Christian needs you to tell him what the sword says."*

*"Yes, I think you're correct," Adam said. "What are we going to do?"*

*I didn't reply right away. I had to think about this. Certainly, if this whole story is true then I can't let Christian obtain the sword, or Adam. The question is, if I don't give him what he wants, then what will he do?*

*Adam was looking at the sword as I put my hand on his shoulder. "Don't worry, Adam. I'm not gonna let*

*Christian take you or the sword. I promise you that."*

*Adam gave me a hug. "Thank you, Grandpa." We hugged each other and chills ran down my spine. Goosebumps popped up on my skin as I thought about the Power of the Sword and the secrets it held.*

*We stood there looking at the blade. Adam said, "You're the only one I can trust, other than Emma. Would you like to know what the writing means?"*

*I thought for a minute. "Only tell me if you really want to."*

*"I have to tell someone who's trustworthy, just in case something happens to me."*

*We bent over the sword. Pointing at the words he said, "This Sword is gifted to the Knights Templar Grand Master by Baldwin the Second, King of Jerusalem. Year of our Lord 1120 A.D."*

*"That's incredible," I murmured.*

*"The treasure contains: One hundred thousand gold coins, fifty thousand silver coins, five hundred golden goblets, one thousand silver goblets, twenty thousand pieces of gold and silver jewelry, ten thousand various pieces of art, and twenty thousand gold crosses."*

*"Is that all it says?" I asked.*

*"No. It also says the Holy Lance, the Sangreal, and the Ark of the Covenant are part of the treasure. There's a date ... 1124 A.D., Year of Our Lord."*

*I touched Adam on the arm. "If this is real and the Ark of the Covenant is part of the treasure, that's amazing. No one knows what type of power the Ark has.*

*I wonder if the Ten Commandment tablets are inside."*

*"It doesn't say what's inside the Ark."*

*"The main story about the Ark is that when Jerusalem was invaded it was taken to Ethiopia. No one has seen it since. Does the writing mention that?" I asked.*

*"No, it only lists the treasure items." Adam flipped the sword over. "Now, let me show you the map. It also gives clues as to the location because the map is not very telling."*

*I pulled out my reading glasses and looked at the blade. There was a map that showed a river and what looked like some mountains. There was a hooked 'X' marking the treasure location.*

*Adam began to tell me a story about the Templars' history.*

*"The Knights Templar were founded in 1118 by Hughes de Payen. This occurred after they had a meeting with King Baldwin II, the King of Jerusalem. His older brother was Godfroi de Bouillon who led the crusaders to victory in the Holy Land twenty years earlier.*

*"The Knights offered themselves as an order that would protect the roadways for pilgrims journeying to Jerusalem. They were given an entire wing of the royal palace for their headquarters. The wing had been built upon the foundations of Solomon's Temple. They received their name 'The Knights of the Temple.' Their real mission was to excavate the tunnels under Solomon's Temple looking for the treasure.*

*"In 1129, the Roman Catholic Church endorsed*

*them as Holy Warriors and the protectors of Christendom. The Templars' reputation for bravery was well known. They were not allowed to retreat from battle and were obliged to fight to the death. They were also pledged to secrecy about the workings of the order."*

*"That's very interesting, Adam."*

*"Oh, there's a lot more, but I'll tell you later."*

*"Now, tell me about this map?"*

*Adam stared at the sword. "I'll explain the clues as best as I can.*

*"Upon arriving at the new land, sail south along the coast. Follow the coast which turns north, where the water is warm. Sail north, along the coast until you reach a great river that flows from the north.*

*"Sail up the great river for three days. Land at the point on the west bank marked by a stone cross where another great river mergers. The cross will point the way.*

*"Proceed west on the cross marked native trail for 40 days until reaching the stone trees. Beware of hostile natives along the way.*

*"Follow the cross west for another eight days to the rock castle.*

*"Go north for 15 days on the marked trail to a fissure in the earth. Here at the head of the trail, leading into the fissure, look for the cross and the Solstice Sun will light the way.*

*"It's signed by Jacques de Molay, Grand Master 1306."*

*I said, "This means the Templars came here in the*

*1300's which was before Columbus."*

*"Columbus was actually searching for the treasure," Adam replied. "Do you have any idea where the treasure might be hidden based on this map and clues?"*

*"No. I though you knew where it was," I said.*

*"Grandpa tried to find it over the years, but he never did."*

*I advised, "We need a real map to see if we can determine what these clues mean. Back in those days the country was crisscrossed with Indian trails. The American Indians traveled by foot and took the most direct path. It appears that the Knights used the Indian paths. Many of our modern highways followed those trails."*

*"Yeah, that makes a lot of sense," Adam replied.*

*"I think that's enough for today, it's getting late. We'll work more on this tomorrow."*

I was really interested in cracking the clues to find the treasure location. Actually going there to find it would be another problem, but the thought did intrigue me.

# ANALYSIS OF
# THE SWORD CLUES
# APRIL 21, 2026

Now I have a small army getting ready to follow the clues on the sword. The first clue stated: *'Upon arriving at the new land, sail south along the coast. Follow the coast which turns north, where the water is warm. Sail north, along the coast until you reach a great river that flows from the north.'*

I had done a lot of research and came to the conclusion that the Templars sailed from England, using a Viking map. They traveled south down the east coast of the United States. Then they sailed around the Florida peninsula, where the water is warm, into the Gulf of Mexico. Following the Florida coast north, they sailed to the great river that flows from the north, which has to be the Mississippi River.

The second clue states: 'Proceed *up the great river for three days. Land at the point on the west bank, marked by a stone cross, where another great river merges. The cross will point the way.'*

The problem is there are two large rivers that enter or merge with the Mississippi. They are the Red River and the Arkansas River. Either one of these could be a three day sail from the mouth of the Mississippi. We will have to look for the cross that points the way, but I doubt that after seven hundred years we'd be able to find any sign of a cross.

Clue three advises: *'Proceed west on the cross marked native trail for 40 days until reaching the stone trees. Beware of hostile natives along the way.'*

I found an old army trail map from 1860 on the ACWWW that showed only one trail that heads almost due west. I overlaid this map with a river map and a modern highway map. The interested thing was that the Red River and the Canadian River, which turns into the Arkansas River, both flow from the Amarillo Texas area.

The maps all converge in the Texas panhandle near Amarillo. This meant that the Templars basically followed a trail near the Red River until it ended and picked up another trail heading almost due west. Or they followed the Arkansas River and then the Canadian River to the same area. Indian trails did follow rivers whenever possible because it made passage easier and it provided a source of water.

In any case, it didn't matter what river they followed, if any. The key location was Amarillo, because the old Army trail and modern highway I-40 both went through Amarillo.

Highway I-40 clearly followed the old Army trail. It was almost an exact match when I overlaid the two. There was another important part of the clue. It was the comment: *'Beware of hostile natives along the way.'*

In those days the most hostile natives in that area were the Comanche Indians. They controlled most of Texas including the panhandle up into Oklahoma. The Knights Templar certainly would have run into these natives who were the 'Lords of the Southern Plains.'

*The Comanche Indians were feared by all the other tribes because of their fighting ability and fierceness. These warriors killed most people who trespassed into their territory. They took no prisoners except for children and women whom they made into contributing tribal members over the years.*

*The Comanche territory, at that time, was the prime feeding area for the American Bison. So they defended this area to the death. I have read stories about them painting their faces black and red to scare their enemies when they went to war. When going to war they always outnumbered the opposing force by a considerable amount, to assure victory.*

*If you were taken alive you could be tortured to death. They considered anyone who surrendered to be coward. Torture at the hands of the Comanche meant a long painful death. Some took pleasure in slowly burning people to death or using them for target practice. Putting as many as 200 arrows into one's body, they tried not to kill you. They wanted to keep you alive as long as possible. Times were different then and they did what had to be done to keep their lands.*

*The last great Chief of the Comanche Tribe was Quanah Parker. Quanah was half Comanche and*

*English-American. His mother was Cynthia Ann Parker, a daughter of a Texas farmer. Cynthia was kidnapped at nine-years-old and was more or less adopted by the Chief of the tribe.*

*When she was older, a Chief named Peta Nocona married Cynthia and Quanah was born. He took the name Quanah Parker out of respect for his mother. He once boasted that he had killed more white-men than any other Indian. Quanah Parker was the last in his tribe to surrender to the United States Government and settle on a reservation. He never signed a peace treaty, but he vowed never to fight again. Since he was a respected leader, his word was good enough for all to believe. Quanah Parker was truly a great Native American.*

Knowing these tidbits about the Comanche Indians, I now assumed that we were on the right track. During our trip we could stop and visit the Comanche Nation located in Lawton, Oklahoma. Who knows, we might find some clue or information about the Templars. Even if the Indians didn't keep any written records, they did keep a detailed verbal history of important events.

Reviewing clue three again, *'Proceed west on the cross marked native trail for 40 days until reaching the stone trees. Beware of hostile natives along the way.'* The other parts of this clue, however, need to be taken into account. Proceed west for 40 days until reaching the stone trees.

I pulled out a modern road map, as Adam sat down next to me, to study it. Adam asked, "If you travel for 40 days, how far would you get?"

I replied, "If they walked at five miles per hour for ten hours, then that's 50 miles a day. Fifty times 40 days is 2,000 miles. But I doubt they could make that kind of speed back then on the old trails. They had to have horses to carry the treasure and equipment. So I guess maybe about 1,200 to 1,500 miles is more like it."

"It says, 40 days to the stone trees. What are the stone trees?"

"I have an idea. Adam, mark off 1,200 miles, heading due west, on the map from where the Arkansas River merges with the Mississippi."

Adam did the mileage check. "Look, it puts us near the border of Arizona and New Mexico."

I scratched my chin and pulled out a thinking stick – my term for a smoke. I dangled it from my mouth, but didn't light it. Gazing at the map I said, "Eureka! The stone trees have to be the Petrified Forest, located just inside Arizona, off of I-40."

"What's the Petrified Forest?"

"I've been there a couple of times. The trees are so old, they turned to stone. That's the stone trees they're talking about. Those petrified trees are thousands of years old. The stone trees had to be there when the Templars came here."

"Good job, Grandpa."

"Well at least we're reasonably sure that the Petrified Forest is the place to start our search. It's a long way from here. Tomorrow we'll tell the Templar Warriors where we're going."

Adam is now thirteen years old and is brighter than most kids his age. He is very well spoken and has a commanding air about him. At this age he just lacks experience and a general knowledge of life. Adam has a good heart and at one time wanted to be a Minister. Being tall for his age, Adam stands almost five foot ten inches tall, so you would think he was older than he really is. He is a natural born leader, in my opinion.

# FINAL DAY ON TOCABAGA
## APRIL 22, 2025

I had wanted to leave on April 21st but there was still a lot of prepping to do. Mainly we had to load up the trucks and double check all our gear and supplies.

Days before, we had all of the trucks inspected and fixed by our mechanics. They provided extra parts for anything that might break from wear and tear, including extra tires.

We painted all the vehicles Army brown with black camo stripes, placed randomly, to break up the silhouette. We were taking four diesel Humvees. Each had a fifty caliber machine gun. We also had five pickup trucks; four of them were F-250's and one big F-350 diesel powered truck which would be used to pull a trailer.

Going on this adventure were the 24 Templar Warriors, which included Captain George Baldwin. Of course, Adam and I were going along with Maggie, who volunteered. We would bring our two best guard dogs, Adolf and Freda, making a total of 28 living beings.

This trip might possibly take as long as three months. We could carry enough food and equipment, but the major problem was fuel to run the trucks. We could never carry enough fuel.

This was a 3,000 mile journey and we would need at least 1,800 gallons of fuel. To complicate the matter, five trucks had diesel motors and the four F-250's were gas operated.

To help solve this problem, we out fitted the five pickups with an extra 100 gallon tank in the bed. We also rigged a 200 gallon tank in the trailer for diesel fuel. We were far short of what was needed, but I figured somehow we'd find the necessary fuel along the way.

It was easy to figure out how much food and water was required. Food was two MRE's per day, per man, and dog. That's 56 meals per day times 90 days, or 5,040 bags. We didn't worry about water because we could filter if necessary. However, we would carry 100 gallons of fresh water just in case we might need it when we get to the deserts of New Mexico and Arizona.

Each man would take care of their own equipment such as: Clothing, rifles, hand-guns, and ammunition. Everyone would bring 3,000 rounds for their M4's and M249's, along with 500 rounds for pistols. The M2 machine guns were also pegged to have 3,000 rounds each. Everyone packed rain gear and cold weather clothes.

We divided up all the gear evenly between each vehicle and loaded up. I didn't want all the food, water, or ammo in one truck in case it was destroyed for some reason. Stranger things have happened.

Captain Baldwin and I had a meeting to discuss the route we would take. We sat down to review the map and Baldwin asked, "What's the plan?"

Pointing at the map I said, "Well, our first stop is gonna be the Comanche Nation, near Lawton, Oklahoma."

"I was wondering if you figured out where the treasure actually is."

"So far, not exactly, but we have determined that one of the clues is the Petrified Forest in Arizona. We're heading there after we visit the Comanches."

"Why are we stopping to see the Indians?"

"They might know something about the treasure, because the Templars had to pass through Comanche territory to reach the Petrified Forest. The Indians were the only ones living there in those days. They didn't have a written language, but maybe some type of verbal history was passed down."

Baldwin shrugged his shoulders. "Ok, if you say so. That was a long time ago."

"Yeah, it was a long time ago, but I think it's worth checking out. Once we reach the stone trees, hopefully it will lead us to the next location."

"After all this time, you still don't know the location of the treasure. I hope we aren't wasting our time going on this trip."

Peering into Baldwin's eyes I said, "George, if I thought that, I wouldn't be going on this quest. Do you think I wanna put all our lives in danger for nothing?"

"Ok, I believe you. I wanna find the treasure as

much as you do. So what route will we take?"

"I think we need to stay away from the big cities, which usually spell trouble. For the most part we'll stay on the Interstate Routes, but when we come to a big city we'll bypass it and take another route."

"Yeah, I agree with that."

"Here, I've marked it out on this map. We take I-75 to I-10. This part should be clear sailing. Once we pass Mobile Alabama, we pick up Route 49 and take it Route 82. Route 82 keeps us away from most of the big cities. Then we pick up Route 281. That leads us right into Lawton and the Comanche Nation."

"Yeah, I'm with you so far," Baldwin commented.

"Leaving the Nation we take I-40 all the way to the stone trees. There's only one large city we have to go through and that's Amarillo."

"Give me your best guess where the treasure is hidden."

"To tell you the truth, I'm not a hundred percent sure. But if we find the Rock Castle, then I'll know for sure."

"Alright, I believe you." Baldwin said.

"Do you have any suggestions for the convoy formation?" I asked.

"That's easy. Two Humvees will lead the convoy and two in the rear. Trucks will be spaced a hundred feet apart. The first Hummer will be a scout vehicle and stay ahead of the group by at least a mile."

"Yeah, that sounds good. Anything else?"

"We'll stop for the night, while it's still daylight,

and make a secure camp. That way we'll know what's around us."

"Ok, then you select the time and locations when we stop each day," I advised.

"Ok good, because it's not that easy. We'll need to pick a spot that we can defend and one that allows us an escape route. I'll ride in the scout truck because I have a good nose for detecting an ambush. We'll scout the camp locations ahead of time to make sure they're safe."

"How many miles a day can we make?"

"If we keep our max speed to 45 mph then the Humvees have a 300 mile range. We'll refuel the trucks when we make camp. That means we'll be on the road for 7 to 8 hours a day."

"Anything else?" I asked.

"No, not right now. Give me a copy of the map to show my men."

"Take this one."

"If we're leaving tomorrow, what time you wanna roll out?"

"How about 9 am."

George stood up and shook my hand. "See you then, Jack."

I went home to have dinner with my family. As we sat down to my last supper on Tocabaga, everyone was quite. I looked around the tables at each person. "Let's pray," I said. Everyone bowed their heads. "Dear God, tomorrow we go in search of your treasure. Please watch over my family and protect them from evil. Amen." That was it, short and simple.

After dinner, Tommy gave me his Cobb 50 sniper rifle. "Here, take this you may need."

I replied, "Thanks a lot. It might come in handy."

*A Cobb 50 caliber rifle fires a big BMG round and can reach out and kill someone a mile away. I call it the superman bullet because it can destroy an engine block. If one of these rounds hits a person it just blows them apart, into big chunks of meat. You're as good as dead.*

My wife and I have two children, Tommy and Amy, who are both in their late thirties. Tommy was a Marine Scout Sniper during the Second Korean War in 2018. He'll be in charge of the family while I am gone.

Amy is a RN and takes care of medical needs for anyone on Tocabaga along with Doc. Scott, our only Doctor. Jim Bo, my son-in-law, and Ron, my brother, would also look after the family. They would be well protected.

As I promised, I wouldn't go on this quest if the Army Rangers hadn't returned to Fort Desoto. Last November they returned in full force, so Tocabaga is well protected with 500 Rangers based at Fort Desoto. The Fort is located on the only island which is connected to ours, by a bridge.

My good friend, Captain Sessions, is the commander of the Ranger base and I was sure he would defend Tocabaga to the death with his men. I was ready to depart on this trip with very little concern for the safety of my family and friends on Tocabaga.

The problem was my family would worry about my

safety, since I was going into the Wild West. My wife, Hemmi, was really worried and told me in so many words, as we got ready for bed. "Jack Gunn, if you get killed I'll never speak to you again." Then she laughed a little, as tears ran down her face. I tried to reassure her that I'd be fine.

My wife fell asleep wrapped in my arms. I couldn't sleep thinking about leaving her behind. Finally, after laying there for a few hours, I drifted off into dream land.

THOMAS H. WARD

# THE QUEST
# DEPARTURE DAY
## APRIL 23, 2026

Hemmi made me breakfast and when I was finished eating she said, "Once you walk out that door, I'm afraid you won't come back. So… don't say good-bye. Just say, I'll see you soon."

Becoming a little teary-eyed, I could only manage to say, "Ok Honey, I'll see you soon." We held each other for a few minutes in a tight squeeze. I kissed her forehead and walked out the door. There were no good-byes. I would try to phone Hemmi using my Army Satellite phone, given to me by Captain Sessions. This was our only way to stay in touch.

Picking up my gear, I walked outside and found Adam waiting next to the truck with Adolf by his side. It was departure time.

Everyone on this adventure would need to be able to defend themselves. Over the last six months I spent a lot of time training Adam in the use of firearms. He has a good eye and is a dead shot. He knows how to clean and use every weapon except for the M2 machine guns.

Adam was bursting with joy. He was anxious to get going. "Come on Grandpa, hurry up!"

If it wasn't for him and the sword we wouldn't be going anywhere. I suddenly wished I had never seen the sword. It was drawing me away from my family. I had never been away from my wife for more than a few weeks. I had a sick feeling running through my gut.

The convoy was lined up in front of my house. I said, "Adam, ride in the last Humvee." I figured that was the safest vehicle for him to be in if we were attacked.

"But, I wanna ride with you, Grandpa."

"Ok fine, then jump in the back." Adam and Adolf jumped in and he carefully placed the box which contained the Sword of Jerusalem under the back seat, next to my Cobb 50 caliber sniper rifle.

Maggie walked up with her dog Freda. "Can I ride with you, Jack?"

"I thought you'd be riding with Captain Baldwin."

Maggie looked at me and shook her head. "No, we don't have too much in common."

I glanced at her with an inquisitive look. "Oh, I didn't know that. Jump in, you're driving."

We would be driving an F-250 four door. I'd rather ride in this than a bumpy Hummer. Our truck was the third truck in line, behind the first two Hummers. Long ago, the air conditioning had stopped working on all the trucks. It was going to be a hot windy ride with the windows rolled down. Daytime temperatures were running in the mid-eighties, but it was going to become a lot hotter by June. In Arizona June temperatures commonly reach over a hundred. I had been there years ago, when it was one hundred-fifteen degrees.

While standing at the side of my truck, Captain Sessions pulled up next to me. I stepped over his vehicle. He said, "You got everything?"

"Yeah, I think so."

"Well, I think you're in good hands with Captain Baldwin." He stuck his hand out the window for me to shake. "Jack, here's a letter signed by me. If you get stopped at any Military checkpoints, show them this letter. It advises that you're on official Army Ranger business and to let you pass without interference."

We shook hands. "Thanks Captain. It may come in handy."

"I wish I was going with you. Good luck and God's speed. Oh, and don't worry about Tocabaga while you're gone."

"With the Rangers here, I never worry." Sessions drove away just as Baldwin was approaching.

Over the last six months Sessions and Baldwin had become good friends. Baldwin and I had informed Captain Sessions of our quest to find the lost Templar's Treasure. He was in full agreement with the mission.

Baldwin came down the line of trucks making sure everyone was set to leave. A crowd of people had gathered to see us off. My whole family was outside saying good-bye except for my wife. I understood her feelings, so it didn't bother me that she didn't come outside to send me off.

As I climbed in the truck, Baldwin yelled, "Move out!"

The convoy started to roll. We rumbled over the Tocabaga Bridge as people waved and shouted good luck. I glanced back, over my shoulder, and spotted my wife standing next to my son. He had his arm around her. I saw her wave good-bye.

Adam shouted, "Here we go!"

Maggie and I didn't say a word. We had been off of Tocabaga many times. We knew how dangerous the outside world was. I was happy to have Maggie riding with me. I knew if we got in a bind, she would watch my back. Maggie is not afraid to kill dirt bags, and believe me she has killed a few.

We passed through St. Petersburg and Tampa with no major problems. We were about an hour and a half out, approaching the Bushnell exit on I-75. I clicked my radio and told everyone we're stopping here for a break to visit the grave of Jack de Molay."

Baldwin replied, "I'm gonna scout up ahead, for a few miles."

Adam's real Grandfather was buried here on the side of the highway. The convoy pulled over and slowly rolled to a stop. There were a few cars and trucks running north and south bound. Most of them went speeding by without stopping or slowing down. A few did slow down to see what the Army convoy was doing. Some of them even waved to us.

Adam, Maggie, and I dismounted with the dogs and crossed the highway to view the grave. The weeds had already grown so high and thick that we could just barely make out the top of the white cross.

It was a bright sunny day with a slight breeze blowing. Adam spoke as he looked at the grave. "Grandpa, we're on the way to find the treasure. If we find it, I'll let you know. Rest in peace." That was all he said.

As we were returning to the truck, I looked down the highway behind us. I could make out a line of cars about half a mile away. Grabbing my binoculars, I zoomed in on them. There were ten vehicles stopped on the roadside. I wondered if they were following us.

Maggie asked, "You see something, Jack?"

Handing her the spy glasses I said, "Here take a look. There's ten cars stopped down the road."

She took a look-see. "It's probably nothing to worry about. They'd be nuts to attack us."

Taking back the binoculars, I took one more glance at the cars. "Yeah, your right, I worry too much." I made a mental note that the first one was a black pickup truck and the next two trucks in line were white. I thought, *I'll keep an eye on them just in case.*

Our convoy continued on with no problems until we reached the intersection of I-10. At this junction we would head west on I-10. Interstate I-10 runs all the way from Jacksonville to Los Angeles. This is the most southern route across the United States. It's the route that illegals take coming from Mexico. Drug gangs, terrorists, and all kinds of dirt bags use this highway.

Baldwin radioed, "Jack, we got an Army checkpoint up ahead. Everyone be alert and tighten up the formation."

I responded, "Are you sure they're really the Army?"

"Yeah, I just pulled up to them. Looks like they're 82nd Air Borne."

At the Interstate junction, Army security was blocking the road. They had a check point set up to help control who was moving around on the Interstate highways. This would probably be the first of many that we might run into.

There were, by my estimate, 30 troopers who were stopping all vehicles heading north, south, east, and west. We slowly came to a stop, behind Baldwin at the checkpoint, following a guard's order.

Glancing around I noted at least twenty cars were being searched or waiting to be searched. There was a small fenced-in area under the bridge, which contained some men apparently being held by the Army.

I watched Baldwin get out of his Hummer so I dismounted, leaving my M4 in the truck, and went to show the guard my letter from Captain Sessions.

The soldiers had shoulder sleeve insignias, indicating they were from the 82nd Air Borne Division, which is based at Fort Bragg, North Carolina. A Sergeant asked Baldwin where we were going. He also wanted to know what we doing with Military Humvees.

*The U.S. Special Forces are trying to clean up the crime and terrorist activities. One way to do that is to make it difficult to travel around the country freely. To stop the flow of dirt bags, gangs, and guns one needs to slowly close in on their strong-holds and then eliminate them.*

I interceded in the conversation. "Sergeant, my name is Jack Gunn. Please read this letter from Captain Sessions, who is the Army Ranger Commanding Officer at Fort Desoto."

The Sergeant nodded his head and opened the letter. After a few minutes he said, "The letter doesn't state what your mission is or why you have Military equipment."

While we were talking, a few of his guards were walking up and down the road next to our vehicles. I noticed some of our people were taking to the troopers, but I couldn't hear what they were talking about. Most likely they were pumping my men for information.

I advised the Sergeant. "Our mission is classified. As for our equipment, it was provided by the Rangers at Fort Desoto."

"I can't let you pass until I know where you're going and what the hell you're doing."

"Sergeant, please ask your Commanding Officer to come here so we can clear this up. I can get Captain Sessions on the horn, and they can discuss it."

The Sergeant sent one of his men to bring their Commanding Officer over. While waiting, the Sergeant said, "Man, you guys are loaded for bear. It looks like you're going on a long trip."

I pulled out a smoke, a Winston light, and offered him one. He gladly accepted it and I lit us up. After taking a drag, I replied, "Yeah, we're going to Arizona. That's all I can tell you."

Baldwin was sitting on the bumper of the Hummer not saying a word. He was just taking it all in and letting me handle the situation. Thirty minutes went by and now all of our men had dismounted and were sitting on the side of the road, trying to keep cool.

Maggie and Adam strolled by us walking the dogs, and the troopers stared at her. Our conversation came to an end, as the troopers goggled her swaying body. They apparently hadn't seen a good looking chick in a while.

Finally a Humvee pulled up and a Captain stepped out of the truck. "What seems to be the problem here, Sergeant Whitehead?" I waited for Whitehead to give his story to the Captain. I watched as he handed my letter over to him. The Captain read it. "Which of you is Jack Gunn?"

"I am, Captain."

"I know Captain Sessions, we went to West Point together. How's he doing anyway?"

"He's doing fine, Sir."

"I've never heard of Fort Desoto. Where the hell is that?"

"It's right near the Skyway Bridge, in Tampa Bay."

"The next time you talk to Sessions, give him regards from Captain Jim Jones. Tell him JJ said hello."

"I'll do that, Captain."

"Which direction are you going?"

"We're headed to Arizona."

"Ok Jack, you're free to go. A word of caution, be careful on I-10, it's very dangerous around New Orleans. There are a lot of shitheads still out there."

"Roger that, Captain. Thanks a lot."

We mounted up and the Sergeant let us pass; half

raising his hand as if to wave good-bye. As we went up the I-75 exit ramp bridge, to access I-10, I made it a point to peer back down the road. I had a good view for about a mile. I was looking for the cars that I thought were dogging us. I was surprised; there were no cars behind us. I guessed they turned off I-75 and were not on our tail after all.

The radio crackled. "Jack, once we get past Tallahassee, I'm gonna scout up ahead for a place to camp. It's getting late. Looking at the map, a good place might be Falling Waters State Park. You know anything about it?"

"No. But if it has fresh water we can get cleaned up."

"I'll check it out and get back to you."

"Roger," I replied.

Our big off road tires continued rumbling down the highway for another hour and a half. We did see some other cars on the road which presented us no problems. From the checkpoint I counted about 200 cars moving east. We had 35 cars pass us going west. All were in a hurry it seemed, zooming by us at more than 70 mph.

Where these people were going, I had no idea. Perhaps they were trying to find families, friends, or just moving to a safer place. People saw our armored Humvees with the big machine guns and stayed away from us for the most part. So far we haven't had a run-in with any dirt bags.

We've been driving now about eight hours and didn't have any encounters with Free Roamers or anyone. We did see a broken down car on the side of the road every now and then. That could mean that things were getting better, at least in Florida. I wondered what we would find as we proceeded further west.

My radio buzzed. "Heads up, everyone." It was Baldwin. "We just checked out the Falling Waters and it looks like a good place to camp tonight. Exit at Route 77 and head south for a mile. Then follow the signs east for about three miles to the park. Once inside follow the road straight back to the falls and you'll see us near the lake."

"Ok, got it George," I replied. We were an hour behind Captain Baldwin.

While driving Maggie said, "Great there's a lake. I can go swimming and clean up."

"Can I go swimming, Grandpa?" Adam asked.

"We'll see. There could be gators or water Moccasins there."

We were all tired and sweaty. A nice cool dip would really feel good, I thought.

"Stop trying to scare us, Jack," Maggie said.

"I'm not trying to scare anyone. There has to be snakes and gators there."

Exiting I-10 on to Route 77, we drove south to the sign that read, 'Falling Water State Park.' Following the road, which wound thought the dense woods into the camp ground area we could hear the thunder of the waterfalls ahead.

The whole area was beautiful, with thick dense trees of all types. Of course, the jungle had almost covered the old cement road since it had not been maintained in years. Even over the noise of our motors, we could hear birds of all species chirping away.

I noticed two RV's, off the road, parked far back in the woods. Maggie spotted a few people along the way who ducked back into the dense forest when they saw us. Other than that, we saw no one else at the park.

Baldwin's truck was parked near a small lake not far from the waterfall. Pulling up, he directed each vehicle exactly how to park. He arranged the trucks into two parallel lines. One line was made up of the combat Humvees, which were located on the north side. The pickup trucks made up the second line, which parked about 100 feet from the shoreline of the lake. The lake assured us protection from the south. The east and west were all open ground which could be easily protected. The trucks were parked facing the same direction to permit us a fast escape in case we were attacked by an overwhelming force.

We set up camp and refueled the trucks. After that, most of the men went for a swim and washed up, while some of us gathered fire wood. We built small camp fires to heat our meals and boil water.

After eating our delicious MRE's, it was dark so Baldwin posted two guards for the night. Adam went to sleep in the backseat of the truck. Maggie and I dragged two old rotted picnic tables close together for our sleeping arrangements.

Adolf and Freda, who ate their MRE's with no problem, because they smell like dog food, were tied to the tables with a long leash. If anyone or anything came around during the night the dogs would let us known.

As I fell asleep, the frogs and crickets were really making a racket. I heard an owl hoot, over and over. It was like music to my ears. It was a beautiful night to sleep under the stars.

Adolf and Freda's growls woke Maggie and me up. I glanced around and saw the dogs looking at something. Grabbing my flash light, I pointed the beam to the edge of the water. My beam picked up its glowing red eyes. The gator was barely out of the water, coming over for some dog food. It was a big one, about 10 feet long. A big gator like that would make a meal of our dogs, so I put them in the truck, out of danger.

Maggie said, "Damn gators, they'll eat anything. Can they get us on this picnic table?"

"I don't know."

"Well, I'm gonna sleep in the truck with the dogs." Maggie picked her sleeping bag and headed for the truck. "Are you coming?"

"No, I'll stay here. I can't sleep now. It'll be daylight soon." A movement caught my eye. It was the gator slowly moving towards me.

*Maggie and I go way back. We're just good friends who trust each other. She volunteered to go on this mission because she likes adventure. She's a damn good fighter and is pretty much fearless. Maggie can drive anything from a truck to a tractor. I recall one time we went to Ellenton to buy a tractor from Farmer Horn. Farmer Horn was a real slimy piece of crap, who lured Maggie there on the pretext that he had a tractor for sale, on the internet. His real intention was to kidnap her. He wanted to use her for breeding stock with his inbred sons. Well to make a long story short there was a gun battle with the Horn clan. It didn't end well for Horn because Maggie shot the big pig in the eye when he grabbed her and wouldn't let her go. That day we probably killed fifteen men from the Horn clan. That's also the day we had a run-in with Federal Agents, who tried to take our guns. It didn't end well for them either, but that's another story.*

I screwed the silencer on my M4 so I wouldn't startle our men awake. To kill a gator you need to pop him in the head, right near the ear. One shot there and he's dead. I waited for him to come closer. The big boy was right next to the table I was standing on. I had never been this close to one before. They are frightening prehistoric creatures. While stalking you they don't make any noise, but just keep watching for you to make the wrong move.

He was trying to figure out how to get up to me. His head was three feet away as I aimed and squeezed the trigger. I hated to kill him, but he pressed his luck. With that big monster around we weren't safe. I shined my light around looking for more gators, but didn't see any.

One of the guards heard the pop of my gun and came over to see what was going on. "Everything ok here?" Pete asked.

*Pete was second in command under Captain George Baldwin. He was one of the most experienced warriors. The other Templars respect him, and follow every order to the letter. Pete looks like a normal lanky guy, standing over six feet tall, but he's fast and strong. He's a lean mean fighting machine.*

"Yeah, I just killed a gator that got too close."

He walked over to it and kicked it. "That's a big one alright."

"Have you seen anything tonight?" I asked.

"There was a truck that came in about an hour ago. That's it."

"Where's it at now?"

"About half a mile down the road, parked under a willow tree."

"Did anyone get out?"

"Yeah, a guy came walking over and asked me what the Army was doing here. I told him we were just camping for the night. He just turned around and left without saying a word. I kept an eye on him until he got back in his truck."

I nodded my head. "You see anyone else?"

"Nope."

"It'll be daylight soon. I'm gonna start a fire and make some breakfast."

"Yeah, it's almost 5 am. I gotta wake up my men."

# INDIANOLA
## APRIL 24<sup>TH</sup>, 2026

After eating breakfast, I pulled out the map. As I was studying it, Captain Baldwin sat down next to me at the picnic table. "Good morning, Jack. I'd like to get an early start today."

"Morning, George. Yeah, I agree."

Baldwin pointed at the map. "I was looking at the map and found a shortcut. If we pick up Route 98 out of Mobile, it will cut off some time. We can take 98 all the way to Hattiesburg and then pick up Route 49 there. It could save us about two hours."

*Once we left Florida our trip would take us through the southern tip of Alabama and across the State of Mississippi, where we would pick up Route 82 right outside of Greenville, at Indianola. Then we would cross the Mississippi River using the bridge on Route 82. I hoped the bridge was still intact. That would take us into Arkansas. We'd drive across the southern part of the state to the little city of Texarkana, located on the border of Texas.*

I followed George's finger on the map. He was right, taking Route 98 was a good short cut. "Ok, George that looks good to me. We'll take 98 to Route 49."

We had four cities, of considerable size, to go through which was Mobile, Hattiesburg, Jackson, and Wichita Falls in Texas. There were also a lot of small towns along the way while going through good-old-boy country.

Baldwin said, "I'd like to make it to Greenville today, and cross the Mississippi before dark."

Checking the time it was 6 am and the sun was coming up. "Ok, that sounds like a plan. I'll get Maggie and Adam ready to roll out by 6:30."

"Ok, 6:30 we move out." Baldwin went to advise his men to pack up.

Maggie and Adam were already set to go. As Maggie was getting in the driver's seat I told her, "I'll drive first today. We'll switch every two or three hours."

"Ok, sounds good to me," Maggie replied.

Adam asked, "Can I drive?"

"Maybe, when we're out in the wide open spaces of New Mexico," I told him.

Since Adam was a big kid for his age, and could reach the pedals, I had been teaching him to drive just in case there was a problem. I have to admit, he's a pretty good driver, but needs a lot more experience.

I commented, "Adam, would you mind riding in Pete's Humvee today."

"Ok, if you want me to."

"We're going into unknown territory and if any

shooting starts, you'll be safer in the bullet proof Hummer."

"Ok. I think it'll be fun." Adam ran over to Pete's Hummer which was right in front of us. I watched him climb in.

Maggie said, "Well, it's just you and me, Grandpa."

"Yeah, just you, me, and the dogs," I said, with a chuckle.

Our little convoy started to pull out of Water Fall State Park. As we rolled past the willow tree, I looked at the truck parked there. It was a black pickup, just like the one I saw dogging us yesterday. I wasn't sure if it was the same one or not, but my sixth sense told me something wasn't right. I gawked at the driver sitting behind the wheel, but couldn't make out his face because of the dark shadows created by the willow tree.

I said, "Maggie, I think that's the same black truck we saw yesterday."

Maggie leaned over, close to me, putting her hand on my leg to look out my window. "Yeah, it might be the same one."

I pushed her back to her side so I could drive. Maggie gave a giggle because she was teasing me on purpose. "Stay on your side of the truck, hot pants," I joked.

"That was an old Chevy. It had spotlight on the driver's side," Maggie said.

"Good eyes, Maggie. I didn't see the spotlight."

We were back on I-10 as I shifted the truck into high gear reaching our standard cruising speed of 45 mph.

I asked, "Maggie, how come you didn't wanna ride with Baldwin?"

"He's kinda weird. I gave him every chance, if you know what I mean, to start something, but he didn't do anything."

I thought about this for a moment. "Maybe he can't do anything."

"What do you mean?"

"Well, maybe he was injured in combat while fighting ISIS. Maybe he can't do anything."

"That's terrible. I never thought of that."

"Yeah, maybe he can't do anything sexual, for some reason, but just desires having a woman to talk to."

"You might be right. Now I feel bad that I didn't ride with him."

Baldwin came on the radio. "I-10 is clear going through Mobile."

Pete replied, "Roger that, Boss. We're right behind you."

Mobile looked like a war zone. All along Interstate 10 there were burned up cars and trucks. Every now and then we'd see a body or two on the side of the road. Maggie was keeping her eyes peeled for trouble. I had to watch the road carefully, looking for debris and junk on the road. I was weaving around a lot of metal and glass to keep from getting a flat tire. From the Interstate we observed buildings burning and heard some gun fire in the distance. I wanted to get out of the city as fast as possible.

Suddenly, two cars entered the freeway, from the on ramp, on our right side. One pulled up, within a few feet, next to us. Maggie looked out her window at them. She yelled, "They got guns! They're telling us to pull over!"

"We're not pulling over. Shoot their tires first and then the cars," I told her.

Maggie racked her M4, leaned out the window, and fired a few bursts at the closest car. "I blew out their tires!" she yelled.

"Good shooting."

I looked at the car as it weaved to the right, and then turned towards us. It was going to ram us. I punched the gas while swerving to my left. The car still hit our right-rear fender spinning us slightly sideways to the right. The tires squealed as our truck pitched back to the left. I punched the gas, and counter-steered to keep from losing control. We were on two wheels for a second, and on the verge of rolling over. I held my breath as our truck bounced back onto all four wheels, wobbling back and forth, as we sped away.

Glancing in the mirror, I saw the attacking car roll to the left side of the road, smashing into the concrete barrier, coming to an abrupt stop. The other car followed it going right in between our truck and the truck behind us in the convoy. They just missed colliding with each other. The second attacking car also collided with the barrier and the other car.

The radio crackled and Pete yelled, "Jeff, blast those assholes!"

Jeff was in the last combat Humvee, at the end of the convoy. He's the third in command of the modern

Templar Knights. Jeff is a dead shot with any weapon. He's the best shooter with the big fifty gun.

All the vehicles in our convoy had made it past the attacking cars. Pete's brake lights came on and the whole convoy came to a screeching stop. We watched Jeff's machine gun open fire on the cars. Their gas tanks exploded and the cars started on fire. No one escaped the deadly rounds from the fifty caliber machine gun. A few men made it out of the flames; but were easily mowed down. Eliminating those dirt bags was easy work for Jeff. The battle was over in a few minutes. It was amazing how quickly the cars turned into huge fireballs spewing black smoke high in the air.

Sitting there watching the action, my hands and feet started to shake. I have to admit, almost flipping over got my adrenaline going. I lit a smoke to relax.

We continued on our way until reaching Route 98. Captain Baldwin was standing in the road waiting for us. We all needed a break and so did the dogs. Maggie let them out to do their business.

Jeff strolled up to me and shook my hand. "Hey, good driving. I thought for sure you were gonna roll."

"Yeah, it was a close one." We examined the damage done to my truck from the collision. The right-rear fender and quarter panel had a big dent, but it wasn't anything serious.

Baldwin called everyone over to his truck. All the drivers huddled around as he leaned on the hood of his Hummer and glanced around at everyone. "What happened back there?"

Pete replied, "Two cars tried to stop our convoy.

Jeff blasted them to hell."

Baldwin nodded his head like it was no big deal and pulled out his map. "Route 98 is gonna be a crude road compared to the Interstate. It's an old country road probably built back in 1920.

"There are a few small towns along the way to Hattiesburg. We'll by-pass Hattiesburg using I-59 and pick up Route 49. I want everyone to stay close, within a few car lengths. That way no vehicles can cut into our convoy, like what just happened. Jeff, since you're the rear guard, don't let anyone pass you. Any questions?"

I asked, "Do you think we'll make it to the Mississippi today?"

"I don't think so, but we'll try. If there's nothing else, take a ten minute break and then get ready to move out."

Maggie gave the dogs some water while I handed out oranges from our farm, to those who wanted one. Maggie commented, "I'm glad you were driving back there. That was pretty scary when we almost rolled over."

"Thanks, Maggie. You drive for a while. I need a break."

She laughed and punched my arm. "Ok, I'll drive."

I saw Pete and Adam talking to each other and sharing a bottle of water. That was a good sign because Adam doesn't usually spend a lot of time talking to the Warriors. I think he feels intimidated because of his young age. Of course, the Warriors intimidate almost any person.

We made it past Hattiesburg using the bypass and

picked up Route 49 taking us into Jackson, Mississippi. We didn't encounter any problems. Some people we passed, shouted greetings or waved as we drove by. Continuing down Route 49, we reached the small hick town of Indianola, Mississippi. It's about 30 miles from Greenville and Mississippi River. This is the junction where we pick up Route 82.

A street sign greeted us:

## WELCOME TO INDIANOLA - HOME OF BB KING, KING OF THE BLUES

It was getting dark when we arrived in Indianola, which was a typical small town that reminded me of the old days. On the main drag was one general store, one restaurant, a couple of closed gas stations, two churches, and a bunch of little stores that for the most part were closed. It was pretty much a ghost town. There were a few people walking around who greeted us with a wave. They seemed down-right friendly because they waved and said hello while we slowly drove past them. I had a good feeling about this place. It was peaceful and quaint.

*Indianola is located at the junction of U.S. Routes 82 and 49W. The town was originally named "Indian Bayou" in 1882 because the site along the river bank was formerly inhabited by a Choctaw Indians. Between 1882 and 1886, the town's name was changed three times before finally becoming "Indianola," in honor of an Indian princess named "Ola." The town developed and grew at this site due to the location of a lumber mill located on the Indian Bayou.*

*The city is 8.7 square miles (22 km²) which includes the bayou. Indian Bayou Waterway runs the length of the city and beyond. The topography of Indianola is mostly flat.*

Captain Baldwin stopped our convoy in front of the little town square. To my surprise, the American Flag was flying, high on a pole, in the public park. That was a good sign for sure. After we dismounted, George told everyone that it was best to stop here for the night. George posted sentries and had trucks lined up in two rows.

Before we could unpack our gear, an elderly man and woman approached us. I eyed them up right away. They didn't have any weapons that I could see. Just the same, I kept my M4 at low ready position.

"Howdy friends," the man said, as he stuck out his hand.

The man was dressed in a plaid shirt with blue jeans, which were held up with suspenders, and a plantation type straw hat. The lady had on a flowery dress with a sun bonnet, which made her look like an old fashioned country housewife.

Maggie was holding onto our dogs who keenly looked at the strangers, but didn't growl at them. The dogs normally have a sense of who's friendly and who's not.

Maggie and I stepped over to them and we shook hands. "Hello, I'm Jack, and this is Maggie."

The man tipped his hat and he pulled a toothpick

out of his mouth. "Hello Maggie, Jack. My name is David Ragsdale, and this here's my wife Alice. I'm the Mayor of Indianola." He spoke in a typical southern accent.

By this time more city people were coming out of the stores. They strolled over to look at our convoy and combat Humvees. "It's a pleasure to meet you Mr. and Mrs. Ragsdale."

"Oh, just call me Mayor, like everybody does."

About thirty people had gathered behind the Mayor, but some just wandered around looking at our trucks. I noticed a few carried shotguns or lever action rifles.

Looking me in the eyes, the Mayor commented, "I don't mean to be nosey, but what brings y'all to our small town?"

"We're just staying for the night, if you don't mind Mayor."

"Heck no, we don't mind. It's great having you Army guys here. We just don't want any trouble."

"We aren't gonna make any trouble. I can promise you that."

Captain Baldwin came moseying over. "Who's this guy?"

"This is David Ragsdale, the Mayor of Indianola, and this is his wife, Alice. Mayor, meet Captain Baldwin the commander of our troops."

"It's a pleasure to meet you, Captain."

Baldwin responded in the same manner. He was going to ask something when Ragsdale interrupted. "If he's the Commander, what are y'all, Jack?"

"I'm the head of this expedition."

"Say, where y'all from, anyway?"

"We're from Tampa, Florida."

Ragsdale stuck the toothpick back in his mouth and nodded his head. "Then y'all are Florida Crackers," he said, with a grin.

Baldwin asked, "Mr. Mayor, do you have any hostiles around here? You know, people who don't like the military?"

"Of course not. We're all Americans here and loyal to the military."

"That's great. Do you mind if we make a few campfires in your park?"

"Nope, go right ahead."

"Ok, thank you, sir. If you'll excuse me, I gotta tend to my troops." They shook hands and Baldwin left to direct setting up camp.

"Miss Maggie, how about if Alice takes you on a tour of our nice little city," Ragsdale said.

Maggie looked at me. I gave a subtle nod that it was ok. "Alright let's go, Alice," Maggie said. They walked away, arm in arm, like two women going shopping, with the dogs by Maggie's side.

Mayor Ragsdale pulled out a bag of chewing tobacco. Putting a handful into his mouth he said, "Glad she's gone. I needed a chew. My wife don't like chewin' or smokin'." He held the bag out towards me. "Y'all like some?"

"No thanks, Mayor. I got a smoke here." I lit up and we both laughed.

"Hey, where y'all headed to?" Ragsdale let out a big spit and wiped his chin off on his brown stained sleeve.

Taking a drag, I held it in a little while and let the smoke out slowly while replying. "We're … going to … Arizona."

"Arizona. Why y'all going there?"

"We're on a secret mission."

Ragsdale let out another big spit on the ground. "What kinda secret mission?"

I pulled out the letter from Captain Sessions and handed to him. "Here, read this. If I tell you what the mission is, then it wouldn't be a secret."

The Mayor read the letter and gave it back to me. "I see, but can't you give me some kinda hint."

Thinking about this for a minute, I stomped my butt into the ground, putting it out. "Do you believe in God?"

"I'm a born-again Baptist and proud of it."

"That's great, but all I can tell you is we're on a mission for God."

"For God? Now y'all really got me curious."

"Mayor, that's all I can tell you."

"What's all you can tell him?" Baldwin asked, walking up behind me.

I turned to face him. "I just told him we're on a mission for God."

"Yeah, that's right Mayor," Captain Baldwin said.

Ragsdale peered at Baldwin, looking him up and down. "Y'all don't look like normal Army to me.

Whatcha carry that big pig-sticker for?"

"You mean this sword." Baldwin touched the handle. "It's to scare our enemies."

"Pray tell me, who are your enemies?"

"Primarily Islamic terrorists like ISIS and al-Qaida. Basically anyone who breaks the law and doesn't honor the Constitution are also our enemies."

Ragsdale nodded his head. "Yep, there's a lot of evil people out there. We're kinda off the beaten path here, so no one bothers us much."

Changing the subject, I asked Ragsdale, "What's up ahead at the Greenville Bridge."

"Y'all planning on going over that bridge are ya?"

"Yeah, we gotta cross the river somehow."

The Mayor spit out some more slimy tobacco laced saliva. He sat down on the bench next to us, as if thinking for a minute. "If you boys are going to the bridge, y'all better be careful."

"Oh, why's that?" Baldwin asked.

"The bridge is guarded by crooks. Bandits that will rob and kill ya. I know many a person that went there and never came back. That's all I can tell y'all."

"So, you've never been there."

"Never been there, and don't wanna go there. Billy Bob went there a few times."

"Who's Billy Bob?" I asked.

"That's my boy. That's him over there by the truck, with the blue shirt on."

"Could we ask him a few questions about the

bridge."

"Sure enough." Ragsdale shouted out. "Billy Bob, get over here!"

Billy Bob came jogging over. "What you need, Daddy?" he said, with a smile.

Billy Bob was a big boy, taller than me, but he wasn't a boy. He appeared to be in his early thirties. He dressed just like his Daddy, including the plantation straw hat. He had dark skin, high cheek bones, and black colored eyes, but his hair was light brown.

"Billy Bob, meet Jack, and Captain Baldwin. Billy Bob will answer any questions you got about the Greenville Bridge. I'll see y'all later, I gotta tend to something." Ragsdale slowly strolled away in the direction his wife went.

Baldwin and I shook Billy Bob's big hand. I noticed he had a strong vise-like grip as he unintentionally crushed my hand. I said, "We're gonna cross the bridge tomorrow and wanna know if we can expect any trouble."

Billy said, "Yeah, if you go there it'll be trouble alright."

"Why's that, Billy Bob?" Baldwin asked.

Billy knelt down on one knee and said, "Where's why." He proceeded to draw a crude map on the dirt sidewalk. "Y'all gotta take 82 through Greenville to get to the bridge. It's a bigger city than Indianola is, so you might run into some unfriendly people along the way."

Billy drew the bridge and made a few X's in the dirt. Pointing at the X's he said, "There are usually four guards at a road block. The guards charge a fee to get across the bridge."

"What kinda fee?" I asked.

"I heard about a thousand dollars per car. But I don't know for sure."

"What's on the other side of the bridge?" Baldwin asked.

"I got no idea," Billy Bob replied, while looking at us. "Where are y'all headed to?"

Baldwin and I glanced at each other. We both knew this crossing could be trouble. We had done some research on the Greenville Bridge. It's is a big four-lane bridge. When built in 2010 it was the fourth longest cable-stayed constructed bridge in the United States, running 4.1 miles long.

Baldwin said, "Our next stop is the Comanche Nation, in Lawton, Oklahoma."

Billy Bob touched Baldwin's arm. "Would y'all let me tag along?"

I said, "Sorry Billy, but I don't think so. It could be a dangerous trip."

"Come on, I'll do whatever you want. I gotta get out of this stinking town."

"What about your Mom and Dad?"

"They're driving me crazy. My Daddy is the big boss around here. He's a slave driver making me work my ass off. Always pushing me to get married, and have kids. I don't wanna get married. I wanna see the world."

I stood there not knowing what to say to Billy because he seemed kind of childish. Baldwin asked, "Billy, you know how to use a gun like this?" He held up his M4 in front of Billy's face.

"I never used one like that, but I'm a good shot and a fast learner. I can shoot the eye out of a possum at fifty yards."

"What do you think, Jack?"

Peering into Baldwin's face and then at Billy, I said, "To tell you the truth, you're too green. I don't wanna be responsible for you."

"What if I can help you cross the bridge? Would you let me come along then?"

"How you gonna do that?" Baldwin asked.

"A few of the guards are friends of mine. I could help pave the way. You know, make it easier to get by them."

While I was thinking about his proposal Maggie came jogging up with the dogs. Adolf and Freda went right up to Billy and smelled him. He got down on one knee and both dogs licked his face. Dogs are good judges of a person's character and they sure liked Billy.

I said, "Maggie, this is Billy Bob, the Mayor's son."

Maggie stared at him and said, "Hi, Billy Bob."

Billy stood up, took off his hat, and bowed. "Pleasure to meet you, Ma'am."

"Billy Bob, excuse us for a minute. I need to talk to Jack and George in private." Maggie grabbed us both by the arm, dragging us about twenty feet away.

"Ok, what's up, Maggie?" I asked.

Maggie whispered, "It's here."

"What's here?"

"That black truck, you dummy. I saw it parked on a side street a few blocks away."

"What black truck you talking about?" Baldwin asked.

"I didn't tell you because I wasn't sure, but now I'm sure. Someone has been following us ever since Florida," I replied.

George scratched his chin and was thinking. I could almost see smoke coming out of his ears. "What do you wanna do about it?"

"Nothing, right now. We'll think about it, after we get across the river."

Maggie grabbed me by the arm again. "That's not all I got to tell you. This Mayor and his wife, Alice, are not the nice people they make out to be."

"Oh, how's that?" I asked.

"Well, Alice invited me in their house. While she went upstairs to change her clothes some woman came out of the kitchen. She seemed scared to death and whispered in my ear, leave this town while you're still alive."

Maggie glanced a concerned look at Billy Bob. "I didn't get a chance to ask her why she told me that, because Alice came back downstairs. She saw her talking to me and yelled at her, 'What did you tell my guest?' Then she dragged the woman by the hair into the kitchen. When I heard screaming, I opened the kitchen door and saw the Mayor beating the woman with a cane. Alice and another woman were holding her.

"He saw me and stopped. Then he came after me. Freda and Adolf stopped him from grabbing me. I pointed my gun at him when he drew a pistol out of his pocket. I came real close to killing him. Then I ran back here to tell you guys."

"Did he say anything?" Baldwin asked.

"All he said was, 'Please don't tell anyone. It's all just a mistake.' I didn't stop to listen to any of his bullshit and got the hell out of there."

I said, "Let's ask Billy what's going on?" Maggie and George both nodded in agreement. We moved back over next to Billy, who was petting the dogs. He stood up as we approached. "Billy Bob, what's going on here?"

"Whatcha mean?"

"Tell him, Maggie." I said.

As Maggie repeated her story to Billy, he hung his head down. "I'm ashamed of that. He's a very cruel man. He beats everyone." Billy lifted his shirt and showed us the cane marks on his torso.

Maggie was shocked by the scars on his skin. "Why do you let him hit you like that?"

"If I tell y'all the truth of what's going on you gotta promise take me with you. If you don't, he'll kill me for sure. Y'all promise?"

With hesitation I said, "Ok, you can come with us."

Billy smiled and shook my hand, crushing it out of joy. "I don't think Ragsdale is my real Daddy. I don't know who my Daddy is, but I don't look like Ragsdale. My mother was a whore who worked for Ragsdale. She was his favorite money maker until she died, a long time ago."

"So what are you telling us?" Baldwin asked.

"Ragsdale owns a bunch of whores and has gambling games. Alice is his Madam who looks after the girls. Ragsdale isn't the real Mayor either. Like I said, he's the Boss Man. This town is under his control." Billy turned his head and scanned his eyes around the park. "You see, only certain people get to carry guns. They work for Ragsdale. You gotta keep an eye on them boys."

"So what does Ragsdale make you do?" I asked.

"I do all his dirty work."

"I take the girls, once a week, to Greenville to make money. That's how I know the guards at the bridge. They always wanna poke my girls. I also collect money from those that owe it from gambling."

"Have you ever killed anyone?" I glared at his face to see if he was telling the truth.

He didn't answer right away. "Yeah, to be honest, I've killed a few bad guys who didn't pay Ragsdale. I had to kill 'em."

I didn't wanna know any details. Most of us have had to kill more than a few bad guys.

Baldwin changed the subject. "Billy, how many gunmen does Ragsdale have?"

Billy Bob counted them out on his fingers. "I guess about twenty guards."

"Here's the big question: Do you think they'll try to attack us tonight?" I asked.

"Well … since Maggie seen Ragsdale doing something bad, he might not cotton to that. Yeah, he might try to take y'all out tonight. He sure would like those trucks and guns, not to mention Maggie."

After telling us about Ragsdale, Billy Bob had gained my full trust.

Maggie said, "I should have shot that asshole."

Baldwin checked the time. "I think they'll attack us when we're asleep, around 2 am. It's 9 pm now. Let's quietly pass the word to get ready to move out. Tell everyone not to make it noticeable. Leave the fires burning, leave some sleeping bags out, and a couple of tents up."

I replied, "Ok, but what's the plan?"

"Everyone be ready to roll out at 11 pm on the dot. The pickups will move out first. The Hummers will provide a rear guard. Once we roll out, head to the bridge." George looked at Billy Bob. "Can we get across the bridge at night?"

"Yeah, I don't see why not," Billy said.

"What will it cost?" I asked.

"Like I told y'all, about a thousand per car."

"Maggie, count out fifteen thousand and give it to Billy to hold. He'll ride with us to the bridge. He'll do the talking and make the payment. We'll cover him in case something goes wrong."

"If something goes wrong we'll blast our way across the bridge. Let the Humvees take the lead across," George commented. Maggie and I nodded in agreement.

"Are we gonna give them the whole fifteen grand?" Billy asked.

"Yes, if we have to," I said. "Billy you stay close to

me until we leave. You'll ride in my truck, along with Maggie."

We broke up the meeting and walked around telling our men the plan. The idea was be in your truck and ready to roll out at 11 pm sharp. We noted that Ragsdale had left five men patrolling around our camp at a considerable distance, so not to be conspicuous.

Slowly, one or two at a time, as 11 pm neared our men started mounting up. Maggie, Billy, and the dogs were already in our truck. I was the last one to leave the campsite. After making sure everyone was ready to roll out, I mounted up, started the motor, and gave a hand wave as a signal to move out.

The sudden movement of all our vehicles speeding away at the same time seemed to take the guards by surprise. They just stood there not knowing what to do. Passing close enough by one guard to see the look on his face, I waved at him with a smile. Maggie yelled out the window, "Bye-bye." Billy Bob ducked down in the backseat so he wouldn't be spotted.

Once by the guards Billy sat up and said, "Keep going straight on Route 82 until we reach the bridge. Stop when you see the road block. Then we'll get out and talk to them."

"How far is it to the road block?" I asked.

"It's around thirty miles."

I said, "Maggie, give Billy the money and your handgun."

Before Maggie could reply, Billy said, "She already gave me the money, and I don't want a gun. I never bring a gun with me when I take the girls to visit the guards."

"Ok, suit yourself!" I shouted over the wind noise, while zooming along at 60 mph. "Both of you listen up! When we stop, Billy gets out first. I'll be right behind him. Maggie, you cover our backs."

"Ok Boss," Maggie said.

"Billy, what are you gonna tell these guys?" I asked.

"Good question, Jack. What do you want me to tell them?"

"Just tell them that I am your Uncle Jack. I have nine trucks that need to cross the river. Hand them the entire fifteen grand. Let them count it."

"They might ask why we wanna cross."

"Just say we're going to see relatives in Arizona who need our help."

"Alright, I got it. Don't worry about a thing."

I slowed down to 30 mph so the Humvees could catch up by the time we reached the bridge.

After slowly coming to a stop about 50 yards from the road block, Billy and I climbed out. We approached to within 20 yards and stopped. It was dark and I could barely make out the shapes of the men.

Billy yelled out, "Hey Joe! It's me, Billy Bob!"

Joe replied, "Who's that with you?"

"It's my Uncle Jack. He's ok."

"Alright, come on up here."

Billy and I started walking up the bridge ramp. Scouring around in the darkness I noted four cars were blocking the road. I could only see four guards on duty.

A man walked up out of the shadows and shook Billy's hand. "Joe, how y'all doin'?" Billy said.

Joe had a smile on his face as he replied, "Say, Billy Bob. What's up? Where the whores at?"

"Oh, they'll be here tomorrow. I had to bring my Uncle Jack here tonight. I promised I'd help him get his clan cross the river."

Joe studied me and so did the other three men. "You in the Army?" he asked.

"No, not exactly. We were at one time."

Joe looked at me closer and commented. "Hey Sam, look at this. He's got a real M4 with night optics." Sam came over and stood in front of me, peering at my guns and uniform.

Joe and his men appeared to be just normal good old boys by looking at their clothes and lever action rifles. One man carried a double barrel shot-gun. They all had on blue jeans and typical farm boy clothes with cowboy boots.

Sam had on a cowboy hat that he took off to wipe the sweat from his head. Putting it back on, he reached out to touch my M4. I made sure the safety was on while dropping the magazine, took it off the three point sling, and handed to him. "Here, take a look," I said, as I slid my right hand to the grip of my Glock 17, and held it there, just in case he might try something stupid.

He smiled, placed the M4 to his shoulder, and scanned around in the darkness. "Joe, look at this night sight. We need this kinda gun." He handed the gun to Joe for a look-see.

"Yeah, that's sweet alright," Joe said, as he handed the M4 back to me. "Here you go, mister. Can we buy a couple of those guns?"

Billy Bob looked at me wondering what I was gonna say. Joe used the word buy and not the word give, which means he was open to some type of negations. That told me these men were not really cut-throat bad guys.

While ramming the mag back in, I said, "Yeah, I think so. We just wanna get across the river. Billy, give him the money."

*I forgot to mention that the money we were using was part of the al-Qaida loot that we captured. Months ago, the Army Rangers and my group of Tocabaga Fighters managed to raid the al-Qaida HQ located near Tocabaga. We found a million dollars in greenbacks and gold. For killing al-Qaida leaders and taking their funds they put a $200,000 bounty on my head. This led to me being shot in the shoulder by an al-Qaida fighter who managed to infiltrate Tocabaga, but that's also another long story.*

Billy handed him the money. "Here you go, Joe. It's fifteen grand for nine trucks to cross."

"Give me ten grand, four of those M4s, and we'll call it even," Joe said.

I jumped in, "Joe, I'll tell you what. I'll give you the fifteen grand and four guns, if you do us a favor."

"What kinda favor?"

"There're some cars following us. One is a black pickup. It has a spot light on the driver's door. All I ask is don't let it cross the bridge. I'll throw in a case of ammo, too."

"Uncle Jack, you got a deal." Joe was all smiles as he shook hands with me and Billy Bob.

I got on the radio. "George, we just made a deal. Bring four M4s up to me."

"What for? We don't have many spare guns." George replied.

"They're part of the deal to cross the river."

George pulled up in his Hummer with Pete's truck right behind him. When Joe saw our big Humvees with mounted machine guns, I believe he said, "Holy shit."

I walked back to the truck and gathered up four guns taking them to Joe and his boys. They were like kids at Christmas time. I provided them some basic instructions on how the weapons operated and in fifteen minutes they were set to go. Joe and Sam had some experience with AR15s so they knew the basics.

As we mounted up Joe said, "You know, you coulda blasted your way through our road block."

I just smiled and said, "Yeah, I know, but we don't want any trouble."

"It was a pleasure doing business with y'all," Sam said.

"One more thing. What's on the other side of the bridge?" I asked.

"Maybe a few gangs, but it's nothing you boys can't handle," Joe replied.

As we drove away Billy shouted, "Y'all take care now."

With two Hummers in the lead we proceeded across the Greenville Bridge and the Mississippi. We were now in Arkansas following Route 82, which runs through the southern part of the state. It would allow us to avoid any big cities. Basically, the state has very few cities and towns. From the Greenville Bridge to Texarkana, Texas is almost 200 miles. With any luck we would reach Texarkana by daylight.

Arkansas presented no problems. We didn't see a single person while driving for three hours in the middle of the night. It made me wonder if anyone was alive in sleepy Arkansas.

Baldwin stopped the convoy to refuel and we took a short break. Maggie and Billy Bob let the dogs out. Most of us hadn't had anything to eat or had a chance to clean up from the day before.

I was tried, sweaty, and hungry as heck. I guessed so was everyone else. As I pumped 30 gallons of gas into the tank the fumes made me nauseous. Now I had the smell of gas on my hands which I didn't like. I poured some water in a dish and washed them off along with my face. It wasn't cold but it was wet. It felt good and woke me up a little.

Maggie walked over next to me. "Jack, do me a favor and pour some water over my head."

I laughed, "Really?"

"Yeah, I'm all sweaty and hot as hell."

I climbed into the truck bed, picked up a 5 gallon bottle of water, and turned around to see Maggie had taken her shirt and pants off. Wow, that was a nice surprise. It was dark but there was a full moon and I could clearly see her. She wasn't totally naked, but when I started to pour water on her, the wet underwear left nothing to the imagination.

The other men in our convoy were on the other side of the trucks eating or relaxing. So they missed the show.

Maggie glanced up at me and said, "You like what you see, big boy?"

I stopped pouring the water. "Ok, that's enough hot pants. You should be cooled off by now. How about getting dressed and make us something to eat."

"Ok, party pooper." She blew me a kiss, put on her clothes, went to the back of the truck and pulled out a couple of MRE's. I thought, *damn that little prick teaser.*

We had just finished eating when Captain Baldwin shouted, "Mount up." Everyone scrambled to the trucks. The convoy started to roll. In an hour and a half we would reach Texarkana and the Texas border.

THOMAS H. WARD

# THE TEXAS RANGERS
## APRIL 25, 2026

The city of Texarkana is divided in half by the Texas-Arkansas state line. Route 82 passes right through the middle of the city, which used to have a population of around 30,000. Texarkana, Texas is located in Bowie County, named after Jim Bowie who was killed at De Alamo.

We finally reached Texarkana just as the sun was coming up. As we approached the Texas border, there were six police cars sitting there with flashing lights. Slowly rolling to a stop at the road block, Baldwin and I approached ten officers who were armed to the teeth. Our M4's were dangling by their slings and we made it a point not to touch them.

The officers held their guns in a low ready position while watching our every move. One of the officer's stepped forward, closing the gap between us to a few feet. "Howdy boys. I am Captain James Walker. What brings y'all to Texas?"

I noticed he was dressed like a cowboy. He had on a white hat, boots, and blue jeans. I spied the shiny badge pinned to his chest. It was a star in a circle that read in big letters: TEXAS RANGER.

Captain Walker had a weather-beaten face full of premature wrinkles and dark skin which I assumed was a suntan. He stood about my height, in seemingly good shape. I guessed his age to be in the mid-fifties. He just looked like a tough old cowboy. The other men appeared to be in their late twenties.

I replied, "Good morning, Captain. I'm Jack Gunn, and this is George Baldwin. We're just passing through Texas on our way to the Comanche Nation and then to Arizona."

He glanced at our Hummers with machine guns and then peered down the line of our convoy. "Are y'all military people?"

"No sir, but we're working for the Army." I handed him the letter from Captain Sessions.

He read the letter and handed it back. "The letter doesn't state what your business is about. You know, we can't let just anyone into Texas, especially people with fire power like you got."

"We're on a classified mission so I can't tell you any more than that. Like I said, we're just passing through Texas, as fast as possible."

Ranger Walker nodded his head and put his hand on his six-gun, while kinda leaning to one side. "Where y'all from?"

Baldwin replied, "From Florida, sir. We got all this fire power cause going across country and you don't know what you'll run into. There are still terrorists out there."

"Yep, we know that. That's why we got road blocks

up on every major highway. We don't want them coming here and making trouble for Texans."

He stood there for a minute looking at us. I said, "Ranger, do you believe in God?"

"Yes. What's that got to do with anything?"

"I can tell you we're on a mission for God to help save the country."

He looked at me like I was crazy. "A mission for God?"

"Yes, that's right." I pointed at the convoy. "These men are the modern Templar Warriors."

"Templars! I thought they didn't exist anymore."

Baldwin spoke up. "We're the new Templar Knights. We've been going around the country killing Islamic terrorist groups like ISIS, for a couple of years now."

"I see. You men seem on the up and up. Let me talk to my Rangers, cause I got an idea." Ranger Walker went back to the road block and we watched them all huddle together.

After about twenty minutes the Rangers came over to Baldwin and me. Walker said, "We wanna help y'all out, so we'll give you an escort through Texas to the Comanche Nation. If any other Rangers saw you with those armored vehicles and machine guns, you'd be stopped for sure."

"That sounds good to me," I replied.

Walker said, "It's about 600 miles to the Nation. It's a long drive. We don't want anything to happen to you, so I'll send two cars with you. One will lead the way and another in the rear. No one will mess with you when they see the Texas Rangers in your convoy."

"Top speed of our Hummers is only forty five. That means it'll take thirteen to fifteen hours, not including piss stops and refueling," Baldwin commented.

Walker said, "Anytime you're ready to leave, let me know."

"Ok, just let us top off our fuel tanks and we'll be ready."

"You don't have to worry about fuel in Texas. We got plenty of stations along the way," Walker said.

*The famous Texas Rangers have a long and colorful history. By the early 1820s, some 700 families had settled in Texas. There was no regular army to protect the citizens against attacks by native tribes and bandits. In 1823 Stephen Austin organized small informal groups whose duties required them to range over the countryside to help protect the people. They became known as the Texas Rangers. The rangers were paid in property since Austin didn't have the funds in cash to pay them.*

*However, it wasn't until 1835 that the Texas Rangers were formally recognized. On October 17, 1835 at a consultation of the Provisional Government of Texas, a resolution was passed to establish the Texas Rangers. They totaled 60 men which was distributed into three companies. They were known by their simple uniforms, which were light dusters. The identification badge was formed from a Mexican Peso into the shape of a star in a circle. Within two years, the Rangers force had grown to more than 300 men. The Texas Rangers were known for always getting their man. They were rugged tough men, who risked death almost daily.*

We rolled out of Texarkana with Captain Walker in the lead. I was surprised at how normal Texas seemed. People were driving around, stores were open, and life was good. Everywhere I looked I saw a Texas Ranger or the Texas Militiaman. Everyone carried some type of weapon for protection. It was clear to me that there was law and order in Texas.

I was riding with Walker to keep him company and to stay in communication with our convoy using my radio. I asked him, "How many Rangers do you have?"

"No one really knows exactly. Any person, man or woman, who wants to be a Ranger can, as long as their record is clean. All they need to do is get sworn in by the Ranger Captain in their county. Texas has 254 counties and we try to have at least fifty Rangers in each county. Some are more and some are less. Of course, no one gets paid anything, unless you're a Captain like me."

"So to maintain law and order you have the Rangers in each county, sheriffs, local police, and the Texas Militiamen."

"Yep, that's about right. Most Texans want law and order."

Texas has more small towns than Arkansas does. It also has 254 counties which is more than any other state. By my calculations, if Texas has fifty Rangers in each county, then there are 12,700 Rangers state wide. That is a considerable force.

"You seem to have everything under control here in Texas."

"Yep, we don't put up with any bullshit from law breakers. Terrorists we shoot on sight. What about in Florida?"

"We still got a lot of problems, but things are a lot better than six months ago. We have the Army Rangers helping to control the situation. They're slowly bringing law and order back."

"We didn't need the Army to help us here in Texas. I am glad however, that the Army removed the President and the commies from office. How long do you think the Army will run the country?"

"I heard from a good source it may take a while. Maybe years before new elections can be held," I said.

Walker commented, "Who woulda thought, the whole country would go to shit."

"Yeah, almost no one saw it coming."

## COMMENTARY ON THE COLLAPSE OF THE GOVERNMENT

The fall of our government didn't happen all at one time. There was no one given moment that signaled the United States was in big trouble. It occurred slowly over a period of years. Like a sandy beach slowly eroding away day by day, as the grains of sand wash away. My best guess is the sand started to erode long ago, in 2001.

Our so-called leaders actually helped make the collapse happen. They destroyed our wonderful country and let the President become a dictator using Executive

Order 13603. It was all for greed and power.

Under this Executive Order, everything belongs to the government. Your property, money, guns, and family are being taken. They tell you where to live and work for the betterment of the State. Much to my dismay, we have gone from being the USA to the USSA (United Socialist States of America). It's a downhill spiral that has plunged our country into deep depression, causing even good people to resort to robbery and violence.

Years before, things were not making much sense, especially when the government took control of the news media. It became state owned so the only news we received was what the Federal Government wanted us to see. Back in 2013, the NSA started to tap our phones, read our emails, and our Facebook pages. We were all being watched, we were all suspected of doing something wrong, we were all having our Bill of Rights violated in the name of government security, and no one did anything about it.

Benjamin Franklin once said, "He who sacrifices freedom for security deserves neither."

Unemployment shot up to 55% and everyone knew that things were changing as more and more acts of violence were reported across the nation. Riots, robberies, shootings, explosions, and even attacks on police stations were common. Some states called up the National Guard to help maintain control as desperate people do desperate things. Just driving to the grocery store was becoming dangerous. You needed to carry a gun for safety or your trip to the store could end up being your last.

Our currency became worthless due to inflation and the government closed all the banks to stop bank runs. A loaf of bread went to a $100 and milk to $150 per gallon, if you can find it. People have run out of money and even if they have any in the bank, they can't get it. Savings accounts were wiped out and if you had any gold or silver in the bank forget it, the doors are locked. The government is taking it all because the country is bankrupt.

For many years, illegal aliens have been coming across the border from Mexico. But not all the people are hardworking Mexicans looking for a job. The fact is, many of those crossing the border are from the Middle East and are related to Islamic radical terrorist groups. How do I know this? Because the US Government has admitted that every year several thousand manage to sneak into the USA.

In addition, the gangs and cartels that smuggle dope were also making inroads into the US selling their crap to whatever idiots would buy it. These gangs have turf wars and during their wars they don't care who they rob or kill. Then there is the drug user who robs and kills to get money to pay for his habit. Finally, we have the radical groups, like the Skinheads, Neo-Nazis, al-Qaida, ISIS, and gangs of all sorts. Everyone is trying to take what you have. People will kill you and steal your property. If you are weak, then you will die.

The government is now controlling the food and there are food lines at every store. You must wait for hours to obtain any food. If you can buy food it's only enough for a few days. You can't feed your family on a loaf of bread. Fresh vegetables and fruit cannot be found.

Our once great healthcare system also came under control of the government. Now we have very few doctors to treat the ill. Hospitals have closed and no one wants to work at them because conditions are terrible. The pay is far below standard wage. Basically our healthcare system is no better than that of a third world country.

Can we change what we've become? There's no country to help us as they've all failed. We're the last hope of free mankind. We cannot forget the Bill of Rights, the US Constitution, and the fact we are One Nation under God.

## END OF COMMENTARY

*Riding along, on our way to Comanche Nation, it occurred to me that now we know what the American Indians felt like. If anyone got a raw deal it was the Indians. They had their lands and homes taken from them by the government. The government lied to them and broke treaty after treaty. Now we were brothers, so to speak, because we are sharing the same misery brought on by the government.*

"I hear tell, that stupid President tried to give Florida to China, to pay the money we owe them. Is that true?" Walker asked.

I replied, "Yeah, that's right. The President was a traitor. We fought off landing parties of Chinese Marines. They had special combat suits which made them invisible. They finally gave up when they lost most of their men trying to gain a foot hold in Florida."

*China now holds 55 percent of all U.S. debt. It is the largest holder of all U.S. debt. If the United States cannot repay the debt in an international currency or gold, then China could demand payment in tangible property, such as real estate. The President signed an illegal agreement and gave Florida to China, because they wanted the oil resources.*

*If you check history, many lands were sold or given as payment of debt. The United States took over Texas, California, Arizona, and New Mexico after the Mexican-American War as payment. We purchased Alaska from Russia. The U.S. purchased land from France in a deal called the Louisiana Purchase. Spain ceded Florida to the United States in 1821.*

"If they were Invisible, how did ya kill them?"

"We found out, they weren't that invisible. We could detect them with lasers. Another big factor was their invisible suits weren't air conditioned so they couldn't take the Florida heat. The sun literally cooked them."

Walker gave a chuckle. "Do our Special Forces have anything like that?"

"Yeah. They have Invisible suits and Talos Warrior units."

"What the hell's a Talos Warrior unit?"

"Putting it simply, it's a suit that turns a man into an Iron Man, but he can't fly."

"I'd like to see one of those."

*An idea came to life in modern days as a comic book and movie called Iron Man. A man invents a suit of armor and becomes indestructible. In 2011 the Army started a program called TALOS. The Army now has the exoskeleton TALOS combat units that are used from time to time for extremely dangerous missions. These TALOS units have developed into fully armored protective suits that a soldier steps into and becomes Iron man. The only difference is the soldier cannot fly.*

*Using the most recent model, a soldier can run at 20 miles per hour all day. They can carry heavy items like big 50 caliber machine guns and 500 rounds of ammunition at the same time. They pinpoint the target and fire by eye movement and brain waves. The most important advantage is one can walk through a hail of bullets and not even get a scratch.*

*A new type of reactive armor has been developed that is more or less painted on top of lightweight thin titanium alloy and beryllium metal, all covered with sheets of Kevlar 10 embedded with a Boron/Silicon Carbide ceramic. The paint is a kind of plastic foam that absorbs energy and behaves like reactive armor. When it is impacted by a high kinetic , it explodes in an outward direction.*

*Boron/Silicon Carbide ceramic is one of the hardest materials known to man. It has been used to make ballistic armor plates since 1986. Typically, it is used in bulletproof vests as well as tank armor. Upon hitting the ceramic, a bullet will shatter into pieces.*

*Titanium is recognized for its high strength-to-weight ratio. It is a strong metal with low density. It has a relatively high melting point (more than 3,000 °F). It is nonmagnetic and has low electrical and thermal conductivity. Some titanium alloys achieve tensile strengths of over 200,000 psi.*

*Beryllium is a hard metal. The modulus of elasticity is approximately 50% greater than steel. Beryllium is two-thirds the density of aluminum. By weight, Beryllium has six times the specific stiffness of steel and Beryllium is non-magnetic.*

*Reactive armor is a type of material that reacts in some way to the impact of a high kinetic projectile to reduce the damage done. The most common type is explosive reactive armor (ERA), but different types include self-limiting explosive reactive armor (SLERA), non-energetic reactive armor (NERA), and non-explosive reactive armor (NxRA). The new foam plastic paint is a combination of all of these types. If damaged in battle, a new coat can be painted on top and it is combat ready in minutes.*

*The TALOS unit is powered by a small atomic battery pack using a new technology no one has heard of. This power system just popped out of nowhere. These little batteries have over a one year operating life and never need charging. The atomic batteries provide the energy to power the electrical - hydraulic servo systems that make movement possible and super feats of strength.*

"Yeah, the Talos Warrior units are really incredible. I've seen them close up. Only the Special Forces use them."

Walker said, "Tell everyone we're stopping up ahead for fuel and food."

It would be a welcomed break since we had been driving three hours already. I got on my radio and advised the convoy as we pulled into a gas station which had a street car diner. The sign above it simply read: 'SALLY's DINER'.

It was a dust-covered little diner out in the middle of nowhere. There were two gas pumps and one for diesel. Behind the diner was a little ranch house.

"Where do you get the gas from?" I asked.

"This is Texas, man. We got no gas shortages here. Let's go in and get some chow. Sally makes the best beef steaks in Texas." Walker replied.

"I haven't had a steak in months."

"We don't have beef shortages either in Texas."

The diner was your typical street car diner from 70 years ago. It wasn't very new, but it was clean. The little mushroom stools at the counter and the seats in the booths were red plastic and every single one had cracks in it from wear. The counter and tabletops definitely showed signs of extreme use.

As we walked in the door Walker yelled, "Sally honey, I brought you some customers."

Sally was a woman in her late thirties with blond hair and a nice figure. She had a real Texas twang to her voice. The dry air and hot sun had taken a toll on her skin, which showed premature wrinkles, but she was still a handsome woman.

Sally ran out from behind the counter and gave

Walker a big hug and a peck on the cheek. "Howdy, Captain. What y'all gonna eat." It was clear that Walker and Sally were more than just good friends.

"Round up beef steaks for everyone, with all the fixin's, Sally."

"How many?"

The Captain nudged me and I replied, "We'll need thirty steaks." I included a steak for each dog.

"Wow, that's gonna wipe me out of steaks."

This was going be a long pit stop. All of our men filed in for lunch, filling the little diner. No one talked much because everyone was tired and hungry. When the steaks came out the men gobbled them down, like a starving wolfs. Maggie and Adam took a couple of steaks out to the dogs.

After chowing down the great food, Captain Walker put the whole bill on his tab. I gave Sally a three hundred dollar tip, which she well deserved.

Checking the time, as we pulled away, I noted we spent two hours eating. It was time well spent because my men were tired from being on the road all night. It was a good rest stop giving everyone much needed energy to continue on.

Still riding with Walker, I commented, "Thanks a lot for picking up the tab. That was great food. Good steaks are hard to come by in Florida."

"It's my pleasure to show you some Texas hospitality. Sally makes a great steak and grilled potato dinner. If you don't have beef in Florida, what do y'all eat?"

"We got beef, but not much of it. We mostly eat fish, chicken, and sometimes a pig. We grow our own fruit and vegetables."

"Fish! Damn, I couldn't live on that."

I laughed. "You get use to it when that's all there is."

Walker laughed and said, "Not me. Pig and chicken is ok, but not fish. I can't stand the smell, nor the taste."

I changed the subject. "Captain, are you related to Sam Walker?"

"You know about Texas history?"

"A little bit. I know Sam Walker was the Ranger who helped invent the Walker-Colt pistol."

"Yep, I am related to him. I'm also part Comanche Indian. That's one reason I wanted to come on this trip. I got relatives at the Nation, whom I haven't seen in a while. So I'm kinda curious why y'all are going there."

Now I had to tell Walker why we were going to the Comanche Nation. I couldn't lie about it. Since he was part Comanche, maybe he could help us out.

"Ok, I'll tell you more about our mission. Adam, my adopted grandson, was given an artifact from his real grandfather when he passed away. This artifact gives clues as to where the long lost Templars treasure is hidden. It also tells what's in the treasure."

"What kinda artifact?"

"It's a sword, called the Sword of Jerusalem."

I paused for a minute waiting for a reply from James. "You got my attention. Go ahead."

"The clues are very vague. However, so far I've

managed to guess that the Templar Knights brought the treasure to Arizona. On top of that they had to travel through Comanche country."

"What year did this happen?"

"Near as we can tell it was 1300 A.D. when they came here."

Walker said, "I doubt anyone will have information going back that far. They didn't keep written records. But we can ask the Medicine man if he ever heard about the Templars coming through their territory."

"Do you know him?"

"Hell yes, he's my Uncle. He also runs the Comanche Nation Museum."

"That's amazing. We run into you and find the man we need to talk to is your uncle. God must be watching over us."

"Jack, tell me, what's the Templar treasure?"

"It's the lost treasure of King Solomon. We believe it contains the Ark of the Covenant."

"You mean the gold box that contained the Ten Commandments?"

"Well, we're not a hundred percent sure, but the sword says it was part of the treasure."

Captain Walker sat there speechless, just nodding his head as he drove us to Wichita Falls.

I dozed off and not much was said after that exchange. Before I knew it, Captain Walker woke me up. "Pit stop, up ahead."

I rubbed my eyes and sat up wondering how far away we were from the Nation. I picked up my radio and advised everyone we were stopping up ahead.

While refueling, Walker met Billy Bob, and while they shook hands, I noticed that they had similar facical features. In the bright sunlight their skin color was also comparable. They both had high cheek bones and dark eyes. They were about the same size and their posture was high and straight. I studied them and was amazed how much they resembled each other.

We arrived at the Comanche Nation at 8 pm without any incidents. The sun was setting as our trucks rolled to a stop at the gate. Ten armed men greeted us as Walker got out and shook their hands. A few of them gave a typical Indian whoop and yelled 'Tu Puuku.' They all seemed to know him and I stood there watching as they exchanged greetings speaking in their native tongue.

Walker didn't bother to introduce me to any of the guards and told me that we could make camp at an empty lot near his Uncle's house. We got back in his police car and the guards, who all wore cowboy hats with two long strands of braided hair hanging down their backs, waved us past the road block.

While we were setting up camp, Walker said, "I'm gonna talk to my Uncle. Ranger Smith and I will sleep at his house tonight, so we'll see you in the morning. You'll be safe here tonight."

"Ok, whatever you say, Captain."

As Captain Walker and Ranger Smith walked away, Baldwin moseyed over and asked, "Where are they going?"

"They're going to his Uncle's house tonight. He

said we'd be safe here."

"Maybe so, but I'm still posting guards."

I nodded my head. "Yeah, I agree."

Everyone was hot, tired, and hungry from the long 15 hour trip. I just wanted to clean up, eat, and hit the hay. Maggie came over and asked, "Where can we get cleaned up at?"

I replied, "I don't have any idea. Where are the dogs?"

"Billy Bob has them over there; doing their business away from everyone." Maggie pointed them out about 100 yards away.

Billy jogged over to us with the dogs. "Jack, there's a motel down the street. Maybe we can get a few rooms for the night."

"Good idea. Maggie, take some money and go over there with Billy. See if you can get twelve rooms for two days. Then we'll be able to take a shower and sleep in a bed."

Maggie said, "That sounds good to me." Billy handed me the dog leashes and they walked towards the motel, a good half mile away.

While they were gone I heated some MREs for the dogs and me. Maggie quickly returned, advising that they were able to get fourteen rooms. She went around and passed out room keys to the Knights.

It was a nice little place called the Comanche Nation Motel. The rooms were plain and the furniture was old. It wasn't a Hilton, but I didn't mind because it was better than sleeping on the ground or in a truck.

We'd be doing enough of that on this journey.

All of us took a much needed shower and we felt human again. It's funny how great a shower can feel. The well water had a little sulfur smell to it, but I didn't mind the stink.

I went outside and cracked open a bottle of JD, which I had been saving. I poured a shot and lit up a smoke. Adolf and Freda were sitting at my feet. Driving just poops me out and a shot of whiskey or two would relax me, so I could sleep.

We ended up sleeping in one room with two double beds. Adam and I had one, and Maggie the other. Billy slept on the floor with the dogs.

THOMAS H. WARD

# BLACK HORSE
## APRIL, 26, 2026

I heard the rooster crow and opened my eyes. It was still dark, as I glanced at my watch, it was 4 am. That damn rooster wouldn't shut up so I got out of bed, took another shower, and went out for a smoke. I peered down the street at our convoy and decided to walk down there to find some coffee. Passing by the motel office, I saw a person was up and moving about.

Opening the door, I walked in and said, "Good morning."

An old man with long braided grey hair turned around and said, "Howdy Mister. You want some coffee?"

"Yes sir, that sounds great."

He poured me a cup of black mud. "Here ya go. My name is Big Bear."

I stuck out my hand. "Hello Big Bear. Pleased to meet you. I'm Jack Gunn." I put the cup to my lips. The coffee was hot so I slowly sipped it. It had a unique taste. "This is good. What's in it?"

"Oh, a little sage, to add some flavor. It's an old

Indian custom."

"I never heard of that before. But it sure is good."

The old Indian took a sip of mud and asked, "So you're friends with Tu Puuku?"

"Sorry, but I don't know anyone named Tu Puuku."

"That's his Indian name. His English name is James Walker."

"Yeah, we're friends."

I pulled out a smoke and offered him one. He took one, looked at it, twirled it around in his fingers, and then smelled it. After that he stuck it between his lips and I lit it for him. "Thanks Mister. It tastes good." I nodded in agreement.

Walker came walking in the door as we were finishing our coffee and smokes. "Hi Jack. Did you sleep here last night?"

"Morning Captain. Yeah, we purchased fourteen rooms."

The old Indian smiled and handed Walker a cup of his sage-laced coffee. "Big Bear, this is still the best damn coffee around."

Big Bear mumbled something in Comanche and the Captain replied back to him. Putting his hand on my shoulder he said, "Jack, you and Billy Bob can speak to my Uncle. He's expecting us after we get some chow."

"Billy don't know anything about what we're looking for."

"I know that, but he wants to meet him for another reason."

"Can I ask why?"

Walker glanced at me. "I think he's part Comanche."

I thought about this for a minute and said, "Now that you mention it, he does appear to have some Indian blood in him. You both have the same facial features."

He let out a little laugh. "You noticed that, did ya?"

Neither of us said another word about the facial similarities.

An hour later, we walked into Black Horse's home. Walker introduced Billy and me to Black Horse. He didn't shake our hands', but just stared at Billy Bob. He didn't say a word for almost ten minutes. He slowly walked around Billy, checking him out from head to toe.

Black Horse appeared to be around sixty years old. His sun-beaten face showed the deep wrinkles of age, but it had a trustworthy appearance. His hair was totally grey with long twin braids which hung to his waist. Black Horse continued to move deliberately around Billy Bob. I liked his half indian/cowboy appearance and calming demeanor. But on the other hand, he was acting kinda weird.

Walker said, "My Uncle's been the Medicine man for 30 years. If anyone knows the history, it's him."

Black Horse was still staring at Billy Bob. He asked him, "What city where you born in?"

Billy replied, "Indianola, sir."

"What was your mother's name?" Black Horse was peering into Billy's eyes.

"Susan, sir."

I could tell Billy was getting nervous and wondered

why this man was questioning him so intensely.

Black Horse ordered Billy to take off his shirt. Billy asked, "Why?"

"Just do as I say, boy." Black Horse pointed his finger at Billy Bob. "Hurry it up."

I really wondered what was going on now, but I told Billy, "Go ahead, take it off." Billy removed his shirt.

I noticed a tattoo of a small horse on his right shoulder. It wasn't just any horse, it was a black horse.

The Comanche Medicine man stood up and looked closely at it. He removed his shirt and pointed to a black horse tattoo on his right arm. "I have same tattoo."

"What does it mean?" Billy asked.

"It means you are my Son. Your real name is Little Black Horse. I gave you that tattoo when you were four years old, so I would always be able to identify you."

"You're … my Father? I can't believe it! I found my real Father."

"Welcome home, my Son." They hugged each other and some tears dropped to the floor.

Walker said, "Welcome home, Little Black Horse." They both smiled at each other and shook hands.

Black Horse stepped over to me. "Thank you for bringing my Son to me. I'll always be in your debt."

"You don't owe me anything. It was the work of God," I replied.

Black Horse nodded his head and put his arm around Billy Bob. "Tonight we will celebrate that my Son is here."

In a soft voice Billy asked, "Father, why didn't you come for me in Indianola?"

"Sit down, I will tell you the story."

We sat down, waited as Black Horse lit up a pipe, took a puff, and passed it around the room. "I met your Mother in Indianola one day when I went there to find work. We were young and fell in love right away." He took another puff and thought. "You were born, but we never got married because she was white and I was Comanche. The Mississippi law would not permit it, but you were born anyway. We lived together for four years, until one day a member from my tribe came and told me my Father was sick. I needed to return to the Nation."

He paused for a few minutes, while gazing up at the ceiling, as if he was thinking. "Susan couldn't leave with me because her mother needed someone to take care of her. So we agreed I would go and return when it was possible. You were only four years old when I gave you that tattoo. I remember you didn't even cry."

"Did you ever come back looking for us?" Billy asked.

"Yes, my Son. But it was a long time later. The years flew by and I became the new Medicine Man of the tribe. When I did return your Mother had already died, maybe from a broken heart. I asked many people what happened to her little boy. No one knew what happened to you. After searching for many days, I gave up and returned home. You were always in my heart. I knew that someday we would come together."

"Yes, now we're together. I will never leave your side," Billy said.

"I was loyal to your Mother's memory and never married or had any children. You are my only son."

I sat there speechless because his story brought a tear to my eye. I glanced at Walker and saw him wipe a tear away.

"Father, I feel at home. The empty feeling I had all those years is gone," Billy said, as he touched his father's hand.

"That is good, my Son. My empty feeling is also gone."

Black Horse glanced at me and wiped a tear from his eye. "Now, let's help Jack Gunn with his problem. Tell me what you want to know, Jack Gunn."

I started by showing him a picture of the Templar Cross. "Have you ever seen this shape anywhere?"

Black Horse put on his glasses and studied the picture. "It looks like some kind of cross."

"Yes, it's a Templar Cross."

"I've never seen one before."

"I know the historians and archaeologists say the Comanche Indians didn't live in this part of the country until fifteen-hundred. Is that correct?"

"No. As far as I know my people have lived here since the beginning of time. We have always ruled the plains here."

I said, "Let me explain more. I believe that in thirteen-hundred a large group of men, called the Knights Templar, came through this area from Europe. If I can prove they were here then it would give me the confidence to keep looking for the treasure they brought.

Do you remember any history about that?"

"There has been many such people from Spain and Europe coming to our land in the past. We always fight with them because they try to change our ways."

I was getting nowhere fast. I pulled out another picture of a Templar Knight in old battle gear, which showed the shield, helmet, and sword. "Have you ever seen anything like this?"

"Yes. We have many such relics taken from the Spanish Conquistadors. Most of them are in the museum but some are here in my house. Would you like to see them?"

"Yes, please." I thought, *now I am getting somewhere.*

"Ok, follow me." We proceed into a bedroom that was filled with old relics.

The room was dark so I took out my flashlight and shined it around. It was filled with all types of ancient items taken from the battle fields. "May I look around?"

"Yes, of course. There's a lot of old junk here that my people collected over hundreds of years."

I viewed the piles of relics. There were scalps, bows, arrows, and many helmets along with a few shields and some swords. Digging in the piles I found old flintlock rifles and pistols.

Black Horse commented, "Jack, you are the first white man to ever see this collection."

"I am honored to be the first," I said, while still digging.

Black Horse, Billy, and Walker went to sit down

while I kept searching in the car size pile of relics. He had a fortune here that any museum would pay money for, when times were good.

After an hour, I had found 12 helmets which were all Spanish, 10 swords, 15 shields, and several old guns. These had to be from the Conquistadors. I walked back into the living room. "I didn't find what I was looking for. Can we go to the Museum?"

"Yes. I will take you now." We walked a few blocks to the Comanche Nation History Museum. It was about 30,000 square feet in size. Black Horse took me to the correct displays showing European relics. There were dozens of metal helmets here and great looking swords with shields. The items on display here were in better shape than the ones in his house.

After another hour, to my dismay, none of the items had a Templar Cross on it. I commented to Black Horse, "Well, that's it. I haven't seen the sign of the cross."

"That's too bad. I really wanted to help you," Black Horse said.

We were walking back to his house and he said, "It just occurred to me that Quanah Iron Coat has some old relics. Do you want to see them?"

"Ok, let's go." We went to Quanah Iron Coat's house, but he wasn't home.

Black Horse commented, "Quanah probably went hunting or is on guard duty. We will talk to him later."

"Is he related to Quanah Parker, the famous Chief?"

"Yes, Quanah Parker is his Great-Great-Grandfather. But most of us are related in some way to Quanah Parker. It is rumored that he had many wives and children. You can find his life story on the internet."

"Yes, I read about him. He was a great warrior who helped his people."

On the way back, to Black Horse's house we passed by many people. Black Horse made it a point to introduce his son and tell each person the story about finding his son. He told the story with joy and cited me as the person who brought his son to him. He advised everyone there would be a celebration tonight at 9 pm in the town park.

Even before 9 pm, people were gathering in the park. I was the only one invited from our group. Captain Baldwin and his warriors stayed close to the motel and trucks along with Maggie, Adam, and the dogs.

I felt totally out of place, since I couldn't understand Comanche and didn't know the customs. It was a big event and I would guess over a thousand people showed up to pay respects to Black Horse and to meet his son. Black Horse introduced me as the friend who returned his son.

Of course, there was an abundance of food provided by the women, who were continually cooking the beef over wood fires. It seemed like a never ending flow of people came to the celebration. They welcomed Billy Bob to the tribe, and then would leave after an hour or so. Almost every person brought a gift of some kind and presented it to Black Horse.

While I was standing next to Black Horse, a tall man dressed in typical old-style Comanche clothing walked up. Black Horse introduced him as the Chief or Head of the Council. It was Quanah Iron Coat himself. I had seen pictures of Quanah Parker and he closely resembled his great-great-grandfather. His bright eyes were the feature I noticed first.

Quanah Iron Coat was a handsome man and his long braided hair was also graying. You could tell he spent a lot of time outside because his facial skin was deeply tanned with crow's feet wrinkles around his eyes. He seemed like a kind caring person as he softly spoke to Black Horse. I didn't understand a word they were saying so I just listened to the wonderful Comanche language being spoken. It sounded almost like music.

I heard Black Horse switch in mid-sentence to English and mention my name. Quanah stepped up in front of me and shook my hand. "So, you are the one to bring Black Horse his son."

I was speechless meeting a great-grandson of Quanah Parker. "Yes, I brought him here, but at the time I didn't know who he was. It's really the work of God or just plain luck."

Nodding his head he folded his arms and looked at me. "So, you take no credit for finding Little Black Horse."

"No, not really. I mean yeah, I brought him here, but I didn't plan it."

"Whether it was fate, luck, God, or the Great Spirit that brought him here, it does not matter. It is important that he is here now. My friend's heart is healed. You made that possible."

"I didn't do anything, but let Billy ride along with me."

"I like you Jack Gunn. You are an honest white

man," Quanah Iron Coat said.

I didn't respond to Quanah because I couldn't think of anything to say at the time. After a minute, Black Horse said, "Quanah, Jack needs your help. He would like to look at the relics of metal Helmets and swords."

"Yes, he may see them, but they are not for sale."

I replied, "I just wanna look at them. I want to see if any have a Templar Cross on them."

"I don't know what a Templar Cross is, but you are welcome to my home to look at them."

"Can we see them now?"

Quanah laughed and replied, "No, not now. It is a night to celebrate the good news for my brother. Come in the morning and I will show you everything."

"How does 8 am sound?"

"That is ok." Without saying another word Quanah Iron Coat walked away, disappearing into the crowd of people.

I turned to observe Black Horse and his son who were now mingling around in the crowd of people. I watched them as Black Horse proudly showed off his son.

I left the party and went to check on my men, most of whom were sitting around a campfire. Baldwin called me over. "I see you got a bunch of happy campers over there."

"Yeah, I'm happy for Billy Bob and Black Horse. It's funny how things work out."

"I take it you didn't find anything indicating that the Templars have been here?"

"No, not yet. Tomorrow the great-grandson of Quanah Parker is gonna show me his collection of metal helmets and stuff. Keep your fingers crossed."

I walked away and went to the motel room because it was already 11 pm. I needed a shot of JD, which was in the room. Opening the motel room door, I found Maggie and Adam there watching an old cowboy and indian movie, named The Searchers. Adolf and Freda were lying on the floor and sat up to greet me.

Maggie glanced up at me. "Well, what did you find?"

"Nothing, so far. Tomorrow Chief Quanah Iron Coat is gonna show me his pile of relics. Maybe I'll find something at his place."

Adam asked, "Can I come along?"

Before I could reply, Maggie said, "I wanna come along."

I poured a shot of JD and took a sip before answering them. "Alright, you guys can come along. I don't think Quanah will mind."

I strolled outside for a smoke, and another drink. After that I went to bed. I couldn't fall asleep thinking about the possibility of finding something that proves the Templars visited here long ago.

# WHITE GHOSTS
## APRIL 27, 2026

The rooster woke me up again at 4 am. I wanted to shoot that damn thing. After a cup of Indian coffee with Big Buffalo and some food, we went to Quanah Iron Coat's house. Adam had hold of the dogs when Quanah opened the door. He was surprised by the dogs. He stepped outside to greet us.

"I forgot you were coming. What's your name again?"

"Jack Gunn, a friend of Black Horse."

He laughed a little. "Yes, that's right. You found Little Black Horse."

Iron Coat's house was a small dwelling which had a two car garage next to it. It was just a normal one-story ranch that was badly in need of a paint job, and possibly a new roof.

I introduced him to Adam and Maggie. Looking at the dogs he asked, "What are the names of these wolf dogs?"

Pointing to each one Adam replied, "Adolf and Freda."

He bent down and the dogs smelled his hand. They let Quanah pet them. Their tails were wagging so I could tell they liked him. That put me at ease. Like I always say, dogs can sense if someone is of good character.

"Tie the wolf dogs up out here and come inside," Quanah said.

Stepping inside I could smell the mold or mildew. It was a musty odor that made me sneeze.

Quanah said, "Welcome to my home. I live alone since my wife passed away years ago. My three sons live 20 miles away, out in the country. I don't get many visitors.

The three of us just stood there viewing the piles of stuff, waiting for his approval to proceed with our search. "Go ahead and look around. There is junk all over the place because I never throw anything away."

I glanced around the room and there was stuff piled in every corner, knee deep. I pulled out a picture of the Templar Cross and showed it to him. "Have you ever seen this symbol on anything?"

He carefully looked at the picture. "Yes, I have seen that symbol, but I don't remember where. Let me think about it."

I thought; *does he have memory problems?*

It was clear that Quanah was a hoarder. His home was filled with all kinds of items, which he cherished. I told Maggie and Adam, "Ok, start looking around for anything that could have a Templar Cross on it, like a helmet, sword, or shield."

Mr. Quanah commented, "I know somewhere … somewhere … I have seen that symbol. Oh, there is also stuff in the garage."

I went to the garage to search. After two hours, my back and hands were killing me. I was only halfway done with the pile of relics and I was beat. I walked back into the living room to take a break.

I heard Maggie ask Quanah if he could turn on the light. He reached over from his chair to pull the chain on a lamp next to him. I watched him pull the chain and the lamp lit up, but it was far from being a bright light.

I asked, "Maggie, any luck?"

"No luck here, but I found a dead rat."

Quanah chuckled and said, "You may keep the rat."

Adam shouted from a back room. "No luck here."

I looked at Quanah and again at the lamp. I did a double take. The lamp had tassels hanging from it. I couldn't actually make out what it was until I moved closer to it. It was a homemade lamp alright. There was something underneath the lamp shade.

I took the shade off. Yes, underneath was a helmet. I carefully rubbed the dust off the helmet. To my surprise there was the Templar Cross etched into the side of it. I shouted, "This is it! Here's a Templars helmet!" Adam and Maggie stepped over the junk on the floor to view it.

Quanah said, "Yes, that's it. Now I remember. Let me see that." Removing the metal helmet from the lampstand, I handed the heavy thing to him. "I made this lamp from the helmet years ago, so I wouldn't lose it. This is very important. Let me tell you the story about this helmet."

"You have a story?" Adam asked.

"Yes, Black Horse is not the only one who knows stories. It is my family story from many thousands of moons ago. It is the story of how the Comanche tribe obtained the first horses from the White Ghosts."

"White Ghosts?"

"Yes, White Ghosts, Wolf Boy," Iron Coat said, with a laugh. "That is my Indian name for you. You are now Wolf Boy because of your wolf dogs."

Adam smiled and said, "Thank you for the Indian name, Mr. Quanah."

"Now, let me tell the story. It is a long story so sit down and listen carefully, because I will not repeat it." We quickly sat down as close as possible so we wouldn't miss a word from the soft spoken old man.

Quanah continued, "Hundreds of years ago, my people were living here on the plains. They had no horses at the time because the horse was not here then. They hunted on foot. They even hunted buffalo on foot which was dangerous and almost impossible.

"Only the fastest runners and best hunters could kill a buffalo using spears and arrows. It became a test of manhood. To become a man, you needed to kill a buffalo by yourself. A good hunter could do this by the age of fourteen."

Adam interrupted, "I'm almost fourteen. I can't imagine killing a buffalo with arrows, on foot. I think it's impossible."

"They had to do it or the tribe would go hungry. They would sneak up on the buffalo dressed as another buffalo. The hunter would need to get within 20 yards.

Usually a group of men would go after one buffalo. It would take many arrows to kill a buffalo. Once it was shot, the buffalo would run so the hunters would have to run after it, until it stopped. Then they would shoot it again. When the buffalo dropped to the ground, then all would run in and stab it in the heart with spears."

Quanah asked for a glass of water which Adam swiftly brought him. "Ok, here's your water Mr. Quanah. Please, tell us more."

"After killing the buffalo, the hunters would cut out the liver and each would take a bite while it was still warm. They hold it in the air thanking the Buffalo Spirit for its life."

The old Indian stopped talking for a minute. As if he was trying to think what to say. "Oh, the women in the tribe cut the buffalo up and dragged it back to camp. Sometimes that would take all day depending how many miles they had to walk."

Maggie said, "Wow, that's a lot of work. One of those buffalo could weight a ton."

"One day the hunters were tracking a buffalo herd when they saw the White Ghosts. The ghosts were riding on the back of some strange animal. Of course, the hunters were surprised and frightened by what they saw. They wondered are these men, spirits, or ghosts? All were dressed in long white robes, their heads and faces were covered by masks, which we call metal helmets. The hunters had never seen anything like this before.

"They decided to follow these ghosts, to see what they were doing and where they were going. According to the story, there were more ghosts than they could count. They also had wagons which were pulled by the big animals. Remember, the Comanche nor any Indians ever used wagons. Indians didn't have the wheel a long time ago. Everything was moved by pulling a pole sled."

Quanah stopped talking and lit up a smoke. I stood up, stretched my legs, and also lit one up.

After a few puffs, he continued the story. "So our hunters wanted to watch these ghosts, which they did while keeping out of sight. They followed them for three days and nights. After that it was clear that they were not ghosts, but some type of man with white skin. They observed how the men took care of the big animals that they rode on. The hunters noticed that the animals ate grass like the buffalo.

"One the fourth day, the white men stopped to carve some stones. The hunters were spotted by the white robes. One of the white robes waved a hand at them to come into their camp. A group of white men rode to meet the hunters, who now were afraid. When the white men came to close, one hunter shot an arrow at him, out of fear. The arrow just bounced off the white man. The hunters thought he was arrow proof."

"The arrow bounced off because of the Knights armor," Adam said.

"The white men on their big animals surrounded the hunters and pointed their long knives at them."

Adam interjected, "You mean their swords."

Quanah gave Adam a look telling him to be quiet. "Yes, swords. When they took out the swords, the small group of hunters submitted, throwing down their weapons. They walked back to the camp of the white men under guard and were given some water."

"Wow," Adam responded.

"They tried to speak to each other but it was impossible. The hunters just sat there and watched the white robes carve a rock for five days."

Old Quanah stopped talking and looked at the helmet. As he rubbed the helmet it seemed his mind was racing back in time. Back to a time of the Comanche hunters, so long ago. I'm sure every time he told this story he held the helmet in his hands. It probably helped him to remember.

After a long pause, Adam asked, "So what did they do?"

"The white eyes fell asleep during the night. The hunters killed two of them and snuck away without being heard."

"That's it?" Adam asked. "What about the horses?"

"Oh yes, I forgot. They took four horses with them and this helmet. That is the story how the Comanche was the first tribe to have the horse."

"Didn't the Knights chase them?" Maggie asked.

"I do not know if they did," Quanah replied. "That is the end of the story. I don't remember any more right now."

I asked, "What about the rock they were carving?"

"Oh, it is still there on a hill, near the old trail."

I stood up and thought, *if the carved rock is still there it may have the Templar Cross carved in it or some clue.* "Mr. Quanah, can you take us to this carved rock?"

"Sure, but it is just a rock. It has the same symbol as

the helmet on it."

"You said the rock is near the old trail. Can you tell us how to go there?"

"Maybe I can remember where it is. Why do you want to see a rock?"

Maggie touched the old Chief's hand and softly said, "Mr. Quanah, the rock, and trail are important for us to see. Will you please take us to see it?"

"Yes, I would like to, but I'm too old for that. It is a two day journey by pony. I have no ponies."

I laughed a little and said, "We'll go by truck."

"I have no truck."

"Chief Quanah, we have a truck."

Maggie spoke up. "Mr. Quanah, we have a truck so you can ride in comfort, so please show us the rock."

He looked at Maggie and patted her head. "Ok, Warrior Woman, who carries a long knife. I will take you. Make ready to leave."

Quanah was referring to the fact that Maggie was dressed in combat fatigues, carried an M4, and had her machete dangling from her waist. She was an imposing figure, so to speak. It was hard to say no to Maggie when she asked you a soft sweet voice for a favor.

We made the truck ready and advised Captain Baldwin where we were going. The only problem was we didn't know exactly where we were going. The Chief just told us he'd remember as he went along.

Pulling away from Lawton we headed north on Route 281 per the Chief's directions. It was almost 2 pm. It was a cloudy day and you could sense that some rainstorms were heading our way.

After about an hour, Iron Coat said, "Slow down and turn left here." I slowed down and started to turn. "No, don't turn here, keep going a little more."

I had my doubts that he could remember where the trail was. At the next dirt road, Quanah told me to turn left. "Is this the correct trail?" I asked, as I stopped the truck.

"Yes, it is. Keep going straight on this road until I tell you to stop."

This wasn't a road at all. It was a single lane dirt trail with big ruts in it. The terrain next to the trail was rocky and contained little valleys or dips. In my opinion, the terrain was impassable, even by four-wheel drive.

We had to slow down to keep from breaking an axle or getting a flat tire on the sharp rocks. The whole truck was rocking and rolling, making everyone hold on to something to keep stable. Our speed was a blazing 5 to 10 mph.

Chief Quanah dozed off and his head was shaking like a bobblehead doll. That disturbed me because if he was asleep, we could drive right past the Templar location and not know it.

The shaking, rocking, and rolling of the truck was getting to everyone. Maggie said, "Man this is a rough road. I'm getting sea sick."

Adam laughed. "It's fun, Maggie."

I said, "Look out the window at the horizon. Don't look at the floor or you'll get sick."

Quanah woke up in a daze. Adam asked, "Mr.

Quanah, how much further?"

"I don't know. This looks different from the old days."

I said, "We're stopping here for a break." I figured that we needed a break, and maybe if Quanah got out of the truck, and looked around it might spark his memory. Maybe riding in the truck was confusing him, since he was probably here last on horseback.

I pulled to a stop on top of a small knoll. We all got out and stretched our legs. The dogs gladly jumped out and started running around. I gave the Chief a smoke, and we both lit up. Maggie handed us all a bottle of water. As I walked around the dirt trail, I couldn't help but think that this was the old Army trail, which was originally an Indian trail. This had been here hundreds of years. If the Knights Templar used this trail, I couldn't imagine how they ever pulled wagons over this. It must have been slow going.

I walked over to Quanah who was sitting on a big stone. "Chief, how do you feel?"

"Better since we stopped. I was getting sick also. A pony is better on this trail."

"I agree a pony is better. Do you know how much further?"

He peered down the trail and pointed. "You see that high hill? The one far away, with the flat top."

"Yes, I see it."

"I think that is Ghost Hill. We'll know if it is, when we get there"

Looking at the hill through my M4 scope, I

estimated the hill was a couple of hours away at the speed we were going.

Mounting up we got moving again. Dark clouds rolled in and it started to rain. If it rained a lot this dirt trail could turn into a mud slick path, making it dangerous as hell. There were cliffs on both sides of the road which meant possible death, if we slid off.

I stopped at the bottom of the big hill and observed the trail had a 30 degree incline. It started pouring cats and dogs. Water was running down the dirt trail like rain in a gutter. The road was being flooded. I dropped the transmission into 4- wheel drive low. Thank God, for big knobby off-road tires.

I muttered, "Everyone hold on, here we go."

My trusty F-250 slowly groaned forward in low gear. The wheels were spinning every now and then. The trail being only seven to eight feet wide didn't leave much room for error. All of a sudden I lost traction and the rear end skidded off to the side.

Maggie shouted, "Oh my, God!"

I stopped as Maggie looked out the rear window. "Jack, this left rear tire is almost hanging over the cliff."

I counter steered just a little while slowly applying gas to inch forward, trying not to spin the wheels. It worked and we inched forward making it to the top of the hill. Of course, as soon as we got on top the driving rain changed to a slight drizzle.

Chief Quanah said, "It is the rainy season." We all laughed at that comment because he seemed unconcerned about the dangerous situation we just had.

Coming to a stop I said, "I need a drink." Getting

out of the truck, I lit up a smoke.

Maggie handed me my bottle of JD. I took two big swigs and handed it back to her. She asked, "Is this it?"

"Yes, welcome to Ghost Hill," Quanah said.

The top of the hill was flat, and was the size of a football field. It was made up of huge rocks protruding out of the ground. These rocks, some the size of cars, were lying all over the top of the hill. There must have been thirty of them.

The Chief was still sitting in the truck. I asked, "Do you know which rock is carved?"

"I can't remember which one."

I ordered, "Maggie, Adam, let's spread out and check each stone."

It was getting dark early, due to the rain clouds. As I walked around checking each rock, I knew we couldn't go back to Lawton tonight with the rain and mud. It was simply too dangerous. I visualized us sliding down the muddy hill, out of control, and going over the cliff.

Adam yelled, "I found one!" Maggie and I ran over to see it. Carved in the top was an arrow. I checked my compass and it pointed due west.

Further to the north, I spotted a gravestone shaped like a Templar Cross. Just the top of it was protruding from the ground. We walked over to it and found another one that was almost completely buried. I said, "Two grave markers means two dead men; just like the Chief told us in his story."

It was a little spooky finding the graves. No one spoke a word because it was almost like we were standing on holy ground.

Maggie checked another big stone near it and found another Templar Cross engraved in the rock. We stood there observing this stone. Adam and I ran our hands over the worn stone. These stones were confirmation that the Knights were here long before any other Europeans. This validated that we were on the right track to find the treasure.

Adam took some pictures of the stones. While standing on top of the rock, he pointed towards the trail. "Look, there's some trucks coming."

I quickly turned around to observe them. I counted eight trucks about a mile away. I ran to get my Cobb 50 out of our truck, because the scope would give me a better view.

Using the high power scope, I could see someone's face, up to almost a mile away. Placing the big rifle's bipod on a stone, I peered through the scope. The first vehicle was the black truck that had been dogging us since Florida.

I used the zoom to gain a closer view. The trucks stopped about 800 yards away, according to my laser range finder. Watching them dismount, the man driving the black truck got out and looked directly at the hill. All of the men had on the Templar white surcoats, with the red cross on the front. I called Adam over. "Adam, here take a look. Who is this guy?"

Adam peered into the scope and replied, "I can't believe it. I think it's Mr. Canfield. It's hard to tell because he's got a hat on."

"I thought that was him. The rat is after you and the

Sword of Jerusalem."

*Canfield is the man who tried to stop Adam and Emma from coming to live with me the night Adam's grandfather passed away. He is a corrupted member of the old order of the Knights Templar. He and Christian de Molay had planned to steal the Sword of Jerusalem in order to find the treasure.*

Chief Quanah walked over and asked, "What is going on?" He peered down the hill and saw the white mantles. "We have brought the White Ghosts back to life. It was not good to come here."

"Quanah, they aren't Ghosts. They're men just like us. Watch, I'll show you." I moved Adam aside. I bent down on one knee, and squinted through the scope at my target. I wanted to take this guy out. I wanted this asshole dead.

"If they are men, like us, why do they come here dressed like ghosts?"

"It's a long story why they're here. I'll tell you later, Chief."

*These were dangerous men who wanted the sword and the treasure for their own profit. I had no choice but to try and kill their leader, Mr. Canfield, and maybe a few others. If I could terminate a couple, from this distance, maybe they would think twice before coming any closer.*

Racking a round into the chamber, I looked through the scope. Canfield's head came into view. I zeroed the cross hairs on his chest. Quickly, I checked the bushes for wind. There was about a 15 mph breeze from the south. I adjusted my scope to compensate for windage, by 3 clicks. I knew this Cobb was zeroed in for 1,000 yards. The 200 yard difference wouldn't matter much, since I was shooting downhill. I decided to aim at his center of mass. It didn't matter much where I hit him, because the 50 caliber round would blow him apart. This was a long shot, almost a half mile, and even a raindrop could cause me to miss.

Iron Coat asked, "Are you going to kill them?"

"Yes, they're here to steal the sword and possibly kidnap Adam. Everyone hold your ears."

"If you can kill the ghosts, I will name you, Ghost Killer."

Canfield was pointing at us on top the hill. I doubted he could see us and saw only our truck. Then he pulled out binoculars and gazed at the hill. Observing him while he was scanning the hill was chilling, to say the least. Little did he realize a bullet would soon rip into him.

Then he looked directly at us. I told Adam to wave at him. Canfield did a double take and then the fool waved back. While he looked at us, I squeezed the trigger. KABOOM, the rifle recoiled, and I pulled back on target for another shot.

I didn't need it because my round flew straight and true, hitting the target, cutting him almost in half. His white robe turned blood red. The rest of his men ducked for cover. I spotted another man sticking his head up on the other side of the black truck, from behind a door. I fired again, KABOOM. The superman bullet went through the door and killed him. The other trucks started to quickly back-up trying to get out of range.

I let them go for now, knowing that come morning we may have to fight our way out of this mess. I had to come up with a plan tonight.

Quanah said, "I have never seen a white man kill another white man."

"Believe me Chief, I've killed many bad white men over the years."

"I believe you, Ghost Killer."

It was going to be a long night. I posted Adam, with my M4, to watch the dirt trail on the east side. Maggie was assigned to the west side of the hill along with Freda.

The Chief was sitting in the truck so he could watch the south. I wasn't worried about the south because it had a 30 foot drop off. I gave him my Glock 17 to use just in case. He smiled at me when I handed him the gun and told him, "If you see any ghosts shoot them." He laughed a little and nodded.

I covered the north side of the hill with Adolf by my side. If they were going to attack us this was the most likely direction they would come from, because the terrain was almost flat.

I wondered, how in the hell did these guys find us. The only thing I could think of was there had to be a GPS bug hidden somewhere. Then it hit me. The most likely place would be in the sword case.

Sitting there, I thought about using my satellite phone to call Baldwin. Maybe he could get a GPS fix on our location and come to our rescue. I turned it on, but with the thick cloud cover I couldn't receive a signal. It was dark now, and the clouds blocked out the moon. A fog was starting to descend on us.

I hunkered down, next to a big stone, with Adolf. He glanced at me, so I rubbed his damp head, and said, "I need to make a plan. Adolf, you got any ideas?"

If they attacked us I guessed it would be early in the morning, about 4am.

It was sometime after midnight and the fog, which now covered the top of Ghost Hill, created a light cold mist. As it slowly moved down the hill, visibility was reduced to a hundred feet, making it almost impossible to see a damn thing.

I told Adolf, "Sit, guard." Giving him that order, he would not fall asleep; he would sit there all night on full alert. Those command words made him raise his ears and visually scan the area. His nose was sniffing the air for the scent of any human.

Adolf, my German Sheppard guard dog, doesn't miss a thing. With him by my side I knew no one could come within fifty yards of me. I sat down next to him and pulled my collar up to keep the wet chilly mist from going down my neck.

*My friend Rick and I rescued Adolf and three other dogs from a kennel, not far from Tocabaga. The trainer and owner, an old German man named Klaus, was murdered by someone and the dogs were running loose.*

*It was just plain luck that we went to his house to purchase a couple of trained guard dogs and found him. Klaus had been a friend of Rick's for five years. Anyway, we saved the dogs and they became valuable allies for us. By the way, we also found the body of a man that the dogs had apparently killed. We assumed it was the same person who murdered Mr. Klaus, because there was a gun in his dead hand.*

Pulling a pack of smokes out of my vest pocket, I noted there were only three left. I lit one up to take off the edge, took a few drags, and then snuffed it out with my fingers to save the butt for later. If I ran out of smokes it would piss me off. I know smoking is bad for you, but when your number is up, it's up. That's the way I look at it. No one can live forever.

I'm not worried about dying because we all die, and I believe there is life after death. I guess that's why I'm not afraid to get into gun fights. I never think about getting killed because if you do, then you will get killed.

There were about fifteen men in the convoy of cars down the trail. Fifteen men against four, doesn't give us very good odds. Our options were: sit here, wait for an attack, and build a defensive line of some kind. Leave the hill tonight, head west on the old trail, and try to out run them, or scout them out and attack them first. We could snipe them off one by one.

Pondering our options, I thought, leaving the hill tonight was just asking for trouble on the mud-slick narrow trail. We could wind-up sliding off the road into a ditch. Then we'd be stuck in the middle of nowhere.

The smartest thing to do is to build some type of defensive line. Picking them off one by one could be the best choice. Yes, it's dangerous but it could put enough fear into them to leave. They had no idea how many men we have on top the hill.

I decided to use two of the options. We'll make a defensive line and snipe off as many as possible. I rubbed Adolf's head. It was soaking wet. He looked at me to give him a command. I said, "Good boy. Sit, guard." He didn't seem to mind a little rain. Every now and then he'd get up and shake off the water.

To snipe these guys without getting caught, I would need a silencer. I had one for my M4, so I needed to get my gun from Adam. That, however, would leave him without a weapon. It occurred to me that Maggie had a pistol with her, so I'd have to run over and obtain it for Adam.

I looked at Adolf and pointed my finger at him. "Sit, guard, stay." Adolf understood my command and didn't follow me as I jogged over to Maggie's position.

I couldn't even see her in the foggy mist. She was well hidden. I shouted in a loud whisper, "Maggie, it's Jack."

After a few calls, she peeked her head out from behind a rock. "Over here," Maggie replied, in a soft tone.

I scooted behind the big rock, sitting down next to her. "How you doing?"

"Ok, just cold and wet."

I explained my plan to her. She said, "I got a better plan."

Surprised, I said, "Ok, tell me."

"We'll leave the two dogs with Adam. He knows how to control them. Adam and the Chief can guard the truck; we'll leave them our pistols. You and I sneak down the hill and kill these guys."

I thought about it for a minute. "Ok, I agree. My guess is these guys are just sitting in their cars waiting for daylight, trying to stay warm and dry. Meet me at the truck. I have to get Adolf."

I figured that two of us going would be better than just one. We could cover each other and it would double our fire power if we got into a fire fight.

Meeting Maggie at the truck, we informed Adam of our plan. He was a little concerned about us leaving him and Quanah alone. I was also a little worried about leaving a thirteen-year-old kid to guard old Mr. Quanah. But, I knew the old Templars were not really after us. They wanted the Sword of Jerusalem and possibly Adam, because he could read the Latin writing.

I unscrewed the flash suppressors on the M4s and put on the silencers. We would have to make head shots to drop our targets quickly before they could fire a round or yell out a warning. Like all snipers say, 'one shot, one kill.' If we could kill five or six of them I'd be a happy camper, or should I say a happy sniper.

Leaving both dogs with Adam, I advised him to use the big rock near the truck for cover. If he saw anyone, then order the dogs to attack. If they get by the dogs, then shoot as many as you can. He had Maggie's Glock, and we gave him twenty magazines.

I woke up Quanah. "Chief, we need your help."

He rubbed his eyes and replied, "What do you need?"

"I need you to stand guard with Adam while Maggie and I go on a scouting mission."

"You are going to leave us here?"

"Yes, for a short time. The wolf dogs will stay with you."

Adam spoke up, "Don't worry, Mr. Quanah, I'm a good shot."

Quanah Iron Coat laughed and said, "That is good, Wolf Boy. Ghost Killer, how long will you be gone?"

As Maggie and I checked our gear, I said, "Maybe two hours. If we hear any gunfire we'll scamper back here fast." I could tell that Quanah was uneasy about us leaving him alone with Adam for protection. He didn't know that Adam was a trained deadly shot. I spent the last six months training him four hours per day the necessary combat shooting skills.

Maggie and I had on our normal black SWAT-like combat gear. Our BPV's could stop an AK round. The M4s have FLIR night vision scopes which allow us to see the body heat of our enemies in the fog and darkness. The main problem is these scopes greatly reduce the distance you can clearly see due to a lack of resolution at over 200 yards. We'd have to be within 50 yards to make a good head shot.

The one item we didn't have with us was our tactical radio gear, which would permit us to communicate quietly over a distance. This meant we would have to maintain visual contact with each other. I suggested we keep no more than twenty to thirty feet apart. I would take the point and Maggie would protect our backsides.

We slowly walked to the north side to make our way down the hill. My plan was to flank them from the north. At the bottom of the hill, the terrain was rocky but mostly flat, covered with small trees, bushes, and knee high prairie grass.

Before proceeding down the hill, we knelt down and scanned the entire area with our night vision for about 10 minutes. I saw a couple of animals, one in a tree, and another on the ground. It looked scary peering into the fog not knowing what the hell was out there.

Satisfied that the bottom of the hill was clear, we slid down the steep wet slope and stopped to scan around again. Maggie and I mudded up our faces, so no white skin was showing. Standing there waiting for Maggie, I took a deep breath and a voice in my head said, *'Go ahead. There is nothing to be afraid of.'*

I calculated we would have to travel east about one klick or 1000 meters, which is 0.62 miles. I would pace that off counting my steps. It's common practice to use 110 paces to equal 100 meters on flat ground. When we reach 1,100 paces we would turn south, towards the old trail where the enemy was located.

Proceeding forward, I checked the compass to make sure we were heading due east. We were moving east, parallel to the trail, and were probably a quarter mile north of it. Maggie was thirty feet behind me. I estimated we could only see about fifty to a hundred feet in front of us because of the thick dense fog. It was slow going because I halted every 10 paces to look and listen for a minute. I kept count of my paces so we wouldn't get lost in the fog.

Finally, after almost an hour of walking, I heard voices. I raised my hand signaling Maggie to stop, and waved her up to me.

We heard one man say, "You guys finish turning around the trucks so we can get out of here. I gotta take a leak."

Peering through our scopes we spotted him walking towards us. Ducking down into the thick mist and high grass, behind a bush, we watched him approach. He stopped right on the other side of the bush we were hiding behind. He was so close we could hear the sound of his urine splashing the ground.

As soon as he was finished, he turned around to walk back to his men. I silently stood up, took aim through my scope, and fired one round into the back of his head. He dropped dead as a doornail. Grabbing him by his feet, I dragged him back into the high grass, about 40 feet away, while Maggie kept a look-out.

Another man yelled, "Hey Marco! Hurry up."

Since Marco couldn't reply, I knew someone would come looking for him.

Maggie and I made ready to pop the next jerk. We spread out, about 50 feet apart. Whoever was closest to bogey would take him out.

He yelled again, but his voice was closer this time. "Marco, what the hell are you doing?"

As he came into view, Maggie had the shot. He was less than thirty feet from Maggie when she popped him. His body stood still, but he didn't fall. Maggie fired again popping him in the melon and so did I. He dropped like a box full of rocks.

We moved forward to obtain a view of the trucks. All the men were inside the vehicles, and the headlights were on. Maggie was on my right flank as we laid in the high grass about fifty feet away from the targets. I whispered, "If anyone else gets out of the trucks shoot them."

Sure enough, a third man climbed out of the last truck, and started shouting for the two we had just killed. I gave the signal to fire. We both started firing short bursts on full auto and he fell dead next to the truck. Another person yelled, "Someone's shooting at us! They just killed Eddy. Let's get the hell out of here!" We kept peppering the trucks with short bursts hoping to kill a few more.

"What about Marco and Greg," another shouted, as they fired wild shots into the foggy night, some of which zipped over our heads. They had no idea we were so close to them.

The last thing I heard was, "We can't help them. Let's get the hell out of here before we get killed!"

They started to pull away and we ceased fire. They didn't have the stomach for a gun battle. As we watched the trucks quickly pull away I thought, *how lucky we were. Or was it luck?*

Maggie and I stood on the trail watching their taillights fade away into the fog and darkness. We turned around without saying a word to each other and started back up Ghost Hill.

Halfway up, Maggie said, "Mission accomplished. I

need a shot of JD when we get back."

Out of breath I said, "Me … too."

"I'm glad they're gone."

"Yeah it was almost too easy. We haven't seen the last of them," I replied. "I'm sure … we'll see a couple of their trucks … in the ravine, on our way back."

We slowly trudged back up the steep hill. Near the top, I shouted, "Adam, we're coming in! Don't shoot!"

Adam and the dogs ran over to greet us. "You guys ok?" he asked.

"Yeah, they left when we started shooting them."

Quanah asked, "Did you kill more Ghosts?"

Maggie replied, "Yeah, but it was no big deal, Chief."

I said, "I gotta eat something to get my energy back."

Maggie broke out the portable stove and started to heat some MREs up for everyone. We had gone all day and night with no grub. While she was cooking, we each had a couple shots of JD.

Maggie handed an MRE to the Chief. He smelled it and asked, "What is this?"

Adam said, "It's Army food."

"It smells like dog food."

"Hold your nose and eat it. It's good for you," Maggie told him. "See the dogs like it." Both dogs had gobbled down the MREs before we even had taken a bite.

Changing the subject, I said, "Ok, here's the plan.

We'll eat and rest here until the sun comes out and dries up the trail a little. I wanna leave by noon."

# POWER OF THE SWORD
## APRIL 28, 2026

The sun was just starting to rise and the sky was clearing up. It looked like it was going to be a nice day.

We cleaned our weapons and were in the process of getting ready to move out, when Maggie spotted some vehicles heading our way. I looked at them using the Cobb 50 scope. To my surprise, it was two of our Humvees coming to the rescue.

Half an hour later, Captain Baldwin, Black Horse, and Walker climbed out of the first truck. I greeted them all with a hand shake. "Boy, I'm glad to see you guys. How did you find us?"

Baldwin said, "Oh, we have our ways. When you didn't come back yesterday, I figured something must have happened."

"Did you see any other trucks on your way here?"

"No, why?"

"Well, we had a little run in with the old Templars last night."

"What happened?"

"I killed Canfield and another guy. Then Maggie and I sniped them, killing three more. Then they left. End of story. Maybe with Canfield dead, they'll stop chasing us for the sword."

Baldwin shrugged his shoulders. "Maybe they will, maybe they won't. We have to find out how they're tracking us."

"Thanks for reminding me. Adam, bring me the sword. I wanna check the box for a GPS bug."

Adam said, "Ok, but there's no bug in it. I know every little thing about that box." Adam got up and went to remove the box from under the back seat of the truck.

He came running over to me. "Something is wrong." He placed the sword box on a rock and opened it. We looked inside and were shocked to see a wooden branch along with a note written in Latin.

Adam read it out loud. "The treasure belongs to those who find it."

"They got the sword and this note means they can read Latin," I exclaimed, while looking at Adam. "How in the hell did this happen?"

"I don't know, Grandpa."

Quanah said, "I know, maybe a ghost took it."

I inquired, "Did you see anyone, Chief?"

"I saw no one."

"Where were you at, Adam?" I asked.

Adam hung his head down. "It must have happened when we took the dogs for a little walk around the hill top."

"Shit, these guys sneak right into our camp and steal the most important item we have." I was upset because I thought Adam would know better than to leave the sword unguarded. On the other hand, it was also my fault for leaving Adam and Quanah alone.

I carefully felt around inside the silk-lined wooden box. Running my fingers over the cloth, on all sides, and feeling the corners. In one corner, I felt a bump the size of a quarter. "I think the bug is here."

Pulling out my knife I made a slit just big enough to remove the item. Adam said, "Please be careful, don't damage the box."

Using my fingers, I lifted it out. It was a GPS bug alright, about the size of a quarter, but a little thicker. I held it up for everyone to see. Then I smashed it into pieces with a stone.

Maggie said, "They must have been watching us. When no one was around, they came to the truck and took the sword."

Baldwin butted in, "Don't worry we'll get that sword back. How long ago did they leave?"

"It was around 4 am," I said.

"Which way do you think they'll go, Jack?"

"If I was them, I'd go back to Route 281, then go to I-40 and head west. They certainly can't go to Lawton. One thing to our advantage is they still have to figure out what the clues mean."

Adam said, "Yeah, that could take them weeks."

"They'll need to stop somewhere and study the sword clues."

Baldwin said, "We can't go back the way we came because our trucks are too slow. We'll never catch them once they're on I-40. Does anyone know where this trail goes to?"

Black Horse replied, "It goes all the way to Amarillo. Up ahead, about 10 miles, it runs into Route 183. We can get on 183 and then it is just a few miles to I-40. There is an intersection there."

"Good, maybe we can cut them off and ambush them at the intersection. Everyone mount up. Let's roll."

Pulling off of Ghost Hill, heading west, the Hummers took the lead. They could make faster time than my F-250 on the bumpy trail. It wasn't long before they were out of sight.

On the way, Adam commented, "If they unsheathe the sword and touch the blade, God will punish them if they're not worthy."

Maggie asked, "What do you mean?"

"I'm just saying something bad could happen. That's why I told Grandpa Jack not to touch the sword blade."

"Oh, I'm not worthy in the eyes of God," I commented.

"Maybe you are and maybe you're not, but that is up to God. I just didn't want anything bad to happen to you."

After seeing with my own eyes, the sword behead Christian de Molay in a flash of light, guided by the hand of an unseen Angel, I knew its power. Adam was right, don't touch the sword unless God tells you to. It sounds so crazy, I can hardly believe it myself.

"What if they are worthy?" Maggie asked.

"Then they will have the power of the sword," Adam said.

"What does that mean?" I asked.

Adam replied, "I don't really know what it means or what will happen. I only know they'll have the treasure map."

Chief Quanah asked, "What the hell are you talking about?"

"It's a long story, Chief, and we'll tell you later," I said. No one spoke after that. Adam's words gave us all a lot to think about. I thought, *maybe we should just let them have the sword.*

Driving along, it occurred to me, that Adam doesn't control the sword, it controls him. What if we find the treasure, then what will we do with it? Will God like the fact that we found his treasure? Will the power of the sword and possibly the Ark of the Covenant strike us down? Are the Bible stories about its power really true?

The more I thought about it, the more I wondered if we were doing the right thing. If God wanted us to find the treasure, why is he making it so darn difficult?

After an hour of a bumpy motion sickness on the old trail, we reached Route 183. I put the pedal to the metal to catch up to Captain Baldwin. He was already at the cloverleaf intersection preparing for the ambush.

We observed various cars and trucks zooming down the highway past our positions, headed west. I carefully peered at each one to make sure they weren't the old Templars.

A couple of hours had gone by, and the old Templar convoy still hadn't shown up. I tried to flag down a car, headed west, but it didn't wanna stop until we pointed our guns at the driver.

The driver, a young looking man who was clearly afraid of us, advised me that he saw some trucks back down the road, at a rest stop. In the car with him were four little kids, and I assumed the woman was his wife. He asked me if we could spare some food for his kids. Maggie gave them a box of MREs for helping us out. The woman thanked us and said, 'God Bless y'all,' and they drove away.

I couldn't help but wonder where this young man was going and why was he putting his family in danger. Driving on the expressway is dangerous because of Free Roamers, terrorists, and just plain terrible people who would kill you for your car and money, if you had any. His kids could be taken and sold as slaves to the highest bidder, or a sicko child molester could get them. They are the scum of the earth and I've killed a few of them over the years, I'm proud to say.

Everyone mounted up and we drove east to find the rest stop and possibly the Templar convoy. After twenty minutes, we spotted them and pulled over to check them out, from half a mile away. Pulling out the binoculars Baldwin and I carefully scanned the group of trucks. From the angle we were at, we couldn't see anyone moving around.

I commented, "They're checking out the sword and licking their wounds."

Baldwin said, "Here's the plan. We'll enter the rest

stop from two sides, using the entrance and exit ramp, cutting them off so they can't escape. If they don't surrender and shoot at us, we'll blast them to hell. Jack, you follow my Humvee."

Everyone agreed with the plan so it was put into motion. We zoomed into the rest area as fast as possible, but saw no people. The Templars convoy was in a single line along the grassy area, next to some picnic tables. We could only see the driver's side of the vehicles and not the passenger side of their trucks.

It was strange that no one was visible. Baldwin yelled, "Be careful it could be a trap!"

Everyone dismounted with guns ready and surrounded the Templars pickup trucks. Adam and the Chief stayed in my truck as we started the search.

Rounding the front of the black pickup, I stopped dead in my tracks, as did the others in my group. On the ground lay the old Templars in their white mantles. They were clearly all dead.

It was a shocking sight as none of them had eyes and their faces were charred black. Lower jaws hung down, leaving mouths wide open, as if they were screaming. I could almost hear their cries of pain. It was abnormal because other parts of the bodies were untouched. The white mantels, which displayed the crimson cross, were not burned in any manner. There wasn't a drop of blood to be seen.

All twelve bodies looked identical, with burned out eyeballs and charred black faces. The old Templars were all laying on their backs, in a distorted twisted manner, with their hollow eye sockets facing the sky. It was an unearthly sight which told you supernatural forces were at work. The bodies were in a semi-circle around the Sword of Jerusalem, which was stuck straight into the ground about four inches deep. The scabbard was a few feet away, on the grass.

I glared at the blade, which was glowing red, pulsating on and off. The metal blade looked red hot, like it just came from a blacksmith's forge. I shouted, "Don't touch the sword! Don't go near it." All our men, including Baldwin, stopped dead in their tracks. Some of the warriors backed away a few more feet. "Adam, come over here right now!"

Adam came running and stopped next to me when he saw the awful sight. He commented, "They touched the sword. God didn't deem them worthy and struck them down."

Adam started to move towards the sword, but I grabbed his arm, stopping him. "Do you think it's wise to touch the sword after seeing this?"

"I need to clean it and put it back in its scabbard. Once in the scabbard, everyone will be safe."

Still holding his arm, I asked, "Are you sure it won't hurt you?"

"Yes, I'm sure, Grandpa. Don't worry so much." I released is arm.

Adam walked up to the sword and it started flashing faster and faster. Adam slowly reached out to take hold of the handle. Suddenly, when his hand touched the grip, the sword turned glowing white, like a light bulb. It flashed the same intense white light as when the sword killed Christian de Molay.

Adam didn't move for a few seconds, it was as if he was frozen. I yelled, "Adam, are you ok?" He didn't reply. I moved closer to my grandson. I wasn't sure what action to take, if any. Was he being hurt by the sword? It sure appeared so to me. His body started to shake and his head was looking straight up at the sky.

Without further concern about myself, I grabbed his arm to pull him away and felt a force, almost like an electric shock. A strong tingling ran through my body. Frozen in place I couldn't remove my hand from Adam's arm. I tried with all my strength to pull my hand away, but I couldn't escape from the connection. I thought, *we're being electrocuted.*

Yet, it was a slightly different feeling. I can't explain it exactly, but it was a force or power that didn't actually hurt. The force was probing my body and brain. Yes, it was probing my brain. It was reading my memory. My life flashed before my eyes. It ran like a 3-D movie in my head. I saw everything I had done. All the good times and bad times of my life were on display. The people I had killed were in the movie. I clearly saw their faces as I killed them for a second time.

There was Leroy, the guy I killed with a shotgun, blowing off his head. Leroy was the scumbag doper who murdered my little brother, Mike, while he was in line at a burger place. Leroy killed little Mike in cold blood and only received a six year sentence. My brother Ron and I made a plan to kill his ass, when he got out of jail.

We ambushed him at a stoplight and I pulled the trigger from ten feet away, as he went for his gun. His head exploded like a ripe watermelon. It was an eye for an eye, because no one was going to murder my brother and get away with it. It was the first premeditated murder I had committed. But, I didn't think of it as murder. To me it was justice. 'Vengeance is Mine,' saith the Lord, and I was his instrument.

I was being judged for everything I ever did in my life, whether it was good or bad. All these memories, some of which I didn't like, were popping up in the front of my head, zooming by incredibly fast.

I faintly heard Baldwin and Maggie yelling at me. Finally, I freed my hand from Adam, and I fell to the ground. Baldwin helped me up, just in time to see Adam pull the sword from the ground, point the blade at the sky, and kiss the ruby handle. The white glow suddenly stopped. He wiped off the blade, and slid it into the scabbard.

Adam asked, "Are you ok, Grandpa?"

"I … I think so. Are you alright?" I replied, still dazed by what just occurred.

"Yes, I'm fine. We were just judged to see if we were worthy to receive the sword."

"Has this happened to you before?"

"Yes, a couple of times."

"Baldwin, how long were we connected to the sword."

"Maybe ten or fifteen seconds, why?"

"Because, it seemed like hours. My whole life flashed in front of my eyes."

Adam laughed and said, "That's right, it was reading your life. Now I know why Grandpa De Molay chose you to be my guardian. He knew you would be worthy to handle the sword."

Maggie asked, "Adam, how does the sword do that? Is it controlled by God or an Angel?"

"I don't really know for sure. The sword doesn't talk. I only know that God has spoken to me in my dreams."

Captain Baldwin said, "Glory to God." All his men repeated it in unison and made the sign of the cross.

Baldwin commented, "You see men, Adam does own the Power of the Holy Sword. This is the second time the sword has helped him."

Adam replied, "I'm only the caretaker of this sword, not the owner. No one can own God's treasure." After saying that, he put the sword in the box, and placed it under the backseat of my truck. I, for one, was glad that he did.

While watching the Templar Warriors dig graves, Chief Quanah and Black Horse were talking to Walker in Comanche. I had no idea what was being said, but I guessed they asked Walker how the sword could glow like it was on fire, and how did it kill all those men?

Baldwin and his men buried the old Templars in shallow graves. He said a prayer over each man, asking God to forgive them for their sins. After that we mounted up and headed back to the safety of the Comanche Nation.

Arriving there without further incidents, we parted ways with our Comanche friends for the night. When we dropped Chief Quanah off at his home, he commented, "Ghost Killer, you will have to tell the tribe stories of our trip. It was exciting for an old man. I need rest now."

We told the Chief good night. With no further comments, he turned and with shoulders slumped, walked slowly into his house.

Maggie asked, "Do you think he'll be alright?"

"Yeah, he's just tired like me," I said.

At the motel room, I pulled out my bottle of JD and had a few drinks to wind down. We were so worn out from the lack of sleep that we didn't bother to eat anything. Adam fell fast asleep on the floor with the dogs nuzzled up next to him. Maggie flopped into her bed still wearing her combat gear.

As I was dozing off, I couldn't help but wonder what the future had planned for us. I'll find out soon enough, like it or not.

*Signing off for now.*

*GOD BLESS AMERICA, LAND OF THE FREE, and HOME OF THE BRAVE!*

*Jack Gunn, a.k.a. Tocabaga Jack*

*If you have any ideas where the treasure is located, let me know.*

Email me at

THOMASHWARDBOOKS@GMAIL.COM.

I WILL REPLY.

# DRAMATIS PERSONAE
# GHOST KILLER

**Adam de Molay** – A future Knights Templar leader. Sent to Jack Gunn, by God.

**Black Horse** – Medicine man for the Comanche Nation and father of Billy Bob.

**Big Bear** – An old Indian who runs the Comanche Nation Motel.

**Billy Bob** – Lost son of Black Horse who lived in Indianola Mississippi.

**Canfield** – A Templar of the old order, who wants to steal the Sword of Jerusalem.

**Captain George Baldwin** – A Knights Templar commander, of the new order.

**Captain Sessions** – Combat officer, commands and controls combat operations in the field.

**Christian de Molay** – Adam de Molay's uncle. A self proclaimed Grand Master.

**Emma de Molay** – The sister of Adam found on Interstate 75.

**Jeff** – Third in command of the new Templar order.

**Grandpa Jack** – Jack de Moley the Knights Templar Grand Master.

**Hemmi** – Wife of Jack Gunn.

**Walker** – James Walker, Captain of the Texas Rangers and nephew of Black Horse.

**Jim Bo** – Husband to Amy and son-in-law of Jack.

**Maggie** – Amazon Warrior from Tocabaga .

**Mike** – Friend of Jack Gunn and Tocabaga security agent.

**Pete** – Second in command of the new Templar order.

**Quanah Iron Coat** – Chief of the Comanche Nation.

**Ragsdale** – A bad guy in Indianola, who runs a whore house. He claimed to be Billy Bob's father.

**Ron** – Brother of Jack Gunn a Retired Navy vet. Part of Tocabaga security.

**Rick** – President of Tocabaga Association, security team member.

**Sally** – Girl friend of Walker, who owns a diner.

**Tommy Gunn** – Son of Jack Gunn and a retired Marine Scout Sniper.

# TEMPLARS QUEST
## THE ANCIENTS

## BOOK TWO
### TEMPLARS QUEST CHRONICLES

THOMAS H. WARD

*This book is dedicated to the Native American Indians who have contributed so much to the United States of America. To understand America one needs to study the history of Native Americans. We are all brothers.*

# WELCOME TO THE QUEST

Another Jack Gunn adventure begins as he is fighting alongside the modern Templar Warriors to find the lost treasure. They are following the clues of a holy relic named, 'The Sword of Jerusalem.'

Young Adam de Molay has now become the Grand Master of the new Templar Warriors. The modern Templar Warriors are twenty-four battle hardened retired Marines, who fought ISIS for years in the middle-east. They were enlightened by God and decided to do the Lord's work and become his warriors. They have pledged to follow Adam because he is the caretaker of the holy sword.

The sword has been passed down in his family line for seven-hundred years. It holds the secrets of the lost Templar Treasure and is the main reason for this quest. The Ark of the Covenant, designed by God, and made by man, is one of the holy items they are seeking. Whoever finds the treasure could very well control the destiny of the United States.

# PREFACE

I am the oldest of three Brothers. We grew up fighting bullies and gang members in a tough neighborhood in south Chicago. My Dad, one of the most honest men I have known, always stressed: tell the truth, and help each other. Never ever be a bully, never steal, and try to protect those who cannot protect themselves. I have always stood up for the people who could not defend themselves. I hate liars and bullies.

Standing six feet tall at 180 pounds, I am in great shape for my age and my body is honed by years of physical training. I keep in shape by lifting weights almost every day and running three miles four times a week. I shave my head two times a week as it is cooler with no hair in the hot south. I sport a gray mustache and goatee that I keep well-trimmed and short. There is a 2 inch scar on my forehead from a knife fight years ago.

I spent four years in the Army as a Military Policeman, and became an expert in the use of handguns, rifles, shotguns, and in hand-to-hand combat. My legs have skin grafts from burns due to an explosion when I worked for the DOD (Department of Defense) doing security work for seven years. I always carry my Glock 17, and Black Bear Cold Steel fighting knife, no matter where I go.

I love our country, freedom, my family, and friends. If anyone messes with my family or my friends, justice will be swift and painful. I have no use for anyone who breaks the law, cheats or steals. For the most part I follow the Ten Commandments, but also believe in The Code of Hammurabi, which is an Eye for an Eye. If you take an Eye, I'll take your whole Fucking Head. I fight to keep our Bill of Rights under the United States Constitution.

That is me, Jack Gunn, and these are my chronicles.

# SUMMARY

Our expedition left Tocabaga Island almost a month ago. We arrived at our first destination, the Comanche Nation located in Lawton, Oklahoma, hoping to find a clue that the ancient Templars had traveled through this Indian Territory. To our amazement we did find relics and a Templar Cross engraved into stones on the top of Ghost Hill. This find verified that the Templar Knights had traveled to America seven-hundred years ago. It was our first real proof that the clues etched into the Sword of Jerusalem were factual.

The old Templar Order, under the control of a man named Canfield, wanted the Sword of Jerusalem to gain power and find the treasure. They had somehow followed us all the way from Florida. To make a long story short, Maggie and I engaged them at Ghost Hill and killed a few. But during the firefight they managed to steal the sword right from under our noses, while we were bivouacked on top of Ghost Hill.

We located the Templar thieves the next day, and were expecting to have a serious battle. But to our surprise the Sword of Jerusalem had already given them the justice they deserved. Adam had warned us that the holy relic would punish those who touched it, if they were not deemed worthy by God.

# THE HOPI
## MAY 20, 2026

My last entry was April 29, 2026. We ended up staying at the Comanche Nation, longer than I liked because Black Horse and Chief Quanah insisted that we visit for a while. I didn't intend on staying twenty days, but somehow you lose track of time living among the friendly Comanches.

Life moves at a different speed here. A much slower and relaxing pace than what we are used to. Here, at the Comanche Nation, there are no threats to contend with or worry about. It was a good life and my whole expedition team was having a well-deserved vacation, so to speak. There was no doubt about it, we were getting soft and weak from this time off. We were losing our edge, or our battle ready sharpness, which has helped us to stay alive in a country gone to hell.

During this time, we went back to Ghost Hill several times, searching for artifacts and other clues that the Templars may have left behind. We also searched along the old Indian trail for miles, to no avail. Many of the tribal members came along to help us find artifacts. They were also curious about Ghost Hill and the stories that Chief Quanah and Black Horse told.

Because the hill contained graves, it was considered improper to dig on sacred land. No one wanted to wake the ghost spirits. Since we couldn't do any digging, nothing of any interest was found, other than a few arrow heads. Any relics there were most likely buried under a few feet of dirt, after seven hundred years.

Once a week, on Saturday night, many tribal members gathered around the fire pit for story night. Chief Quanah told the story about Wolf Boy and Ghost Killer that foggy night on Ghost Hill. He spoke of how Ghost Killer shot and killed the white ghosts so far away that you needed the eye of an eagle to see the target. He made the story sound exciting but I noticed he took the liberty to change it from time to time.

Black Horse told how his son, Billy Bob, was brought here by the Great Spirit under the protection of Jack Gunn. He advised everyone the sad story of how he had lost his son and future wife so many years ago. Black Horse had dreamed that one day they would be united by a stranger.

Adam was requested to tell the story about the Sword of Jerusalem. He called it the holy long-knife. Of course, no one believed the stories of how the sword beheaded a man, and terminated the old order of the Knights Templar. Not one person really believed its power and many questioned the truthfulness of the stories. That is until Chief Quanah and Black Horse told the tribe they had seen the magic of the sword with their own eyes. They had seen the sword glowing red, as if it was on fire, and the burned skulls of the twelve old order Templar Knights.

It was a chilling supernatural event that made everyone a believer in the Power of the Sword. Adam has control of the sword, *I think*, and is not afraid of handling it. After the sword scanned my brain, to see if I was worthy, it spooked me for sure.

I thought back to that even, and this is what transpired.

*We had tracked down the old Templar order who had stolen the Sword of Jerusalem from our truck on Ghost Hill. They were stopped at an I-40 rest area. We dismounted to surround them and upon rounding the front of their black pickup, I stopped dead in my tracks as did the others in my group. On the ground lay the old Templars in their white mantles. They were all dead.*

*Adam had warned us, if they unsheathe the sword and touch the blade, God would punish them if they were not worthy.*

*After seeing with my own eyes, the sword behead Christian de Molay in a flash of light, guided by the hand of an unseen Angel, I knew its power. Adam was right, don't come in contact with the sword, unless God tells you to. It sounds so crazy, I can hardly believe it myself.*

*The more I thought about it, the more I wondered if we were doing the right thing. If God wanted us to find the treasure, why was he making it so darn difficult?*

*It was a shocking sight as none of them had eyes and their faces were charred black. Lower jaws hung down, leaving mouths wide open, as if they were screaming. I could almost hear their cries of pain. It was abnormal because other parts of the bodies were untouched. The white mantels, which displayed the crimson cross, were not burned in any manner. There wasn't a drop of blood to be seen.*

*All twelve bodies looked identical, with burned out eyeballs and charred black faces. The old Templars were all laying on their backs, in a distorted twisted manner, with their hollow eye sockets facing the sky. It was an unearthly sight which told you supernatural forces were at work. The bodies were in a semi-circle around the Sword of Jerusalem, which was stuck straight into the ground about four inches deep. The scabbard was a few feet away, on the grass.*

*I glared at the blade, which was glowing red, pulsating on and off. The metal blade looked red hot, like it just came from a blacksmith's forge. I shouted, "Don't touch the sword! Don't go near it." All our men, including Baldwin, stopped dead in their tracks. Some of the warriors backed away a few more feet. "Adam, come over here right now!"*

*Adam came running over to me and stood there in disbelief at the awful sight. He commented, "They touched the sword. God didn't deem them worthy and struck them down."*

*Adam stepped slowly towards the sword, but I grabbed his arm stopping him. "Do you think it's wise to touch the sword after seeing this?"*

*"I need to clean it and put it back in its scabbard. Once in the scabbard, everyone will be safe."*

*Still holding his arm, I asked, "Are you sure it won't hurt you?"*

*"Yes, I'm sure, Grandpa. Don't worry so much." I released his arm.*

*Adam walked up to the sword and it started flashing faster and faster. Adam slowly reached out to take hold of the handle. Suddenly, when his hand touched the grip, the sword turned glowing white, like a light bulb. It flashed the same intense white light as when the sword killed Christian de Molay.*

*Adam didn't move for a few seconds, as if he was frozen. I yelled, "Adam, are you ok?" He didn't reply. I moved closer to my grandson. I wasn't sure what action to take, if any. Was he being hurt by the sword? It sure appeared that way to me. His body started to shake and his head was looking straight up at the sky.*

*Without further concern about myself, I grabbed his arm to pull him away and felt a force, almost like an electric shock. A strong tingling ran through my body. Frozen in place I couldn't remove my hand from Adam's arm. I tried with all my strength to pull my hand away, but I couldn't escape from the connection. I thought, we're being electrocuted.*

*Yet, it was a slightly different feeling. I can't explain it exactly, but it was a force or power that didn't actually hurt. The force was probing my body and brain. Yes, it was probing my brain. It was reading my memory. My life flashed before my eyes. It ran like a 3-D movie in my head. I saw everything I had done. All the good times and bad times of my life were on display. The people I had killed were in the movie. I clearly saw their faces as I killed them for a second time.*

*There was Leroy, the guy I killed with a shotgun, blowing off his head. Leroy was the scumbag doper who murdered my little brother, Mike, while he was in line at a burger place. Leroy killed little Mike in cold blood and only received a six-year sentence. My brother Ron and I made a plan to kill his ass when he got out of jail.*

*We ambushed him at a stoplight and I pulled the trigger from ten feet away as he went for his gun. His head exploded like a ripe watermelon. It was an eye for an eye, because no one was going to murder my brother and get away with it. It was the first premeditated murder I had committed. But, I didn't think of it as murder. To me it was justice. 'Vengeance is Mine,' saith the Lord, and I was his instrument.*

*I was being judged for everything I ever did in my life, whether it was good or bad. All these memories, some of which I didn't like, were popping up in the front of my head like a movie screen, zooming by incredibly fast.*

*Then I saw the time we rescued three kids from the Federal green zone. We were on a recon patrol in downtown St. Petersburg searching for MIA Army Rangers. Behind office buildings, in the alleyways, is where all the trash is kept in big dumpsters. Long ago garbage trucks would come once a week, empty the dumpster, and take the trash to be burned or put in a land fill. Many bums or homeless people would hang out in the alleys to pick up any food that may have been thrown away. We called it dumpster diving because you literally had to dive into the big metal container.*

*As we passed by one dumpster, I heard a noise from inside. The lid was open so I peeked over the top, and looked inside while holding my Glock. I thought maybe there was a rat or raccoon inside. As I peered over the edge with my night vision goggles on, they saw me and huddled together in fear. I must have been a scary looking sight with my face painted black, looking like I had on war paint.*

*"Please don't hurt us, Mister," one said, in a high female voice. Three kids were sitting on a pile of rotten garbage that made me gag from the stench. In their hands they had some kind of rancid looking food.*

*I took off my night vision goggles, advising them, "Don't be afraid kids. I'm here to help you." I held out my hand and waved my fingers for them to come over to me. "Come on kids, I'm not gonna hurt you. I have some food for you." I pulled three power bars out of my pocket and held them up.*

*Now the rest of my crew came over and looked in the container. Willis asked, "Now what are we going to do?"*

*I told Willis, "We're gonna help them."*

*The three kids hesitantly climbed out and I handed each one a power bar which they ripped open and gobbled up in a few bites. I asked them, "Where are your parents?"*

*The girl replied, "Our parents are dead. We lived in the Green Zone and there wasn't enough food. They were killed by the Federal Police for stealing food."*

*"How long ago was that?"*

*Looking at them you could tell these kids have had*

*a tough time. Their clothes were filthy and so were their bodies. As a matter of fact they smelled like garbage. The girl's hair was matted and falling out, probably due to malnutrition. She was a skinny-looking thing and her hands were shaking from the lack of food. Her face was sunken in and I thought she could be close to death. The two boys didn't look any better. I gave them each another power bar, which they quickly devoured.*

*The girl said, "I think about a year ago our parents were killed. I've been trying to take care of my brothers but there isn't enough food here. We don't have any other place to go. Who are you guys?"*

*"We're with the Army Rangers. What are your names and how old are you?"*

*I handed her a bottle of water which she passed to the smallest boy before drinking any herself.*

*"I'm 15, my name is Rosie. Billy is 13 and Peter is 9 years old."*

*Billy said, "Would you Army guys please take my sister with you because the men around here make her trade sex for food? One guy hurt her so I hit him in the head with a pipe. If he touches her again ... I'll kill him. My brother and I can make it ok. I just want my sister to be safe."*

*"Billy, you look pretty beat up. How did you get those black eyes?"*

*"The guy I hit with the pipe had his friends beat me."*

*"Where are they now Billy?"*

*"Oh ... they're around somewhere. They're tough mean guys and they run this part of town."*

*"Don't worry about them, Billy, you're all gonna be safe now. You can come with us to Tocabaga."*

*"I've of heard of Tocabaga but I didn't think it was real. Isn't that an island where people live?"*

*Peter asked, "Do you have food there?"*

*"Yes. We're all going there tonight," I replied.*

*"That sounds great. Do you think I can become an Army Ranger and fight the bad guys?"*

*"Probably, when you're old enough."*

*Speaking to my recon team, "We can't leave these kids here alone; they'll die for sure. You three complete the mission and I'll take them to the extraction point and wait for you there."*

*Hammer replied, "I don't like it, but we need to help them."*

*Tommy and Willis concurred so I explained to the kids what we were going to do. "Ok, we have to walk about three miles to our truck. Kids, you stay close to me and do what I do. If I stop then you stop, if I hide then you hide. You guys got it?"*

*"Yes sir, Mister," said Rosie.*

*"My name is Gunn, Jack Gunn. You can just call me Jack."*

*Billy said, "Yes sir, Mister Jack."*

*We headed out toward 3$^{rd}$ Street where we would part ways with the recon team. They would continue straight to the airport. We would turn south on 3$^{rd}$ St. and go to 22$^{nd}$ Ave. heading west to the extraction point at Interstate 275.*

*Upon reaching 3$^{rd}$ Street, I wished my recon team*

*good luck and we parted ways. As we were walking along, I noticed that Peter was limping and dropping behind. He couldn't keep up so I asked him, "Peter, what's wrong with your foot?"*

*"I cut my big toe real bad on some glass and it hurts a lot."*

*"Let me see it." We stopped behind some bushes next to an old building. Peter sat down and took off his worn out tattered shoe. He didn't have any socks on his feet; none of them wore any socks. He held his dirty foot up and I shined my flashlight on it. It was a badly infected cut, swollen red, festering with yellow puss running out of it. It smelled like rotten meat. I washed it off with water and put some antibiotic cream on the wound. Peter winced in pain as I wrapped a bandage around it and helped him put his shoe back on.*

*"Jump on my back I'll carry you for a while to give your foot a rest. Billy, can you carry my backpack for me?"*

*"You bet I can, Mr. Jack." I took it off and handed the 30 pound pack to him. I kneeled down and Peter wrapped his arms around my neck then put his feet around my waist. I guessed that Peter was only about 35 pounds. A kid his age should be at least 60 pounds, but he was just skin and bones.*

*"Peter, when we get back to Tocabaga we'll have the Doctor look at that cut. Ok kids, let's get going. We still have a long hike ahead of us."*

*I didn't want to tell Peter but I thought gangrene had set in and he could lose his toe or maybe his foot. He could lose his life if it wasn't treated soon.*

*I could tell these kids were polite, kind children. They helped each other stay alive in the concrete jungle for a year and that's not easy to do. I can only imagine what Rosie had to endure. It made me want to kill every dirtbag that ever touched her.*

*We had no sooner stepped out from behind the bushes with Peter on my back, when standing in our way were four men with handguns. They were about fifty feet away from us and one of them yelled, "Hey! What y'all doing with my kids?"*

*Billy whispered, "That's them, they're the ones that hurt my sister and beat me."*

*After putting Peter down I told the kids to get behind the bushes. I flipped my safety off putting the M4 on full automatic. I yelled back to them, "Oh, these are your kids. Sorry, I just wanted to have some fun, you know what I mean."*

*Another jerk asked me, "You're dressed up like an Army guy. Who do you think you are ... GI Joe?" They all laughed at the comment.*

*I was out-numbered but not out-gunned. I looked at their handguns to determine the caliber. I couldn't tell in the dark but they looked like small caliber guns. I figured my bulletproof vest would stop those rounds if I got shot.*

*The same dork yelled, "Hey Rosie, you little whore, get out here where I can see you." Of course Rosie didn't come out from behind the bushes.*

*The four men were starting to spread out, to create space between them, and were moving closer to me. As they were moving closer I thought, now is the time to take them out.*

*The same asshole yelled to me, "Mister, hand over your gun! You're no match for the four of us. We've killed a few guys like you before. Give us your gun and we'll let you go."*

*"You mean this gun," as I pointed it at them and pulled the trigger firing on full auto, creating a spray pattern of deadly bullets.*

*I dropped down to one knee to reduce my target size and kept firing, taking careful aim at each man. I heard one or two of their guns fire and saw flashes but they missed me. Three scumbags fell to the ground but the fourth dork was running for cover across the street. I slowly took aim, putting my laser on him, and squeezed the trigger ... BAM ... my bullet hit his head, exploding it like a ripe watermelon.*

*I knew he was dead so I got up and walked over to the three jerks laying on the ground. Two were dead but one was still alive and cried, "Please don't kill me, Mister!" I kicked the gun away from his hand.*

*The three kids stepped up next to me. Billy pointed at the man and said, "He's the guy. He's the one that hurt Rosie."*

*This jerk looked like a real piece of shit. He had long matted hair and a dirty beard that was gray in color. He was kind of scary looking with his long witch-like nose and beady eyes. His face was almost black from all the grime on it. I wanted to blow his head off and kill him on the spot. I told the dork, "I'm not going to kill you. I'm going to hurt you real bad then God is going to kill you for what you did to these kids."*

*He had at least two wounds in his upper torso. He was as good as dead so I thought I might as well help him suffer a little more. I fired four more rounds into his legs. With each shot his body jumped in the air and he screamed in pain. Then I pointed the M4 at his crotch, pressed the barrel on it, and fired one more round. That really made him jump and scream. That was the least I could do for a bully and child molester. They should all be shot on sight.*

*We stood there a few minutes watching the life drain from his body until the worm finally died. The kids stared at the bodies, and didn't say a word as I walked around picking up the handguns, tossing them down the sewer drain in the street. I commented, "They won't be hurting any more kids. They're going to hell."*

*Rosie started to cry and I put my arm around her. "It's ok, Rosie. He'll never hurt you or anyone again."*

*Wiping the tears away, she replied, "I hate to say it, but I'm glad he's dead."*

*"Me too, Rosie." I picked up Peter and we started walking.*

*Billy told me, "I wanna be tough guy like you, Mister Jack." I didn't say a word, but deep down inside I felt good, real good, knowing four child molester dirtbags were dead. They would never hurt another kid. Rosie, Billy, and Peter were going to live with my family on Tocabaga, which made me feel great. I had done my job well.*

*Just as this 3-D movie in my head ended, I faintly heard Baldwin and Maggie yelling at me. Finally, I freed my hand from Adam, and fell to the ground.*

*Baldwin helped me up, just in time to see Adam pull the sword from the ground, point the blade at the sky, and kiss the ruby handle. The white glow suddenly stopped. He wiped off the blade, and slid it into the scabbard.*

*Adam asked, "Are you ok, Grandpa?"*

*"I ... I think so. Are you alright?" I replied, still dazed by what just occurred.*

*"Yes, I'm fine. We were just judged to see if we were worthy to receive the sword."*

*"Has this happened to you before?"*

*"Yes, a couple of times."*

*"Baldwin, how long were we connected to the sword?"*

*"Maybe ten or fifteen seconds, why?"*

*"Because, it seemed like hours. My whole life flashed in front of my eyes."*

*Adam laughed and said, "That's right, it was reading your life. Now I know why Grandpa De Molay chose you to be my guardian. He knew you would be worthy to handle the sword."*

*Maggie asked, "Adam, how does the sword do that? Is it controlled by God or an Angel?"*

*"I don't really know for sure. The sword doesn't talk. I only know that God has spoken to me in my dreams."*

*Captain Baldwin said, "Glory to God." All his men repeated it in unison and made the sign of the cross.*

*Baldwin commented, "You see, Adam does own the Power of the Holy Sword. This is the second time the sword has helped him."*

*Adam replied, "I'm only the caretaker of the sword, not the owner. No one can own God's treasure." After saying that, he put the sword in the box, and placed it under the backseat of my truck. I, for one, was glad that he did.*

That's the true story of what transpired.

We were getting ready to leave the Nation in a few days. Tonight was our last story night. Black Horse sat next to me and advised, "Jack, you must visit our brothers, the Hopi Tribe. They are near the Four Corners area."

I asked, "How can the Hopi help us?"

"The Hopi have lived there since the start of time. They would know if any Templars passed into their hunting grounds. They have a long history and keep stories alive by rock writing."

"Rock writing? You mean petroglyphs or hieroglyphs."

"I do not know what those are, but the Hopi write and draw on rocks. They may have something to show you. I was there years ago and know they will help you. Hopitun Shi-nu-mu means peaceful people. They are also called Pueblo People along with their brothers, the Navajo."

"Yeah, maybe you're right. We should visit them."

Pointing at a man walking a horse who was coming our way, Black Horse said, "Here is the man I want you to meet."

A man, whom I had never seen before walked up to

us leading a horse with a brown-haired mutt by his side. The horse was a fine looking Mustang with a Mexican silver-studded saddle on its back. Black Horse said, "Jack, I want you to meet White Feather. He just returned from a hunting trip. He knows the Hopi Nation very well and can be of help to you."

The man certainly didn't look like a Comanche because his skin was darker and his facial features were different. His black hair was cut shoulder length and he had a black band of cloth wrapped around his head. For clothing he wore a plain green-colored long-sleeve shirt and blue jeans. He wore high-top brown leather boots. In his arms he cradled what appeared to be an old Henry lever-action rifle. I guessed him to be in his mid-forties.

Usually, I can size someone up in a minute. Call it intuition or judgment but I can tell right away if someone is trustworthy. I stood up to shake his hand. "White Feather, it's a pleasure to meet you." He was a little shorter than me and a lot thinner. I gazed into his tiny dark eyes, but couldn't get a good read on him.

His grip was weak, almost girly like, as we shook hands. When I squeezed his hand, a little more than normal, he didn't return the squeeze and withdrew his hand. He was weak so I suspected that he couldn't be trusted to cover your back, if needed.

White Feather replied, "Hello, Jack Gunn. I heard you brought us many good things, including Black Horse's son."

Black Horse said, "I told Jack he needs to visit the Hopi Nation and see the rock writing."

"Yes, if he is interested," White Feather replied,

while looking at me. "I hear you are seeking a lost treasure."

"Yeah, that's right, we're on an expedition to find the Templars treasure. Do you know anything about the Hopi rock writing?"

"Yes, I know it. I am part Hopi and lived many years with the tribe on the three mesas."

"What can you tell me about it?"

"It is very complicated to tell all about it since there are more rock writings than stars in the sky. The most important one is named Prophecy Rock."

Billy Black Horse, standing behind his father, blurted out, "Why don't we go there with you, Jack."

Thinking for a minute, I said, "I don't think that's a good idea. We have no idea what we'll run into. Furthermore, we don't know when we'll be coming back."

"Maybe my son has a good idea. Why not go with you? It is a chance to be with my son and see this treasure you seek," Black Horse commented. "White Feather can show us the way."

"Let's let White Feather continue his story," I said.

"Well, located near old Oraibi there is a Prophecy written into a large rock. No one knows how old it is."

I interrupted, "What is Oraibi?"

"Oraibi is an old Hopi village located on the Third Mesa on the Hopi Reservation near the Kykotsmovi Village. It was founded before the year 1100 AD, according to the archeologists. We Hopi know it is older than that."

"What is the Third Mesa?" Billy asked.

"We Hopi have 12 villages located on the reservation which is divided into three regions: First Mesa, Second Mesa, and Third Mesa. Our language, customs, and traditions are almost the same, but each village conducts its own ceremonies and is unique from others."

White Feather paused for a moment and patted his horse. "Please tell us more," I said.

"The First Mesa contains the villages of Walpi, Sichomovi, and Tewa. Walpi is the oldest and most historic and has been continuously inhabited for more than 1100 years. Walpi is 300 feet above the valley which provides for a good view of anyone coming. Walpi does not have running water or electricity. Residents must walk to Sichomovi to wash and get water."

I nodded and sat down. "Interesting, please continue."

"The Second Mesa includes the three villages of Shungopavi, Mishongovi, and Sipaulovi. Over a thousand years ago, Hopi clans began to arrive at this location. According to Hopi legend, Shungopavi is one of the first Hopi villages established on Second Mesa.

"The Third Mesa contains the villages of Kykotsmovi, Old Oraibi, Hotevilla, and Bacavi. Forty-five miles to the west of here, near Tuba City, is the Hopi village of Moenkopi."

"How many Hopi are there?" I asked.

"Currently, around 10,000 people live in the Hopi Nation. Hopi are a matrilineal society that is organized into clans. In the Hopi Nation clan relationships are more important than blood lines."

I asked, "Who discovered the Hopi Tribe?"

White Feather gazed up into the sky and thought for a minute as if he was annoyed. "Well, the historians claim that Don Pedro de Tovar did. He was part of the Coronado expedition in 1540. They were searching for the Seven Cities of Gold, which of course did not exist."

"Yeah, I read about the Seven Cities of Gold," Billy said. "So ... there was no gold there?"

"Of course they found gold, but there is no Seven Cities of Gold. Gold is everywhere and if you search long enough you can find it. We Hopi believe the Spanish were seeking the golden treasure."

I sat up in disbelief at what I had just heard. "What golden treasure?"

"The golden treasure made by the Ancients."

Now I was really curious. *What the hell was he talking about?* "When you say the golden treasure, what do you mean and who are the Ancients?"

By this time Chief Quanah had started telling his story and the crowd went silent. White Feather whispered, "I can explain more tomorrow. Please excuse me now. I must feed my animals and clean up. I have traveled a long way today."

I replied, "If it's ok, let's meet here at 10 am to finish this discussion." White Feather nodded and bid us good night, as he slowly walked away.

I asked, "Black Horse, can we trust him?"

"How much can you trust any man? We trust, but

use caution. That is the Comanche way. White Feather comes and goes like the wind. No one really knows him."

I couldn't wait to tell Maggie, Adam, and Captain Baldwin about this new important clue. I returned to the Motel room and found all three in the room watching a movie called the 'Terminator' from years ago. Our dogs, Freda and Adolf, were laying on the floor and jumped up to greet me.

I cracked open my bottle of JD, poured at shot, and went outside to have a smoke. The dogs, right behind me, took off when I opened the door to relieve themselves.

It wasn't long before Baldwin came outside and asked, "What's up?"

I took a sip of whiskey and then a deep drag, blowing out smoke rings. "Oh, not much. I only found the biggest clue yet where the treasure might be."

Adam came outside and asked, "Where is it?"

"I don't know yet, but we could find out tomorrow."

"You always say that. What's gonna happen tomorrow?" Baldwin asked.

"Tomorrow we have a meeting with a man named White Feather. He's half Hopi Indian and knows something about a golden treasure made by the Ancients. We'll meet him at 10 am in the park to find out more information."

"That sounds promising. I'm ready to move on because we're getting lazy sitting around here," Baldwin replied, as he walked away. "See you guys in the morning."

I took another swig of booze and said, "Adam, hook up the Sat phone to the computer and do some research on the Hopi Indians for me. Use the ACWWW (Army Command World Wide Web)."

"Yeah sure, Grandpa, but what do you wanna know?"

I thought about it for a moment. "See if you can find anything about a treasure. Also, check out their petroglyphs or hieroglyphs. Just find out as much information as you can."

Maggie, who had followed Adam outside said, "I'll help you, Adam." She grabbed my bottle of JD and took a big swig.

They went to work researching the Hopi. I had another drink and went to bed.

# THE PROPHECY
## MAY 21, 2026

The rooster woke me up again at 4 am. I'm gonna kill that bird yet. I can't wake up until I've had a cup of black mud and a smoke. I noticed on the table there were a lot of handwritten notes.

Adam heard me moving around. "Morning, Grandpa. You gotta read my notes on the Hopi and the Grand Canyon."

"Ok, I will after I have a coffee and wake up."

I went to the motel office to see if the manager, Big Buffalo, had made any coffee. Sure enough he had some java already made. After greeting him, I grabbed three cups to bring back to the room.

Arriving back at the room, Maggie was up and I handed her a coffee. "Jack, you won't believe what we found out."

"Ok, you guys tell me, because I don't wanna read all those notes. I can't understand your scribble anyway." I took a sip of the sage-laced black mud. Damn, it tasted good.

Adam and I went outside while Maggie took a shower. "What did you find out?" I asked him.

"The Hopi believe they came from the earth inside the Grand Canyon. They emerged from some cave and came above ground. Furthermore, there's still a Hopi Clan living in the canyon."

"Did you find anything about a golden treasure?"

Just then Maggie walked out. "Did Adam tell you about the treasure?"

I looked at my watch and it was already 8:30. "Tell me later, I gotta take a shower and shave. Then we gotta eat before our meeting with White Feather."

By the time everyone was cleaned up and ate breakfast it was almost 10 o'clock. Baldwin came in our room as Adam was just about to tell the story of the treasure. Baldwin said, "Ok, let's go meet this White Feather."

"This story is important," Adam said, with a disappointed look on his face.

"I believe you, but I don't wanna keep White Feather waiting. You can tell us later." We left the motel and moseyed over to the meeting place at the city park.

Adam had our dogs on a leash as we walked to the park. I noted that White Feather was already sitting there. Peering at the dogs, White Feather said, "So, you must be Wolf Boy. Chief Quanah told me about you." He couldn't take his eyes off of the big German Shepherds. He stood up and stuck out his hand to pet them.

Both dogs let out a low soft growl. Adam ordered, "Sit, stay," as he tugged on their leashes.

"They must smell my dog," White Feather commented as he withdrew his hand and backed up a few feet.

The thought ran through my mind, *the dogs don't trust him for some reason.*

I said, "Good morning, White Feather. This is Adam, Maggie, and Captain Baldwin members of our expedition. I brought them along to hear your story."

White Feather didn't even say hello or offer to shake hands. "I was going to tell you about Prophecy Rock." He pulled a hunting knife out of its sheath, knelt down on one knee, and proceeded to make a crude drawing in the dirt, using its point. It looked something like this.

"I will explain the drawing as best as I can," White Feather said. He pointed his knife at the largest figure. "This is the Great Spirit. The bow near his left hand represents his intent for the Hopi to lay down their weapons. His right hand points to a timescale line in thousands of years. The point where the Great Spirit touches the line is the time when he will return."

We all sat there listening intently to his story.

"There are two life paths established by the Great Spirit. One is a lower path, which is continuous with nature. The other is the upper path, which is influenced by white man.

"The bar, above the small cross, is connecting the paths. That point marks the coming of white men. The cross stands for Christianity. The circle slightly below the cross represents the continuous Path of Life.

"Four small figures on the upper path represent the past three worlds and the present one. It shows that some Hopi have followed the white man's path.

"The swastika inside the sun and the Celtic Cross represent the two helpers of Pahana, who is the True White Brother.

"The thicker line that runs between the upper and lower path is the last chance for people to turn back to nature before the upper road is destroyed.

"The small circle above the lower path line is when the Great Purification will happen. After which corn will grow in abundance again and the Great Spirit returns. This lower path of life continues forever. Well … that is all I can tell you. Are there any questions?" White Feather asked.

"Yeah," I stated. "How old is this Prophecy?"

"No one knows for sure."

"I'd sure like to know how they knew about the swastika and the Celtic Cross, as you call it."

"That is all I can tell you. If you wanna go to the Hopi Nation, let me know."

"What about the golden treasure the Ancients brought?"

"We Hopi need to keep some secrets from you white eyes." With that comment White Feather proceeded to leave the meeting. No one said a word after his comment about white eyes. I sensed he had some bad dealings with white men in the past.

We were standing there gazing at the drawing and when he was out of earshot, Adam said, "The swastika is an Egyptian or Buddhist symbol. It's been around for thousands of years."

I said, "Yeah, that's true. Hitler copied it, for some unknown reason, and made it the Nazi symbol. It's one of the most hated symbols in the world because of him."

"I agree with Jack, that's a Templar cross alright. So what the hell does it all mean?" Baldwin asked.

"It all depends how old the Prophecy is. If it was drawn seven hundred years ago then the Templars did visit the Hopi. It's also possible that some Buddhists or Egyptians were here a long time ago."

Maggie replied, "On the other hand, the Prophecy could have been made within the last 40 years by some nut case."

"I asked, "What is the Pahana or True White Brother?"

Adam excitedly said, "Wait, I have to tell you what I found. This whole thing is so weird, you won't believe it."

"Ok, shoot."

"In 1909, the Phoenix Gazette published a story about a man named Kincaid who found a cave in the Grand Canyon. I read the story and Kincaid claims that he found mummies, statues, and gold artifacts that were oriental in appearance.

"Mr. Kincaid was an explorer and hunter all his life. He worked for thirty years for the Smithsonian Institute. Let's go to our room and I'll show you more on the ACWWW."

We hooked up the Sat phone, and Adam typed in 'Kincaid's Cave' and the article popped up.

As I read the newspaper article, a number of points popped out at me: *It stated the cave was found by accident while searching for minerals. Its general location is forty-two miles up the river from the El Tovar Crystal Canyon.*

*The cave is hidden from view because it is about 1,500 feet down the canyon wall and is set back blocking its view from the river. It is also located on government land where visitors are not permitted.*

*Kincaid determined it was clearly a manmade cave and found mummies deep inside the cave. He stated that he took a picture of one. He gathered up a few relics and took them to Yuma for shipment them to Washington D.C., which is the headquarters for the Smithsonian. Kincaid advised that because of the relics further explorations were undertaken under the direction of the Smithsonian, by Professor S. A. Jordon who was reported to be Kincaid's boss.*

*G. E. Kincaid went into great detail of the cave construction and its tunnels, which I didn't care about. He advised that he found an idol sitting cross-legged with a lotus flower in each hand. Kincaid thought it resembled Buddha.*

I commented, "Now, this is interesting to me because everyone knows that Buddha sits cross-legged and has a lotus flower in his hand. This had to be an idol of Buddha. No other idol even comes close to resembling Buddha." I continued reading.

*Around the idol there were many smaller images carved out of marble. On the urns, tablets, walls, and doorways strange hieroglyphics were painted or carved.*

*The last clue stated that laying on the floor everywhere were yellow cat's eyes. Each one was engraved with the head of what appeared to be Malay type person.*

I commented, "The cat's eye stone was well known and used by Egyptians. The cat was a protected animal and considered to be a goddess. The cat's eye stones where used for protection from evil things. Spreading them around on the floor meant some type of danger was in the cave system.

"Kincaid went to great lengths in the story, stressing how inaccessible the cave was. Yet he was able to climb up and down with a handful of relics. If such a find was made, why would anyone want to reveal its location? I think he's lying about the location."

*These points made me wonder, was he telling the truth. In every truth there is non-truth. In every fiction there is non-fiction.*

Baldwin replied, "I think you're right, Jack. Kincaid wasn't telling the whole truth."

Maggie asked, "But, why would he lie about it?"

"Who knows," I told her.

"Here's the kicker," Adam said. "Kincaid disappeared and no one has ever found the cave. The Smithsonian claims he didn't work for them and they have no knowledge about any cave in the Grand Canyon containing artifacts. Furthermore, the Smithsonian says they never heard of Professor S. A. Jordan. He was never employed by them."

"Wow, someone is covering up something," I said. "Maybe the Smithsonian is doing a cover up job."

"Why would they do that?" Baldwin asked.

"If the Egyptians were in the Grand Canyon it would change the history of the world. Or maybe there was a golden treasure so valuable that they wanted to keep it a secret."

"Do you think the treasure we're looking for is the one they found?" Maggie asked.

"I don't know for sure. I only know I smell a rat. We have to follow the clues on the sword to find out. We don't even know if the Templars Treasure is in the Grand Canyon."

"Here's another tidbit," Adam said. "There's an article about John Westly Powell that states in 1869 he was the first white man to travel down the Grand

Canyon by boat. It says he found a cave with Egyptian hieroglyphs on the cliff walls near the cave entrance."

I said, "That's interesting because Powell was there 40 years before Kincaid and he saw Egyptian hieroglyphs."

"Oh, I found out what the Pahana means," Adam responded. "Simply put, the Pahana is the older White Brother who left the Hopi Tribe and traveled east. He promised to return and help the tribe. When he returns, life will be improved for the Hopi Indians."

"Older White Brother, what does that mean? Was he a white guy? Maybe he was a Templar."

Adam shrugged his shoulders, and Baldwin said, "This is all bullshit. I say we move out tomorrow and continue our quest following the sword clues."

Everyone agreed with that idea. I said, "The next place we need to go is the Petrified Forest. The question is, should we bring Black Horse, Billy, and White Feather along?"

Maggie commented, "Yeah, why not? Maybe they could help us somehow."

"I don't trust White Feather. He just looks sneaky to me," Captain Baldwin advised.

I said, "Yeah, there's something about him I don't like either and I get the feeling he doesn't care for us."

Then Adam made a good point. "We might need him to go into Hopi country in the Grand Canyon."

"Good point, Adam. We'll bring him along and keep an eye on him."

Baldwin said, "Ok, it's settled, we'll leave

tomorrow. I'll tell the men to be ready to roll out by 0800 hundred."

Our meeting broke up and everyone started to check their gear and pack up. I went to tell Black Horse, Billy, and White Feather that they could ride with Pete in the second Hummer, in front of our truck. Adam and Maggie, along with the dogs, would ride with me.

I couldn't wait for tomorrow to continue our quest.

# SANTA ROSA
## MAY 22, 2026

As usual, the rooster woke me up at 4 am so I went to have a coffee and smoke with Big Buffalo. I also paid him for the fourteen rooms we rented over the last few weeks. It was the only income he had made in a year.

When I handed him twenty thousand dollars he smiled, showing several missing teeth. I liked him a lot because he was an easy going guy, whom you could tell was at peace with the world.

As I finished my coffee, Big Buffalo said, "I will miss you, Jack Gunn. I wish you a safe journey."

"Don't take any wooden nickels and never trust the white eyes," I said. We both laughed, as I walked out the door.

Back at the motel room I pulled out a map. It seemed to me that it would be faster to take Route 281 north to Interstate 40. Using this route would save us some miles. We would pass through Oklahoma and back into the Texas panhandle to Amarillo. Captain Walker, of the Texas Rangers, who led us to the Comanche Nation, provided me a letter before he went back on duty. The letter was a pass, allowing us to move through Texas unimpeded by law enforcement. Who knows, it may come in handy in any state. This letter, along with the one from Captain Sessions, of the Army Rangers, should keep us from having any problems with the local law enforcement.

Of course, there aren't many real law enforcement officers around anymore. Mostly, it's vigilantes taking the law into their own hands and they aren't trustworthy. Then you have the Free Roamers, as I call them, who roam around stealing what they need to survive. They usually travel in small groups of five to ten, and won't hesitate to kill you to steal what they want. These Roamers like to prey on the weak and helpless because they can't fight back.

There are gangs of all types to contend with, along with Warlords and Drug Lords. The worst ones are ISIS and al Qaida terrorists who kill anyone not of their faith. They rule by fear and cut off the heads of those that oppose them. Make no mistake, they will slowly hack your head off with a small dull knife.

Captain Baldwin and his Templar Warriors fought these radicals for eight years in the Middle East. That is why he carriers a sword himself. It's not just any sword; it's a samurai sword which is designed to cut off heads in a single blow.

Baldwin claims that radical terrorists fear getting their heads cut off. If their head is gone then the spirit cannot pass into heaven, where seventy-two virgins are waiting for them. With no head, they cannot enjoy the heavenly virgins.

Baldwin and his men understand these terrorists and know how they think in combat. Actually, in combat you just need to kill as many of them as possible, before they kill you. The terrorist's battle tactics lack fundamental skills and strategy. However, this being said, they aren't afraid to die, and will sacrifice themselves to kill any infidel.

Our plan was to pass through Oklahoma non-stop, enter Texas where we would refuel, and stop for the night. The next day, at first light, we would proceed across New Mexico, a distance of 340 miles.

As we rolled out of Comanche Nation, about a thousand people gathered to see us off. Many of them brought some kind of gift such as a dream catcher, eagle feathers, or medicine bags to bring us good luck.

The trip was uneventful and no one spoke much during the drive. The rumble of the big off-road tires lulled everyone to sleep. One fuel stop and twelve hours later, we arrived in Texas. The Texas Rangers guarding the border on Interstate 40 read the letter from Ranger Walker and let us pass into Texas with no problems. Like I said before, Texas was under control. Everyone here obeys the law. If they don't then Texans take care of the problem – cowboy style.

Arriving in Amarillo, we took a much needed break. Amarillo is the most populated city in the Texas panhandle with a population of over 100,000 people. It was once the Helium capital of the world because of its vast natural helium reserves. It is located in the Llano

Estacado, or start of the high plains area.

*The Llano Estacado lies at the southern end of the High Plains of North America. It is part of the American Desert. The Canadian River forms the Llano's northern boundary, separating it from the northern High Plains. To the east, the Caprock Escarpment is the boundary between the Llano and the Red Plains of Texas.*

*Robert G. Carter an Army officer, who received the Medal of Honor, described the Llano Estacado in 1871 while pursuing Quanah Parker. "It appeared to be a vast, almost limitless expanse of prairie. As far as the eye could see, not a bush or tree, a twig or stone, not an object of any kind or a living thing, was in sight. It stretched out before us as an uninterrupted plain, only to be compared to the ocean in its vastness."*

Passing through Amarillo with no problems, we stopped at Adrian, Texas which had a population of about fifty people. *Hee-haw!* Lucky for us it did have a gas station and a local diner. After refueling, we made camp behind the station and had some good homemade chow at the little diner.

While at the diner, two Texas Rangers showed up and we started a conversation. Of course, they wanted to know where we were going and why. We told them to Arizona to find some friends. The Ranges advised us some news about New Mexico. According to them, ISIS had taken over large parts of the state. They hadn't seen any traffic coming east, into Texas, on I-40 for over a week. They strongly warned us that crossing New Mexico could be very dangerous.

According to New Mexico authorities, the only safe areas are Albuquerque proper and Santa Fe. They classified I-40 and I-25, the only two Interstate Highways in New Mexico, as death traps because ISIS controls these two major routes.

After eating, I hunkered down with Baldwin, observing the map of New Mexico. The Rangers told us there were an estimated 5,000 ISIS fighters in the state. A travel-at-your-own-risk warning was issued. We laughed at this because that's the way it had been for a few years. We always travel at our own risk.

Baldwin commented, "We have a lot of fire power with our 50 caliber guns and M249s. The terrorists usually travel in teams of around a twenty to thirty men. The problem is the terrain. If we get ambushed at any point where they control the high ground, we'll be in a world of shit. If they have RPG's, then we really got problems."

"Yeah, I agree. They're probably just waiting for a fat juicy convoy like ours," I said.

Baldwin said, "I know how these guys think. Their main forces are probably keeping near Albuquerque and Santa Fe to pick off anyone who dares travel the highway near the city. They're also doing sneak attacks into the city for food and supplies."

"That makes sense. Even with 5,000 men that's not enough to overtake a city the size of Albuquerque but they can still do a lot of damage using hit and run tactics."

Baldwin nodded in agreement while gazing at the map. "There aren't any good roads to bypass I-40. If we don't use I-40 it'll take us days to cross New Mexico."

I pointed at the map. "Look at this. At Santa Rosa we could pick up Route 54 and take it south to Route 60 and then to I-25. Then take Route 6 back to I-40. That way we bypass the outskirts of Albuquerque. "

Baldwin peered at the map. "Yeah, that seems to be the only good route. The problem is we have to cross the Pecos River, at Santa Rosa, on Route 54. My guess is ISIS will have a roadblock there. Santa Rosa is a small town of only a couple thousand people so ISIS probably owns the town."

"Well, what about Route 64? We could turn off on this before the Pecos Bridge. That also takes us to State Route 60."

"But then we're backtracking, wasting time, and fuel. We should just take the shortest route and do a night recon to check out the bridge on Route 54. We'll find out what kind of forces are there."

"I don't care for that idea."

"Why not, Jack? If there's only ten or twenty guards we'll blast our way through their roadblock, if there is one. That's why we need to do a recon."

"George, I see your point, but I don't think we should take any chances. Getting into a gun battle is the last thing we need. One of our people could get killed by a stray bullet or lucky shot. That could screw up our whole expedition."

"Jack, the way I see it, we have no choice. You and I can recon the bridge. If we don't like what we see then we'll backtrack on Route 64."

"Ok, I agree. What's your plan?"

"From here to Santa Rosa is about 120 miles. I suggest we leave here tonight at 11 pm. Remember, we have to go past the little town of Tucumcari. Interstate 40 runs right by it and my guess is ISIS will have some spotters there who will radio ahead that cars are headed their way. If we're lucky they'll be asleep when we roll past the town around 2 am."

"George, there's still the small towns of Montoya, Newkirk, and Cuervo."

"That's right, but we don't pass directly through them. They're off of the Interstate, on old Route 66, so we'll zoom right by them. Once we get past Cuervo, we'll conceal the convoy, on the side of the road, while we do the recon."

"Ok, sounds good so far."

"We'll proceed to within two miles of the bridge, dismount, and go on foot from there. Bring your sniper rifle. My idea is Pete and I will move forward and snipe anyone we see with an RPG first. Then we'll terminate the rest of them so we can cross the bridge. You'll set up about 600 yards away and cover us."

"You want me to play God."

*'God' is the expression used to name snipers doing over watch duty. He watches over the troops from a high point and terminates any possible threat using a long range fifty caliber rifle.*

"Right, you cover our backs. So the team will be you, me, and Pete. We need one more man to team up with you. Once we secure the bridge, we'll radio the convoy to move up."

"I'll bring Maggie." I figured Maggie was the best choice to watch my back. We had been through a lot together over the last few years. She knew what to do, and in a bind, she would not let me down.

"Alright, that sounds good. Let's get ready to move out. It's already 9 pm."

Baldwin called a meeting and advised everyone of the plan. We would roll out at 11 pm with Baldwin's Hummer taking point. The convoy would run with lights off at 45 mph and keep a 100 foot spread between trucks. At 45 mph it would take us about three to four hours to reach our turn off to Route 54. That's assuming we have no problems along the way such as a flat tire, or a gun battle with any bad guys.

It was a chilly cloudless night, with half a moon shining in the starlit sky, and the wind was blowing out of the west at 20 mph. I could smell the sage brush, dirt, or sand in the air. Little particles were stinging my face every now and then.

Billy Black Horse would ride with Jeff in the bulletproof Hummer, along with his Dad and White Feather. Jeff is third in command of the Templar Warriors and he has my utmost trust. My grandson, Adam, would ride with me, Maggie, and the dogs.

As we were packing up, Adam advised me of some new information he had found on the ACWWW. "I was reading about the Kensington Stone. You ever heard of it?"

"Yeah, a long time ago. Refresh my memory," I said.

"A big stone was found in 1898 by a farmer in Minnesota, near the town of Kensington, hence the name. Anyway, the 200 pound stone had writing carved into it. The theory is, it was carved by the Knights Templar because it had hooked X's in the writing. It's a known fact the Templar Order used the hooked X."

"That's interesting. What did the writing say?"

"This article says the writing translates as follows: *'Eight Swedes and twenty-two Norwegians on an exploration from Vinland to the west. We had camp one day's journey north from this stone. We were out to fish one day. After we came home found ten men red of blood and dead. Ave Virgin Maria save us from evil.'* That was the main text."

I asked, "Is there more?"

"On the side of the stone it said, *'We have ten men by the sea to look after our ships, fourteen days' travel from this island.'* Here's the amazing thing, it's dated 1362."

"Wow, that's around the same time period that we thought the Templars came here."

As Adam packed up the phone and electronics gear, he said, "Maybe they were part of the same group and they split up for some reason."

"Yeah maybe, but the important thing is the stone proves the Templars did come to America in the thirteen hundred time period."

"I got some other things to tell you, Grandpa."

"Ok, shoot."

"Well … this whole thing is becoming very

complicated. I found an article written about Burrows Cave, located near Olney, Illinois. It showed pictures of the artifacts found by Russell Burrows in 1982."

"What type of the artifacts?"

"Egyptian artifacts, or at least that's what the article said. It's really weird because the more I check into a lost treasure, the more stuff I read about Egyptians coming to the United States."

"Ok, let's finish packing. It's almost time to leave. Once we're on the road, hook up the Sat phone and get on the ACWWW. You can fill me in while I'm driving."

Maggie slammed the hood of the truck down. "Oil and water are ok. You want me to check the tires?"

"Nope, I think they're alright." Just to be sure, I walked around and kicked each one. The toe of my boot bounced off the hard tire, indicating the inflation was about right.

"You want me to drive?" Maggie asked.

"No, I'll drive tonight and you ride shotgun." Riding shotgun meant keeping your eyes open and your weapon at the ready. Her eyes are better than mine. With us both watching the road, we'd be a lot safer driving in the dark, without headlights.

Baldwin gave the signal to move out and the convoy started to roll. Adam plugged the Sat phone into the jumper outlet and connected the computer.

Once we were off the dirt road, back on I-40, Adam said, "Listen to this, it's crazy. The first Egyptian King to visit America was King Zaphnath, or Joseph, as he is mentioned in the Bible. The story goes, Joseph was given the name Zaphnath and the right to rule under

King Sesostris because he saved Egypt from a terrible famine. Joseph became the number one advisor to King Sesostris and then he became King on the death of Sesostris."

Driving along, half listening to the boring story, I said, "So, what about it? The first modern humans were estimated to come to North America 18,000 to 20,000 years ago across the land bridge from Asia. If people came here that long ago, it's not so hard to believe that Egyptians came here."

"This article claims that King Zaphnath, or Joseph, came to America in 1744 B.C., by a boat with wings. It says he had a map that showed the new world called Ophir, which is the United States. Joseph came here when he was 26 years old. It says he made twelve trips to the new world. He died when he was 110 years old."

"It says he came here on a boat with wings?" I asked.

"Yes, the translation clearly says wings and not sails."

"That's weird because they knew the difference between wings and sails. Maybe it was some type of flying machine." Adam and Maggie laughed at my comment.

"Come on Jack, a flying machine back in 1,000 B.C.," Maggie commented.

"Hey, we don't know what they had. I do know something about the Great Pyramid. It was built in 2,560 B.C. when Khufu was Pharaoh. How in the hell could men in 2,500 B.C. build a Pyramid? How did they even think of a Pyramid? How did they design it? There are no written records or drawings. It was the tallest manmade structure on earth until the Eiffel Tower was constructed in 1889."

"Really? I didn't know that," Adam said.

"Most people don't know that. The pyramid is estimated to have 2.3 million block stones in it and each one weighs anywhere from 2.5 tons to 15 tons each. These are huge blocks of stones the size of cars. Now, why would anyone, even today, build such a thing? When we build homes or buildings they are box-shaped because they're easier to manufacture."

Adam replied, "That's true."

Taking both hands off the wheel, I lit up a smoke and took drag before continuing. "To me, this is interesting because no one really knows how the Great Pyramid was built by people who just crawled out of the Stone Age. They lived in mud huts. How did they move car-sized stones and lift them into place?"

I took another drag on my smoke and a sip of water. I glanced at the road sign as we rolled past it. Maggie let out an evil laugh, "Ha-ha. Welcome to New Mexico, the Land of Enchantment and … terrorists."

I continued with my lecture. "Now, ask yourself these questions. Why would you make a pyramid-shaped building? It is one of the most difficult structures to build. Why would you use large stones, weighing tons, and not small ones? Why would you want to build something so difficult and so large when you didn't have the skill, knowledge, or the tools?"

"Well, they must have had some type of tools we don't know about," Adam said.

"Right, I agree. The Egyptians claim it took twenty years using 20,000 men to make the Great Pyramid. Someone, I can't remember who, calculated if the pyramid has 2.3 million stones, then to build it in 20 years, workers would have to put one block in place every two and a half minutes. That's impossible unless they had some kind of special tools, or they had some help from Aliens."

"What kind of Aliens?" Maggie asked.

"Ancient Aliens, you know, little green men."

"How long do you think it took to build?" Adam asked me.

"Well, using simple math and logic, let's just say they put one stone block in place every two and a half hours, or every 150 minutes. That's 60 times longer than two and a half minutes."

Adam, sitting behind me, touched my shoulder. "That sounds more reasonable."

"Yeah, but if you use the same time period of 20 years and multiply times 60, it would take over 1,200 years to complete the construction, assuming there are 2.3 million stones. So no one knows for sure how it was built. Myself, I believe they had Alien help. The Aliens designed it and helped them built it for some reason. We don't know why, but it wasn't for a tomb."

"If they aren't tombs, what are they?" Adam inquired.

"I don't know but there are theories about it. But this brings us back to the point about the boat with wings. If the translation said wings and not sails then they had a flying boat. They didn't have a name for a flying object so they called it a boat because it held people. These people certainly knew the difference between wings and sails."

"That sounds crazy," Maggie commented.

"Ok, where did Joseph get a map from? How did he know where the United States was located? If he actually used a boat the trip would take years. I say he flew here, crazy as that sounds."

Maggie turned around in her seat and looked at Adam. "Who wrote this article?"

Adam replied, "It doesn't say. There is no official author. But the title of the article is 'Egyptians in America'. It has a lot of pictures."

"What kind of pictures?" she asked.

The radio buzzed and Baldwin came on. "We're stopped on the out skirts of Tucumcari. I don't see anyone. We're gonna scope the town out. Over."

The radio hissed again. "Boss, we're about ten klicks behind you," Pete, number two in command, advised.

"When you reach the city limits, stop and wait further orders. Over."

"Roger that."

We were heading down, off the high plains, or Llano Estacado, into the desert and the temperature dropped. Adam complained he was getting cold so we rolled up our windows a little. That's the way the desert works. It's hot as hell in the day and freezing at night.

A short time later, the convoy rolled to a stop at the Tucumcari city limit sign. We sat there in silence, peering out into the darkness, searching for any sign of life, scanning for anyone who could be an ISIS spotter. Everyone had out their FLIR night vision glasses or M4 scopes, scanning the entire road ahead.

Turning off our motors, the night air became dead silent, except for the freaky low howling of the wind, blowing across the desert sands. Maggie said, "That's sounds spooky."

I replied, "Yeah, it sounds like coyotes. Just sit, look, and listen." I rolled the windows down so the dogs could smell the air. If a person was within a hundred yards, they would let us know.

We had been sitting there almost an hour listening to the wind when suddenly the radio crackled and it startled us, making Maggie jump. "We cleared the town. Move out," Baldwin advised.

Our guard dogs, Adolf and Freda, were sticking their heads out the window and whining. Adam said, "They want out."

"Ok, let them out to do their business, but hurry up."

Adam opened the door and both dogs jumped out. They stood there for a minute sniffing the air, and then suddenly took off at a full run, into the darkness of the starlit desert. Adam was running after them, yelling for them to stop.

Jumping out of the truck, I took off after Adam. "Adam, wait up!" Adam stopped as I caught up to him. "Be careful, there's something out here because Adolf and Freda never take off like that." I flicked my M4 safety off and handed Adam my Glock 17.

We slowed down to a walk, being careful where we stepped. I didn't want to step on any rattlesnakes. Raising the M4 FLIR scope up to my eye, I peered around in the darkness, trying to see the body heat of our dogs.

Sagebrush was growing everywhere, making it difficult to see very far. The terrain was rocky, making it difficult to walk without making any noise. We heard the dogs barking and growling directly in front of us, but they were still out of sight. We started jogging toward the noise.

Freda and Adolf both stood there with the hair on their backs standing straight up, while growling in a low tone. Then we saw what they were growling at. There was a pile of bodies, surrounded by five coyotes, which were there for the dead meat. I quickly estimated there were over a hundred bodies – men, women, and children laying there decomposing. It was a massive killing field. The stench was over whelming.

Adam started to gag and we stopped in our tracks. "We're close enough," I said, and shouted in a deep alpha male voice, "Adolf, Freda, come!" They turned, looked at me, ran over, and sat at my feet. "Adam, put their leashes on and let's get the hell out of here."

As we walked away, the coyotes went back to their feast. "Who were those dead people?" Adam asked.

"I think that's the town of Tucumcari. That's why Baldwin didn't see anyone. ISIS killed everyone in the little town."

Adolf started to pull Adam toward some bushes. He couldn't hold Adolf back, so we followed his lead. I held my M4 in low ready position as we moved slowly forward. Shortly, we found out what Adolf was going after. Under a bush, there was a man who appeared to be dead.

Bending down, I checked his pulse. "He's alive," I said. Visually checking his body, it was clear that he had been shot, at least twice, in the gut. Gut shots cause a lot of pain and a slow death.

I placed a bottle of water to his lips, pouring just a small amount in his mouth and on his face. He opened his eyes so I gave him a few more drops of water. He said in a soft whisper, "Gracias."

Bending close to his face I asked, "Entiendes Ingles?"

"Si señor.*"

I knew we could not help this man. His wounds were just too severe, but maybe he could still help us. He was an old man, whom I guessed was at least sixty years old, by the wrinkled skin on his face and silver gray hair. "Who did this to you?"

He mumbled out one word. "ISIS."

"How many are there?"

"Dos hombres." He coughed up some bright red blood. Taking his bandana, I wiped his mouth and then provided him a little more water.

"Where are they?"

"He raised his hand slightly and pointed. "Hotel." His hand dropped and he let out a last and final breath. After pushing his eye lids closed with my index finger, I made the sign of the cross.

Adam said, "Now what are we gonna do?"

"We gotta get back to the truck and tell everyone."

By the time we arrived back at our truck, most of the convoy had already left. Maggie was sitting in the driver's seat. "Come on guys, what the hell you doing out there?"

I noted that one Hummer stayed behind for security and it was Jeff's. He walked up to me. "What the hell happened?" I advised Maggie and him what the dogs had found. "Yep, that sounds like ISIS' work to me."

I grabbed the radio. "Captain we found a group of people killed by ISIS out in the desert. Maybe it was the whole town. One old man was still alive and told us two ISIS fighters were at the hotel. Did you see any ISIS fighters? Over."

"Yeah, we found two bastards at the hotel and killed them."

"Did you get their heads?"

"Yeah, I whacked off their heads. Why?"

"Good. I just wanted to make sure you beheaded the dirty bastards for murdering the whole town."

"They're dead and headless, so don't worry." I heard Baldwin let out a little chuckle. "Get your butts up here. Over."

Jeff said, "Hey, we better get going."

We finally caught up to the convoy which was pulled off the highway about two miles from the Pecos River Bridge, on the eastern side Santa Rosa proper.

*Santa Rosa is located in Guadalupe County, New*

*Mexico. Population at one time was just over 2,000. At the time it was mostly a Hispanic populated city, strongly oriented in Catholicism. The city is just west of the Llano Estacado, in eastern New Mexico. The first European settlement here was in 1865. It was named Aqua Negra Chiquita or Little Black Water. The name was changed in 1890 to Santa Rosa which means Holy Rose.*

While the convoy was being concealed off the road, in the bush, our sniper team, Baldwin, Pete, Maggie, and I had a brief meeting reviewing the satellite map. Route 54, which was named Parker Avenue within the city limits, took a dog leg to the southwest which provided a half mile of straight road leading to the bridge.

Maggie and I would find the tallest building and position ourselves on the roof. Baldwin and Pete would proceed to the bridge within 200 yards, and start to eliminate targets using silenced M4's.

We found an eight story warehouse located on the north side of Parker Avenue at 5th Street. All of us cleared the perimeter of the building. Maggie and I entered the building with ease since the doors were not locked. We carefully checked the empty building. Satisfied that no one was there, we locked the doors from the inside and proceeded to the roof.

The roof was flat, making it a perfect shooting platform. I popped down the Harris Bipod legs and set-up the Cobb fifty on the edge of the roof, facing the bridge. Maggie guarded the stairs and patrolled around the roof, watching for any bogies.

Looking through my low-light scope, I could see the bridge which had four trucks blocking the four lanes which crossed the bridge. I zeroed in on the people and counted four men. One did have an RPG and the others carried rifles of some type.

I spotted Baldwin and Pete moving towards the bridge. Baldwin was on the north side, and Pete was on the south side of Parker Avenue. This would allow them to create crossfire.

I radioed Baldwin and Pete. "Four bogies are on the bridge, right near the trucks. One man has an RPG. Over."

"What are they doing?"

"They're just sitting there talking and not paying any attention to Parker Avenue. Over."

"Roger that. Keep us informed of any movement. Over and out," Baldwin replied.

I kept my eye glued to the scope watching these guys, while also scanning the entire area for any other terrorists. I checked out each building on both sides of the street. I didn't see any other radicals. Checking the time, it was almost 5 am, which meant the sun would be coming up in an hour.

Captain Baldwin had better make his move soon, before the break of dawn. We had driven all night and needed some rest. Lying there, I almost dozed off. Maggie woke me out of my daze as she kicked my foot. "I wish they'd hurry it up."

"Yeah, me too," I told her.

"How far is it to their trucks?"

"The range finder shows 600 yards."

"That's an easy shot for you, Jack."

"Maggie, you got good eyes so do me a favor, look through this scope. Tell me if you see four or five men by the trucks." I needed to give my eyes a rest for a minute because I thought I saw another man.

"Sure." I stood up and Maggie laid down to scan the area with my rifle. "I see four men by the trucks."

I lit up a smoke to take the edge off my nerves and stretched my legs. I dowsed my bandanna with some water and wiped my face off, trying to wake up.

Standing on the edge of the roof, I glanced down the street at the bridge and thought I saw movement near some trees. "Maggie, you see anyone moving down there?" Before she could answer, a bullet zipped by my head. I heard the zing loud and clear. It was too close for comfort. I dropped flat to the roof top. "Where did that come from?"

"I don't know. I didn't hear any gun fire," Maggie said.

"Shit, there's a sniper out there. Maybe he also spotted Pete and Baldwin." I grabbed the radio. "Guys, we have a sniper out there taking pot-shots at us."

"Where's he at, Jack?" Baldwin asked.

Just then another round impacted into the side of the building at the edge of the roof, near my head. I scooted back a foot. "Maggie, did you see where that came from?"

"Negative."

I got on the radio. "Guys, he just took another shot

at us."

"Where is he?" Baldwin asked.

"I guess he's somewhere near the trees on the north side of the street."

"Roger that," Baldwin replied. "We'll find him. Over."

"Jack, what the hell we gonna do?" Maggie asked.

"I got an idea but it's risky. One of us has to be bait for him to shoot at."

"Bait! Are you nuts?"

"No, hear me out, I'll be the bait. We can't see or hear him because he's got a silencer. But using the M4 FLIR scope maybe we can detect his heat signature or that of his gun."

"What are you gonna do, stand up and let him shoot at you?"

"Basically, yes. He has to make a mistake. We have to have him heat up his barrel or show us some body heat."

I glanced at the other buildings and thought this was the tallest one in the area. He had to be within 500 yards, knowing the types of weapons they use. But maybe he had a .308 or 30.06, and a good old American quality rifle. In any case, wondered how I was going to be the bait without getting killed. More than likely he had a FLIR scope that detected heat or an old-style night scope that used the ambient light of the moon. If he had an old-style night scope I had a chance.

The sniper must've been located somewhere lower than we were, otherwise he'd be shooting at us now. I had to conclude that he couldn't see the top of our roof. That's why he only fired when I stood up near the edge of the roof. I thought, m*aybe if I move back ten or twenty paces from the edge and stand up he won't be able to see me. Then that could give me some idea how far away he is by using some simple trigonometry by line of sight.*

Maggie asked, "I wonder why he doesn't have his buddies come after us?"

"He doesn't know who we are or that we have weapons. More than likely he thinks we're just some people roaming around looking for food. We're just infidels he wants to kill."

"Well, what's the plan, Jack?"

"I'm gonna back up from the edge of the roof about twenty steps and then stand up. If he sees me, he'll shoot. You use the FLIR on your M4 and see if you can detect him. You're looking for a small heat signature, or a bright sudden flash."

"If I see him, should I shoot?"

"Negative. We'll radio Baldwin and let him do the kill."

I crawled back across the roof until I was about twenty paces away. Then I radioed Baldwin, advising what I was doing. We set a time that in two minutes I would stand up.

"Maggie, are you ready?"

"Yep."

I started a countdown out loud from ten seconds. On one, I slowly stood up and quickly ducked down. I didn't hear the whine or whizz of a bullet going by. That meant he must be closer to us, so I moved forward toward the roof's edge by ten steps.

Baldwin came on the radio. "Jack, we didn't see a thing."

"He didn't fire so I'm moving closer to the edge of the roof by ten steps. Count down, one minute." I also moved about ten feet to the right, so if he did have a fix on me he would have to sight in again.

The minute went by fast, and I stood up once again just for three seconds. As I was ducking down I felt something hit my head. My hat flew off and I picked it up. To my surprise there was a bullet hole in the top. Half of an inch lower and I would have been dead meat. I felt the warm trickle of blood running down my face. The bullet had grazed the top of my head. I wiped the blood off and felt the wound with my finger. It was a very small graze that started to burn. After pouring a little water on it I put my hat back on.

Maggie shouted, "I spotted him."

As I crawled back next to Maggie I said, "Good, paint him with the laser."

She looked at me, touching my face. "You're bleeding. Are you ok?"

"Yeah, it's just a slight graze."

Clicking the radio, I advised, "Baldwin, Maggie has him painted. Do you see the laser?"

"Roger that, he's ours now."

Picking up the fifty, I looked at the laser spot through my scope. The sniper was in a tree 300 yards away, close to Baldwin's location, on the north side of the street. I could see Baldwin moving in for the kill. I could make out the shooters arm and rifle. He was taking aim again, directly at us.

I glanced over at Maggie and she had her torso showing. He was going to kill her for sure. I leaned over and shoved her to the ground just as the bullet zipped overhead.

"Stay the hell down, Maggie, and keep him painted."

I had a fix on this jerk and wanted to put a big fifty caliber round into his body, blowing it apart. The problem was, if I fired my big cannon, his buddies on the bridge would be alerted and come running to his aid.

I peered once again into my scope and saw he was now aiming at Baldwin. I had no choice but to fire. I grabbed the radio. "Baldwin, look out, he's got your number!" Baldwin quickly rolled to one side, but he had no cover.

Flicking my safety off, I took aim and squeezed the trigger. KABOOM! One shot, one kill. I scanned over to the bridge and sure enough, the four men on the bridge were running this way. I had to warn Pete and Baldwin. "Four bogies from the bridge are coming your way! The sniper is dead."

Pete replied, "I see them." He started to fire.

I told Maggie, "Now you can shoot them."

"Hot dog! I finally get to kill one of these jerks," Maggie replied with glee.

It was like shooting fish in a barrel. Pete and George had them in a cross fire as the ISIS men dressed in black came running to their death. Maggie was firing her M4 at them, but I couldn't tell if she hit one or not.

The action happened so quickly I didn't have a chance to zero in on another target. All the bogies were dead. They didn't even get off a shot at us. I heard Captain Baldwin radio the convoy to move up to the bridge. In the meantime, Maggie and I came down off the roof.

Baldwin, Pete, and I checked the bodies and vehicles. We put another bullet in their heads, just to make sure they didn't return to life, like the walking dead. Pete collected the weapons, including an RPG with a dozen rockets, and piled them on the side of the street. Maggie stood guard just in case another raghead popped up out of nowhere.

Thirty minutes later, the convoy showed up. We moved the ISIS trucks out of the way and disabled them by tearing out the spark plug wires, stabbing the tires, and throwing the keys into the Pecos River.

After loading up the confiscated weapons, we proceeded across the Pecos River Bridge on State Route 54. A bright yellow sun was just breaking the horizon. There wasn't a cloud in the sky, which meant it was going to be a hot day.

# JESSIE ROSEBUD
## MAY 23, 2026

We would follow Route 54 south to State Route 60 and head due west to I-25. After reviewing the map, I only counted four small cities between Santa Rosa and the Interstate.

According to our map, the largest city on Route 60 was Mountainair, located 90 miles from Santa Rosa in Torrance County. Population of this little city was about 1,000 people in 2010. It's located at an altitude of 6,495 feet in the Pedernal Hills area.

The route soon proved not to be so good, with steep hills and a winding narrow highway. It was a two lane country road that hadn't been maintained in years. From the appearance, it seemed that it hadn't been traveled either. We passed through two deserted small towns, and didn't see a soul for the next 90 miles until we reached Mountainair, two hours later.

At the city limit sign there was a roadblock made up of two pickup trucks. Eight men dressed like cowboys flagged us down. We rolled to a stop about a hundred feet from their vehicles. Baldwin and I dismounted and approached them with our M4's slung on our chests, holding our hands slightly raised.

We were within twenty feet when one of the guards said, "That's close enough boys." They all pointed their weapons at us.

We stopped and I said, "Gentlemen, good morning."

The guard replied, "Morning. What do you boys want?"

"We're just passing through, on our way to Arizona."

"Why are you using this route?"

"Because we heard I-40 is blocked going into Albuquerque by ISIS."

He nodded his head. "Yeah, we know that. We had to fight them a couple of times. Are y'all in the Army?"

"We're on a mission for the Army." I reached into my pocket to show him the letter written by Army Ranger, Captain Sessions. I held it up. "Here, read this letter."

The man stepped forward and took it from my hand. After reading it he asked, "How long you gonna be in Mountainair?"

"Well, we need somewhere to rest for a while, and if possible, get some grub and fuel. We've been driving all night. But if you don't want us to stick around, we'll just pass through. We don't want any trouble."

He peered straight into my eyes to see if I was telling the truth, and then at Baldwin. He glanced at the armored Hummer. "How many trucks and men you got?"

"We have thirty men, two dogs, and nine trucks."

The rough looking cowboy stuck out his hand and said, "I'm Jessie Rosebud, Sheriff of this county. You're welcome to visit Mountainair for a while."

I firmly gripped his hand and shook it. "Thanks, Sheriff. I'm Jack Gunn and this is Captain Baldwin." They nodded to each other.

Jessie had to be about fifty years old, and judging by his beer belly was a little over weight. Maybe he ate too many donuts. He was a little shorter than Baldwin and I. He spoke like a straight shooter and carried himself with confidence. Jessie wore a white neatly-pressed shirt, blue jeans, a white hat, and of course, cowboy boots. He carried an AR-15 and a cowboy-type holster on his hip with a black handled revolver. The pistol appeared to be a Colt Anaconda.

Jessie replied, "Jack, just a friendly warning, if you're up to no good, you'll be the first one I kill." Then he let out a chuckle. "Follow me into town."

"You got nothing to worry about, Sheriff," I told him.

Highway 60 runs right through the center of the city. Upon first entering the old town I was surprised to see a lot of people milling around on the streets. The city itself was a quaint looking place. We slowly followed the Sheriff, at 10 mph, into the heart of downtown, passing the Tomahawk Service Station, the old Greyhound Bus Station, finally coming to a stop near the Shaffer Hotel, down the street from the Rosebud Saloon.

Baldwin had his men line the trucks up in a neat row, bumper to bumper. Pete and Jeff posted guards at both ends of the convoy and in the middle. Jessie commented to Baldwin, "Captain, you don't need any guards here. No one will steal anything in Mountainair."

"I know, but its protocol for my men. We do it out of habit."

Everyone dismounted but stayed with their vehicles, awaiting further instructions. Adam and Maggie were standing next to our truck with the dogs, which needed to go for a walk.

Jessie said, "There are two places to eat, the Rosebud Saloon, and the Shaffer Hotel. Either one is good but the Rosebud has home-made beer."

I asked, "Do you own the Rosebud?"

"No, my brother Jimmy does and he's the Mayor. My family owns most of the town and property around here."

By now a crowd of people had gathered across the street. They were closely observing our combat Humvees. Baldwin looked at Jessie with a concerned expression. "Sheriff, do we have anything to worry about?"

"No, don't mind them, they just don't see many strangers. Let's get a beer."

Baldwin and I put our M4's into the truck and followed him into the Rosebud Saloon while our men stayed by their vehicles. We both wore Glock 9mm guns and kept them with us. Of course, I had my Black Bear Bowie fighting knife strapped to my tactical vest.

The saloon was a quaint old place, and judging by the looks, it hadn't been remodeled since it was built. The bar looked like something out of a John Wayne western movie. Yeah, it was old alright. It reeked with the odor of beer and whiskey. The tables, chairs, and bar stools were made of wood that showed a lot of wear.

Another man behind the bar, who looked just like Jessie, walked over. Jessie said, "This is my twin brother Jimmy. He runs this bar and he's the Mayor."

Jimmy and Jessie were dressed exactly alike, except for their guns. Jimmy had a shoulder holster under his left armpit which carried some type of semi-auto handgun.

We all shook hands. Jimmy said, "Have a seat. I gotta talk to my brother for a minute." They walked away through a swinging door into another room, which appeared to be the kitchen.

A short while later, another man came out of the kitchen with a young lady who had a beer in each hand. "Hello," she said. "My name is Maria. This is Carlos," as she placed the beers in front of us, on the table.

Baldwin and I said hello and Maria put her hand on my shoulder. She was dressed in a short black mini-skirt, red high heels, and a red low-cut blouse, which revealed her ample sized breasts. Maria was a shapely young woman whom I guessed was in her late twenties. She was pretty alright, with long black hair and an exotic face with full red lips. She smoothly swayed around like smoke blowing in the air.

Maria said, "If you gentlemen need anything, just let me know."

"Ok, we'll do that," I replied.

Maria squeezed my shoulder a little. I looked up at her and she winked. "If you see something you like …

let me know," as she winked again.

Baldwin replied, "We get the idea honey. We don't need anything right now."

Carlos, an older man, probably about fifty, smiled and said, "Si señor, we understand. Maria let's go back to the kitchen and leave them alone while they have a drink."

I didn't care for the way Carlos looked. He had a sneaky demeanor about him. He was a small skinny guy with beady dark eyes and was always smiling. His clothes were dirty and he looked a mess.

As they walked away, Maria smiled at us. "Remember, anything you want, let me know."

I watched her nice butt sway as they entered the kitchen and the door swung shut. I had to watch her, after all, I am not dead.

Baldwin said, "That was weird."

As I looked at my beer I said, "Yeah, I guess she's a hooker."

I picked up the beer to take a sip and it was warm so I smelled it. It didn't smell right, so I took a tiny sip of foam off the top. It tasted bitter and had an odor about it that I had smelled before, but couldn't place it. I didn't like the nasty smell.

Baldwin held his beer mug up, "Cheers."

I stopped his hand before he could take a drink. "Wait … I think the beer is laced."

Baldwin smelled it. "I agree it doesn't smell normal. You think they're trying to poison us?"

"I hate to say it, but yes."

"Why would they do that?"

"George, they want our weapons and trucks."

With that comment Baldwin stood up, went to the window, and peeked outside. "The crowd is getting bigger. There must be two-hundred people out there now."

Just then, the Rosebud brothers came out of the kitchen. "What are you looking at?" Jessie asked.

George turned and replied, "Just checking on my men." He walked back to the table and sat down.

Jessie nodded and sat down next to Baldwin. Jimmy scooted a chair up alongside of me. "Y'all didn't drink your beers," Jimmy said.

I replied, "Sorry, but we don't drink."

"You don't drink! Come on now. Let's have one drink as friends. Carlos, bring Jessie and I a beer."

"Si, Jefe," Carlos yelled.

A few minutes later, Maria strolled over to the table with two more beers, placing them in front of our hosts. Following behind her was sneaky looking Carlos. Maria stood directly behind me and once again placed her hand on my shoulder and squeezed it. Carlos stood behind Baldwin.

We don't like people standing behind us, especially people we don't know. Call us paranoid, but you never know what could happen.

The Rosebuds picked up their beers and said, "Cheers." George and I just sat there and didn't say a word. "Come on, you boys gotta drink up!" Jessie said.

"Like we told you, we don't drink," Baldwin said.

Jimmy changed the subject. "Well, how do y'all like Maria?"

"Yeah, she's a looker alright," I said.

"Jack, go ahead, take her upstairs, and have some fun."

Maria replied, "Si Mr. Jack, I would like that," as she grabbed both my shoulders massaging them, while digging in her nails.

"Sorry honey, I can't do that."

"Are you a queer?" Jessie asked. Carlos laughed at the comment.

Jimmy said, "Yeah. Are you queers? Shit, we don't cotton to queers around here." With that comment he pulled his gun out of its shoulder holster, placing it on the table.

"Why'd you pull that out?" I asked.

"Shit, you won't drink our beer, or take Maria, so we can't trust y'all. Maybe you want another lady? Maria, bring two more ladies here, pronto."

"Jimmy, that's not necessary. The truth is, we're happily married men and don't fool around."

"I understand now. You guys are pussy whipped." The Rosebud brothers laughed out loud, as did ugly little Carlos.

"I think it's sweet, they're loyal to their wives," Maria commented.

Jessie growled, "Shut the hell up, Maria. Nobody asked your opinion." He reached over the table and slapped her hard in the head.

"Sheriff, that's no way to treat a lady," Baldwin

commented.

"Shit, she's no lady. She's my whore and I own her."

With that comment, Baldwin and I looked at each other. It was becoming clear that the Rosebud boys were not very friendly people. I suspected we were going to have a run-in with them before we left the good town of Mountainair.

"You can't own anyone, it's against the law," I replied.

"Law! We are the law around here," Jimmy said. "We're the judge and jury also."

"Yeah, we don't need no stinking badges," Jessie replied. Both of them starting laughing until tears ran down their cheeks.

I peered over at Baldwin and he had a disgusted look on his face. I knew he wanted to kill these guys as much as I did. These jerks had no respect for the law or the United States Constitution.

I noticed that Jimmy reached out, placing his hand on the gun sitting in front of him. It was a Smith and Wesson M&P 9 mm. I kept my eye on him, closely observing his face and hand. I was planning some type of action in case he actually pointed that gun at us.

"Why are you boys going to Arizona with armored Hummers and big machine guns?" Jimmy asked, as he twirled the gun around on top the table.

This was clearly a threatening move he was making. Jimmy was reminding us he had his gun out and would use it if necessary.

I replied, "We're on a mission to rescue some family members for the Army and take them back to Florida with us." I had no choice but to lie to the dirtbag.

"Where in Florida?" Jimmy asked.

"Tocabaga Island."

"Never heard of it. Where's that at?"

"It's near Tampa Bay," I replied, not wanting to tell him the exact location.

"You boys are a long way from home. Now, let's discuss our fees."

"What kind of fees?"

"Well, to safely pass through Mountainair, it will cost you. It's a simple fee system; $5,000 for every man, so that comes to $150,000. Each truck will cost you $10,000. That comes to $90,000, which brings it to a grand total of $240,000."

"Are you crazy?" Baldwin asked.

Jimmy stopped twirling the gun. "You think we're crazy?" Jimmy asked.

Jimmy was sitting right next to me. I could quickly reach out, grab the gun, and turn it on them. However, firing it might attract the attention of the crowd gathering outside around our vehicles.

I advised, "Your price is a little steep. We didn't expect you'd charge us for passing through your town."

"We gotta make money somehow," Jessie said. "Do you have that much money?"

We did have that much, but it would drain our cash resources. I certainly wasn't going to give it to these dirtbags.

"No, we don't have that much," I told Jessie.

"How much do you got?"

"We can give you $50,000 cash."

"Ok, we'll take that and one of those Hummers to make up the difference."

"You're nuts," Baldwin said.

Jimmy pointed his gun at Baldwin. "If you call us crazy again, I'm gonna shoot you in the face." Jessie and Jimmy both had a shit-eating grin on their face.

Now that was clearly a threat to kill Baldwin and me so I calculated the odds of grabbing his gun before he could shoot me.

Jimmy said, "Looks to me like you boys got no choice."

All of sudden the front door opened and Maggie walked in. "Jack, there's a lot of people out here! I suggest … we leave," as she sized up the situation, Maggie stopped speaking.

Jimmy and Jessie both turned to observe Maggie and I made my move. I swiftly grabbed the gun, twisting it out and away of his hand. Jimmy jumped up, and I swung the barrel cold-cocking him hard as I could in the face. The blow knocked him to the floor.

Jessie made a move to draw his gun but Baldwin beat him to the draw, getting the drop on him. He submitted by raising his hands. To my surprise, Jimmy wasn't fully knocked out and grabbed my leg, trying to drag me to the floor.

I tossed his gun to Captain Baldwin and pulled out my Cold Steel knife. Dropping down, slamming my right knee into his chest, I stabbed Jimmy in the center of the throat, and in one smooth fast move, sliced it open so he couldn't yell. He would slowly bleed out and die in a minute or two. You could hear his blood gurgling as he gasped for air.

Jessie yelled, "You bastard! You killed my brother!"

Jumping up I told him, "Shut the fuck up or you're next," while holding my knife to his throat. I pulled his gun out of the holster and tossed to the other side of the room.

I noticed Carlos and Maria suddenly made a dash towards the kitchen. I shouted, "Maggie, get them!"

Maggie, like a lioness on the hunt, quickly leaped down two stairs and flew past our table on a full run, catching Maria before she made it to the kitchen door. Maggie drew her Barong Machete and whacked Maria in the right arm, just below the shoulder, almost severing it. It was hanging by the skin as she fell to the floor screaming, with bright red blood squirting from her stump.

After pausing for a second to observe Maria, Maggie ran through the kitchen door after Carlos. The door banged shut. We heard pots and pans banging around or being thrown, along with a lot of yelling. A few minutes later, the shouting and banging stopped and all was still.

The kitchen door slowly opened. Maggie walked out holding his head up by the hair. "I got the little bastard!" She dropped the bloody head next to Maria.

Laying on her back bleeding out, Maria whimpered,

"My arm is gone. I'm worthless ... I beg you ... please help me."

I glanced over at Maggie who placed the tip of her machete on Maria's chest. Maggie looked at me and I nodded approval. With one strong fast thrust Maggie shoved the big blade into Maria's chest, and the beauty was instantly dead. She felt no pain. I made the sign of the cross as she let out her last breath.

I didn't wanna kill Maria, but she was right, without her arm she was worthless. She would probably die a long painful death from infection or continue to live as a one-arm sex slave.

I felt regret for killing Maria. Maybe I should have stopped Maggie from cutting off her arm, but it all happened so fast I didn't know she was going to do that. On the other hand, Maria probably would have run to warn the others that I killed Jimmy. What's done is done, and it can't be changed. I wondered how God would judge our actions. I should have known better than to release the lioness.

Maggie walked over to me and asked, "What's wrong with these people?"

Jessie, sitting there with his hands up in shock, asked, "Who's this bitch?"

I replied, "She's an Amazon Warrior, your worst nightmare. Shut your face!"

I noticed she had been cut across the forehead and her left sleeve was sliced open. Blood was dripping down her hand.

*Years ago, when I sensed the country was changing*

*for the worst, I started training women how to shoot and fight so they could defend themselves against any evil-doers. I started training Amy, my daughter first, and then Maggie. Slowly but surely, other women became interested in self-defense. Now we have a select group of twenty women warriors who can shoot with the best. They train every week at the farm. I call them the Amazon Warriors, and believe me, you don't want to mess with any of them. They would cut your balls off and hand them to you on a plate.*

*The legendary Amazon Warriors are believed to have lived in a part of modern day Turkey. There they formed an independent all-woman kingdom ruled by a Queen. They were also called the Androktones, or killers of men. No men were permitted to reside in Amazon country. Once a year, to prevent their race from dying out, they would visit a neighboring tribe. Any male children who were born from these visits were killed or sent back to their fathers. The girls were brought up by their mothers and trained in the art of war. When they went to war, men would be taken as slaves or killed. When they grew tired of a man, he would be killed or forced to leave their country.*

*My Amazon Warriors, or Androktones, are the police force for Tocabaga Island. They all carry the deadly Barong Machete, which they have been fully trained to use. The Barong is shaped like a small sword. The 14 inch sharp blade has a point so the user can stab, slice, or dice the enemy.*

Baldwin said, "Maggie, let me see your arm." She moved next to him while I guarded Jessie. Ripping open her sleeve, she had a deep cut across her forearm. The wound on her head was most likely caused by a flying pot or pan during the fight. "This arm might need some stitches."

Baldwin patched her up, cleaning the wounds with antiseptic and placed a bandage on them. He tightly wrapped her cut arm with tape. Maggie is one tough cookie. She can handle almost any man and for sure any woman. I've see her in battle and she's fast as lighting, strong, and knows just about every combat move in the book.

"Jack, there's a lot of people out there. How are we gonna get out of here?" Maggie asked.

"Mr. Rosebud is gonna give us safe passage."

Jessie replied, "Go fuck yourself. You'll never get out of Mountainair alive."

I pressed my blade to his throat until it cut the skin and started to draw blood. Jessie winced in pain. "Jessie, I can make this very painful for you. I'm somewhat of an expert with knives. I like what they can do to pricks like you."

I started to slice his face slowly, one cut at a time. No deep cuts, just enough to make him bleed. If you slice just about skin deep the blood really flows out. He tried to fight back but I stabbed him in his gun hand and that really hurt him as blood ran out of the veins. Jessie yelled, "You bastard! I'm gonna kill you."

"No, Jessie you got it all wrong. I'm gonna kill you and then we'll blast our way out of this dump. Maggie, zip tie his hands behind him."

Maggie pulled out zip cuffs and tied his hands

behind him. I kept slicing his face and blood was freely flowing into his eyes. When blood flows into your eyes it burns and blurs your vision.

"Maggie, find me a salt shaker," I said. She went behind the bar and tossed me one. I sprinkled the salt directly into his wounds. Boy does that smart! He started to yell, so I shoved my bandana into his big mouth to muffle his screams.

I said, "Now I'm going to cut off one of your ears, then the other, and finally your nose unless you co-operate. If you don't co-operate, I'll cut off every digit you have including that little dick you got."

Baldwin was guarding the door as Maggie ran over next to me. "Jack, let me cut off his little prick."

"OK, go ahead. Here's my knife."

"I'll use my machete. Should I cut off his balls, too?"

"Yeah, why not? Balls are no good without a prick." We started to laugh, except for Jessie who looked terrified, as Maggie started to unfasten his belt.

Jessie had just witnessed Maggie kill Maria and Carlos so he knew Maggie wasn't messing around. Jessie started to mumble something so I took the rag out of his mouth. "You say something, Jessie?"

"I'll do whatever you want just don't cut me anymore."

"Don't believe him, Jack," Maggie said. "Let me cut that little prick off."

"Jessie, you better do what I say or Maggie will cut it off."

"Ok, whatever you say," Jessie stated. His face was a bloody mess. I could tell he was broken from the torture. Of course he didn't want to lose the family jewels.

"Maggie, wipe his face off with some water so he don't look like a bloody piece of meat."

Baldwin warned us, "Hurry up, some people are coming this way."

After his face was cleaned off I pulled Jessie to his feet. Drawing out my Glock, I held it to his head while holding onto his hands tied behind his back. "Jessie, we're going out so tell your minions to back off or I'll kill you on the spot. You'll be the first one to die. That's a promise."

He softly replied, "Ok."

"I'll go out first with the little prick and he'll tell his men to back off. Maggie, you cover one direction and George the other, but first radio our men to be ready to roll out fast and provide us cover."

Baldwin got on the radio and told our men to start the engines and be ready to roll out fast. He warned them to be prepared to defend the convoy.

I walked out the door holding Jessie tightly in front of me. Following right behind us, Maggie covered the south side of the street and George the north. The crowd just looked at us as I poked Jessie in the head with my pistol. "Tell them to back off now and let us leave. Otherwise, I'll kill your ass."

Jessie complied with my orders. He shouted, "Everyone back off and let these people leave or they'll kill me. They already killed Jimmy, Carlos, and Maria."

The crowd stopped approaching us, following his orders.

We climbed into the back of my pickup bed and stood up, holding my gun to Jessie's head for all to see. The mob started to close in as our convoy quickly pulled away. They ran after us for a few hundred feet, but we were soon out of their range. The good thing was no shots were fired.

Reaching the western edge of town, our convoy stopped before reaching another roadblock. I told Jessie, "You did a good job back there. Now get us through this road block. I give you my word, I'll let you go on the other side."

Jessie told his men to move the roadblock and let us safely pass or we would kill him. The guards followed his orders so we quickly drove past them. The truth was the eight man guard team was no match for us. We could have gunned our way through the roadblock, but I didn't want to risk any of us getting shot.

We were safely down the road about 600 yards when I radioed the convoy to stop so I could release Jessie. Cutting off his zip cuffs, I told him to beat it. I watched him run down the middle of the highway until he was about 300 yards out.

Walking up to the last Hummer, driven by Jeff, I told him, "Ok, open fire on them. Kill Jessie and the guards." I gave Jessie my word to let him go. I didn't give my word that I wouldn't kill him.

Without asking me any questions, the big fifty caliber M2 machine gun opened up. I got the satisfaction of seeing Jessie fall to the ground. The rounds started to hit the trucks and men at the roadblock. They were getting peppered because 600 yards is well within killing range for an M2. After a few hundred rounds, Jeff stopped firing.

I don't know if we killed them all or not, but I was sure they wouldn't be chasing after us. I mounted up and we moved out, continuing on Route 60.

As I was driving, Adam asked, "What was that all about?"

"Those guys were nuts and wanted us to pay them for going through their town. They weren't good people." That was all I told him about the situation.

"Maggie, are you ok?" I asked. She nodded her head and didn't say a word. I wondered if killing Maria was bothering her.

Thirty miles later, Baldwin pulled the convoy to the side of the road. We could see Interstate 25 about a mile ahead. Everyone dismounted and Baldwin called a driver's meeting.

Baldwin asked, "How's everyone on fuel?" Consensus was we could use some fuel to top off our tanks, if we could find it.

I said, "George let's see if we can find some fuel along I-25. Look at the map, we could head south. Route 60 and I-25 blend together going south for about 30 miles and then SR-60 breaks off heading west to Arizona. I suggest we stay on sixty until we get into Arizona."

Gazing at the map, Baldwin replied, "Yeah, good idea that way we stay away from the terrorists up north. You're right, maybe we can find some fuel along the Interstate."

My greatest fear was running out of fuel. We had enough to travel for another day and night but it's best to keep our tanks topped off. You never know when you'll find the next fuel stop. My hope was that Arizona would not be full of terrorists like New Mexico.

"Alright, let's get out of New Mexico while it's still daylight," Baldwin said.

Arriving at I-25 we headed south to where SR-60 turned west. We found a few stations along the way and some abandoned cars that allowed us to scavenge gas and diesel fuel. It wasn't enough, but we'd have to make do. Daylight was running out and we still had an estimated 120 miles to reach Arizona.

Traveling all day, we didn't see any other cars, but we did spot some people on foot. When they saw us, however, they beat a path into the bush and hid. I can't say that I blame them; I'd hide from a convoy with four armored Hummers. This is very dangerous country, especially with ISIS fighters running around.

We wound through the Gallinas Mountain Range and the Datils Mountains. The road was mostly up one hill and down the other side. This was a beautiful area which contained scrubland consisting of pinyons, ponderosa pines, and grasslands. Shrubs included yucca, cholla, and Apache plume. While driving, we saw off in the distance several elk and mule deer, along with quails and other birds. The entire area was teeming with wild life.

Normally we would have stopped and went hunting. But considering we were in ISIS country we kept on the move.

It was 7 pm when we finally reached the Arizona border. Swinging north, we passed through the tiny town of Springerville, which appeared abandoned, but we weren't sure. We decided to head for Lyman Lake State Park to spend the night. It was out in the middle of nowhere and we guessed it would be a safe place to rest up. Looking at the map the lake was a considerable size. We could go swimming and take a bath in the pristine lake, which was fed by the Little Colorado River.

The lake was about a 30 mile drive from the Arizona border. Baldwin took the lead to scout the park before our arrival. Everyone one was exhausted after driving almost 36 hours straight with little to no sleep. We hadn't had much to eat, other than energy bars.

Our radio came on. "The park is clear. No one is here. It looks great so hurry up," Baldwin told us.

A bath in the lake, some MREs, a couple shots of JD, and some sleep would make me feel a lot better.

Pulling into Lyman State Park, we saw the large lake with its abundance of fresh water. Adam asked, "Grandpa, can I go swimming?"

"Yes, of course. There aren't any gators here, just snakes. We'll all go swimming. Maybe I'll go fishing."

"What kind of snakes?" Maggie asked.

"Rattlesnakes … maybe some Water Moccasins."

Maggie glanced at me with a pouting face. "Gee whiz, I hate snakes." Adam and I laughed at her comment, razzing her a little.

*Lyman Lake is at 6,000 feet elevation, and is*

*located in Apache County, Arizona. This lake was created as an irrigation reservoir by damming the Little Colorado River. The river is fed by snowmelt from the slopes of Mount Baldy and the Escudilla Mountains. The park had a dozen old cabins and trailers, indicating that at one time some people had lived here.*

As he normally does, Baldwin had the vehicles line up in a double row formation with the Hummers guarding the ends of the rows. Once we turned off our truck motors it was dead quiet. Everyone went about their business either making some chow, going for a swim, topping off the fuel tanks, checking their trucks oil and water, washing clothes, or starting a campfire.

I checked Maggie's arm and used surgical super glue to seal the wound shut, making it waterproof. Satisfied that she wouldn't get an infection, Maggie, Adam, and I went swimming. Since we didn't have swim suits our underwear had to suffice. As usual, Maggie looked sexy as hell, wearing just a bra and panties that looked like a two piece bikini. I just couldn't keep my eyes off her toned muscular figure. She has normal size round firm breasts, a washboard stomach, muscular arms, great looking legs, and a small shapely butt. Like I said, I may be old, but I'm not dead.

We washed our clothes and took them back to the camp to hang up, knowing that the dry mountain air would suck the water out of them over night. Our dogs, Adolf and Freda, loved jumping in the water, and running around the park, after being in the truck all day. Adam spent most of his time playing fetch with them.

The sun was setting over the mountains to the west, causing the sky to glow shades of red. Adam collected wood and made a fire. Maggie heated up some MREs and I sat down, lit a smoke, and cracked open a new bottle of JD.

White Feather, Billy, and Black Horse came over to our campfire. White Feather said, "We are close to the Stone Trees."

"Yes, I think about two hours away. We should be there by 10 am tomorrow."

Adam interjected, "Grandpa, I just saw someone up there near that cabin," as he pointed at the hill about a half mile away with a lone structure on it, on the other side of the lake.

I grabbed my binoculars to take a peek. After carefully scanning the hill for movement, I didn't see anything. "It was probably just a coyote," I said.

"It was pretty big. It didn't look like a coyote."

"Well, if it comes around here the dogs will let us know." I took another look just to be sure nothing was there. Maybe the setting sun created some shadows that spooked Adam.

*The coyote is native to North America. It is smaller than its close relative, the gray wolf. They can run up to 45 mph and when fully grown can be two feet high and weight 45 pounds. We've had a lot of experience with coyotes on Tocabaga. They can be dangerous to pet dogs or cats and other small animals. Given the chance, the will also attack small children. They are smart crafty animals who generally avoid contact with humans.*

We were all sitting around the fire as the darkness closed in. White Feather asked me, "What are you looking for at the Stone Trees?"

"We're looking for a clue of some kind that proves the Templars were there. Maybe the clue will give us some direction to find the lost treasure."

"You mean the golden treasure of the ancients."

"I don't know if it's the same treasure or not."

Adam butted into the conversation. "Hey, maybe there are two treasures."

"Now, that's an interesting thought," I commented. "White Feather, can you tell us about the treasure of the ancients?"

"I only know it is in the Grand Canyon. Some of it was brought there and some of it was made in the canyon. Rumor has it the treasure is located in one of the following: Isis Temple, Temple of Ra, Tower of Set, Osiris Temple, Horus Temple, or the Cheops Pyramid. All pyramid-shaped mountains in the canyon have an Egyptian name."

"Why is that?" Adam asked.

"No one really knows for sure. I can only tell you that the Hopi have used these names before the white man came here to explore."

I replied, "If that's true it means the Egyptians had to be at the Grand Canyon."

"If that's true then my theory about two treasures might be correct," Adam commented.

I lit up a smoke and took a big sip of JD while thinking about what Adam had just said. I thought about the last two clues that were written on the Sword of Jerusalem: '*Follow the cross west for another eight days to the rock castle. Go north for 15 days on the marked trail to a fissure in the earth. Here at the head of the trail, leading into the fissure, look for the cross and the Solstice Sun will light the way.*'

I asked, "White Feather, do you know what the rock castle is?"

"Why do you ask?"

"One of the clues on the sword says proceed west from the stone trees for eight days to the rock castle. I figure that eight days by foot puts you somewhere near Sedona." I pulled out a map to show White Feather.

Looking at the map, running his finger over the paper, he said, "It is not directly west of the stone trees. But there is a place we call City of Stone. You call it Montezuma's Castle."

I bent over, peering at the map with his finger pointing at the castle location. Yes, that had to be the rock castle. Taking the map, I plotted a route north and calculated that traveling north, on foot, for 15 days to the fissure puts you at the Grand Canyon. *That's it, the fissure has to be the Grand Canyon.*

I have been to the canyon eight times in the past. It is one of the most awesome sights in the world. Made by nature, ground out by the Colorado River, so they say. But now, I wonder if man was involved in creating some of the formations.

I didn't say another word about this conclusion to the group. I said, "Well gentlemen, it's been a long day and I need some rest. You're welcome to bed down near our fire if you like."

White Feather replied, "No thanks. We'll head back to our truck." Black Horse and Billy agreed and we bid them goodnight.

After our friends left, I advised my thinking to Maggie and Adam. "I think Adam is correct and there are two treasures. Maybe both are buried at the same spot or close to each other."

"I think that's right, Grandpa," Adam said.

"Adam, let's look at the sword again." The three of us walked over to the truck and Adam unsheathed the sword. He laid it on the tailgate while I shined my flashlight on it, looking for any clue we may have missed.

"What are you looking for?" Adam asked.

"We're looking for something subtle, or small that we just overlooked it."

Adam gazed at the side of the shiny blade, which listed the treasure artifacts. Then he turned the sword over to the side that contained the clues and map etched in it. "I don't see anything," Adam said.

Maggie pointed at the sword. "I don't know anything about this stuff, but is that a map?" It was the first time for Maggie to see the holy sword close up.

She got her hand to close to the blade. "Maggie, be careful! Don't touch the blade," Adam warned her.

"I know, I'm not a dummy."

"Yes. It's a map of the fissure, which I now believe is the Grand Canyon," I said.

"It doesn't make any sense to me," Maggie

commented. "What's that tiny mark?"

"What tiny mark?" Adam and I looked very closely at the blade.

"That tiny mark," she said, while pointing at it.

"It looks like a scratch of some kind. I'll get a magnifying glass," I replied.

Bringing the glass back, we took turns looking at the small almost invisible mark. I looked at the whole map again using the magnifying glass. The map made sense now that we knew the fissure was the Grand Canyon. It became crystal clear that the river was winding through the canyon next to the mountain-like formations.

Observing the tiny mark under 10 x magnification, I saw a Hooked X sitting on top a very tiny rock, or at least I assumed it was a rock. The rock was pointed and shaped like a very small pyramid. How they managed to etch this so small was beyond me.

The location of the Hooked X was clearly lined up with one of the mountains, which was directly across the river. The mountain was shaped like a pyramid.

Adam and Maggie both looked at the sword using the eyeglass. I asked them, "What do you see?"

Maggie replied, "It's an X."

"Yeah, I agree," Adam said.

"It's not just an X, but a Hooked X which is a sign of the Templars. Look at the shape of the rock under it. It looks like a pyramid," I said.

Adam looked again. "Yeah, you're right. The small rock is shaped just like a pyramid."

"Now, look at the alignment of the X to the mountain in the middle of the map. There's another Hooked X in the center of the mountain."

Looking again, Adam said, "Yes, it does line up directly with the mountain and the other Hooked X. Why didn't we see that before?"

"It's so small it looked like a scratch in the metal," Maggie replied.

I said, "This means that the mountain is where the treasure is. Once we get to the canyon we'll need to find a Hooked X on a small pyramid-shaped stone. We need to find this before the Summer Solstice date."

"Ok guys, here's your homework for tonight. Get on the ACWWW and find a map or pictures of the canyon, and determine which mountain that Hooked X is on. Next, find out all you can about the Egyptian treasure and its location. Finally, find out how many trails lead down into the canyon toward that mountain. We're going to need to check out each trailhead to find the stone with the Hooked X."

Adam and Maggie started doing the research right away. They weren't tired since they took cat naps during the day, as I was driving. I, on the other hand, was exhausted. After one more shot of JD I fell asleep, while sitting in the back seat of the truck.

# THE STONE TREES
## MAY 24, 2026

It was 5am and I was having a cup of coffee when my trusted friend, Baldwin, moseyed over to my truck. I poured him a cup of hot java. "How you doing, George?"

He nodded ok and took a sip of mud. "Jack, there's no need to hurry today since we're just a couple of hours away from the Petrified Forest. I figured we'll camp there overnight and make it a short travel day."

"That sounds good to me. What route are we taking?"

"We'll just follow Route 180 north, because it takes us right there. There's only one small city we have to go through, named St. Johns."

"George, we cracked the clues. The treasure is definitely in the Grand Canyon."

Suddenly, we heard the roar of jets echo over the lake. Baldwin and I looked up, to the south, but by the time we glanced into the sky they were blasting away with a roar that shook the ground.

Captain Baldwin yelled out to his men. "Everyone put the US Flag out so they can see we're friendly." Every truck carries a flag just for this reason. Our men scrambled to put them out before the jets returned.

"George, they wouldn't bomb us, would they?" I asked.

"They're watching us to see if we're friendly. So we gotta let them know we are. Generally they'll do two or three flybys to check us out. If they think we're the enemy, then we're dead. These are most likely Air Force Reserve planes on a scouting patrol.

Baldwin was right; in a few minutes, they returned. Watching them drop out of the sky, we all waved at them and the flags were spread out on top of the trucks. Passing low overhead, at about 300 mph, they did a wing wave indicating they recognized our group wasn't a threat. They hit the afterburners and zoomed away with a tremendously loud blast that vibrated our skin and ear drums.

Baldwin commented, "Those were F-22 Raptors. They're capable of flying at 2,000 mph and they carry air to ground missiles. I'm glad they're on our side."

"Yeah, me too. So what time you wanna leave here?" I asked.

"There's no need to hurry. We'll leave when everyone is ready."

The jets woke up Adam and Maggie. "What the hell was that?" Maggie asked.

"It was two Air Force jets checking us out to see if we're friendly. But it makes me think there must be some bogies around here that they were looking for," I said.

"Maybe so, but they could just be on patrol," Baldwin commented. "Jack, you were saying before the jets came, that you cracked the clues and the treasure is in the Grand Canyon."

"Yeah, we did. After the Petrified Forest we're heading directly to the canyon."

"Grandpa, you won't believe what we found on the web last night," Adam said.

Pete, second in command, came jogging over to us and interrupted the conversation. "I don't wanna break up your meeting, Captain, but we got company," he said, while pointing to the lone cabin on the hill across the lake. It was the same one where Adam thought he saw someone yesterday.

Peering in his binoculars, Captain Baldwin said, "Ok, it looks like you were right, Jack. We got about twenty armed men moving this way on foot. Everyone break camp and mount up. Pete, provide a rear guard and start shooting those bogies to buy us some time."

Pete and Jeff moved their Hummer to the edge of the lake and started firing the big fifty caliber machine gun, keeping the men at bay, about a half mile away. The lake was between us and them, so they would have to circle around it to reach us. We were well out of their range and Pete made sure they didn't get any closer. You could see the big fifty rounds hitting the dirt around the men as they all scrambled for cover.

Everyone was mounted up, ready to roll in 10 minutes. Baldwin gave the signal and we moved out at full speed. As we rolled away, Maggie asked me, "Who are those guys?"

"I don't know for sure but they could be ISIS fighters. Maybe they're the same men the jets were looking for. I wonder why they don't have vehicles." I was hoping we wouldn't run into them again anytime soon.

About an hour later, Baldwin radioed the convoy. "Listen up, there's a broken down truck up here, pulling a trailer. It's an old man and his wife. Help them out if you can. I'm proceeding to St. Johns to check it out. Over."

The entire convoy pulled over and stopped behind the broken down truck which was pulling a camper trailer. I noticed it had New Mexico plates. An old man was trying to change the left front tire. I walked up to him. "Hi Mister, you need some help?"

He stood up, glanced at me, and said, "I can't get these … damn wheel nuts off. Can you give me … a hand?"

I noted that he was probably in his mid-seventies, a little overweight, and he was huffing and puffing from exerting himself. His wife was sitting in the truck, out of the hot sun.

"Yes sir, I'll help you out. Sit down, relax, and have a drink of water while I change your tire."

"We greatly appreciate your kind help mister."

I grabbed the tire wrench and asked, "Why are you pulling this big trailer?"

His wife commented, "It's our home. It's the only place we got to live."

"Are y'all from New Mexico?"

The old guy replied, "Yep. We had to get out of there cause of the terrorists. They were killing everyone. They killed the whole trailer park and our two boys."

"Where are you headed now?"

"St. Johns. We heard that it was a safe place. It's guarded by Christians."

As I finished changing the tire, my radio hissed. "St. Johns is a friendly city full of armed Christians. I've cleared the way so the roadblock will let you pass," Baldwin advised.

I heard Pete reply that we'd be there in less than an hour.

The old man shook my hand and thanked me. I told him we would follow him to St. Johns for his protection. The old man and his wife reminded me of my Grandparents, on my father's side.

I thought about my Grandparents because of what the old lady said, about the trailer being their home.

*Grandpa started working in the coal mines, taking care of the mules that pulled the coal cars when he was ten years old, after his Dad got killed in a mining accident. He became the bread winner for his Mother and four younger brothers. Of course, Grandpa had to drop out of school in third grade to work in the mines. He could never read anything more than a comic book.*

*They were tough old birds who never had much money and just barely made a living. Grandpa and Grandma were married for 62 years, she was fifteen and he was seventeen when they tied the knot. In those days, if you worked in the mines your whole family became miners. They didn't know anything else. The mining companies owned your ass and it was almost impossible to get out of their debt.*

*At the old age of twenty-two, there was a mining accident. A coal car jumped the track and landed on my Grandpa. It busted his back and he was never able to work in the mine again. He couldn't stand up straight and always leaned to one side to ease the pain. They moved to Chicago to find easier work where he became a bulldozer driver.*

*What sparked me to think of my Grandparents was the trailer. My Grandparents lived in a trailer until the age of 65 when my Father finally purchased them a small house for $10,000. I'll never forget that day because it was the first time I ever saw my Grandpa and Father cry. When my Dad gave him the keys to his new house, they both cried out of happiness. It was my Grandpa's retirement gift. He only received a meager retirement income of $250 per month, so my Dad supported his parents. I was young at the time and didn't have any sense of money. I remember staying with my Grandparents in that little old trailer every summer for two weeks. It was the only thing they owned, other than a beat up old 1950 Chevy. The trailer was their home no matter how small it was.*

I decided to help these old folks out and give them some of our proceeds. I wanted them to live in dignity and not be homeless.

We finally arrived at the St. Johns road block, where Baldwin was waiting for us.

*St. Johns is the county seat of Apache County, Arizona. It is located along U.S. Route 180. The 2010 census showed a population of 3,480. The elevation is about 5,500 feet in the dry desert mountains. St. Johns is a close nit, family first community, known as a "Town of Friendly Neighbors" and it seems to be an appropriate motto.*

I had Maggie give me $50,000 in bills. After putting the money in a paper bag, I walked up to the old couple. "Here's a gift from us to you."

The old guy looked in the bag, and said, "We don't need anything."

"I know you don't, but please just take it."

"You're very kind, thanks a lot."

We shook hands and the old lady said, "God Bless you, mister." It occurred to me I didn't even know their names, as I walked back to my truck.

St. Johns was a nice little city. The people here were well-armed and we could tell they were friendly. Everyone said hello or waved to us as our convoy passed through the city streets. I knew these old folks would be safe living here.

Leaving St. Johns we were about 40 miles from the Petrified Forest. We would arrive there in about an hour with no problems.

Adam said, "Grandpa, you did a good deed giving

those old people some money. Why'd you do that?"

I told Adam and Maggie they reminded me of my Grandparents because they had an old trailer. I told them the story of my Father's parents.

"You're tough on the outside, but you're a softie on the inside, Jack Gunn. That's why I love you," Maggie said, as she punched me in the shoulder.

Changing the subject, Adam said, "Ok, here's some more information we found about the Egyptians. This is a very confusing and twisted story. It's a known fact that King Solomon's treasure and the Ark disappeared when Nebuchadnezzar II invaded Jerusalem. At that time, Zedekiah was King of Jerusalem.

"Egypt had some kind of special relationship with the Kingdom of Judah and Israel, which was composed mostly of Hebrews. No one knows what that relationship was so I did some research. It seems King Solomon became allied to Pharaoh of Egypt by marriage. He married the Pharaoh's daughter and brought her into the City of David, which is now Jerusalem, around 965 BC."

"So what's that got to do with the Ark and treasure?" Maggie asked.

"Very simply, Egypt and Israel were now related. It's ironic that the son of a former Egyptian slave was now the son-in-law of the Pharaoh. This was a common political practice back in those days to help keep countries from going to war with each other. It also helped increase trade and benefited the local people."

"So what's the point?" I asked.

"Well, I think this alliance carried on for almost 400 years."

I said, "Yeah, maybe so."

Adam continued, "In 588 BC, Hophra the Pharaoh, also known as Apries, dispatched a military force to Jerusalem to protect it from the Babylonian forces of Nebuchadnezzar. The story goes that Hophra's forces were quickly defeated and returned to Egypt. Following an 18-month-long siege, Jerusalem was then destroyed by the Babylonians. The city was sacked and looted. They burned it to the ground, and took key people as prisoners back to Babylon, holding them for 70 years. Of course, many of them died during this time."

"Wait … why did God let the Babylonians take Jerusalem?" Maggie asked.

"I read some scriptures in Jeremiah, chapters 34 through 44. It seems that the people of Judah had violated their covenant with the Lord. Some of them also worshiped the Egyptian Gods, which included the Sun God Ra. Anyway, God told the Hebrews he would punish them for this sin. God did this using the military forces of Nebuchadnezzar."

"So what happened to the Ark?" I asked.

"There're a lot of theories about what happen to the treasure and the Ark of the Covenant. One theory is the Ark and treasure is buried under the old original temple, which is now covered by the Dome of the Rock," Adam said.

"If the Ark and treasure are there, you would think they would have already found it 500 years ago," I commented.

"Yeah, you would think so because Jerusalem was rebuilt 70 years later, after it was destroyed by the

Babylonians, and so was the Holy Temple. So you would think that someone knew the treasure was buried in the caves under the old temple."

Maggie asked, "Why didn't they make a new Ark?"

"Good question, Maggie," I replied. "Most claim that the Israelites did not build a new Ark because it would be meaningless without the two stone tablets, made by the finger of God, known as the Ten Commandments. They were kept inside the Ark."

Adam said, "Yes, that's right. I think they didn't make another Ark or a copy of the Ten Commandments because they were afraid of what God might do to them for losing the Ark."

Ok, what's another theory?" Maggie inquired.

Adam replied, "The Ark was taken and hidden in a cave in the nearby mountains."

"Well, if that's true, why didn't they go find it?" I said. "You don't just misplace the most Holy item in the world. That was their channel to God. It doesn't make any sense to me."

"I agree," Adam replied. "They wouldn't forget the location after only 70 years. You would think someone knew its location and would bring it to the new Temple they built."

We all nodded in agreement. Maggie asked, "What if, what's his name … Nebuch … took the treasure and the Ark?"

Adam said, "There are no records of any great treasure or the Ark of the Covenant being taken by the Babylonians. If they took it, believe me, they would have made a big deal of it. It would have been written in the history books for all to see for sure. It was well known that the Ark was the most holy artifact of the Jewish faith."

"Well, that pretty much rules that theory out," I said. "I agree, if Nebuchadnezzar had the Ark he would let it be known. Furthermore, look what we know about the Sword of Jerusalem. You can't touch it unless you are deemed worthy by God. I would assume the same would hold true for the Ark."

Adam nodded yes and commented, "Another theory is that it went to Ethiopia and that's where it is now."

"Ethiopia? How's that possible?" Maggie asked.

"The story is that King Solomon was visited by the Queen of Sheba, also named Makeda. She became pregnant and had a son named Menelik. I read two different accounts about this.

"They credit Menelik with bringing the Ark of the Covenant to Ethiopia, following a visit to Jerusalem to meet his father upon reaching adulthood. This made the entire country of Ethiopia turn into believers of God. I don't think that King Solomon would ever let the real Ark leave Jerusalem.

"The story I believe is that Solomon gave him a duplicate Ark as a gift, and sent him on his way to be first Solomonic Ruler of Ethiopia. You have to remember that this all happened in 950 BC, which is long before the Ark went missing in 586 BC."

I commented, "I heard a story about a church in Ethiopia that claimed to have the Ark. But no one has ever seen it. Maybe that's the duplicate that Solomon made and they think it's the original one."

"Yes, that's exactly what I think," Adam said. "Who knows, maybe there was more than one duplicate of the Ark. So the theory that the real Ark is in Ethiopia is can't be correct."

"So how does all this relate to the Knights Templar?" I asked.

"The most common theory or rumor is that the Templars found the treasure and the Ark in Jerusalem, under the temple. Then, they whisked it off to Europe. When the Knights Templars came under attack by the King of France and the Pope, they moved it to America. If this was true, I think someone would have let the cat out of the bag while it was still in Jerusalem."

"I agree, it would have been almost impossible to take the Ark out of Jerusalem without someone knowing it.

"I also heard that for years people have searched a place called Oak Island looking for a treasure. I always wondered, why would you hide an important treasure on an island that could possibly get washed away by a hurricane? If not washed away, the storms would damage the island, destroying any landmarks."

Maggie said, "Yeah, that makes a lot of sense."

I said, "Ok, let's look at our facts. We have the Sword of Jerusalem, which we know is real. It has a map and lists the treasure items. We found that the Templars were at the Comanche Nation. We're going to check the petroglyphs made by the Ancient Indians in the Petrified Forest area."

Adam spoke up. "Yes, and we know the treasure is in the Grand Canyon, or at least we think it is."

"So what are we looking for in the Petrified Forest?" Maggie asked.

While holding up a picture on his computer tablet screen, Adam said, "This petroglyph of the Ark of the Covenant." The picture showed, what appeared to be, a representation of the Ark pecked out on a stone. The lines and detail of the pecking was remarkable.

I asked, "Where is that located?"

Adam replied, "I found this picture on the Army Command web. It's located in the Petrified Forest at the Puerco Pueblo ruins, which is off the main road, just south of Interstate 40. Some people believe this is the Ark, and others don't. If you look at it and then at a modern hand drawn illustration of the Ark, it seems to me, this is pretty close in appearance."

"Man, if we find that petroglyph, that proves the Ark was here and the Indians saw it."

Adam continued, "Look, it has two 'V' shaped winged figures on the top of the lid, which would represent the cherubim, or winged angles. There is a border on the top similar to what we see on modern Ark illustrations. And, oddly enough the length appears to be two times the height, which is the same ratio as the Ark."

I interjected, "You're right. Look at the other petroglyphs. They're completely different. So who would spend the time to peck out something in the shape of a box with wings on top of it? Why would someone do that unless they saw the Ark, and it made an impression on them?"

Maggie commented, "What if they did see an Ark?

Adam, you even said there might be two or even three Arks. Maybe this wasn't the real one."

That statement made us start thinking. It was a good point. We have some fairly good evidence that the Ark was in control of the Templars at one time, based on the Sword of Jerusalem. We have evidence that it is located in the Grand Canyon. The problem is, we don't know if it is the original Ark of the Covenant, which contains the Ten Commandments.

Adam replied, "There's only one way to find out and that's to locate the Ark and open it. Now listen, to my theory about the treasure and the Ark.

"When Hophra sent troops to help Jerusalem, they didn't go there to battle the Babylonians. They went there to save the treasure and Ark. They removed it from the city, taking it to Egypt for safe keeping."

"Yeah, that's possible. But why let them take it?" I asked.

"They were allies and trusted each other. For some reason the Babylonians didn't threaten to attack Egypt."

Maggie asked, "If the Egyptians took the Ark for safe keeping, where did they hide it?"

Adam said, "I think they hid it in the Sphinx."

"The Sphinx! Why there?" I asked.

"Why not? It's one place that no one would ever look. The Sphinx is carved out of the bed stone. It's a one piece statue and everyone in those days believed that. However, modern Investigations by Florida State University and Boston University have located various anomalies underground, around the monument.

"In 1995 workers digging a new parking lot uncovered tunnels and pathways underground, close to the Sphinx. In 1992, while using a seismograph, a team found evidence of hollow chambers a few meters below the ground, between the paws. The Egyptian Government then stopped all further testing around the Sphinx."

"Who build the Sphinx?" Maggie inquired.

"That's also a mystery," Adam said, while wiping the sweat from his head.

In the desert, this time of the year, temperatures can reach 100 degrees. I guessed it was about 90 degrees now, and it wasn't noon yet. I took a drink from my water bottle and handed it to Adam in the back seat. He in turn gave some to the dogs and then passed the bottle to Maggie.

"Adam, you were telling us about the Sphinx," I commented.

"There was a debate years ago on the age of the monument. An author named, John West, first noticed weathering patterns on the Sphinx that appeared to be caused by water erosion rather than wind and sand. These patterns were not found on other structures on the Giza plateau. West called in Geologist Professor Robert Schoch, who after examining the Sphinx, agreed there was water erosion.

"Although Egypt is desert today, 10,000 years ago it was a swamp or jungle, which received a lot of rain fall. So, Schoch concluded that in order to show effects of water erosion, the Sphinx would have to be about 10,000 years old."

"That means the Sphinx was built before the Great Pyramid," Maggie said.

"Yes, and no one knows when it was built, who built it, or why. There are no records of it being built by the Egyptians."

"How does this tie into the Templars?"I asked.

"Hophra secretly hid the treasure and Ark in a chamber near the Sphinx paws. He died before the Israelites returned to Jerusalem 70 years later. They might have known the Ark was in Egypt but didn't have any idea where it was hidden. They couldn't do anything to find it. They couldn't just walk into Egypt and start searching around the pyramids or the Sphinx. Oh, sure they could have gone to war with Egypt, but they didn't have the manpower or the army to do so.

"So it was lost forever until the Knights Templar discovered a clue in the old Temple ruins that it was in Egypt. They went there to search for it around 1250 AD. At that time, Egypt was in disarray so nobody objected to the Templars digging around looking for the treasure. I suspect that the Coptic Christians in Egypt helped the Templars because at that time they were a powerful group. So the Templars would have enlisted their aid. This is why the Templars were able to smuggle the treasure out of Egypt to Europe, with no one knowing."

"Why didn't they give it to the church?" Maggie inquired.

Adam replied, "I think the Templars believed the treasure belonged to the Israelites. They didn't want to give it to the church. The Templars became rich and powerful, which the Pope and King of France didn't like. They suspected that the Templars became rich because they found the holy treasure. This is why most of the Templars were rounded up and many were killed on Friday the 13th in 1307. After the attack on the Templar's locations in Europe, they decided to move the Ark and treasure to the New World, which was more or less discovered by the Vikings."

"Is that why Friday the 13th is considered an unlucky day?" Maggie asked.

"That's right."

"That's a pretty good theory, Adam. It makes a lot of sense," I told him.

We pulled up to the south gate of the Petrified Forest National Park and our conversation came to an end. The gate was locked and chained shut. A sign read: 'CLOSED UNTIL FURTHER NOTICE. TREPASSERS WILL BE PROSECUTED.'

Adam asked, "What are we gonna do now?"

Everyone had dismounted and was standing there reading the stupid sign.

Baldwin asked, "Jack, what now?"

I pulled out the map, showing it to Baldwin. I said, "I don't think anyone is here. I don't see any guards, so let's proceed. We're going to the Puerco Pueblo ruins, about 10 miles away."

"This is federal land, or used to be. Maybe no one is here now but someone is watching us," as Baldwin pointed to a camera high on top a metal pole, about 50 feet away.

I looked up at the camera. "So what. Even if they're

watching us what can Park Police do about it? Let's roll out. Once we get to the ruins we'll set up camp and take a break."

Proceeding around the locked gates, we arrived at the Puerco ruins without any incidents. We were surprised there was a visitor center, so we broke in. The center was dusty and we proceeded to clean it up so we could spend the night. It seemed no one had been here in a few years.

The water wasn't working until one of Baldwin's men found a generator and a pump that was connected to an underground well. He managed to get the generator started, and to everyone's delight, it also ran the air conditioning system. Maggie was especially happy that we had water for the washrooms, which contained two shower stalls.

Baldwin's men tested the water and determined it was very safe to drink. I took a sip and was elated that the water was actually cool, but it did have a well water taste.

*Adam and I browsed around the center, looking at the information displays about the ruins and people that lived here a long time ago. Reading the information, it was clear that the Petrified Forest area had a long human history dating back to 13,000 years ago. Historians claim that people came to the area in nomadic groups after the Ice Age. The Petrified Forest in located on the southern side of the Painted Desert. It's a beautiful dry colorful landscape that one would not want to cross on foot, or even by horse.*

*During this time, the local area was very fertile and had plenty of rainfall. The literature showed there was a river which was a reliable source of water. This enabled the people to farm maze, beans, and other crops close to the river. The river was also used for travel, creating a trade route with other tribes.*

*Then, a series of droughts came in the 1300s. The natives of Puerco Pueblo started to leave the area in search of better land to grow their crops. The area was just about abandoned by 1400 due to climate change.*

Adam said, "If people lived here until 1400 that means they had to see the Templars who passed by here around 1350."

I commented, "Yes, the dates match up pretty close. The petroglyph showing the Ark proves the native Indians saw it."

Maggie replied, "Yeah, everything comes together alright."

It was getting late so we set up camp and Captain Baldwin posted sentries for the night. We took turns taking a shower and using the washrooms. The air conditioning felt great. It was a sure bet that everyone would sleep inside tonight.

Peering at a large map of the park hanging on the wall, we discussed how we would proceed with our search tomorrow. Adam, White Feather, Billy, and Black Horse would be one team. Maggie, Baldwin, Pete, and I would be another team. We would fan out and check every rock and stone that we could. The remaining

Warriors would provide security for the expedition. We didn't want anyone sneaking up on us while we were busy concentrating on petroglyphs.

After making our plans, I went outside for a smoke and a shot of JD. It was a half moon and the night sky was crystal clear. I sat down on a huge petrified log and pondered the information we had found over the last month. I was pleased that the clues we found supported what the Sword of Jerusalem had written on it. We had to be on the right track.

Maggie came outside. "It's a beautiful night. Look at all those stars."

"Yeah," I replied. "Here, have a drink," and I handed her the bottle of JD.

After taking a big swig she said, "I'm glad I came with you on this expedition." She wrapped her arm around mine as we sat there glaring at the night sky.

"Once we find the petroglyphs we'll move on to the Grand Canyon."

She squeezed my arm. "I can't wait to see the Grand Canyon."

"It's incredible, just simply incredible."

We continued to watch shooting stars, like the ancients did, late into the night.

# MISSING
## MAY 25, 2026

The morning came around fast. Everyone was up before sunrise and ready to go before it was even daylight. Each group had a radio and all of us carried a supply of water in our Camel Backs.

The teams gathered at the large map hung on the wall. We divided the area in half, running a line east to west. Adam and his group would hunt for petroglyphs or artifacts north of this line. My group would cover the southern part of this area, which was about three miles square. The plan was to take a picture of the Ark petroglyph to verify it was real, along with any other interesting items. To do this we would have to walk around and visually check each stone, tree, or rock. We would meet back at the visitor center at 2 pm to review our findings.

It was a sunny day and the temperature was just right at 75 degrees, but by 2 pm it would be over 90 degrees. In the bright sunny desert it gets hot. The air is dry and it saps your energy slowly, draining the body of moisture. You don't sweat because it evaporates so quickly. It's easy to become dehydrated and then sunstroke could set in.

For security, Baldwin's warriors were positioned two miles north and south of the visitor center, guarding the main road. Three men would remain at the center protecting our supplies and weapons.

We headed out and my group spread out, four in a line. We would sweep the area proceeding up and down the zone. Adam's group would follow the same procedure. This country is rugged stone and sage brush covered ground. I cautioned everyone to be on the lookout for rattlesnakes.

After searching for an hour, the radio hissed. Adam said, "We found the Ark petroglyph."

I replied, "That was fast. Where is it at?"

"I was just following the trail to the pueblo ruins and there it was. There's even a sign showing the location."

"Ok, that's great. Keep on looking."

"Roger that."

My crew hadn't seen one thing of interest after walking for two hours. I stopped to light a smoke and take a drink. I heard Baldwin yell, "Jack, over here! I found something!"

After putting out my smoke, I wandered over to Baldwin. "What you got, George?"

"Look, another box or Ark."

I bent down on one knee to get a better look. It was a box alright, shaped very similar to the picture of the Ark Adam showed me. This one, however, was very crude in appearance and seemed unfinished. There were no wings on top or any raised decoration on the lid.

Sticking out like a sore thumb next to it, was a cross. I couldn't believe what I was seeing. There was no doubt it was a cross, very similar to the Templars Cross. I concluded that these petroglyphs were crude because the artist wasn't that good. I snapped a picture to show Adam.

We continued on and soon found a pecked drawing of two men. Well, they didn't exactly look like men with necks as long as their bodies and tiny heads. They had long spindly arms and legs. One of the figures was waving with one hand held in the air. These were very weird looking people, if they were people. I wondered why would someone draw a man that didn't really look like a man? It looked more like an alien from another planet. *Maybe it was an alien.*

Proceeding on, turning back toward the visitor center, Pete spotted another weird looking drawing. This one had two man shaped figures with horns on their heads. They wore what seemed to be some kind of suit. Were these glyphs of the Templars or more aliens?

We saw other glyphs of sheep, snakes, and other animals. These were of no interest to me because they looked like a kid made most of them. We continued back to the center to rest and get out of the blazing sun. I noted that the one thing we didn't bring was suntan lotion.

My group arrived back at camp about the same time as Billy and Black Horse. Adam and White Feather were not with them so I asked Black Horse, "Where's Adam?"

He replied, "Adam went with White Feather to view some more stones further down the trail. They should be coming soon."

We sat down and had some cool water and I showed everyone the pictures I took. I commented, "It's too bad but we didn't find any Hooked Xs."

Billy said, "Adam found a Hooked X near the Ark drawing."

"That's great. It's getting late. Where the hell are they?" Checking my watch it was already 6 pm. Everyone else had returned and some were heating up MREs for dinner.

I noticed that Black Horse had a radio with him. "Does Adam have a radio with him?"

"No, this was his radio. I just carried it for him," Black Horse replied.

"Does he have a gun?"

Billy said, "No, but White Feather does. So don't worry."

"Shit! He doesn't have a gun or radio." I grabbed my binoculars, went outside, and climbed up on the roof to see if I could spot them.

After scanning the area for several minutes, I spotted a bright flash, like a mirror flashing far off in the distance. I saw the flash several times, then it disappeared. I kept looking in that direction for about ten minutes. I thought, *maybe we should go and search for Adam before sun goes down.*

I made my mind up to start searching. Approaching Black Horse I asked, "Can you take me to where you last saw Adam?"

"Yes, of course. But do not worry, he's safe with White Feather."

"I don't think so. Let's go now because it'll be dark in a few hours. Anyone else wanna come along?" Baldwin and Maggie stood up and grabbed their M4's along with some water.

Maggie said, "Let's go find them."

Putting Adolf and Freda on a leash I picked up one of Adam's shirts and let them smell it. I gave the order, "Search. Find Adam."

The dogs led the way pulling me along. They had Adam's scent and everyone followed us single file, Indian style over the rough terrain, weaving around cactus and bushes as the sun beat down.

Now you're wondering why we didn't take a truck. Simple, the terrain was too rough and driving across it we could have broken an axle or damaged something. We'd have to drive so slow that walking would be faster. Besides, with the truck we couldn't use the dogs.

An hour had gone by and Black Horse said, "Wait, here is where I saw them last." He pointed northwest. "They headed that direction. Here are their tracks." Black Horse started to follow footprints in the soft desert dirt.

Every now and then the tracks would disappear when we came to some rocks or a hard surface. The dogs would sniff around and pick up the tracks again. The sun was fading fast; in an hour it would be dark.

The dogs stopped when we came to a dirt road. They had lost the scent. I asked, "Where's this road go to?"

Black Horse looked in both directions down the road. "I don't know, but it seems to run north and south."

We walked around, looking at the tracks. There were a lot of footprints and a set of tire tracks in the sandy road. "Black Horse, what do you make of these tracks?" Baldwin asked.

"There was a truck here and four other men. It seems that Adam and White Feather got into the truck. It looks like they headed north. Maybe they are friends of White Feather."

I replied, "Maybe they're not friends. We gotta go back to camp, look at the map, and find out where this road goes to. We'll rest tonight and pick up the trail in the daylight."

We made it back to camp after 10 pm. Baldwin and I immediately went to the map hanging on the wall to find the dirt road or trail. We noticed that the dirt road was located about a quarter of a mile off the main park road. The two intersected about eight miles north of our location. If they were driving on the main park road, which was paved, we would not be able to track them.

Now I was really getting worried. Why would White Feather take Adam and leave with some strangers? Maybe they were not strangers. Maybe White Feather wanted Adam to tell him the secrets of the Sword to find the treasure.

Maggie tried to console me. "Don't worry, Jack. We'll find him tomorrow. Try to get some sleep." She patted me on the back and walked away, leaving me alone to think.

I started to clean my M4, getting ready to do battle. Popping the rear takedown pin out and removing the bolt carrier, I paid special attention, cleaning every surface. Satisfied my M4 was spotless, I pulled out my Black Bear knife. Slowly I ran the edge of the blade back and forth over the honing stone. After an hour, I tested the sharpness by shaving the hair off my arm. It was razor sharp, ready to draw blood.

I couldn't sleep because I was already plotting what I was gonna do to the men who kidnapped my Grandson. When I find these dirtbags they will suffer. If they hurt Adam, then they will die.

*Signing off for now,*

*GOD BLESS AMERICA, LAND OF THE FREE, and HOME OF THE BRAVE!*

*Jack Gunn, a.k.a. Tocabaga Jack*

*If you have any idea where the treasure is located, or who took Adam,* Email me at:

THOMASHWARDBOOKS@GMAIL.COM.

I WILL REPLY.

# DRAMATIS PERSONAE
# THE ANCIENTS

**Adam de Molay** – A future Knights Templar leader. Sent to Jack Gunn, by God.

**Black Horse** – Medicine man for the Comanche Nation and father of Billy Bob.

**Big Bear** – An old Indian who runs the Comanche Nation Motel.

**Billy Bob** – Lost son of Black Horse who lived in Indianola Mississippi.

**Canfield** – A Templar of the old order, who wanted to steal the Sword of Jerusalem.

**Captain George Baldwin** – A Knights Templar commander, of the new order.

**Captain Sessions** – Combat officer, commands and controls combat operations in the field.

**Carlos** – A little jerk that worked by Jimmy Rosebud.

**Christian de Molay** – Adam de Molay's uncle. A self proclaimed Grand Master.

**Emma de Molay** – The sister of Adam found on Interstate 75.

**Jeff** – Third in command of the new Templar Warriors.

**Grandpa Jack** – Jack de Moley the Knights Templar Grand Master.

**Hemmi** – Wife of Jack Gunn.

**James Walker** – Captain of the Texas Rangers and

nephew of Black Horse.

**Jessie Rosebud** – County Sheriff, brother of Jimmy and all around bad guy.

**Jim Bo** – Husband to Amy and son-in-law of Jack.

**Jimmy Rosebud** – Mayor of Montainair, brother of Jessie, and scumbag.

**Maggie** – Amazon Warrior from Tocabaga .

**Maria** – Hooker who was owned by Jessie Rosebud.

**Mike** – Friend of Jack Gunn and Tocabaga security agent.

**Pete** – Second in command of the new Templar order.

**Quanah Iron Coat** – Chief of the Comanche Nation.

**Ragsdale** – A bad guy in Indianola, who runs a whore house. He claimed to be Billy Bob's father.

**Ron** – Brother of Jack Gunn a Retired Navy vet. Part of Tocabaga security.

**Rick** – President of Tocabaga Association, security team member.

**Sally** – Girl friend of Walker, who owns a diner.

**Tommy Gunn** – Son of Jack Gunn and a retired Marine Scout Sniper.

**White Feather** – Half Hopi Indian.

# REFERENCES

https://en.wikipedia.org/wiki/Pharaoh%27s_daughter_(wife_of_Solomon)

https://en.wikipedia.org/wiki/Menelik_I

http://www.ancientlosttreasures.com/forum/viewtopic.php?f=26&t=698

http://www.crystalinks.com/gc_egyptconnection.html

http://www.bibliotecapleyades.net/esp_orionzone_9.htm

http://www.philipcoppens.com/egyptiancanyon.html

https://sites.google.com/site/ancientegyptiansinamerica/ancient-egyptians-grand-canyon

http://www.pahanalives.com/hopi.html

http://beforeitsnews.com/alternative/2013/11/vikings-freemasons-hooked-x-the-knights-templar-2814840.html

http://www.crystalinks.com/ark.html

https://en.wikipedia.org/wiki/Kebra_Nagast

http://www.keelynet.com/unclass/canyon.txt

http://www.nps.gov/pefo/learn/historyculture/puerco-pueblo.htm

THOMAS H. WARD

# TEMPLARS QUEST
# LUCEM SANCTAM

## BOOK THREE
TEMPLARS QUEST CHRONICLES

# PROLOGUE

J ack Gunn is fighting alongside the modern Templar Warriors to find the lost treasure. During a time of turmoil, chaos, and mayhem they battle their way across the United States, following the clues on a holy relic named 'The Sword of Jerusalem.' Did the ancient Knights Templar find the lost treasure and bring it to the New World in 1350 AD? Read "The Templars Quest" and discover what really happened to the treasure and the Ark of the Covenant. It is the greatest mystery of all times.

The Sword of Jerusalem and the hand of God, along with a Native American Indian, have led Jack Gunn and his blessed step grandson, Keeper of the sword, to a secret cave.

*As we walked into the cavern, I had a plan. I said, "Adam, when we're in front of the glowing pedestal, draw the sword and point it in the air."*

*"What do you think will happen?"*

*"I don't know for sure. Maybe the Ark and treasure will be revealed to us, or maybe not. We might even meet*

*God or he could speak to us. The worst that could happen is God kills us, like the others."*

*"Why would he kill us? We believe in him."*

*"Like I said before, God works in mysterious ways."*

*We were almost at the large pedestal. It was still glowing with the dim yellow light, as were the walls. Stopping in front of the four foot high plainly craved large block of stone, I took hold of Adam's left hand, squeezing it slightly.*

*I asked him, "Are you ready?"*

*"Yes Sir, I am ready." He slowly started to draw the sword out.*

It is a known fact that King Solomon's treasure and the Ark disappeared when Nebuchadnezzar II invaded Jerusalem in 586 BC. There are no records of any great treasure or of the Ark being taken by the Babylonians. If they took it they would have made it well known. It would have been written in the history books for all to see. So how did the treasure and the Ark disappear into thin air?

In 1909, the Phoenix Gazette published a story about a man named Kincaid who found a cave in the Grand Canyon. In the story, Kincaid claims that he found mummies, statues, and gold artifacts that were Oriental or Egyptian in appearance. Kincaid advised he worked for the Smithsonian and sent some of the artifacts to them. He also claims that the Smithsonian mounted an expedition to the Grand Canyon to conduct further research.

Kincaid disappeared and no one has ever found the cave. The Smithsonian claims he didn't work for them and they have no knowledge about any cave in the Grand Canyon containing artifacts.

# PERSONA OF JACK GUNN

I am the eldest of three Brothers. We grew up fighting bullies and gang members in a tough neighborhood in South Chicago. My Dad, one of the most honest men I have known, always stressed, "Tell the truth, and help each other. Never ever be a bully, never steal, and try to protect those who cannot protect themselves." I have always stood up for the people who could not defend themselves. I hate liars and bullies.

Standing six feet tall at 180 pounds, I am in great shape for my age, and my body is honed by years of physical training. I shave my head two times a week as it is cooler with no hair in the hot south. I sport a gray mustache and goatee that I keep well-trimmed and short. There is a two-inch scar on my forehead from a knife fight years ago.

I spent four years in the Army as a Military Policeman and became an expert in the use of handguns, rifles, shotguns, and in hand-to-hand combat. My legs have skin grafts from burns due to an explosion when I worked for the DOD (Department of Defense) doing security details for seven years.

I love our country, freedom, my family, and friends. If anyone messes with my family or friends, justice will be swift and painful. I have no use for anyone who breaks the law, cheats, or steals. For the most part, I follow the Ten Commandments, but also believe in The Code of Hammurabi, which is an Eye for an Eye. If you take an eye, I'll take your whole head. I fight to keep our Bill of Rights under the United States Constitution.

I've been shot two times, burned from explosions, and stabbed multiple times by the forces of evil. It's a wonder that I am still alive. But I keep on fighting because there is no other choice. It's fight or die in this screwed up world.

I have killed a lot of men in my lifetime. Killing always came easy for me. Some I killed in cold blood, but I never killed anyone who didn't deserve it, so I feel no remorse or guilt.

That is me, Jack Gunn, and these are my chronicles.

# INTRODUCTION

Yesterday Adam went missing along with White Feather in the Petrified Forest while searching for petroglyphs that could prove the Knights Templar had been to this God-forbidden part of the country seven-hundred years ago.

We tracked them to a dirt road using our dogs, but lost the trail. It appeared that they were abducted by four men in a vehicle. Judging by the tire tracks it was some type off-road truck or jeep.

Since we were on foot and darkness had set in, we returned back to the bivouac area, which was the visitor center building located at Puerco Pueblo Ruins. We needed to review the park map to determine where the dirt road led to. We would pick up the trail in the morning and continue our search.

I was really concerned for Adam's safety. Why would White Feather take Adam and leave with some strangers? Maybe they were not strangers. Maybe White Feather wanted Adam to tell him the secrets of the sword to find the treasure.

As everyone was getting ready to bed-down for the night, Maggie tried to console me. "Don't worry, Jack. We'll find him tomorrow. Try to get some sleep." She patted me on the back and walked away, leaving me alone to think.

I started to clean my M4, getting ready to do battle. Popping the rear takedown pin out and removing the bolt carrier, I paid special attention, cleaning every surface. Satisfied my M4 was ultraclean, I pulled out my Black Bear knife. Slowly I ran the edge of the blade back and forth over the honing stone. After an hour, I tested the sharpness by shaving the hair off my arm. It was razor sharp, ready to draw blood.

I couldn't sleep because I was already plotting what to do to the men who kidnapped my Grandson. *When I find these dirtbags they will suffer. If they hurt Adam in any manner, then they will die. Maybe I'll kill them just for taking Adam. Yeah, that's what I'll do.*

# THE SEARCH
## MAY 26, 2026

Finally, I dozed off and managed to grab a few hours of sleep. Waking up before sunrise, I went out for a smoke. Captain Baldwin, commander of the Templar Warriors, was already outside with a few of his men getting the trucks and weapons ready for our search mission.

Captain George Baldwin and I had grown to become really close friends. No, not close friends, best friends. He is a trustworthy man who believes in God and isn't afraid of anything. He's the type of man who would give his life to protect his troops and friends. George is not afraid of dying. He once told me, 'If you think about dying, that's bad juju. When your time is up, you can't do anything about it.'

Since George is our battle field commander, I defer most combat situations to him because of his experience. I said, "Morning George. What's the plan to rescue Adam?"

George turned around, stopping what he was doing. He put his hand on my shoulder and asked, "Did you get any sleep?"

"Yeah, a couple of hours."

"Good let's get some chow, and then we'll go over the plan. I already have Pete and Jeff doing recon, while it's still dark. Hopefully they'll find some clues."

We walked back into the visitor center. George yelled, "Everyone up! It's time to rock and roll!" His men, along with Maggie, crawled out of their sleeping bags. Freda and Adolf, our Shepherd guard dogs, jumped up to attention.

We heated up some coffee and five MREs, giving one to Maggie and one to each dog. They ate what we did simply because there was no dog chow. Besides, the MREs are good healthy food. After eating, Maggie took the dogs outside for their morning walk.

*Freda and Adolf were trained by Klaus Tummel in Florida. He was a famous guard dog trainer. Klaus was killed by a Free Roamer in Gulf Port, Florida. We went to his home to purchase trained guards dogs for use on Tocabaga Island. While there, we found his dogs running loose purely by accident. After we buried Klaus the dogs came with us to Tocabaga. They are well trained smart canines who took a liking to us right away. They follow every order, and I think they can sense who is evil and who is not. I swear they can understand every word you say.*

I was sipping some coffee while looking at the satellite map. George commented, "This park is pretty big. There are a lot of dirt roads that run out into the middle of desert. Who knows where they go? We're gonna split up to expedite the search."

Nodding, I looked at George. "Yeah, I agree with that idea."

As George pointed at the map, he replied, "The tactical Hummers will take the lead. I want one Hummer to run all the way to the park HQ, located here," as his finger followed the road to the park's headquarters. "In the meantime, two will follow behind and search the Painted Desert Lodge."

"There's a lodge here?"

"Yeah, we don't know how big it is or if anyone lives there, but we'll find out."

I observed the map and noted that six dirt roads spun off of the Petrified Park Highway. Each one would have to be checked for tracks.

Baldwin continued, "The rest of the convoy will check out the six dirt roads. Any comments?"

"Are you taking the lead truck to the park headquarters?"

"Yeah. You know I always lead the way."

"I wanna ride with you."

"Ok. You'll be with me. We need one more man."

"I suggest Maggie and the dogs ride with us."

"Alright, that sounds good. I'll give the assignments to my men. Be ready to roll out in one hour."

As I was packing up my gear, Maggie walked in with the dogs. I informed her of the plan and told her to get ready to move out.

While we were waiting the radio hissed. It was a message from Pete who was doing recon. "Based on the tracks coming off the dirt, it appears they headed north on the main road." Baldwin acknowledged the message and told him to stay there until we arrived.

As the sun was breaking the horizon, our Hummer took the lead. We reached a blazing speed of 45 mph. That's the top speed of the combat Humvee due to the weight of the armor. The other units followed behind us. Baldwin's idea was to move in fast on the park HQ and the lodge. If anyone was there, he wanted to surprise them. Catch them off guard so to speak. I was driving; George sat in the machine gun turret with Maggie as back-up and ammo feeder.

The paved road went over the Burlington Northern railroad tracks and then over Interstate 40. From I-40 it was only a few miles to the park HQ. As we passed over I-40, we didn't spot any other vehicles moving on the Interstate. Because the park was closed to the public, there was no traffic inside the park.

*The main park road runs directly north from Route 180 passing over the railroad and I-40. Then it continues north for five miles until it loops back south to the main entrance, where the main Visitor Center and Headquarters are located. The road is shaped like a reversed question mark when observing it on a map. It's about 25 miles long.*

Rounding some sharp curves the road wound around the foot of some high cliffs, before turning south again. The scenery of the Painted Desert was awesome.

*The Painted Desert is a spectacular colorful sight, for a desert. It is a bleak but colorful landscape due to the iron and manganese compounds in the dirt, which causes the soil to have various colors such as pink, blue, and white. It looks like someone painted it, hence the name. It is also known as the Badlands of Arizona.*

We passed by the Desert Inn on the left side of the road. Looking in my mirror, I observed Pete's Humvee and another one pull into the parking lot. A few minutes, later we pulled up to the Park Headquarters.

I was surprised, as was Baldwin, at how large the HQ complex was. "Damn, this place is huge."

Baldwin replied, "Yeah. I think we need some help to search this place." He got on the radio and asked for another Hummer to come help us out when they were done searching the Inn.

Maggie said, "The government sure knows how to waste money. This place must house thirty people."

I said, "All this to take care of a desert and some petrified trees. What a waste of money. No wonder the country went bankrupt."

"These guys were living high on the hog for sure, until the government ran out of money," Baldwin commented. "We never had it this good in the military."

We sat in the Humvee waiting for reinforcements to come. From this position on the road I counted: five condominium one story type buildings, two main buildings, which were the visitor center, and one garage with gas pumps.

I asked, "George, where do you want to start searching at?"

"I'm not sure. Pull around back, let's see what's there."

Pulling around back behind the main buildings, on the service drive, we counted three big double-wide trailers which appeared to be living quarters, four actual adobe type houses, and three garages which contained fire trucks.

George commented, "It may take a while before Pete comes to help us, so here's what we'll do. Jack and I will clear each building along with the dogs, starting with these trailers. We'll sweep all the buildings heading west until we get to the visitor center. Maggie, you take the truck and park on the main road. Man the M2, and keep your eyes peeled for anyone. Shoot first, ask questions later."

Maggie nodded ok, and pulled away after we dismounted with the dogs and our weapons.

Baldwin's plan was a good one. We would open the door on each building or trailer and let the dogs search for people inside. No one could escape or hide from Adolf and Freda. After the dogs did the initial clearing we could go in and take a look-see.

We proceeded with Captain Baldwin's plan. Most of the building doors were unlocked, but a few we had to bust in. After a fruitless search of all the buildings and trailers, we arrived at the main building which contained the HQ and Visitors Center.

The doors were locked so we popped open a window to gain entrance. That set off an alarm bell that was louder than hell. Baldwin quickly found the alarm control box and cut the wires, disabling it. I let the dogs search the building, and after checking all the rooms, we determined no one was inside. I radioed Maggie it was all clear, advising her come in.

The radio buzzed, it was Pete. "We didn't find anyone at the lodge. We're on our way over to you now."

I replied, "Take your time, this place is empty."

Baldwin shouted, "Jack, come here and look at this!"

"Where you at?"

"In the main office."

After roaming around the 30,000 square foot building for a while, Maggie and I found the main office far in the back of the building. Walking in the door, Baldwin was sitting at a control panel with computer monitors mounted on the wall.

Maggie asked, "What are those for?"

"These are security monitors. My guess is there must be eight cameras mounted out in the park since there are eight screens here," Baldwin replied.

"Can we turn them on?" I asked.

"Yeah, we got electric power. I'm gonna check the disk from yesterday for each camera. Maybe we can spot Adam and the guys who took him."

I lit up a smoke and watched George work on it. One by one the monitors came on. It was showing us real-time displays of what was going on in the park. While pointing at a monitor, Baldwin said, "Look, our convoy is coming this way."

"Can you run yesterday's recording?"

"I'm trying to figure it out now."

Just then, Pete came in the door. "What you guys got here?" he asked.

Baldwin moved out of the way. "Pete, you're good at this computer crap. Figure out how to run the camera recording from yesterday."

Pete sat down and in about five minutes figured it out. "There's eight cameras and each one has its own memory. That means there are eight screens to watch."

We were watching the monitors, trying to get a view of Adam or the men that took him and White Feather. Pete put the re-play on fast forward to speed up the process, so we wouldn't be there all day. The picture was in black and white.

Pete said, "Look, monitor five shows a truck moving near the Puerco Pueblo Ruins on a dirt road. My guess is it will show up on monitor four next. I think monitor one is located here, at the HQ."

Sure enough monitor four showed the truck on the main road. The problem was we couldn't make out who was in the vehicle. I could see that it was a dark-colored truck that appeared to be shaped like an old Ford, but it was hard to tell.

Monitor three showed the truck pull up to the Desert Inn. Everyone got out and I saw Adam with White Feather, along with four armed men. White Feather wasn't carrying his rifle. The men pushed them to the entrance of the lodge. The picture was dark because it was taken at night, so I couldn't clearly make out their faces. I could however, make out that the weapons which appeared to be M16 rifles and AK47s. I also observed three other trucks parked in the hotel lot. The video didn't have any sound.

I said, "Well, at least they're alive."

Baldwin said, "Yesterday they were alive."

We continued to watch the video as it turned to daylight, which would be this morning. We saw everyone get in the trucks and leave. Adam was with them but White Feather wasn't. We counted a total of ten men, two in each truck and four in the truck with Adam. They headed toward the park HQ.

Monitors one and two picked them up very clearly, but since they didn't stop and get out of the trucks, their faces were not defined. I did see the driver of the truck Adam was in. He had an eye patch over his left eye and a bandana on his head, but that was all I could make out. Watching the monitor, we noted they left the park, and headed west on Interstate 40. The time was 7 am.

I checked my watch, it was 9:50 am. That meant they had a two hour and fifty-minute lead on us. Maggie said, "At least we know which way they went. Let's go get them."

Captain Baldwin replied, "Yeah, but we don't know where they're going. Besides that, they have a big lead on us." George had a worried look on his face as he put his hand on my shoulder.

The radio squawked. "This is Black Horse. We found White Feather walking down the road. He looks beat up and needs help. I think he's in shock."

I replied, "Bring him here, to the headquarters, right away! I need to ask him a few questions."

"We're on the way."

"He better have a good story why Adam isn't with him," Baldwin commented.

"Yeah, or he's dead," I said.

While we sat waiting for White Feather, I pondered how to handle the situation.

Fifteen minutes later, the truck pulled up and two of our men helped White Feather into the building, sitting him down on a bench. I carefully observed him, but didn't utter a word. He had a black eye and some cuts on his face. His clothes were torn in different places and were extremely dirty.

White Feather asked, "Can I have some water?"

The room was quiet as I walked over to him. Maggie and Baldwin watched me, wondering what I was going to do to him. I handed him a bottle, which he quickly gulped down.

When he finished, I asked, "What happened?" I was really trying to contain myself. I didn't want to show my anger and hate for him. He was free and Adam was still captive.

White Feather said, "Yesterday Adam and I were looking for glyphs. As we came to a dirt road there was a truck with four men. They greeted us and seemed friendly enough. They asked what we were doing here since the park was closed. We told them and they offered us a ride back to our camp."

"What did you tell them?"

"Adam told them we were searching for glyphs that proved the Knights Templars came to this area. He showed them the glyph picture of the Ark."

"What did they say?"

"Not much at the time. Then I mentioned the treasure and they really became interested, wanting to know more."

Baldwin said, "So, you told them about the treasure in the Grand Canyon. That was pretty stupid."

"I didn't think it would hurt anything. Anyway, that is when they pointed their guns at me and took us prisoners."

"Ok, then what did they do?" I asked.

"They blindfolded us and tied our hands. We were taken to some building, and they asked me many questions. If I didn't answer they'd beat me and threaten to kill me."

"What did they do to Adam?"

"Adam was locked up in a room. Then they locked me up and started talking to Adam. They asked him many questions about the treasure. They wanted to know exactly where it was located."

"Did they hurt him?"

White Feather said, "I do not know for sure, because I managed to untie my hands and escape out a window. I hid until I saw them leave and then started walking back to your camp."

"Did they search for you?" Baldwin asked.

"Yes, they searched all night for me. But I know how to hide very well."

Maggie asked, "Who are these guys?"

White Feather looked at her and replied, "I do not know exactly. But this is called the Badlands by the local people. In the Badlands there are groups we call Nomad Bandits. That's who they are."

"Bandits?"

"Yes, bandits, who rob and kill people. They are nomads and don't live in any one place to long."

"White Feather, do you know any of these men?" I asked.

"No, of course not."

"Are they Indians, or Hopi?"

"The men who captured us were not Indians. But I only saw a few of them because of the blindfold. The Hopi would never do such things."

"One final question. Do you know where they're going?"

"Maybe the Grand Canyon. I don't know for sure."

I said, "I don't think so. They can't find the treasure until the summer solstice, which is June 21$^{st}$. That's 25 days away."

Baldwin spoke up, "They only had ten men here, so maybe they're going to their camp before going to the canyon."

"Yeah, I think you're right, George. The question is, where's their camp at?"

"Let's look at the map," Maggie said.

While we were looking at the map, I noticed that Black Horse was talking to White Feather. I kept an eye on them, because I didn't trust White Feather.

The radio came on. "We got company. Two Sheriff trucks just pulled up."

Baldwin, Maggie, and I went outside to meet them. They were staring at our armored Humvees. Four Deputies peered at us and one said, "Are you men with the Army or Special Forces?" They stopped about thirty feet away, facing us. The Deputies guns were at low ready as they glanced around at our group of warriors, wondering who the hell we were.

The problem was we didn't know if they were real Deputies. They might be fake ones, which was a common trick used by bad guys. Everyone was on edge and ready to take action.

George told a little white lie. "We're Marine Special Forces assigned to the Army."

The same Deputy replied, "Semper Fidelis."

*This has been the Marine motto since 1883. It is always spoken in Latin and means 'Always Faithful.' When a man says Semper Fidelis it usually means he was in the Marines. Once a Marine, always a Marine.*

George repeated the motto back to the man, who had some stripes indicating he was a Sergeant. After shaking hands and introductions, Sergeant Smith asked, "Did you break in here?"

Baldwin lied again. "No, we found it this way. Four pickup trucks were here before us. They must have done it. They headed west on I-40. Did you come from that direction?"

"Yes, but we didn't see any pickup trucks. We only spotted a few cars and some business trucks. The guys that broke in here must have been the bandits we've been chasing."

"How many bandits are around here?"

"We don't really know."

I said, "We counted ten men."

Smith replied, "Yeah, they run around in small groups."

"How often do you get out this way?"

"We try to make it here once a week. By the way, where are you heading to, Captain?" Sergeant Smith asked.

Pointing at me, Baldwin said, "Jack, you tell him."

"Yeah sure … we're going to Flagstaff area looking for missing Army families."

Deputy Smith nodded his head. "How many people are you looking for?"

"I think twelve, but there might more. We don't know for sure."

"Sergeant, how safe is Arizona?" Baldwin asked.

"What do you mean safe?"

"Are the cities safe so can people go about their daily business without being killed by gangs or bandits?"

"Mostly, but you still need to carry a weapon for protection. You never know what's going to happen. Most towns have a Police Force and the state has the Highway Patrol and National Guard on duty."

"So, you still have problems, but not as bad as New Mexico."

"Yeah, that's right. New Mexico has problems because they didn't have any National Guard troops and very few active Police Officers. The Governor didn't think they needed them. Here in Arizona we still have a lot of trouble down near the Mexican border."

I asked, "What about Flagstaff area?"

"It's pretty safe, if you stay on the main highways," Smith advised. "With your firepower I doubt anyone will screw around with you."

Deputy Smith's radio came on and interrupted the conversation. After talking for a few minutes he advised, "Gentlemen, we have an emergency call and have to go. Do me a favor and lock this place up before you leave."

"Ok, will do. Stay safe out there," Baldwin told them.

Smith yelled back, while getting into his truck, "You too, Captain," as he waved goodbye and sped away. We stood there a minute watching them leave.

"Jack, why didn't you tell them that Adam was kidnapped?" Maggie asked.

"Because I don't want the police involved in this. It's family business and we'll take care of it."

"Let's look at the map again," Baldwin said. "We have to figure out where these guys went."

I said, "My guess is, if the Sheriff didn't see the four trucks, then they turned off I-40 somewhere and are taking back roads."

I moseyed over to White Feather who was talking to Black Horse on the couch. They glanced up at me and I asked, "White Feather, do you know this part of the country?"

"Yes, I do. What would you like to know?"

"If you were these guys, where would you hide at?"

White Feather scratched his head as if thinking. "This is Navajo country. They might know where these men are."

"Who can we talk to about this?" Baldwin asked him.

"I know several people we can speak to. They live in Indian Wells and Dilkon City, on the Navajo Reservation."

"Where exactly are these towns?" I asked. White Feather was pissing me off. Getting information out of him was like pulling teeth. You had to pry it out of him, he didn't volunteer it.

Mr. Feather stood up and advised, "Not far from here," as he slowly walked to the map and pointed at the two towns. "If they went by these towns then someone saw them."

Indian Wells was on Route 77, just north about 50 miles. Dilkon City was just west of Indian Wells, on Navajo Route 15.

Studying the map, it was clear, we needed to proceed west on I-40 for about five miles and exit on Route 77. Then go north for 50 miles to Indian Wells. All of a sudden a bell rang in my brain. This could be the route the bandits took. Maybe some Navajos did see them.

Baldwin peered at me and said, "Are you thinking what I am?"

"Yeah, this could be the route that the kidnappers took."

"Bingo! Baldwin shouted, "Everyone, get ready to move out!"

Glancing at my watch it was already 11 am. Baldwin gave orders for the convoy to keep in a tight formation. We mounted up; as usual Maggie and the dogs were riding with me. It felt weird that Adam wasn't sitting next to me.

As we were about to roll out, Black Horse came up to my window. "Jack, I think you should know that White Feather is acting strange. He told me when we get to Indian Wells he wants to leave and go to the Hopi Nation. It is not far from Indian Wells, just 10 or 20 miles away."

"Ok, thanks for telling me, Black Horse." As he returned to his truck I thought, *White Feather isn't going anywhere until he helps us find Adam.*

Maggie overheard Black Horse. "I can't believe that White Feather wants to leave our group. Are you gonna let him?"

"Of course not," I replied. "He's not going anywhere until we find Adam."

I punched the gas as the convoy took off at a top speed of 45 mph. Damn it, I wish these Hummers were faster.

Once we entered the reservation, Route 77 changed into Navajo Route 6. An hour and a half later, we arrived at the small town of Indian Wells, without incident. It's actually located about half a mile off of Navajo Route 6, on Navajo Route 15.

*Indian Wells is a small town out in the middle of nowhere. It's an unincorporated community located in Navajo County on the Navajo Reservation. The scenery is spectacular. This area is part of the Painted Desert, and it has many high buttes popping up in the colorful landscape. A picture is worth a thousand words. Words can't describe the beauty and peacefulness found here. Driving over 50 miles we hadn't seen a single person.*

To our surprise, nothing was in Indian Wells other than a few homes, a couple of businesses, and a school. The convoy pulled over, and stopped on the side of the road, next to the school. White Feather was riding in the pickup behind mine, along with Black Horse and Billy.

I approached the truck and opened the door. Peering in at White Feather, I asked, "Where should we go?"

"You wanted to speak to someone to see if the trucks passed by here. Then this is the place. The guard at this school is my friend. If they came by here, then he saw them. His name is Jimmy Two Times."

"How'd he get the name Two Times?"

"In the old days he would shoot everything two times to make sure it was dead. It's his nickname. He used to be a Navajo Reservation Police Officer."

White Feather and I walked up to the school's front door. As we approached, a man dressed in a blue uniform, wearing a black cowboy hat, came outside. He carried an AK47, which was pointed at us, and wore a revolver on his hip. I stopped and raised my hands, showing I meant him no harm.

White Feather yelled, "Jimmy Two Times, put that gun down! It's me, White Feather."

He replied, "White Feather, what are you doing here?" Jimmy kept walking towards us until he was within a couple of feet. He still kept his gun pointed at me, which was making me a little uneasy. "Who is this man?"

"He is my friend. The white eyes came here searching for some nomads who kidnapped his grandson."

Jimmy pointed his weapon towards the ground. I reached out my hand. "Hello, my name is Jack Gunn." He shook my hand with a firm grip. Jimmy was an older man whom I guessed to be about 60 years old. His facial characteristics clearly looked different than White Feathers.

"Howdy, Mr. Gunn. I am Jimmy Two Times. Sorry to hear your grandson was taken. There are a lot of bad people out there. That's why I stand guard here at this school. How can I help you?"

"We're looking for four pickup trucks that might have passed by here this morning."

"A lot of pickups pass by here. What time do you think they went by here?"

"I guess around 8 or 9 am."

He pulled a little book out of his pocket and scanned the pages. "My memory is not so good, so I write everything down." He kept flipping the pages in his little book. "Yep, got it right here. Four pickups went by here at eight-thirty today. One was green and three were white."

White Feather said, "Jack, the truck that picked us up was green."

"Which way did they go, Jimmy?" I asked.

He pointed west. "They went that way, on Route 15, like they always do."

"They come by here a lot?"

"Nope, but they pass by every now and then. I hear they purchase supplies over in Dilkon City. Are they the ones that took you grandson?"

"Yeah. Do you know who they are?"

"Hell no, but I think they're nomads."

"Who can we speak to over in Dilkon City?"

"Stop at Dilkon Market and talk to Charlie Wilson. He's the owner, and if anyone knows anything about these men, Charlie does. He's a nosey old coot."

"Thanks for your help, Mr. Two Times. We have to get going."

"I hope you find your grandson and kill the dirty bastards. That's why I stand guard here. You never know who could come around."

Turning to walk away, I noticed that White Feather was still talking to Jimmy. I reached my truck and yelled, "White Feather, we gotta go!"

White Feather ignored my shout and kept talking to Jimmy. I shouted again but he didn't reply. After a minute or so I walked back to both of them. "White Feather, what are you doing? Let's go."

"Jack, I will stay here with Jimmy tonight. Tomorrow I will go to the Hopi Nation to see my wife and children."

"I didn't know you had a wife and kids."

"You did not ask me. I have not seen them for six months."

His story kind of made me feel his pain, but I had my own pain. "White Feather, you were with Adam when he was kidnapped. You escaped leaving him alone with the bandits. So, in my opinion, you're responsible and need to help us."

"I'm sorry, but I cannot be of further help. I wish you good luck and hope Adam is safe."

Now I had a real dilemma. If I make him come along by force it might not be acceptable to his friend, Jimmy. He could try to protect White Feather, which could develop into a gun fight with the man who just helped us. I stood there for a few minutes contemplating what to do.

Neither of them said a word as Black Horse came over to join the conversation. "Hello, I am Black Horse, of the Comanche Tribe." Jimmy shook his hand and introduced himself.

"What's the problem, White Feather?" Black Horse asked.

"I told Jack that I will not go with you. I need to go home to my family."

"That is not a good, White Feather. Jack Gunn needs your help and experience to find his grandson. Remember he found my son, Billy, and brought him to me. So we owe him a big debt."

*This is what really transpired when I first met Billy, the son of Black Horse. About a month ago, we were going through Indianola, Mississippi on our way to the Comanche Nation. We had a run-in with the self-made Mayor, David Ragsdale, who was a crook. Maggie and I suspected that the friendly Ragsdale was up to no good. So, I asked Billy, then known as Billy Bob, the son of Ragsdale, what was going on? He seemed like as person I could trust.*

*Billy told us, "If I tell y'all the truth of what's going on you gotta promise to take me with you. If you don't, Ragsdale will kill me for sure. Y'all promise?"*

*With hesitation I said, "Ok, it's a deal. You can come with us."*

*Billy smiled and shook my hand, crushing it out of joy. "I don't think Ragsdale is my real Daddy. I don't know who my Daddy is, but I don't look like Ragsdale. My mother was a whore who worked for Ragsdale. She was his favorite money-maker until she died, a long time ago."*

*"So, what are you telling us?" Baldwin asked.*

*"Ragsdale owns a bunch of whores and has gambling games. Alice is his Madam who looks after the girls. Ragsdale isn't the real Mayor either. Like I said, he's the Boss Man. This town is under his control." Billy turned his head and scanned his eyes around the park. "You see, only certain people get to carry guns. They work for Ragsdale. You gotta keep an eye on them boys."*

*"So what does Ragsdale make you do?" I asked.*

*"I do all his dirty work."*

*It seems that when Black Horse was a young man, he went to Indianola to find a job, fell in love with a girl, and had a kid. He returned to the Nation after four years, to take care of his sick Father. A couple of years passed by and he went back to Indianola a few times searching for his girlfriend and son but could not find them. Ragsdale had hidden them and used them as slaves, more or less. Black Horse gave up his search and returned to the Nation to become the Medicine Man for the tribe, after his father passed away.*

*We took Billy Bob to the Comanche Nation with us, and by accident, he met his real father, Black Horse. Black Horse had given his then four-year-old son a tattoo. It was a black horse, on his right arm, which was the same as Black Horse's. That was the final proof that was needed to unite father and son, after I introduced them at the Comanche Nation. It was a great reunion.*

"Black Horse, you owe him a big debt, not me," White Feather replied.

"But you were with Adam when he was kidnapped. That makes you somewhat responsible," Black Horse said.

"I have done my best to help. I can do nothing more. That is all I have to say."

"You bring shame to me and the Comanche Tribe. In that case, do not come to visit my Tribe anymore. You are not welcome in our land." Black Horse reached out, touching my arm. "Jack, let us leave this coward, who is no longer my friend."

"Ok, let's go," I said. I knew from the first time I met White Feather that he was not trustworthy, just by the way he weakly shook my hand.

Before leaving, I told Maggie and Baldwin what was going on. They both agreed we didn't need White Feather. We mounted up and headed for Dilkon, which was 15 miles away, at full speed.

Dilkon City, according to the information we have, had a population of around 1,100 people. That made it three times larger than Indian Wells. Dilkon is a Navajo name meaning smooth black rock. The name comes from the rock formations found around that area.

Arriving at the city, we located the Dilkon Market, a small general store, which probably sold everything you could think of. As I opened the door, a small bell hanging on it rang out, noting our entrance.

Baldwin, Maggie, and I walked in and were surprised at the amount of inventory and goods for sale. However, there weren't any fresh fruits or vegetables. Almost everything was a can good of some type. They had ammo, guns, knives, and all types of mining gear for sale. One of the walls was lined with bottles of booze and cases of beer stacked in a cooler.

Walking over to the cooler, I grabbed three cases of beer and four bottles of Jack Daniels, placing them on the counter. An old man standing behind the counter was watching us like a hawk. He commented, "We only accept greenbacks or gold."

I said, "We'll pay in greenbacks."

"You need anything else?"

"Maybe, let us look around a while." I noted that Maggie and Baldwin were browsing around the aisles checking out the goods.

The old man asked, "Where y'all from?"

Peering into his dark, almost black-colored eyes, I could tell he was a Navajo. Navajos are a handsome looking people. I replied, "We're from Florida. Are you Charlie Wilson?"

Wilson was at least 80 years old. He was a little short fat man who wore wire-rimmed glasses. He didn't have any facial hair, but had long silver-black hair hanging down his back, tied in a braid. Charlie wore a white cowboy hat with an Eagle feather stuck in the hat band.

"Who wants to know?"

"I'm Jack Gunn. Jimmy Two Times and White Feather told me to contact you."

"Contact me for what?"

"Well, it's a touchy situation, Mr. Wilson. We need some information." I glanced around the store to make sure no one else was around.

Maggie and George came up to the counter with a cart full of canned fruits, Spam, and vegetables. I guessed they had about 100 cans of stuff. Maggie said, "We wanna buy these goods. We're tired of eating MREs and could use a treat."

"Ok," I replied. "Mr. Wilson, ring us up."

While Wilson was ringing us up he asked, "What kind of information do you want?"

Just as I was getting ready to tell him what we wanted to know when I heard the tiny bell ring, alerting us someone had just walked in the store. We turned to see who it was. He looked like a Navajo, but it was hard to tell because of the wide- brim straw hat he had on. He wore a pistol on his hip. As he walked toward us across the room, his cowboy boots clacked on the wooden floor. He was a man who walked with confidence. Then I saw the shiny star pinned on his chest.

The Officer walked over to the counter and asked, "Charlie, everything ok here?" The Officer glared at us and our weapons.

Charlie said, "Yeah ... everything is fine, Dan. These people are just buying some supplies."

I peered back at Dan, looking him right in the eyes. He was a clean-shaving man, about five foot eight and a little overweight, maybe from eating to many donuts. He avoided eye contact and looked at the goods we were purchasing.

Dan said, "I'm the law around here. I assume those are your trucks with the machine guns. What brings you to Dilkon City?"

I replied, "We're just passing through."

"I hope so because we don't want any trouble here. Where you headed to?"

"We're headed to Flagstaff area looking for missing Army family members."

"That's good. Just keep on moving because this is Navajo country, and people get nervous seeing Army Humvees running around here."

"Ok, we get your point. As soon as we load up these supplies we'll be on our way."

Lawman Dan didn't say another word as he turned and left the store. The bell rang, signaling his departure. I commented, "He isn't very friendly."

Mr. Wilson said, "No, he isn't. He thinks he's the King around here, but he's just the Captain of the Navajo Police in this area. Anyway, what do you want to know?"

Wilson handed me the bill for the supplies. I looked at it and each can was four bucks which totaled $450.00. One bottle of JD was $150.00. The beer came to $400. The grand total was $1,450.00. It was a little steep, but I didn't complain about the price, because I really wanted some information.

As I counted out the greenbacks, I asked, "Have you seen four pickup trucks come by here today?" I laid the cash on the counter. "Here you go," as I slid it over to him.

Wilson gave me a surprised look. "Why you wanna know that?" He asked, as he counted the money.

I slid him an extra five hundred bucks. "They kidnapped my grandson yesterday and we're after them."

Wilson glanced at the pile of money and took it. "Yeah, they stopped in here about 9 am to buy supplies. I didn't see any kid with them. They're a strange bunch of ruff-neck nomads. I think they pay off the police to let them pass through Navajo land."

"Can you tell us where these guys were going or where their hideout is?" I handed him another five hundred to entice him, which he took with some hesitation.

"I know these bad guys. They've been coming in here for about two years. White Feather used to hang out with them."

"White Feather used to hang out with them?" I asked.

"Yep, that's right, until he met a nice Hopi woman, got married, and started a family."

"So, White Feather isn't a real Hopi?"

"No. He's not even an Indian, as far as I know."

"I see, now I know why he didn't wanna come here with us," I commented.

"If the nomads find out I told you anything, they'll kill me for sure," old man Charlie said.

Baldwin said, "Don't worry about them, Mr. Wilson. We have a small army that will deal with them."

"Yeah, kidnapping means the death sentence where we come from," I told him.

Charlie quickly glanced around the room as if someone was watching us. He leaned in super close to me and said, "I'll tell you in one word. That's all I'm gonna tell you." He looked around the room again and I noticed his hands shook a little. I could tell he was afraid of these nomads.

"Ok. What's the word?"

He replied in a whisper, "Wupatki."

"Jack, do know what that means?" Maggie asked.

"Yes, I know what it is. Let's go." When I reached the door and opened it, the tiny bell rang. I stopped, glanced back at old Charlie, and raised my hand, giving half a wave. "Thanks for your help, Mr. Wilson. Have a great day."

Stepping outside, we noticed two police cars parked across the street. They were watching us for sure. I told Baldwin let's get out of town so we can study the map, without the cops watching us.

We left, heading west, but the cops dogged us for several miles, until they were finally convinced we were leaving. After the cops were out of sight we pulled over to the side of the road. Maggie handed out a beer to everyone and a can of Spam, along with some canned fruit. That was our lunch.

While eating, Maggie said, "How about that dirty rat White Feather."

I replied, "He better pray that I don't see him again. I knew something was funny about him."

"But he did help us out by putting us in the right direction to find Adam."

"Yeah, he probably knew I'd kill his ass if I found out about him. That's the only reason he helped us. He wanted to get away from me."

Baldwin finally asked, "Ok, what does Wupatki mean?"

Maggie also asked, "Yeah, what the heck does it mean?"

I started to chuckle. "Wupatki means 'Tall House', in Hopi."

Maggie said, "I never heard of it. What is it?"

"It's a group of ancient ruins located at Wupatki National Monument, north of Flagstaff, near Sunset Crater. They're ancient structures built by the Pueblo People, who were known as the Anasazi, or Ancient Ones."

Maggie asked, "How do you know that?"

"I've been to the ruins four times. The first time was with my Dad, when I was only twelve."

"How old are these ruins," Baldwin asked.

"If I remember correctly, Indians started moving to the area in 500 AD and by 1300 AD they moved away because of water shortages. But who really knows. They might have been around when the Templar Knights came here in 1350."

Baldwin said, "Let's check this place out on the Army Command Website. Jack, do you know where this place is?"

"If we stay on Navajo 15 it turns into Leupp Road. Then we pick up Townsend-Winoma Road and that takes us directly to Route 89. It's about 70 miles to Route 89 from here. Once on 89 we turn north for 10 miles to the south entrance of Loop Road, which is the southern route to the park HQ. The northern entrance to

Loop Road is another 10 or 15 miles further up Route 89."

"Jack, what did you do, memorize the map?"

"Of course, I got a photographic memory."

Maggie pulled out the SAT phone and up-linked the computer tablet. She typed in Wupatki and it popped right up, showing us a map. Using a portable digital laser scanner, she made copies for all our men on special plastic paper, which is waterproof. Basically it can't be destroyed, except by fire.

As our men gathered around, we studied our maps. "Ok, everyone, listen up!" Baldwin said. "The map shows there is only one road in and out, which is called Loop Road. But you can come in from the southern or northern entrance off of Route 89. We're gonna block both exits with our Hummers and trucks."

*Sunset Crater and Wupatki Ruins are located along the 34 mile scenic Loop Road that takes you through open meadows and the beautiful Ponderosa pine forests. It winds through Juniper grasslands and provides a view of the Painted Desert before reaching Wupatki National Monument. The road's general direction takes it north and south but since it curves around so much you also travel east and west to some degree. It is a two lane paved road that the National Park Service used to maintain in the old days. The park HQ is between the north and south entrance on Loop Road.*

"Jack, since you've been there before, where do you think they'll be bivouacked?"

"Most likely they're at the park's visitor center or HQ," as I pointed to it on the map.

"Are you sure about that?"

"I'm pretty sure because I would hold up there. It's more comfortable than living in a 1,000-year-old ruin. Besides that, maybe it has lights and air, like the Petrified Forest center had."

Baldwin said, "We'll split into two teams. Squad one will move in from the south entrance and squad two from the north entrance. Two Hummers and three trucks will take the south entrance on Loop Road. The other two Humvees, with the remaining trucks, will proceed to the north entrance. Both teams are to move within three miles of the visitor center and wait for further orders. The Humvees will block the road at that those points terminating anyone who tries to pass. Four men will be positioned at each roadblock."

"Sounds good," I commented.

Baldwin continued, "Alright, Pete and I will recon from the south with squad one. Jack and Maggie, you're with squad two, and will be coming from the north entrance."

"The squads will be support for the recon teams. Eight men will be in Jack's squad, and eight in mine. The squads will surround the target area providing over-watch protection for us."

"Is everyone with me so far?" The warriors all nodded as he peered into their eyes, one at a time, searching for any negative reaction. None of the warriors spoke a word, as they waited for Captain Baldwin to continue. "Now here's the key point, no one is to fire until I give the order. You have to wait until the rescue team is in place to extract Adam. Is that clear?"

A question came from Jeff. "Boss, which way will you extract, north or south?"

"It depends … but let me make it clear, we'll extract the direction that is the safest, be it north or south. Your job is to make sure it is safe and cover our backs. Any comments?"

No one said a word, so I spoke up. "Let's take a closer look at the grounds, the buildings, and how they're positioned."

*This type of operation requires special attention to the details. You have to know the best way in and the safest way out. You need to know the layout of the buildings, inside and outside. The terrain needs to be known, so you can take advantage of strategic locations to use for cover. Timing is critical, so everyone needs to set a schedule and have go/no-go signals. The entire rescue operation needs to run like a well-oiled machine. If a mistake is made, some of our men or Adam could be killed, and that is not acceptable.*

*However, we do have the advantage over the bad guys. They don't know we are coming for them. They don't know we're going to kill most of them before they even see us. Using our night vision gear, we own the night.*

I grabbed a piece of plastic paper, a marking pen, and drew the following rough diagram, based on the map and from my memory. I wanted everyone to know more details about the area. Maggie made copies for everyone to study.

I said, "The X's mark the suggested locations for the squads to take assault positions. The top of this diagram is due west and the bottom is east.

"Building 1 is the main Visitor Center. Building 2 is for storage. Number 3 is a repair shop. Numbers 4, 5, and 6 are resident houses."

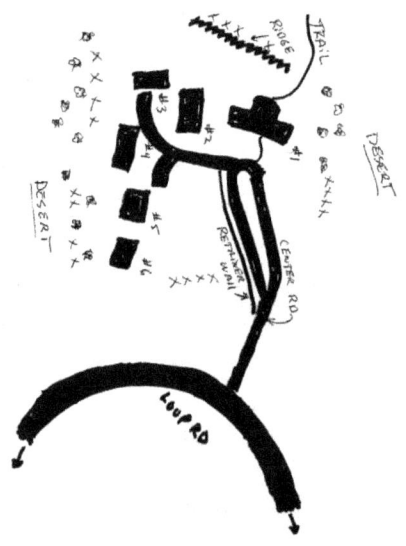

I commented, "There are two ways into the Visitor Center, as noted by the trails. There's a front door on the eastside and a back door on the west side of the building."

Baldwin commented, "Thanks, Jack. Now, everyone note, as soon as we arrive, squads one and two set up and wait for my command to open fire. But you hear us fire, then open up if you see a target. If you're spotted, defend yourself. Pete and I will proceed to the back door, while Jack and Maggie cover the front."

I interjected, "There are big windows in the front and back, so it's easy to see inside if the lights are on."

"Ok, when Pete and I breach the rear door and enter the building, you and Maggie follow in through the front. Before entering, we need to locate Adam," Baldwin advised.

Maggie asked, "What if he's not in the main building?"

"Good point," Baldwin said. "If he's not in the main building then we'll need to carefully search each one until we find him. Our job is to find Adam before any assault begins. The squads will provide overwatch protection. They got our backs."

I looked at the time because the sun was getting low in the sky. It was 6 pm and Baldwin said, "Let's proceed to Route 89. We'll stop there to rest, eat, check our weapons, and review the plan again before proceeding. I'd like us to be in position at the target shortly after midnight."

We drove on, 70 more miles, to the Route 89 intersection and pulled to the side of the road, out of sight. We were well-concealed from any traffic that might pass by, which could possibly give us away to the nomads.

Here for the next few hours, we made ready to do battle with the nomad bandits. Everyone checked their gear, guns, radios, ammo, and water supplies.

THOMAS H. WARD

# WUPAKTI
## MAY 27, 2026

It was just after midnight on the 27th of May, as my squad rolled onto Loop Road, at the northern entrance to Wupakti ruins. We stopped about three miles from the Visitor Center. Everyone knew what to do and how important this mission was.

The two Hums, short for Humvees as I call them, set up a roadblock on Loop Road, as planned. Four men would remain there, guarding the road not letting any vehicles or persons pass during this operation. It was after midnight and we figured that anyone driving around that late would be a bogie, so we would shoot first and ask questions later.

It was a little chilly with a slight breeze blowing across the open desert. The sky was clear, exposing millions of stars and a half moon. It was surprising to me just how much the stars and half-moon lit up the night. Once your eyes adjusted to the darkness, you almost didn't need night vision. But our night vision is the best FLIR system money can buy. It shows the body heat of a target as small as a mouse. You can't hide behind a bush to be safe from our rounds.

I was very anxious and wanted to find Adam quickly, praying that he was still alive, and had not been beaten or tortured. If he had been, there would be hell to pay. As I have always said, I hate bullies and people who harm children in any manner. The only justice for these sick bastards is a bullet in the head. That solves everything, in my opinion.

We were getting ready to move out on foot for the three-mile hike. Maggie asked, "Should we bring the dogs?"

I thought about it for a minute. If we bring our guard dogs, Adolf and Freda, they could give us away with one bark. On the other hand, if we can't locate Adam, they could sniff him out no matter what building he was in.

"I don't wanna risk bringing the dogs. They could give us away with one bark and blow the mission, getting Adam killed and maybe some of us," I said.

Maggie nodded her head in agreement, and put the dogs back inside the truck so they wouldn't follow us. Our squad was made up of ten people. Maggie and I along with eight Templar Warriors, who would be our support team and cover our backs. They would take positions on the east side and the south side of the visitor center compound. Baldwin's men would be on the west and north side.

We were dressed in our standard black SWAT-type combat gear, which made us look like Ninjas. We would blend in with the shadows even on a star-lit night, making us invisible to the enemy.

Our men would select the best positions to cover us once they arrived at the target zone. My crude map with the X's only suggested positions for the over-watch crews to locate. They would decide the exact spots based on their experience.

We would approach the Visitors Center, staying off the main road in case there were any cameras. Once the Warriors had located their over-watch positions, Maggie and I would proceed to the rendezvous point, meeting up with Baldwin and Pete. We had to circle around to the north side, crossing over the visitor center driveway, to link up with them.

A little more than an hour had passed. The radio crackled. "We're in place," Baldwin said. "Over."

I pushed the radio button, "Our men are in place. We're on the way over to you now. Don't shoot us by mistake. Over."

The radio hissed, "Ha, ha. Jack, we wouldn't do that. Over."

"Very funny, asshole."

Maggie and I kept a low profile and crossed the driveway, meeting Baldwin and Pete with no problems.

Baldwin got on the horn again, speaking to everyone. "If anyone has an eye on a bogie, speak up." No one replied. So far we have not seen any nomads.

The four of us were about a hundred feet away from the building, kneeling behind some small shrubs. We could see dim lights in the main room and in one of the housing units located on the northeast side. Thank God these stupid jerks didn't have any security posted. They must have felt smug as a bug in a rug.

Baldwin said, "Pete and I will proceed to the back door and try to get a look-see inside. I'll radio you when I do."

"Roger that. We'll sit tight until you give us the ok to move up."

Maggie and I watched as they kept low moving across the desert, and around the building to the rear door. I scanned the front door using my FLIR and didn't see a soul.

I said, "Maggie, keep your eyes open."

Then, a body flashed by the front window, blocking the light for an instant. It was just a shadow-like figure. I radioed George. "I just saw someone walk by the front window."

A whisper came back. "Roger that. I got eyes on him. It's the guy with the eye patch and black head bandana."

"Adam has to be in that room."

"He is, Jack. Move your butts up to the front door fast, because we're going in. I count six bogies. Two are awake and four seem to be asleep."

Maggie and I ran the 100 feet in record time. I radioed George, "We're here." I peeked in the window with Maggie to determine exactly where these jerks were at.

"Going in now, Jack."

"Roger that. We're right behind you." We observed George open the rear door and open fire on the two men sitting at the front desk. Maggie and I quickly entered the room and opened up on the four sleeping on the floor, but now they were awake. Startled, they reached for AK47's. We gunned them down before they could turn a weapon on us. Everyone was quickly terminated without them firing a single shot.

I wish I had a video of it. The four of us firing M4s on full automatic pumping lead into these dirt bags; watching the bodies jumping around as if an invisible string was making them move. Blood was splattered all over the room, covering the white walls with spots of crimson red.

We stopped firing. Pete went to make sure the rest of the building was clear. I glanced around the room. Adam wasn't here. George told me he was here. I panicked and grabbed George by the shoulders. "Where's Adam at? You said he was here."

"Take it easy, Jack. He's here alright."

Then the restroom door squeaked opened. I raised my M4 putting my finger on the trigger getting ready to squeeze. Baldwin grabbed my arm and stood in front of me.

"You don't wanna shoot your Grandson, do you? He ran into the washroom when we entered to keep from being shot by the bad guys. Smart kid."

Suddenly we heard gunfire from outside. The radio hissed, "Boss, five tangos are terminated. It's all clear out here. Over."

"Roger that. It's all clear in here." Baldwin replied. "Hold your positions until further notice. There's no need for an extraction."

Adam ran to me and we tightly embraced each other. Then Maggie joined in hugging us both. Captain Baldwin joined in, making it a big group hug.

Adam had tears in his eyes. He said, "I knew you would come for me, Grandpa. I told them you would kill them all for kidnapping me. They laughed at me."

I held Adams face in my hands and carefully examined it. He had some bruises and a black eye. I said, "They beat you."

"Yeah, a little but I'm ok. They wanted to know where the treasure was."

"I know, White Feather told them about the treasure."

"Yeah, that's right. How did you know that?"

"We found White Feather and he told us. We also found out White Feather was friends with these guys at one time."

Adam said, "I could tell he knew them. They were friendly to him at first. But when they hurt me he did step in and tried to stop them. Then they beat him up pretty good. Somehow he escaped, and boy that pissed them off. They searched for him all night."

"Well, I have to admit White Feather did help us find you by providing some information."

"Is he here?" Adam asked.

"No, he chickened out."

Adam glanced around the room at the dead bodies. He counted them and said in a whisper, "One man missing."

"Are you sure?"

"Yeah, I'm sure. There were seven men here and there are only six bodies."

Walking over to George, I advised him in a whisper what Adam had just told me. Baldwin nodded and hand signaled Pete. They went to perform another sweep of the building.

I spun around, turning in circles, peering at the room wondering where someone could be hiding. Then I saw it. It was blended into the wall so closely that you could hardly spot it. It was a door to somewhere. I thought, *most likely it's just a closet, with no exit.*

Holding my finger to my lips, I warned Adam not to speak. I spoke loud enough to be heard and said, "Well, we got these guys." I hand motioned for Adam to move to the washroom and waved Maggie over to me.

Maggie came over. "What's up?"

I pointed to the hidden door and held my finger to my lips. I said loudly, "They're all dead so let's get out of here." Whispering in her ear, I told her someone is hiding behind that door, so follow my lead, as I pointed at the wall.

We shuffled our feet and walked past the door, while observing it. I didn't see a doorknob, so I figured it was the kind of door you push in a little and it will pop open on its own.

We very quietly moved back in front of the door. I hand signaled Maggie to make ready her M4. She stood back a few steps, off to the side. The problem was, I didn't know what side the hinges were on, which would determine whether the door would open to the left or right. I guessed the hinges were on the left, based on the layout of the room. That meant that Maggie had a good position for a shot.

I pushed on the door and it popped open an inch, just as I thought it would. Grabbing the door frame I swiftly pulled it open. The nomad was standing inside the small room with his hands up. He mumbled, "Don't shoot. I surrender." He didn't have a gun.

I said, "Hold our fire, Maggie, while I zip tie this bastard up."

"Come on, Jack, let's kill the asshole now."

"No, not yet. I want some information."

This guy was a dirty looking creep with curly black hair and beady eyes. He wore a plaid shirt and blue jeans. His facial features looked Mexican or Mexican-Indian to me. He had a black bandana tied around his forehead. He was a short little asshole, about five foot four, weighing around one-hundred thirty pounds.

I pulled out a zip-cuff, dragged him out of the closet, and ruffed him up a bit. I gave him a gun barrel to the gut, hard, that made him double over and fall to his knees. Then I cuffed him really tight. I knew the cuffs would cut off the circulation to his hands in a few minutes. They would turn numb and he would lose all feeling after an hour. In the meantime, he would be in real pain from the cuffs.

He said, "Hey man, these cuffs are killing me."

"Shut up, dork." I didn't give a shit about his pain. I wanted to inflict more pain on this piece of crap. I yanked him up by the cuffs, almost dislocating his shoulders in the process. He screamed loudly which made me feel good.

Adam came out of the washroom, and at the same time, Pete and Baldwin returned.

"Hey, you found him," Pete said.

"Yeah, he was in that hidden closet," I replied, as I pointed to the open door in the wall.

Adam said, "He's the guy who beat me."

"I'm sorry, but I had to, kid. I didn't really hurt you and I could have," he said.

"You're a liar! Grandpa, he's one of the leaders."

"What's your name," I asked.

"Pablo."

"That's a Mexican name. Is your gang made up of Mexicans?"

"Some are, but not all."

"Well Pablo, your gonna tell me what I want to know. If you don't, I'll hurt you real bad. Hold on to your teeth because this is gonna hurt." I took the butt of my M4 and slammed it into his face as hard as I could. He fell to the floor knocked out cold from the blow. I wanted him to know that I would hurt him.

Maggie dribbled some water over his face to wake him up.

He came to in few minutes. Blood was flowing out of his mouth as he mumbled, "You're going to kill me anyway … so why should I talk?"

"I'll make you a deal. If you talk and tell the truth, I won't kill you. If you don't talk, you will suffer unbearable pain before you die." I pulled out my trusty Black Bear fighting knife and waved it in front of his face. "Pablo, I know how to make people talk."

In a swift move, I grabbed his left ear and sliced it off. It was like cutting warm butter. He screamed, "You're crazy! I'll talk … I'll talk!" Blood ran down the side of his face and neck.

I held his ear up to my mouth and shouted into it. "Yes, I am crazy! Can you hear me?" He nodded his head yes, very quickly up and down. "You know, it makes me sad that you wanna talk because I wanted to cut off more body parts." I threw the bloody ear into his face.

Maggie commented, "Yeah, it also makes me sad, because I wanted to cut off his little prick." She pulled out her Barong Machete and swung it in a circle over her head.

*This is Maggie's favorite weapon. It is the weapon of choice for the Amazon Warriors who guard our island home, named Tocabaga. The Barong is made from 1055 hardened steel and has an 18-inch long leaf-shaped blade. It is so sharp you can shave with it. Maggie is very skillful with this weapon. She has killed several dirtbags by slicing off their heads, as well as other body parts.*

We both laughed, acting like we were really nuts. Pablo looked at us with wide open eyes and said, "Ok …

I'll tell you … whatever you wanna know." His voice quivered in fear as he spoke.

"Pablo, then we got a deal. I won't cut you or kill you as long as you talk."

"Does that include me?" Maggie asked.

"Maggie, you can't cut him as long as he talks."

"Damn it anyhow, Jack. You always ruin the fun."

I asked, "Mr. Pablo, tell us who's in charge of this group of misfits?"

"Your boy is right. I am one of the leaders. There are three of us," Pablo replied.

"What are the other names?"

"Pancho and Aba."

"Where are they now?"

Pablo laughed and said, "They went to find the treasure In the Grand Canyon, which your boy told us about." He started to laugh louder.

I slapped him in the head with the barrel of my carbine. "What's so funny ass-wipe?"

He stopped laughing. "Nothing really. I just thought it was funny that they'll beat you to the treasure because your boy told us everything."

Adam was watching the interrogation and said, "That's not true, Grandpa."

I waved my hand at Adam and told him, "It's ok, it doesn't matter. These nitwits couldn't find shit, even if they stepped in it."

Baldwin said, "We're going outside to check on my men, and explore this compound. Maybe we'll find something."

"Ok, take Adam with you."

Captain Baldwin nodded and said, "Grand Master, please come with me."

As they walked outside, I heard George get on the radio ordering the trucks to move up to the Visitor Center.

*I had never heard Captain Baldwin call Adam the Grand Master before. He would always just bow and really never gave him a title of superiority. It was true that Adam was the Grand Master of the modern Templar Warriors. The Warriors all vowed to follow him after they had witnessed the Sword of Jerusalem behead Christian de Molay, thereby protecting Adam. It was clear that the holy relic had supernatural powers, and in the hands of Adam, it made him invincible. Maybe Adam had gained a little respect after having under gone the terrible kidnapping without any complaining. Adam is only thirteen years old, but it seems he took it like a man.*

I continued my questioning. "How many men do they have?"

Pablo said, "Fifteen men went to the canyon."

"How many men total do you have?"

"We had twenty-seven, including me, until you killed everyone here."

"What are they looking for in the canyon?"

"You know, the Hooked X to find the treasure."

It seems that someone, either Adam or White Feather, told them about the Hooked X. I'll ask Adam later just how much he told them. But in reality, it didn't matter, because they couldn't find the treasure until the summer solstice, which was in June.

"How well do they know the canyon?"

"Pretty well. Aba has been down in the canyon many times. He's somewhat of an expert, because he knows all the trails."

"What about you, Pablo, do you know your way around the canyon?"

"No. I usually stay on top."

"So, you know your way around the rim of the canyon."

"Yeah, that's right, the rim."

"Why did Aba go into the Grand Canyon in the past? What was he looking for?"

"Gold and treasure. There's a lot of gold you can mine if you can find it."

"Has he ever found any treasure?" I asked.

"No, but the Indians tell a lot of stories about ancient treasures hidden in a cave somewhere. But no one has ever found any."

"So, Aba goes mining for gold. Do they have mining equipment and climbing gear?

"Hey, I'm telling you everything. You're not gonna kill me, right?"

"That's right, Pablo I won't kill you. Just keep talking. What trail do they usually take down?"

"Man, my hands are numb. Come on and loosen these cuffs up, please."

Maggie said, "Hey Pablo, I might have to cut those hands off due to lack of circulation. Then you can't pick that big nose of yours." Maggie laughed, thinking that was funny, but so did I.

I cut the cuffs off to make him feel better, so he'd talk more about his buddies. "You feel better now?"

"Yeah, thanks a lot."

Maggie said, "If you make any sudden moves, little creep, I'll cut your ugly head off."

"What trail do they usually take into the canyon?" I asked.

Pablo replied, "Usually they take the Bright Angel Trail because it is wide enough to use the ATVs. But sometimes they use the South Kaibab Trail and go on foot."

"They got ATVs. That's a good idea."

"Yeah. It beats the hell out of hiking. The trip up is a killer. We used mules until they all died, or the Indians ate them."

"I've hiked down the canyon, so I know all about it. How many ATVs do they have?" I asked.

"Hey, how about some water?" Pablo asked.

"When we're done here I'll give you some. I asked you, how many ATVs do they have?"

Pablo, who was on his knees, sitting on the floor said, "How about letting me sit in a chair."

"Answer the question Pablo. You're starting to piss me off, and you don't wanna piss me off or there's no deal."

"Ok Boss. They got five ATVs. What else do you wanna know?"

"Since you're an expert on the canyon rim, how many trails lead into the canyon?"

"Crap, I don't know. A few of them are small and steep, like goat trails. The major trails are: Bright Angel, which is the only one wide enough for an ATV, Hermit Trail, South Kaibab Trail, which is steep, and North Kaibab Trail, which is on the north rim. They never use the North Kaibab trail because it's too far away."

Checking the time, I saw it was almost 3 am. I was tried and we needed to get some rest. We couldn't sleep in this room because of the stinking bloody mess and dead bodies.

I said, "Pablo, that's enough questions for now. I want you to drag the bodies outside about 200 feet away and then clean up this room."

Pablo objected, "Hey man, that's not my job."

After I hit him in the head with my gun barrel, he came around to my line of thinking. I ordered Maggie to watch him. I said, "If he tries anything funny, blow his head off."

"Don't worry, I will," Maggie said. "What are you gonna do, Jack?"

"I'm gonna have a smoke and a drink."

I had just lit up a smoke, when Pete walked in the room, followed by Captain Baldwin and Adam. "The

Captain wants me to destroy any surveillance equipment in case they got us on video."

"Go ahead, Pete. Have at it; I'm taking a break."

Baldwin saw Pablo dragging out the first body. "What's he doing?"

"I got him cleaning up the room so we can rest here for a few hours."

"Did you get any good intel?"

"Yeah, I did. I found out they probably entered the canyon on Bright Angel Trail and they use ATVs. That's smart thinking, because it beats the hell out of hiking the canyon. Oh, I almost forgot. They sent fifteen men to the canyon."

"That's not good. There's fifteen more of these guys we have to deal with. Using ATVs is a good idea. Where are we going to get ATVs from?"

"We'll have to go to Flagstaff or maybe even Phoenix to find them. Believe me, we'll need them to go into the canyon. Hiking in by foot is a bitch. Besides, if we find any treasure we'll need ATVs to carry it out."

"So tomorrow we go hunting for ATVs?"

I nodded my head. "Yeah, we have a lot of time before the solstice occurs. We could just rest here for a few days."

"Yes, we could do that, but what if the law comes around and finds us here with these dead bodies?"

"Good point, George. That wouldn't look too good."

"I say we stay here today and tonight. Then move out tomorrow and find the ATVs."

"Ok, I agree, George. "By the way, what did you do with the bodies outside?"

"My men put them in the garage, out of sight."

Pablo was dragging out the last body. Maggie followed him out the door. I heard her tell him. "Come on, you little shit, move it."

Pete approached Captain Baldwin. "Sir, I destroyed all the video equipment, as you ordered."

I took a swig of JD and lit another smoke. Baldwin said, "Jack, that stuff is gonna kill you someday."

"We all die of something. You can't live forever," I replied.

Maggie came back in with Pablo and he mopped the blood off the floor and cleaned the walls, as best as he could. Maggie took him back outside to empty the bloody bucket and clean the mop.

About thirty minutes later, Maggie came back inside, but there was no Pablo. I asked, "What happened to Pablo?"

"Oh, he tried to escape, so I killed him."

Baldwin said, "I didn't hear any shots."

Maggie unsheathed her Barong showing the blood-stained blade. "I don't need a gun to kill a piece of shit like him." She gave a smile of self- satisfaction.

Baldwin and Pete gazed at her wearing a skin-tight black SWAT outfit. She was one sexy woman gladiator, or I should say Amazon Warrior. But she is also deadly as a Black Widow Spider. Pete said, "No wonder you like her on your team, Jack."

Maggie and I think so much alike. She knew I wanted her to kill Pablo. I promised him I wouldn't and I'm a man of my word. She saved me from having to give the order. It was like she was reading my mind.

I said, "Good job, Maggie. Here, you need a drink." I handed her the bottle of JD. She took three big chugs and let out a loud belch.

I must admit that Maggie is a little blood thirsty. She likes to use the blade because I assume it gives her a feeling of power. She likes to watch the scumbags suffer before they die. I can't say anything bad about what she does. I'm just glad she's on my side.

I'm not sorry that we killed all these dirtbags. It actually made me feel good knowing Adam was safe and some his kidnappers were dead, which gave me closure.

It was almost 5 am. I said, "Adam, let's get some rest. Go out to the truck and bring in our gear and sleeping bags. After that, take the dogs for a walk. They missed you."

After a few hours of sleep I woke up, made some coffee, and went outside for a smoke. Adam and Maggie were still asleep so I tried not to make too much noise. I walked over to the pit that the bodies were thrown into. Pablo's head was sitting on top of a rock, marking the spot. Maggie had a sense of humor alright, even if it is a little sick.

The Warriors were all awake, including George, who approached me. He said, "They have two cars here, so my men disabled them just in case anyone comes back."

"So what's the plan today?" I asked.

"We have to do maintenance on the trucks. Change the oil and so forth. That will take most of the day. Also, I want everyone to clean their equipment and weapons. Then we just relax and rest up."

"Then tomorrow we can go to Flagstaff and find some ATVs. By the way, we also need rope and climbing gear."

"Roger that. Climbing gear is a good idea," Baldwin said.

I wondered, *would we run into any trouble in Flagstaff?*

# FLAGSTAFF
## MAY 28, 2026

The Templar Warriors and I were up before the break of dawn. I heard the coyotes howling during the night, meaning they had found the bodies. Yesterday the vultures, ravens, and ants were feasting, now it was the coyotes turn.

As I was drinking a coffee, Baldwin said, "I suggest we burn those bodies."

As I lit up a smoke I said, "Yeah, go ahead, but it will stink."

"When we're ready to leave we'll lit them up using some gas. We checked our gas supply and we need to top off our tanks. Maybe we can find a station in Flagstaff."

"I'm sure we can. What time you wanna move out?" I asked.

"How about 9 am?"

"That's fine by me. I'll pass the word."

I took the dogs out the front door for a walk while Maggie and Adam were still asleep. They were sniffing the air and could smell the bloody bodies. I kept them away from the killing pit. You never know, one of those coyotes might have rabies.

I felt sorry for Adolf and Freda because this trip has been hard on them. Big dogs like these don't really like riding in a truck all day. But they never complain and just do their job. Dogs are great friends and these are the best of the best.

After feeding them each an MRE, I made some breakfast for myself. I sliced up a can of Spam, heating it up until it was golden brown, using a small one burner camp stove. I popped open a can of mixed fruit, opened a box of soda crackers, and sat down in a corner to enjoy my breakfast. I washed it down with a can of beer. Man that was good stuff.

Adolf and Freda smelled the Spam and came over, tails wagging, begging for some. I told them sit. With that Adolf let out a couple of barks, waking everyone up. I opened another can and gave them each half. They didn't even chew it, but wolfed it down in one bite.

Maggie, still in her sleeping bag, said, "That smells good. Whatcha cooking?"

"Fried Spam, you want some?"

"Yeah!"

Adam piped up, "Hey, I want some, too."

"Maggie, that was a good idea buying these can goods."

"Of course, I always have good ideas," she said.

I threw them each a can of fruit and cooked up some more Spam. I commented, "After eating, get ready to roll out. We're going to Flagstaff today."

Pulling out my map, I turned the pages to find Flagstaff. One time, in my distant past, I wanted to live in Flagstaff. It's a great location that has snowy winters, but also long warm summers.

*Here's what I know about Flagstaff. It's only an hour and a half from the south rim of the canyon or about 80 miles. At 7,000 feet elevation, it is located near the largest Ponderosa Pine forest in America, up against the San Francisco Peaks. Flagstaff is surrounded by extinct volcanoes in Coconino National Forest.*

*Population used to be around 69,000 people, with about ten percent being Native Americans. The story goes that Lumberjacks celebrating the 4th of July in 1876 hoisted a US Flag on top of a tall ponderosa pine. They named the little town Flagstaff. The city was actually founded in 1881. Since this was a major pass to proceed west, the railroad came in 1882 and the city slowly grew.*

We rolled out of Wupakti Ruins at 9 am sharp. We followed the north route on Loop Road out of the ruins and turned south on Route 89, which took us directly into Flagstaff. It connects with Alt. 40, which is the same as the old Route 66.

Observing the map, only four major roads run into Flagstaff, making it easy to protect. Sure enough, at the intersection of 89 and Alt. 40, there was a roadblock set up by the Flagstaff Police, along with a few Sheriff Deputies.

As we rolled to a stop, it occurred to me that I didn't know what to tell them. They would certainly ask us what we were doing here in four armored Hums with M2 machine guns.

Baldwin's Hummer was first in line. I picked up the radio. "Hey George, what are we gonna tell them? We can't tell them we're looking for treasure in the canyon."

"You're right about that. Think fast."

Maggie said, "Just tell them we're looking for nomad bandits who stole military equipment and weapons."

"Damn good idea, Maggie. Here, tell that to George," as I handed her the radio. She repeated her idea to Baldwin as I stepped out of the truck to greet the officers with Captain Baldwin.

Moving up to his truck, he got out and we slowly approached the roadblock. The six officers were gawking at our convoy and Hummers. I said, "Let me do the talking. But jump in anytime you want to."

With M16 rifles pointed at us, we both held our hands up in the air. We left our M4 carbines in the trucks. However, just looking at our body armor and gear, it appeared that we were some type of special military tactical unit.

One officer stepped forward, about 20 feet, to meet us. He said, "Morning, gentlemen. What can we do for you?" Judging by the stripes on his sleeve, he was a Police Sergeant.

I replied, "Morning Officer. My name is Jack Gunn and this is Captain Baldwin. We're just passing through Flagstaff. We need to obtain some supplies and fuel."

"Are you with the military?"

"Yes, we're on a mission to recover stolen military equipment and weapons for the Army Rangers. We're tracking some terrorists."

"Where are you from?"

"Believe or not, we're from Florida. We're based at Fort Desoto."

"Never heard of it." The officer turned around and yelled to his men, "Anyone ever hear of a Fort Desoto?" No one answered.

Captain Baldwin said, "It's a secret Ranger base located on Tocabaga Island. I suppose you never heard of that either."

"No, I haven't."

I pulled out the letter Captain Sessions gave me, which was on official Army Ranger letter head. I said, "Here Officer, read this," as I handed it to him.

After reading it, he replied, "Ok, that's all well and good, but exactly what do you want and where are you going?"

Baldwin spoke up. "We need fuel, supplies, and some equipment."

"What kind of equipment?"

"We need to buy at least five ATVs."

"Ok, but where are you going?"

This bullshit questioning was starting to piss me off, but I had to keep my cool.

"I said, "We're heading north, towards the canyon.""

The officer said, "Is that where the bad guys went?"

"Yes, that's right. They went in that direction."

The officer glared at me while still holding my letter. "How in the hell do you know that?"

Jumping in the conversation, Baldwin said, "We know that because a satellite is tracking them."

"Wow, that's pretty impressive. What kind of equipment and weapons did you say they stole?" The officer had a cocky attitude. He was a cop whose power had gone to his head. I knew how to handle this guy.

I changed the subject. "What's your name?" I leaned in to read is his nametag. "Officer Stevens. Look we didn't say what they took because it's classified. If we told you, we'd have to kill you. Only the Captain and I know what it is. Our men don't even know."


Steven's jaw dropped. He said, "Holy shit! It's a nuke, I bet. Some of those terrorists got hold of a nuke, didn't they."

"Hey, I didn't' say that."

"You don't have to. I'll be right back. Let me talk to the Chief."

As Stevens walked back, he huddled up with his men and then got on a radio, which I assumed linked him to the Chief of Police. Baldwin whispered, "Smart move, Jack."

Officer Stevens returned and advised, "The Chief says to give you whatever you want and for us to fully co-operate."

"That's great," I said.

"Yeah, whatever you need is on the Flagstaff Police Department."

"We really appreciate that, but it's not necessary," Baldwin said.

"My Chief insisted that it's on us. Thanks for coming here to help protect Flagstaff. Now, if you follow me, we'll put you up at the Flagstaff Hotel until we can obtain those ATVs. On the way, there's a Mobile station if you need to refuel. Here's my name card. Just tell them to bill the Police Department. Use this to buy anything you need."

I took his card and thanked him. Returning to our vehicles, we mounted up and followed him to the hotel. On the way, we made a stop and topped off our tanks.

Flagstaff seemed to be a city that was under control. There was law and order here and most citizens I saw carried some type of weapon. That made me feel better and confident that we wouldn't have any trouble here.

While refueling, Officer Stevens commented, "We have two ATV stores here. One is a Polaris store that sells ATVs and snowmobiles. The other is owned by a guy named Joe and he sells different brands. You got any idea on the size and type you need?"

After thinking for a minute I replied, "Actually, we need something small, like a Polaris two-seater sportsmen. We want them in black, Army green, or brown. No bright colors. If possible, we'd like five of them along with trailers so we can haul them."

"By the way, why do you need the ATVs?"

"The terrorists have five ATVs. If they go off road, we have to follow them. We suspect that's what they're gonna do."

"What else do you need?"

"Climbing gear," I told him.

"There's a sporting goods store near the hotel that carries climbing stuff."

We finished refueling and pulled into the hotel parking lot, 20 minutes later. Captain Baldwin set up security to protect our trucks. Officer Stevens took off, along with Pete, to purchase the ATVs. Jeff went to the sporting goods store to obtain climbing gear. The rest of us checked into the apparently empty hotel.

I showed the police name card for payment and the clerk didn't bat an eye until I signed in as Jack Gunn, Special Forces. He curiously studied us. We acquired twelve rooms, all on the ground floor near the trucks. The clerk did ask how long we were going to stay. I told him one or two nights, at most.

Going to our room, I asked Adam to look up on the ACWWW more information about the canyon. I wanted him to verify how many trails went into the canyon and advise the locations. Maggie volunteered to help him.

The room phone rang, I answered it. "Jack Gunn."

"Mr. Gunn, this is Ed Seibert, Chief of Police."

"Hello, Chief. What can I do for you?"

"I'd like to have dinner with you and a few of your people tonight, along with Officer Stevens, to discuss what's going on."

"First of all, I'd like to thank you for your kind support and help. It's our pleasure to have dinner with you tonight. I'll bring along Captain Baldwin and my right-hand man."

"Fine, we'll meet you at the hotel dining room at 7 pm. Is that ok?"

"Yes sir, that sounds ok to me. See you then."

"Great, we'll see you later, Mr. Gunn."

"Goodbye."

I knew this was going to happen. The Chief wants information about what's going on. Baldwin, Maggie, and I will have to sit down and make up some bullshit story to tell him. Maggie always has good ideas and is a great liar. Besides that, she'll take the tension out of the meeting by giving the Officers something to look at. She's eye candy, so to speak. It's hard not to look at Maggie because she's so damn sexy.

The three of us had a meeting to get our story straight. We'd tell the Chief basically the same thing we told Officer Stevens. I would embellish it a little bit to make it seem we gave the Chief more information than he should know. After all, we have to tell them something because they are paying the tab.

It was around 5 pm when Pete came back. He advised us that five ATVs would be ready with trailers by tomorrow at 2 pm. He told us the problem was finding trailers.

Adam and Maggie had been working on the Army Command Website, looking up information. Adam said, "We found out that Havasupai Indians live in the canyon."

"Living there now?" I asked.

"I imagine they're still living there."

"Well, we'll find out soon enough. I just hope they're friendly."

Maggie said, "Did you ever notice how much the Indians look like Egyptians?"

I replied, "They don't look like Egyptians. Look at picture of Akhenaten. Now that was one weird looking dude. Tell me he isn't from another world. His head is cone shaped and he has elongated facial features. His wife, Nefertiti, looks more normal than him. All the Egyptian Kings had slanted eyes, making them appear to be oriental. They all wore conical shaped crowns to cover up the cone head."

"No, I didn't mean they look like the old Kings. I think some of the American Indians have a lot of facial features similar to the normal Egyptian people. Especially the Havasupai, who are living in the Grand Canyon."

"I don't know about that. Someone who's an expert in facial features should study that. But you might be right."

Adam interrupted, "The Havasupais have lived in the canyon over a thousand years. Who knows, maybe they've been there a lot longer than that. Historians don't really know that much about them."

"If so, then they might have seen the Knights Templar. We need to talk to them and find out if they have any stories about that. Maybe they know where the cave is. Tell me more about them," I replied.

"It says here that the Havasupais lived along the Grand Canyon's South Rim, planting crops and tending the orchards in Havasu Canyon. They also grew food in other places within the Grand Canyon during the summer. In the winter, they forage for game on the rim. They refer to themselves as Havasu 'Baaja. In English it comes out to Havasupai. It means "people of the blue-green waters." Havasu, which is what their land is called, has beautiful waterfalls which provide clean water. Their city is named Supi and is located at the bottom of the Havasu Canyon. It says here that about 600 people live in Supi City and it can only be reached by using Havasu Canyon Trial. The trailhead is located west of the Bright Angel Trail. It's a private trail on the Indian Reservation."

Adam continued, "Listen to this, there is another tribe called the Hualapais. The reservation is just west of the Havasupais. They have about 2,500 tribal members. It seems that both of these tribes revere the Colorado River as a life source and backbone of their beliefs. They believe that they were created from the sediment and clay from the river. The name of their God is Tochopa. It doesn't say here what that means."

"Do they mention anything about the Egyptians?" I asked.

"No, I haven't seen anything about that. But, would they even know about the Egyptians? I mean, these were simple people who had no written history. When the Egyptians conquered a people, they selected just a few of the locals who spoke the native language and taught them how to speak Egyptian. These guys became the local over-lords, so to speak. They were the ones who controlled the normal people, not the Egyptians. The Egyptians avoided contact with most of the salves. The Indians would think the Egyptians were a superior tribe from somewhere. Maybe they even thought of them as Gods."

"Yeah, that makes sense," Maggie said.

Adam said, "Here's something of interest. Pack-i-tha-awi, is the man who made the Grand Canyon. There was a big flood covering the earth. He took a knife and cut into the ground to drain the flood waters into the Ocean. This cut created the canyon."

I let out a laugh, and said, "He must have been one big dude with a big knife to dig out the Grand Canyon. But what's interesting is they mention a flood that covered the world. It reminds me of the great flood and Noah. That information helps to verify there really was a great flood."

Maggie said, "Gee, I think you're right, Jack."

Captain Baldwin walked in and said, "Time to go to dinner, kids."

"Thanks, Daddy," Maggie replied. "Just give me a minute to fix my hair and put on my face."

I said, "Come on Maggie, hurry up, you're not going on a date." I lit a smoke and cracked open a bottle of JD, taking two big gulps right out of the bottle. "Adam, while I am gone, take the dogs out for a walk and keep doing research on the canyon."

"Ok, will do, Grandpa."

"I'll send you up a steak."

By the time I finished my smoke, Maggie was ready, so we proceeded to the dining room to meet the Chief. Maggie looked pretty damn good. She cleans up nicely for a warrior.

We walked into the dining room and our hosts were having a drink. The drinks looked like gin or vodka martinis because they had olives in them. They stood up to greet us and everyone shook hands. After introductions, the Chief asked, "Is this beautiful woman your right-hand man?"

I said, "Yes. I don't go anywhere without her." Stevens and the Chief couldn't keep their eyes off her. Maggie had on her skin tight black SWAT clothing with a sidearm strapped on her hip. We never go anywhere without a weapon. Sitting down we ordered a round of drinks. Maggie had what I did, a double shot of JD on the rocks. George just had a glass of water.

Chief Seibert said, "Cheers gentlemen, and Maggie." We raised our glasses and repeated cheers. "Now tell me, who are you people?"

"Well Chief, I'm in charge of this expedition and the weapons expert." The Chief looked at me with a doubtful expression. "Captain Baldwin is in charge of the Special Ops force. Maggie is my bodyguard and dog handler."

"And what is your rank, Jack?"

"I'm not in the Military. I work for the DOD Weapons Retrieval Unit."

I pulled out the letter from Captain Sessions of the Army Rangers and handed it to Seibert. He read it and handed it back to me.

"That letter doesn't tell me shit about you guys and what you're looking for."

The waitress came over and interrupted our discussion. We ordered dinner and I requested an extra steak to be delivered to room 107 for Adam.

Chief Seibert took a sip of his drink and said, "I checked with the Arizona National Guard and they don't know anything about you guys. So, who are you and what are you doing here?"

Maggie said, "Hey, can I have another drink? I didn't know this was gonna be a business meeting."

Seibert said, "Honey, this isn't about business. It's about National Security."

I said, "Ok Chief, here's the story. We're based at a secret location in Florida called Fort Desoto, on Tocabaga Island. Don't ask where it is because it's classified. A little over a month ago some top secret weapons were stolen by terrorists from Mac Dill Air Force Base, in Tampa. We were assigned to retrieve those weapons and terminate the terrorists, at any cost."

"Ok, now we're getting somewhere. Please proceed." Seibert said.

"This Special Ops group is the best of the best that we have for this type of operation. We've tracked these guys all the way from Florida, and know they are headed north towards the Grand Canyon."

"What type of weapons are they?"

"I can't tell you that because it's classified."

Stevens said, "See Chief, that's what they always say when a nuke is involved."

"Is it a nuke, Mr. Gunn?"

I looked him directly in the eyes. "That's classified information. You understand that, don't you, Chief?"

"Yes, I understand what classified means. At least tell me why are they going to the canyon?"

"We don't know for sure, but there are two big dams on the Colorado River. There's the Glenn Canon Dam in Utah and the Hoover Dam in Arizona. I can only tell you what we're after could change the destiny of the United States, if we don't stop them."

"Well Jack, you convinced me that this is a serious problem. How else can we help you? You need some more men?"

Baldwin spoke up, "Thanks for the offer. No offense, but your men would just get in the way. We're a well-oiled team that moves light and fast."

I butted in, "Chief, there is something you can do. We need you to block all the roads going up to the canyon. Stop all the traffic until we return or notify you because it's going to be very dangerous up there."

"Shit, we already have roadblocks up so that's not a problem. There's only four major roads leading to the canyon and we have each one covered. It makes wonder how these terrorists got by us?"

I said, "They came across the desert thought Navajo country and got on Route 89, bypassing Flagstaff."

"Yeah, that explains how they got around us."

Just then our dinner order came. We enjoyed a beef steak dinner with a baked potato and green beans. I dripped a little steak sauce over some of it. The steak was an inch thick juicy Porterhouse, which melted in my mouth.

While eating, Seibert asked, "So, what's your story, Maggie?"

Maggie glanced up with her mouth full, chomping away. She couldn't speak a word as she washed down the steak with a drink of water. Maggie licked her red lips and let out a giggle. "Excuse me, but I haven't had a steak this good in a year."

"I'm glad you're enjoying it," the Chief replied. "What is a beautiful woman like you doing with the Special Forces?"

"Well, it's kind of a long story." Maggie thought for a moment. "I'm a dog trainer so I decided to join the Army. I was selected to join the Special Ops group because of Jack and Captain Baldwin. They needed some super dogs and that's what I train."

"And you're also Jack's personal bodyguard. How did that happen?"

I took Maggie off the hook by telling him, "Maggie is one tough cookie. Don't let her looks fool you. She has terminated more men in the last year than anyone I know."

The Chief nodded in approval and asked, "How many terrorists did you say you're following?"

Baldwin answered, "Originally there were twenty-six of them. We terminated eleven of them, so fifteen are still on the loose. We'll terminate all of them sooner or later."

"Let's hope it's sooner." Siebert raised his glass. We raised ours and Maggie said, "Here's to sooner."

After finishing up dinner, the Chief said, "I'm satisfied our money is being well spent helping you men out."

We all shook hands and I said, "Thank you for your support, Chief. We'll be in touch." He gave Maggie a hug.

"Thank you, gentlemen. God Bless you and good hunting. Anything you need let Officer Stevens know."

"Roger that, Chief," Baldwin said. "See you tomorrow, Stevens."

After bidding them a goodnight, we proceeded to our rooms. Baldwin said, "Goodnight, I'm gonna watch a movie."

Maggie, who was sleeping in the same room with Adam and I, proceeded to our room with me. She stopped me from opening the door by touching my arm. We were standing in the hallway, outside our room. Maggie said, "That went … pretty well." Maggie was slurring her words from too many drinks.

"Yep, it sure did," I said.

Maggie grabbed me by the shoulders and pulled me in towards her, kissing me hard on the lips. "I love you, Jack Gunn."

"I know, and I love you, Maggie. But we can never be lovers."

"Damn you anyhow. You're so righteous, so pure. I know you want me, so do something about it."

"Maggie, you're drunk. I admit that I want you. Any man would, but then we wouldn't be friends anymore. I value your friendship and loyalty. Let's go to sleep, it's been a long day." Maggie didn't say another word as I opened the door, but she did give me a friendly punch in the arm.

As we entered the room, Adam excitedly said, "I found out some important stuff." I noticed the empty plate and the dogs gnawing on a steak bone. "Oh, thanks for the steak, it was great. I shared it with the dogs."

"What did you find out?" I asked, as I rubbed his head messing up his hair.

Adam turned on the computer pad. "I found out that the Havasupai and Hualapai have found a lot of caves in the canyon. They stated that some of the naturally made caves were modified by man. Someone, it doesn't say who, interviewed the Indians who said many of the caves had strange markings or writing on them."

"I think we need to talk to these people."

"I agree. They might be able to help us," Maggie said, after she flopped on the bed.

"Maybe, but these people don't like talking about the caves. They won't go in the caves because they considered them off limits, due to their beliefs," Adam commented.

"So you're telling me that the Indians have never gone into any of the caves," I said.

"That's what it says. But maybe some were curious and did go in the caves."

I nodded in agreement. "Yeah, you bet they did. Probably the Chiefs and Medicine men went inside the caves to try and gain knowledge for themselves. They wanted to be more powerful than the common person.

Knowledge is power, so they sought to gain any type of information that would give them an edge."

"Maybe the Indians took the treasure. Maybe they took the Ark," Maggie said.

Adam replied, "Maybe, but I doubt it. They would believe it was the property of the Gods. I don't think they would touch it and I don't think God would let them touch it."

"So which tribe should we visit first?" I asked.

"I think the Havasupai Tribe is the best to visit first. If we don' find anything out, then we'll go to the Hualapai Tribe. Of course, they are very close to each other since they are neighbors. They probably marry women from each other's tribes to keep from inbreeding."

"Do they speak English?"

"Yes, I believe so. As far as trails go, here is what I found. On the rim, the main trails and roads are: Rim Trail, Hermit Road, Desert View Road, and part of Bright Angel Point Trail. Trails going down into the canyon are: Hermit, Hulalapai, New Hance, North Kaibab, South Kaibab, Tanner, Bright Angel, and Havasu Canyon Trail.

"The only trail that you can take an ATV into the canyon on is the Bright Angel Trail. It's the only one wide enough. The other trails are too steep, narrow, and dangerous, even on foot."

"Bright Angel is the only one?"

"Yes, but you can go to Supai City on the Havasu Trail, but that's not part of the National Park property.

It's owned by the Havasupai Tribe. After Supai City the trail gets too narrow for an ATV."

"What's Supai City again?"

"It's the capital of the tribe and is at the bottom of Havasu Canyon, which is really part of the Grand Canyon. Most of the tribe lives there. The Havasu River runs down the cliffs and through this canyon into the Colorado River."

It was getting late so Maggie and I had one more drink and we all hit the hay. Tomorrow was going to be a big day because we would arrive at the Grand Canyon before sunset. We'd have to be on our toes watching for the nomads who wanted to steal the treasure of God.

# ONGTUPQA
## MAY 29, 2026

We obtained five ATVs, compliments of the Police Chief, hooked the trailers up to our trucks, and took off to the canyon. Maggie and Adam were excited to see the canyon because I had told them so much about it. It's a two hour drive from Flagstaff, reaching an altitude of about 7,500 feet.

*The Grand Canyon was carved by the Colorado River, so they say. Most people know it is located in the state of Arizona. It is managed by National Park Services, the Hualapai Tribe, the Havasupai people, and the Navajo Nation. Each have their own areas to manage and maintain.*

*The Grand Canyon is 277 miles long, up to 18 miles wide, and attains a depth of over a mile deep. The processes that formed the Grand Canyon are still debated by geologists. Most believe the Colorado River started carving out the canyon five million years ago.*

*For thousands of years, the area has been inhabited by Native Americans. They can be traced as far back as 1,200 BC, as proven by the artifacts found in the canyon. There are an estimated 2,000 unexplored caves. The natives considered the Grand Canyon a holy site. History books say the first known European to visit the Grand Canyon was Garcia Lopez de Cardenas, in 1540. He was a conquistador from Spain. We now know he wasn't the first, since the Knights Templar visited the canyon in 1350.*

I've been to many places in my life. In my younger days I visited the Great Wall, the Pyramids, Niagara Falls, the Black Hills, and Yellowstone Stone, to name a few. Only one place made me say, 'Holy shit!' The Grand Canyon is the most spectacular sight in the whole world. It is a holy place where you are humbled by power of God and nature.

Entering the park, I noted a sign that read: CLOSED. Of course, the park was closed since the collapse of the Federal Government because there was no money to support the National Park system. The gates, which should be shut to keep people out, were busted open. We drove past the gates and observed a few cars running around on the main park road.

We arrived at the South Rim Visitor Center. There were a few cars in the visitors' parking lot. Everyone, including the Warriors, ran to see the spectacular sight. I walked behind them, but I could hear what they said. They uttered the same words that I did when I was twelve years old.

*The sight of the canyon brought back memories. In the old days, very few people went to the Grand Canyon, mainly because it was a transportation issue. You had to have a good car or truck. You had to be an adventurer. My Dad didn't have the best car but he took care of it and knew how to fix it. It was a 1954 Chevy with a six cylinder motor. Dad wasn't afraid of anything, especially going on a three-week camping trip to the middle of nowhere. He knew how to do everything.*

*I recall we camped out in a Sear's tent and cooked over the open fire. If my memory serves me right, only four other campers were at the canyon at that time. Everyone had tents, because RVs didn't exist. You didn't need a reservation or permit to camp.*

*When we went camping, everyone had a job to do. Dad gave us boys the privilege of putting up the tent and digging a drainage ditch around it in case of rain, which we did with great pride. Then we had to blow up the air mattresses and lay out the sleeping bags inside the tent. My brothers and I collected firewood from the dead pine trees. Since I was the oldest, I got to start the fire. I thought that was the most important job. Dad taught me how to start a fire and keep it burning. Those were some of the best days of my life. Thanks, Dad.*

Maggie shouted, "Jack, this is incredible! It's the most beautiful thing I have ever seen."

About twenty other people were meandering about the rim, looking at the sights. When they saw us dressed in our SWAT gear, loaded down with weapons, they quickly beat a path back to their cars.

Adam said, "The canyon is really massive."

I asked, "Baldwin, what do you think?"

He replied, "I've seen a lot of things, all over the world, but this takes the cake. It's so large I wonder where to start looking for the treasure."

"Ok, I got some ideas. Let's mount up and head to the Bright Angel Lodge. We'll make that our HQ and operate out of there, because it's close to the trail we're going to use."

Needless to say, the lodge was officially closed, so we opened it. The stores and concession stands had been looted and ransacked. The lodge rooms were cabin-like structures, and we took twelve of them, making ourselves at home. We had to clean the rooms up because they hadn't been used in a while. Baldwin posted security, covering the cabins and vehicles. He had his crew unload the ATVs and bring them to the cabins.

I called a meeting with Baldwin, Pete, Maggie, and Adam to discuss our plan. Adam printed out eight copies of a satellite map which showed the canyon and trails.

I said, "George, what I suggest is have your men do a recon on Hermit Road, Rim Trail, and Desert View Road before it gets dark. You and I will take a look at Bright Angel Trail to check for ATV tracks."

Pete asked, "Boss, what do you think?"

"Take two ATVs to cover each trail and use two men on each patrol to recon those roads. Have them report in if they see any nomads," Baldwin ordered.

"Roger that, Boss." Pete left to hand out the maps and give his men Baldwin's orders.

After grabbing some binoculars, Baldwin and I walked outside, heading towards the Bright Angel Trailhead. Walking up to the canyon rim, we stood there observing the sight. He said, "Look at that tower shaped like a pyramid," as he pointed in a slight easterly direction.

"That, my friend is Isis Temple. The treasure could be hidden in a cave on Isis." We proceeded to look at the temple through the binoculars.

"That thing is gigantic."

"Yeah, it's big alright."

Proceeding down the trail we ran into a few people hiking up Bright Angel, so I stopped them and asked, "Are you coming from the bottom of the canyon?"

One replied, "Yes, why?"

"Did you see anyone else, a group of men on ATVs?"

"No. We didn't see anyone else. Why, is there a problem?"

I advised them to leave the park because we had reports that terrorists were here. They quickly walked away. I was sure they would also tell others about the terrorists. The last thing we needed was for some innocent people to become involved in this mess.

"George, radio your men and advise them to tell everyone they see that terrorists are here. Tell them to leave the park immediately to be safe." George thought that was a good idea, and he did so.

Reaching the trailhead I said, "One thing that bothers me is the area here on the rim was a lot different back in 1350. We might have trouble finding a Hooked X, here."

"Yeah, good point. We'll just have to keep our eyes peeled."

Proceeding down the trail, it starts off gradually and then becomes steeper before you pass through the first tunnel. We saw the ATV tracks in the soft dirt. The nomads had definitely gone down Bright Angel Trail.

We both looked down the trail using the spy glasses but didn't see a soul, except for a few people who were hiking down into the abyss. Turning around, we started back up.

Bright Angel Trail is supposed to be an easy one compared to the others. We only went down about half a mile on the eight-mile long trail. The incline is pretty steep, and at an altitude of almost 8,000 feet, it takes the wind right out of you. My smoking didn't help matters any, or the fact that I had on 30 pounds of gear.

I recall hiking this trail with my son and daughter years ago. Even at a much younger age, and in better shape than now, it kicked the shit out of me. It took me two days to recover from sore muscles and dehydration. I was glad we had the ATVs.

Hiking back up, reaching the top of the trail, I said, "George, I gotta rest a minute." We sat down on a bench and I took a drink of water.

George commented, "That's a tough little hike. It reminds me of the mountains in Afghanistan. Actually, the whole terrain does with its desert-like appearance."

"Let's scan around in the canyon and see if we can spot these guys."

George said, "I doubt we'll see anyone, but let's give it a try."

I was looking at the base of Isis Temple while we strolled past the cabins, stopping in front of the looted stores. I commented, "It's a shame they looted and ransacked this place. It used to be a nice place for people to eat and relax, while viewing the canyon."

As we were scanning the canyon, five men came around the building, laughing and shouting to each other. When they saw us, about fifty feet away, they suddenly shut up. I saw that they were well armed with AK47s. I noticed they had black bandanas wrapped around their foreheads, similar to those worn by the nomads.

They froze, glaring at us. Baldwin and I turned to face them. I said, "Hi guys. Do you know that the park is closed?"

One of them spoke up, "No, we didn't. Actually we're waiting for our friends to come back out of the canyon. We can't leave without them."

"When did they go down?"

"They went down other day. Are you guys cops or something?"

"Yeah, kind of," I said.

The biggest of the bunch said, "Well, let's see your badges."

Baldwin said, "We're with the Army, so we don't have any badges."

"The Army? What are you doing here?"

"Just checking on everything and asking people to leave because the park is closed."

"You don't have any jurisdiction here?"

Baldwin replied, "Oh yes we do, my friend. This is government property and we're assigned here."

Our M4's were hanging on three point slings in front of us. I moved my hand to the pistol grip and flipped off the safety with my thumb. Out of the corner of my eye, I saw George do the same.

The five men also saw us put our hands on the pistol grips. We didn't point our guns at them, but I was getting ready to. George and I knew who these men were.

I told them, "Put your weapons on the ground and don't try anything stupid."

"Why do you want us to do that," the big dope asked.

"Because we said so," Baldwin replied. "Put the weapons down, now!"

The same jerk said, "There's five of us and two of you. You put your guns down."

"Look, you guys don't wanna fuck with us, you don't stand a chance. Put your weapons down now!"

It was a tense situation as we stared each other down. Then they made a dumb move. Three of them started to raise their AK's. My sixth sense told me they were going to fire.

Before they could level their guns and fire, Baldwin and I got the drop on them, because we were expecting them to do that. Swiftly, we swung our M4s around, aiming from the hip, and let loose with short bursts. Three dorks immediately fell to the ground. The other two men, on the left, dropped their AK's like hot potatoes, raising their hands, surrendering to us. The gun fight, if you can call it one, was over in five seconds.

Baldwin ordered, "Get down flat on your stomachs, with hands over your head." They complied instantly and he zip-cuffed each one, with hands behind their backs, while I stood guard. George stood them up, one at a time, and frisked them. No other weapons were found, but one had a radio.

I said, "It looks like we have a couple of prisoners to interrogate."

By this time, a few curious people wandered over to check what was going on. Baldwin told them, in a commanding voice, "There's nothing to see here. Everyone should leave the park because it's not safe." With that comment, everyone beat a path away from us. Hopefully they left the park.

We were standing in front of a concessions store. George dragged the three bodies inside, out of sight, while I watched the two dirtbags.

We took them inside and told them to sit down at the counter. I sat down and lit up a smoke. I offered one to them, but they declined. No one said a word for about five minutes. The nomads closely watched us. I could tell they were afraid and would tell us everything we wanted to know.

These guys were young and I placed them to be twenty something. They were greenhorns and had probably never been in a gun battle, let alone killed anyone.

George asked, "Do you have any other buddies here?"

The young man with blond hair and child-like face replied, "Yeah. They went into the canyon."

"How many are in the canyon?"

"Ten went down on ATVs."

"Are any more up here with you?"

"No, it was just us five. They left us here to guard the trucks."

The numbers added up because we knew there were fifteen of them. I asked, "Where did they go in the canyon?"

The dark-haired ugly one spoke. "We don't know exactly. They went looking for a treasure or something like that."

"They don't know shit so let's just terminate them now," George said.

The blond punk said, "We don't know anything, so you don't need to kill us."

The other one said, "Please don't kill us! We'll leave and won't come back."

I said, "I'm sorry, boys, but we can't take that chance," as I walked behind them and drew out my Glock.

"Come on, Mister, please give us a break."

"I am giving you a break … a break from life." I swiftly shot each one in the back of the head. They flopped over on the countertop banging their heads as they hit. Blood splattered around the area, messing up the counter, but no one was going to eat there anyway.

George and I dragged the all bodies into a back storeroom and locked the door with a key we found. I didn't feel any remorse about killing these little punks. If you play with the big boys, that's what can happen to you. Besides, kidnapping means the death penalty in my book. Baldwin didn't say a word. He knew we had no choice but to kill them.

We found the bandit's cars in front of the lodge and disabled them. It was getting late, so we walked back to the cabins.

It was almost dark when the patrols came back. They reported there weren't any signs of nomads. We told them about our encounter and advised them we were on the right track.

Baldwin set up security by assigning two men to guard the trucks, two men to guard the cabins, and one man to watch Bright Angel Trial in case the nomads came back up during the night. They would rotate every two hours with the other Warriors so everyone would get some rest.

I went to the room and Adam was still on the computer. He said, "The Indian name for the Grand Canyon is Ongtupqa."

"What does that mean? " I asked, as I poured a double shot of JD.

"I don't know I'll look it up tomorrow. I'm too tired now and I have a headache." I gave him some aspirin and we went to sleep. Maggie was already in dreamland.

I couldn't sleep and stayed up for a while longer. I thought, *it was too bad those young men chose a life of crime.*

# THE HAVASUPAI
## MAY 30, 2026

Baldwin and I had a meeting at 7 am. I said, "The nomads will be coming out of the canyon any day now. They'll run out of food."

"Yeah, I've been thinking about that. The Bright Angel Trail is a perfect killing zone," George stated.

"What do you mean?"

"Come on, I'll show you."

We hiked back to the start of the trail. Baldwin said, "From here we can see more than a mile. These guys are coming up on a narrow trail with no place to hide. Once they come around that bend, on the trail down there, we'll terminate them before they get to the tunnel. I killed a lot of Isis guys using the same method."

"Yeah, good idea. That's about 800 yards away. I could use the Cobb 50."

"Yes, for sure. But don't fire at the lead vehicle. Fire at the last ATV first, taking them out in reverse order. That blocks the trail so they can't back up and escape. Since there has to be two men on an ATV, maybe you can kill two with one shot. I've done that many times. The big fifty bullet will rip right through both men. Anyway, you shoot the last one first and then move forward, taking one out at a time. Most likely the ATVs in the lead won't hear the shots over the noise of the motors. They probably won't even turn around to look behind them on that narrow trail because they're afraid of going over the cliff. That's at least a 2,000-foot drop."

"That makes a lot of sense, George."

"Then, if any men do make it to the tunnel, we'll be waiting to ambush them. Once inside the tunnel it's a perfect killing zone."

"Ok, that's a good plan. We can see them coming miles away so that gives us time to set up."

"Now, what else do we need to do today?" Baldwin asked.

"We need to start looking for the Hooked X located somewhere on the rim. It's a big job and there's a lot of ground to cover. We might not even find one because this place has changed so much since the time of the Templars."

"So, what should my men be looking for to find the X?"

"They need to check every large stone or rock, along the rim, that sticks up enough that the rising sun would strike it. We'll cover the south rim first and if we don't find it we'll have to go around the canyon to the east and north."

"Man, that's a lot of ground to cover."

"Yes it is, but we have 20 days to find it."

We had nineteen men to search for the Hooked X. Ten would proceed using the ATVs, and nine would search on foot, working in teams of two or three.

Baldwin said, "Hey, I just remembered we got the nomads radio so we can listen in. I'll have one of my men monitor it. Maybe they'll tip us off when they're heading up."

"Good idea, that'll give us a jump on them." We hiked back to the cabins to get some chow.

Maggie and I needed to meet with the Indians to find out if they knew anything about the caves, treasure, Templars, or Egyptians coming to the canyon. If they did, would they tell us.

Adam stayed in the cabin, searching for information on the Army World Web. Maggie and I mounted up to make the drive to the Havasupai Reservation which is about 200 miles by car, but only 20 miles by the way the crow flies. It's not easy to get there by car. We drove one of the Hummers and brought along the dogs for added protection.

The Havasupai capital is named Supai Village, which is located within Havasu Canyon, on the Havasu River, which is a tributary on the south side of the Colorado River. The village is not accessible by road. The Havasupai Tribe administers the land, which is outside the jurisdiction of Grand Canyon National Park.

To get there we had to backtrack south on Route 83 to I-40 and then proceed west to Seligman exit. There, we pick up Indian Route 18, which takes you to a parking lot and the end of the road, bringing you to the reservation. This is the start of the dirt trail that leads to Supi Village.

We arrived five hours later, at 2 pm, because the top speed of the Hummer was only 45 mph. Just as I suspected, a group of Indians were sitting at a roadblock, in the parking lot, at the head of the trail.

The Indians were positioned about 100 feet away from where we parked. They were watching as Maggie and I jumped out of the Humvee with the dogs and stretched our legs. We clipped our M4s on the slings and put the dogs on a leash. Right away, they took a much needed leak. Speaking of leaks, I had to take one also. I glanced around the parking lot and saw a porta-potty on the side of the lot, about 50 feet away, near the Indians.

I said, "Maggie, I gotta take a leak."

"Me too. You go first and see if it's safe."

I went in to relieve myself. Coming out, I glanced over at the Indians. They sat in the shade of a tree glaring at us.

"Jack, is it safe for me to go in?"

"Yeah, it's ok. It smells bad, but the only snake I saw was a trouser snake." I let out a chuckle.

"Very funny."

A few minutes later, Maggie came out with a disgusted look on her face. "That thing was fifthly."

Maggie was holding both dogs as we walked up to the Indian greeting party. The Indians didn't stand up or speak to us until I said, "Hello, my name is Jack Gunn and this is Maggie. We're with the Army and we're staying for a few weeks at Grand Canyon Park."

I glanced around at the men. Most of them appeared to older, except one man who looked to be in his twenties. They all wore cowboy hats and had long black hair.

Speaking perfect English, the young Indian said, "I am Eddie Moon. What do you want?" He stood up and stepped over to me.

Eddie was a good looking man, about 6 feet tall. He was thin, but strong looking. His hair hung straight down from under his white cowboy hat. His skin was dark from years of exposure to the bright sun. He wore a blue long-sleeve shirt and jeans. I noticed he had on hiking boots. Eddie had a friendly looking face, which made a good impression on me.

"We'd like some information," I said.

"Ok shoot, what do you want to know?" Eddie asked.

"Has anyone ever heard of a treasure being in the canyon?"

"Of course, a treasure is a big rumor or lie that the white man made up." All the older men laughed at his comment.

"Ok, so there's no treasure."

Eddie said, "Look, if there was some big treasure, do you think we'd be living in this place?"

I pulled out a picture of the Knights Templar dressed in the old-style armor. "Do you have any legends of men dressed like this coming to the canyon a long time ago?"

Eddie turned around and he spoke to the other men who stood up to see the picture. The conversation went on for a short time. It seemed to me some of the men appeared to be very interested.

Eddie Moon said, "Yes, we have heard stories from our Chief and Medicine Man about men dressed in metal coming here long ago. They were thought to be Gods at the time."

"Are you talking about the Spanish?"

"No, this is long before the Spanish. The men helped us and gave us horses and seeds to grow beans."

"Did they bring anything with them?"

"The story goes, they went into the canyon on Bright Angel Trail with supplies and came out many months later. Many of them did not come out. They were buried in the canyon caves, proving they were not Gods. That is the story."

"Do you know where these caves are?"

"Yes, they are in the temples. That is all can tell you. We never go to the caves because it is not good to bother the dead spirits."

Pulling out a picture of the Egyptian hieroglyphs, I showed it to him. "I have one more question. Have any of you ever seen these symbols carved in a canyon wall or cave entrance?"

Eddie said, "Before I answer, what do you have for us? It is not polite to obtain information without giving something in return." Eddie looked at the dogs. "How about, one of those dogs?"

"No, we can't do that because they're my family."

"Then how about one of your guns."

I thought about it for a minute. "These are the only guns we have. How about, I give you a thousand green backs."

Eddie hesitated for a minute. "Ok, I agree."

Maggie pulled the money out of her pocket. It was all in hundred dollar bills. She handed it to me and I passed it to Eddie Moon. He smiled, took the money, and passed it to an old man sitting behind him.

"We have seen the strange writing in many places in the canyon. If you look for it, you can find it."

"Thank you for the information, Eddie Moon."

"You are welcome, Jack Gunn. By the way, three days ago some other men came here asking about caves and treasure. I told them the same thing."

"Ok, thanks again."

"Hey, if you need a guide around the canyon, let me know. They hired my friend, Stephen."

"Eddie, those are dangerous men, so I fear your friend may be in danger if they find any treasure."

"Thank you for that information. But I think Stephen can take care of himself."

"How much is your guide service?" I asked.

Eddie said, "For me, it's a thousand per day."

"Ok, you're hired. Can you leave now?" I had a good feeling about Eddie Moon. I thought he could be a big help to us finding our way around the canyon, because we didn't know crap about the canyon trails.

"Yes, I am ready to go. Just let me get my gear and gun."

"Good, let's go."

Eddie collected some gear, he put in a small bag, and followed us to the truck. I glanced at his gun and it was an old 22 caliber Winchester rifle.

We beat it out of the reservation. I wanted to get back before it got dark. While riding along, Maggie asked, "Eddie, how well do you know the canyon?"

"I know it like the back of my hand."

I asked, "How well do you know Isis Temple?"

"I know a secret trail that goes up Isis Temple. Without me you would never find it. But I will not go into the caves with you."

"You said caves. Do you mean there is more than one?"

"Yes, many are in Isis Temple. I will not go inside them."

"That's ok, I understand. I am glad I hired you."

The dogs were in the back seat with Eddie and they seemed to like him. Observing Eddie in the mirror, he was petting them. He asked, "What are the names of your dogs?"

While pointing at them, Maggie replied, "The big one is Adolf and the other is Freda."

If the dogs liked Eddie, that made me more certain he was an alright guy. He seemed to be a straight shooter, so to speak. Someone I could trust.

We arrived back at the canyon just before twilight. I introduce Eddie to Baldwin and Pete. Eddie noticed that we had ATVs. He commented, "These will make the hike out a lot easier."

"I've hiked the canyon before so I know how hard it is," I said.

As the sunset and the canyon grew dark, the colors given off were spectacular. Maggie, Eddie, and I watched the show as we sat on the edge of the cliff in front of the cabins.

Eddie said, "The Hopi and us call the Grand Canyon, ONGTUPQA."

"What does it mean?"

"The Canyon of Life. We believe human life started in the canyon."

I commented, "I've always loved the Grand Canyon. It's so amazing. You're lucky to live here."

"You may think so, but I do not. I want to get a real job and see the world," Eddie said. "I've been trapped here my whole life."

"Eddie, believe me, you are lucky. It's a mean world, full of people who would do you harm. Remember, the grass isn't always greener on the other side of the fence. Here you have security and your tribe to help each other. Your life is not complicated, so you can enjoy God's wonders."

Maggie said, "He's right, Eddie."

"I like you guys," Eddie said. "I think I can trust you because you seem like honest people."

I told him. "I like you, Eddie."

"I like you too," Maggie said.

"My problem is I can't find a wife here. There are no women available to marry, who are worthwhile. It is very frustrating. My mother and father died years ago, when I was fifteen. I want my own family."

"Well, you need to find a wife at another tribe," I said.

It was as if he heard our conversation. Out of nowhere, Black Horse appeared from the darkness. "Jack, who is this new man?" he asked.

"Black Horse, I'd like you to meet Eddie Moon. He's from the Havasupai Tribe, located here at the canyon." They shook hands, while checking each other out. "Black Horse is the Medicine Man for the Comanche Nation, in Oklahoma."

Eddie said, "It is nice to meet Black Horse. I have heard many stories about the Comanche Tribe. Your tribe was once the most feared by whites as well as the Indians."

"Yes, in the old days we Comanche' were a very powerful tribe, until the white man came."

"I would like to visit the Comanche Nation in Oklahoma. I have never been outside of Arizona. Do you have many young women who are free to marry?"

Black Horse laughed. Yes, we have many women because our tribe is very large. You are welcome to come and visit anytime."

It was getting late, and I was tired from driving eight hours. I needed a drink to relax. I said, "Eddie, you can sleep in cabin number fourteen, because it's empty."

"If you like, you can sleep in my cabin with me and my son. His name is Billy," Black Horse said.

"Thank you very much, but I will sleep outside under the stars." Eddie opened his bag, pulled out a blanket, and laid it on a big flat rock. "That is my bed tonight."

Maggie said, "Jack, before we go to bed let's have snack because we didn't eat all day."

"Yeah, good idea, cause I'm hungry. Do we have any Spam left?" I asked.

"Yep, I'll bring out a few cans with some crackers. You like Spam Eddie?"

"I like it better than steak, but we don't eat much Spam."

After sharing a meal with the two Indians, we retired for the night. Tomorrow would be another busy day.

# HOLY LIGHT
## MAY 31, 2026

The birds woke me up. It was 5 am and they were chirping away. I peeked out the window and spotted Eddie sitting on the edge of the canyon. After I made two cups of mud, I went outside and gave him one.

Eddie said, "Thanks, Jack."

I sat down next to him and lit up a smoke. I held the pack out in front of him. "Here, you want one?"

"No thanks. I don't smoke. When are we going into the canyon?"

"You told me that your friend Stephen left with those men a few days ago."

"Yep, that's right."

"Well, we're waiting for them to come up before we go down. But don't worry, you're getting paid for every day that you're with us, even while sitting here on the rim."

"Wow, that's great."

"I told you yesterday that the men Stephen went with are really bad guys. They are very dangerous and are trying to steal the treasure of God."

"You keep talking about this treasure. What is it exactly?"

"It's the most important treasure the world has ever known. Whoever finds it could control the destiny of the United States and maybe the world. If it gets into the wrong hands, it could be disastrous. Do you know what the Ark of the Covenant is?"

"Wasn't that the golden box that the Israelites carried around. It had the Ten Commands in it. That's about all I know."

"Well you're right, but it was also a powerful weapon which was controlled by God. God would talk to the people using the Ark. It's one of the most holy items that Israelites and Christians believe in."

"How does that affect the destiny of the United States?" Eddie asked.

"No one knows for sure what could happen if it got into the wrong hands and someone opened it. We just wanna make sure no one does that. We just want to make sure the Ark is safe."

"I understand your concern. But what makes you think it is in the canyon."

"We believe that the Knights Templar brought it here with other treasure items in 1350. We have a holy relic called the Sword of Jerusalem which has a map that pointed the way here. This sword was made seven-hundred years ago. It's a holy item blessed by God. It has strange wondrous powers if you believe in our Lord."

"I know nothing of your God. Most Havasupai do not believe in such a thing."

"Here's a question. Have you ever seen a Hooked X?" I drew a picture in the dirt.

Eddie looked at it and replied, "I think so, but I don't recall where. What does it mean?"

"It was used by the Knights Templar. It is the symbol they used to mark that they had been at a location. When you see this mark that implies that the Knights were involved."

"Ok, let me think about."

Maggie came out of the cabin and yelled, "Hey, you guys wanna eat. I made some surprise MREs."

"Let's get some chow, Eddie," I said.

We walked into the small cabin and I introduce Eddie to Adam. They shook hands and Adam said, "After breakfast I have some more information for you, Grandpa."

"That's great, Adam. I hired Eddie to be our guide in the canyon. We'll let him listen to what you have to say."

I grabbed an MRE and gave it to Eddie. He asked, "What is this?"

"Breakfast, you dummy. It's good, just open the bag and eat it."

Eddie sat down on the floor, Indian style, and opened the Beef with Noodles MRE. After a couple of spoonfuls, Eddie confirmed he like it.

I said, "This is what we normally eat. Spam is a treat."

Eddie replied, "This is a treat for me."

After eating, Adam pulled out the computer pad, which was linked to the SAT phone. "Grandpa, here's an interesting story. It's about two backpackers who came into the canyon hiking. They were going to Isis Temple and on the way found a small pyramid made of stones. They wondered who made it and how old it was. It was strange that no one had mentioned this since it appeared to be very old."

Eddie said, "That is true. I have seen this little stone pyramid."

Adam continued, "Once arriving at the foot of Isis, they climbed to an estimated elevation of about 800 feet above the river. From this point they were able to see several caves above them. The openings in the caves appeared to be sealed shut and they were curious about it. They wondered why they were sealed shut."

Eddie said, "All the caves have been sealed by someone."

"Interesting," Adam said. "Since they were expert rock climbers they proceeded further up Isis to the view one of the caves. Reaching the entrance, it was also blocked. The cave entrance appeared to be man-made. On the entrance walls they observed strange writing. It appeared someone had tried to chisel out the writing making it unreadable. Most people didn't believe their story, but as one person said, why would anyone make it up."

"That is very interesting," I said. "It confirms there are caves in Isis. What else you got, Adam.

"I told you there are caves in Isis," Eddie commented.

Adam continued, "There isn't much about a hidden treasure in Isis Temple. There's an article that states how strange it is that Egyptians names were given to many of the carved out mountains in the canyon. It's also strange that all are located in the so-called forbidden zone. This is the area that hikers are not permitted. Also, all the caves are off limits. No one is allowed inside the caves."

Eddie commented, "Our tribe can go anywhere we like."

"Interesting. Go ahead, Adam," I said.

"One article stated that it's weird there are no maps showing trails in the area of Isis Temple or any of the so-called temples," Adam said.

Eddie spoke up. "There are trails going to Isis. I don't know why they aren't on a map."

"The government doesn't want anyone going there, that's why," I said. "Look, we don't know if the treasure is at Isis Temple or not. It could be somewhere else, but it certainly isn't in the cave that G.E. Kincaid found. That cave has already been looted by the Smithsonian Institute."

Adam advised, "Speaking of that, a couple of articles stated that the location of the cave given by Kincaid was a lie. He provided a false location so people wouldn't go to the real location, which is Isis Temple, according to the article."

"What about the other Temples? Did you read anything about them?"

"Yes, there is a YouTube video that shows the Temples and Towers with Egyptian names. The peaks clearly match the star pattern of the Orion Constellation. They match the position of the Orion stars perfectly, which suggests the canyon pyramids were not entirely formed by natural erosion from the river. They were helped by man or aliens. You have to watch this video; it's all mapped out to see."

I said, "That is very weird because the belt of Orion is what the pyramids in Egypt match. The Orion Constellation is a key. If the formations in the canyon match exactly the star pattern of Orion, then it can be assumed that it has something to do with aliens, or where the so-called Gods came from. This proves a connection to the Egyptians. That's incredible."

"I have two more stories from an article in Treasure Magazine. Some men claim they found Montezuma's treasure in the Grand Canyon, so they think."

"Montezuma was the King of the Aztec's in Mexico, which was invaded in the 1500's by Hernando Cortez, who was from Spain," I commented.

"Yeah, that's right. Anyway, these stories are believable. The article states that in 1867 a man named James White drifted ashore on a make-shift raft close to a small farming town, south of the canyon. It is believed that he passed through the Grand Canyon on this flimsy raft. He was in pretty bad shape and the town people nursed him back to health.

"The story goes that he was prospecting north of the canyon and was attacked by Indians, losing all his gear. Making it through the rapids, he was washed ashore in the canyon and wanted to escape the heat. He spotted a cave and crawled inside to rest. A day later, he was found in the cave by some Indians holding torches inside the dark cavern. Looking around the large cavern he saw piles of golden idols, masks, and weapons of all types. The hilts were embedded with gems and made of gold. White had never seen such weapons or jewelry. For some reason, the Indians did not kill him, but gave him some food and sent him on his way down the river. White tried to find the cave again over the years but never did."

I said, "If that story is true, the cave was near the river. He was in bad shape, so he couldn't hike up the cliffs to a cave. But back then, the level of the river was a lot higher than it is now, maybe by a hundred feet. What's the next story?"

"In this story, a man claims he found an Aztec treasure in the canyon. In 1902, a guy named Jake Johnson, who was also a prospector, broke his leg while mining near St. George, Utah. He was near death when he was found by a Paiute Indian and his squaw. They nursed him back to health and he gave them his camping gear for helping him.

"One day while the brave was out hunting, a mountain lion attacked the woman. Johnson happened to be there and killed the cat before the woman was severely injured or killed. Johnson and the Indian became good friends. While Johnson was still recovering, the Indian told many stories about his people. One story was about a great treasure hidden long ago.

"The legend states that an expedition, made up of many warriors, came from the south escorting a long line of men carrying wooden boxes full of treasure. They went into the canyon, descending down the main south rim trail. The treasure was hidden in a cave somewhere. Half of the men came back out of the canyon with just their weapons. The other half of the men remained there guarding the treasure. After many years, the remaining guards married into the local Indian tribes, and started a new life."

"I have heard this story. It is true because some of our people are lighter skinned than others," Eddie said.

Adam glanced at Eddie. "That's interesting. We should a DNA check of those people."

"Yeah, that's a good idea, Adam," I said. "Continue the story."

"Anyway, Johnson didn't believe the treasure story and begged the Indian to see the treasure to prove it really existed. Finally, the Indian agreed to take Johnson to the treasure for saving his wife's life. The Paiute took him on a five day trip by horse. On the fifth day, at sunrise, he blindfolded Johnson and took him down a steep grade. After several hours, they stopped.

"The blindfold was removed after they entered a large cave and he saw a golden treasure from the light of the touches. The Indian told him he could take whatever amount he could carry on his body. Johnson stated that it was clear they were in the Grand Canyon. He had managed to obtain a peek outside the cave, spotting high cliffs and a river. He filled his pockets with gold before he was blindfolded again when they left the cave. After climbing up a steep trail, the blindfold was removed many hours later, when it was dark.

"After this trip the Indian and Johnson parted ways. Johnson went to the town of Pipe Springs and received about $15,000 for his gold. He spent the next seven years searching for the treasure, but never found it again."

I said, "Wow, that's a good story. But there is no proof that it was a treasure brought here by the Aztecs. The Indians didn't even know who the Aztecs were. What is important is the warriors went down the main trail on the south rim. Maybe they went to Isis Temple, and maybe they were the Templars and not Aztecs."

"There's no mention of treasure hidden in any of the other pyramid formations, except for Isis," Adam said. "That's all I have to report."

"Excellent report, Adam. There are many stories about treasure hidden in the canyon, but very few stories about the Templars."

Eddie, who had paid close attention, to the stories, asked, "So, when are we going into the canyon?"

"Like I said, not until your friend comes up with his clients."

"Does Stephen know the secret trail to Isis?"

"Yes, of course. We have been on the trails many times together."

"What does he look like?"

"He looks like an Indian, like me."

What color shirt did he wear?"

"Why do you ask that?"

"Listen to me very carefully. We're going to kill whoever comes out of the canyon. If we know what color of shirt he has on and what he looks like, it may save his life."

Eddie glared at me with a strange expression on his face. It was one of disbelief. "He has long black hair down to his waist. It hangs down straight. He has on a white cowboy hat. He'll either have on a red or blue shirt. Those are the only two colors he will wear."

"Ok, I'll pass that along to the men so they don't shoot him. You may have saved his life."

"Tell me, why do you want to kill these men?"

"Eddie, they're bad guys. They are bandits, kidnappers, and probably murders. They may just kill your friend when they find what they want. Or if they don't find what they want, they might still bump him off. Either way, he's in big trouble."

"Then we need to find Stephen and save him."

Adam said, "We can't do that right now because we're looking for the Hooked X here on the rim."

"What does this Hooked X look like again?"

Adam pulled up a computer picture of the Hooked X carved into a big stone. "It looks like this picture."

Eddie stared at the colored picture for a few minutes. "I have seen that mark."

"Yeah, you told me that already. But where have you seen it?" I asked.

"You will not believe this ... but I think ... at Isis Temple. It was carved above a cave entrance."

"Are you sure? You're not just saying that so we go rescue Stephen, are you?"

"No, honest, Jack. When Adam showed me the picture carved in the rock it jarred my memory. Please, believe me, I would never lie about something like that."

"Ok, I believe you."

By now it was 8 am. Picking up the radio I got ahold of Baldwin, advising him we found the Hooked X. This meant we didn't have to wait for the summer solstice. About thirty minutes later, all the warriors showed up at the cabin, with the exception of those working security.

Eddie told everyone the story how he had seen the X before. Then he added some more information. "It's going to be difficult to ride those ATVs down the trial. They are almost as wide as the trail. The hike up Isis will not be an easy one."

I said, "Yeah, it won't be easy. Eddie, you're used to climbing up and down the canyon at this altitude. The air is very thin. Your lungs and leg muscles have developed so you can hike the canyon with no problem. We're not in as good of shape as you are, so you'll need to take it slow with us tagging along."

"I see your point, Jack. Once we get down to the bottom you can only take the ATVs to the river. It's impossible to cross the river on the Silver Bridge because it is too narrow. We can leave the ATVs at the bottom on this side of the river. After we cross the bridge, there is a hidden small dirt trail. It has hardly been used, so it is not noticeable to most people. It will take us to the cave with the Hooked X. The trail will be difficult to hike with your guns and gear."

"Ok, what else can we expect?"

"I can't explain all the details, but once we get to the base of Isis the trail becomes very difficult and steep."

"Ok, let's pack up and get ready to move out," I said. "Adam, I want you to stay here."

"Grandpa, are you kidding? I have to come along."

Putting my hand on his shoulder, I could see the disappointment in his face. "It's safer if you stay here."

"You don't understand. I had a dream last night. God told me I must go to the cave and bring the sword."

If Adam had a dream and God spoke to him, then I believed him. He has a connection to God that normal people don't have. I have seen his dreams turn into real-life events, like when the Sword of Jerusalem beheaded Christian de Molay.

"Ok then, Adam, you ride with me." I glanced at Maggie and Eddie Moon. "Eddie, you ride with Maggie. Maggie, you take the lead and follow Eddie's directions. George, pick out six men, including you, for the trip to Isis."

Baldwin told Pete he was coming along and ordered him to select four more men. That meant we had a total of ten people on five ATVs going on this adventure. I left the dogs with the Warriors, working security.

After packing up the guns, gear, supplies, and water we motored to Bright Angel Trail and started the descent into the abyss. I had hiked this trail thirty years ago and forgot how bumpy it was. I didn't remember all the stone steps the Park Service had put in. Maybe the steps weren't here when I made the trip. I don't recall.

Of course, when you're on foot you don't notice the bumps and holes in the trail. The path was just wide enough for our small ATVs. The wheels were missing the large rocks, lining the edge of the trail, by inches on both sides. Any slight mistake could spell death if you went over the 3,000-foot cliff. We moved at less than 5 mph most of the time.

*Isis Temple is a pyramid formation north of the south rim. It is about 5 miles directly north of Grand Canyon Village. It lies north of the Colorado River, and is just north of Middle Granite Gorge. Trinity Creek flows due-south at its western border, and its northeast border is flanked by Phantom Creek were Phantom Ranch is located.*

*Isis Temple is part of an uplifted rock formation about 3.5 miles long by 2.0 miles wide. It is a little over 7,000 feet in height. A sub-peak near Isis is named Cheops Pyramid, which is 5,392 feet tall. The Isis Pyramid is erosion resistant cliff-forming Coconino Sandstone.*

We didn't know exactly where we were going, because Eddie never told us. All we knew was we were headed to Isis Temple, but none of us had ever been there, except for the Indian. I did know that the canyon trails are not well-marked and some trails have no markings at all. I directed Adam to use his GPS and mark way points once we arrived at the bottom of the canyon. That way we could find our way back safely if something happened to the Chief.

It was a two-hour bumpy ride, but a scenic one down Bright Angel Trail. Upon reaching the Silver Bridge at the bottom, we spotted the nomads ATVs parked under some trees. We decided to hide our ATVs in the bushes, about a mile away from the bridge. Baldwin damaged the nomad ATVs by stabbing the tires and ripping out the spark plug wires, throwing them into the river.

It was a clear day at the bottom of the canyon and the temperature was a comfortable eighty degrees. We crossed the Silver Bridge over the Colorado River and proceeded up to the northwest, or so it seemed. It was hard to tell because the trails wind around and are not straight. One minute you're heading west and the next east or north. After an hour of climbing, we stopped for a break. Everyone found a rock to sit on and rest.

Eddie said, "From here the hike becomes a little harder, so we'll take a break for a while."

I asked, "Eddie, exactly where is the cave located?" I only knew we were proceeding around the west side of Isis Temple.

"I can't tell you exactly. But it is on the north side, about half way up the mountain. You cannot see it from anywhere until it is in front of you. To reach it, we must hike about three hours until we reach the stone steps. Then we go up the steps which takes us to the cave."

"How much longer till we're at the cave?" Baldwin asked him.

"I think about four hours. Let's move before it gets too hot."

This trail had no markings. It didn't even look like a trail because it was not worn. We started climbing north or northeast on a steep slope. The trail was full of switchbacks until we reached a fifty-foot high vertical cliff. The cliff had hand and footholds to use for climbing.

Eddie warned us. "Be careful, there are a lot of loose stones." We watched him reach the top and then we slowly made our way up, one at a time. The loose shale and unsecured small rocks made your foot slip out of the footholds, raining stones on those below. It was a dangerous climb – one slip you could be badly injured or killed. It was clear that someone had made these footholds, but who?

By the time I reached the top, my arms and legs were shaking from the strain. My fingers were bleeding from being cut by the sharp little shale stones. Once on top, the almost invisible trail continued north-northeast and then it became flat again. It was a good place to take a break considering everyone was exhausted. I opened a bottle of water and took a few big gulps.

The trail was still winding in a general north-northeast direction as we came upon huge boulders, or large blocks of stones, the size of cars that we had to climb over. We could not go around them because on each side there was a cliff that dropped at least 800 feet.

Climbing over these boulders zapped our strength once again.

Finally we reached a flatter area that was very large, but it slanted slightly up hill. The trail appeared to be more or less straight from this point. This area was covered with some grass and Prickly Pear cacti. I assumed this was the top of an Isis arm. We took another break.

Looking up, I could see a sheer wall of rock far ahead. Eddie commented, "It's not much further to the stone steps."

After a thirty-minute rest stop, we proceed up the flat area. The problem was, it went from flat to steep. It became steeper and steeper the further we proceeded up. Because of the loose gravel and shale rocks, each step we took we slid back half a step. We had to bend over and use our hands some of the time, crawling our way up the hill on all fours, like an animal.

We were all out of breath and dead tired, but the Indian kept up a fast pace as we dropped far behind him. It was getting steeper and I estimated the angle was at least 45 degrees now. After taking three or four steps you had to stop and catch your breath. My heart was pounding so fast I could feel it thumping in my chest.

Adam grabbed my arm. "Here Grandpa, I'll help you."

"Thanks, Adam … I'm out of shape for this hike. I forgot … how tough the canyon can be." Neither of us said another word as we gasped for air.

Up ahead we could see the shear wall of rock that was extremely high. It went straight up, making me wonder, *how in the hell are we going to climb that?*

We finally reached the base of the rock wall where everyone plopped down and took in some much needed water. It was much hotter up here and I was sweating like a pig. Looking down the trail, I guessed we were about 3,000 feet from the floor of the canyon.

I asked Eddie, "Are we on Isis now?"

"Yeah, we have been for the last couple of hours."

"How are we gonna get up that cliff? It must be 300 feet high."

"Actually, it's probably higher than that."

Baldwin asked, "So, are we gonna climb that?"

"I already told you. We'll use the stone stairs," Eddie replied.

Glancing around, I said, "I don't see any stairs."

"Of course not. They are not visible from here."

After resting 30 minutes, Eddie got up. "Follow me to the staircase."

Baldwin told everyone to lock and load because the nomads were probably at the top waiting for us. He asked, "Eddie, can they see us down here or when we're going up the stairs?"

"No, because the staircase has switchbacks, and it ends about 200 feet east of the cave, out of sight of the entrance. You cannot see the cave even when you reach the top."

Moving along the vertical cliff, all the stones looked the same, making it appear to be a confusing maze or puzzle. You had to be careful, as we followed in single formation, not to slip or you could tumble down the steep grade to your death. The heat of the sun was radiating off the stone wall making it even hotter. It felt like an oven blasting me in the face.

Eddie abruptly stopped. He said, "Here are the steps."

As I rounded a slight indent in the cliff wall, I turned my head to the right peering at where Eddie was pointing. At first I didn't see them, and then as if by magic the steps appeared in front of me. The stone staircase was an incredible sight. The steps were carved out of the sandstone rock. They looked so much like a natural part of the cliff. They were hidden in plain sight. Many people had probably passed by here and never noticed them, hiding in the open. The stairway was covered with small rocks, stones, and rubble. It was not obvious they were steps, and without Eddie we would have walked by them.

The steps were about three feet wide. Each one was at least twenty inches high, which forced us to climb one step at a time. You had to put your right foot up and then the left one. Moving one leg at a time was very slow-going and strenuous. The stairs seemed to be carved out for giants. They were almost vertical, with a seventy-degree angle, winding back and forth like a snake every ten or twenty steps. Because of the sharp switchbacks, it always appeared that the stairs ended at the point of a sharp turn. The rocks all looked the same, so it fooled your depth perception, which made me feel dizzy.

Baldwin and Pete had taken the point in case someone was waiting at the top. Eddie was behind them, then me, Adam, and Maggie. The rest of the Warriors followed behind. Finally, after almost an hour, we reached the top. As I climbed up the last step, I fell to the ground on a large ledge, gasping for air. Everyone else did also, except for Eddie.

Looking up, I saw the stone cliff continued up, but I couldn't see where it stopped. I surmised it went straight up, at least another 500 feet.

Then I noted Eddie was standing next to a body. I saw a white cowboy hat on the ground and Stephen, Eddie's friend, was next to it. I went to check him out. He had been shot in the face. "You were right, Jack. They are bad men. Stephen never hurt anyone," Eddie said, with a tear in his eye, as he gazed at his dead buddy.

I put my hand on his shoulder. "Don't worry, Eddie, we'll get the guys who did this. Maybe they're still here."

Pete and Baldwin stood guard, watching both sides of the ledge we were on, while the rest of us, following Eddie's lead piled rocks on top of the body. It was Eddie's way to bury his friend, because we could never carry him off the mountain.

Once we were finished, Baldwin asked, "Eddie, which way do we go?"

Eddie pointed west. "Go around the point. After rounding it, the cave is directly to your left, in a corner."

We were standing on a ledge about fifty feet wide. Looking east, the ledge seemed to disappear into nothing, after an estimated 100 feet. Looking to the west, the ledge narrowed to a few feet and went around a bend along a sheer cliff. You could see how it curved around, a little, but you couldn't see what was on the other side.

Baldwin took the lead and moved forward disappearing around the bend with Pete closely behind him. They had to be careful because it was a 500-foot drop off the narrow ledge. I was next in line, and as I came around the bend, hugging close to the cliff wall, I didn't dare look down for fear of falling. I expected to hear gunfire, but there was none. Rounding the point put me in front of the cave, which was back in the corner about 50 feet away from the edge of the cliff, which we had just climbed.

Right away I saw them, just outside the cave entrance. Four dead bodies were scattered near the entrance and they had been burned. Not just burned, but charred to the bone, similar to when the Sword of Jerusalem zapped the old Templars who had tried to steal it from Adam.

Their clothes were not burned; only the heads and bodies were charred. All that was left was a burned up skeleton. You would never be able to tell who they were. It took an intense, strange type of heat to do this kind of damage to the human body. It was the 'Fire of God' which burned up the flesh, but not the clothing.

I gave the all clear for everyone else to come around the bend. Adam was next to come around. Seeing the charred skeletons he said, "That looks just like the sword did it."

"Yes, that's exactly what I thought."

George said, "It looks like they found God."

I grabbed Adam's shoulders and turned him to face the entrance of the cave. I pointed and said, "Look, the Hooked X. We made it!" The X was carved above the entrance. It was about a foot high and clearly visible.

George said, "We didn't make it yet. Someone has to go inside and check it out."

It was hot and I guessed the temperature was near a hundred degrees. A breeze was blowing and an occasional strong gust of wind blew up. I looked up at the sky, made the sign of the cross, and said to myself, 'Thank you, God.'

Baldwin went to the cave entrance, shinned his flashlight inside, and said, "A wall of rocks is blocking off part of the entrance, but we can still get by them." He slowly proceeded inside.

I noted that outside, near the entrance, was a pile of large rocks. I wondered why they were there?

Adam and I followed Baldwin, while everyone else remained behind. The entrance was just wide enough to allow us to pass. We squeezed by the stone wall blocking the entrance. This explained the big pile of rocks outside. The entrance had been sealed up. The nomads had removed just enough of the large stones to make a small passageway. It must have taken them hours to do so since the wall of stone, blocking the entrance, was eight feet thick. Each stone probably weighed fifty to a hundred pounds.

I shined my light on the walls. I said, "Look, those are Egyptian hieroglyphics."

"Yeah, that's amazing," Adam said. "That proves the Egyptians were here also."

"Yes, the Templars must have used the same cave as the Egyptians."

Passing by the blockage, we found three more charred bodies. We shined our lights down the tunnel, which was about ten feet wide, seven feet high and thirty feet long. The tunnel appeared to make a sharp turn to the right.

The cave smelled of burned flesh, which almost made Adam vomit. The air had a faint haze of smoke still lingering. I noticed what seemed to be a faint glow coming from the far end of the tunnel, where it turned.

I said, "Turn off your lights." Baldwin and Adam complied. "Look, the cave is glowing, down there where turns." It was a very faint yellow light that looked like a lantern. We slowly advanced to the turn, not knowing what to expect, with our weapons at the ready.

Reaching the bend, Baldwin got down on one knee and peeked around the corner. He pulled back and glanced up at me. I whispered, "What do you see?"

He softly said, "Take a look."

I peered around the corner. The cave opened up into a large chamber that was most likely 100 feet long and 50 feet wide. The whole room was glowing. It was basked in a faint yellow light which seemed to be radiating from the walls.

As I stepped back, Adam asked, "What's there? What's making that light?

I said, "You won't believe it." I stepped around the corner with Adam, as Baldwin followed.

Adam uttered. "Lucem Sanctam."

I knew that was Latin, but I didn't know the meaning. Adam was pretty fluent in Latin because he was taught by his real Grandfather, Jack de Molay. The clues etched in the Sword of Jerusalem were all written in Latin. At one time Latin was one of the main languages.

I asked him, "What does that mean?"

"Holy Light. It's God's Holy Light."

The three of us stood there, dumbfounded at what we observed. Slowly, we advanced toward the light. Maybe it was more similar to that of firefly, twinkling bright and then diming. Sparkling on and off in a uniform rhythm.

The yellow light was slightly pulsating, becoming brighter then dimmer every few seconds. It reminded me of a heart beating.

As we approached the end of the cavern, Adam said, "Nothing is here. What happened to the Ark and treasure?"

Nothing was in the cavern but the glowing yellow light, and a solid stone pedestal which was about five feet high, eight feet long, and eight feet wide. There was nothing fancy about the pedestal, other than it was also glowing yellow. It appeared to be just a smooth large block of stone.

Over in the corner, behind the pedestal, we found three more charred bodies. That accounted for all the nomads that came here.

Adam commented, "I think the Ark was probably sitting on this pedestal," as he rubbed his hand across it.

I said, "Yeah, it probably was. But nothing is here now except for these burned bodies. What the hell happened to the Ark?"

Baldwin commented, "Furthermore, what's causing the room and pedestal to give off this weird yellow light."

"Search around the cave for a hidden door or opening somewhere."

We spread out and began searching, touching the walls and floor, feeling for anything unusual. After thirty minutes or so, Baldwin said, "There's nothing."

I examined the pedestal very carefully. I looked for seams, buttons, levers, or anything that would give an indication that it could be opened. It seemed to be one solid piece of stone with no hidden openings. Satisfied it was just a solid block of stone, I said, "How could the Ark disappear into thin air?"

"Look what I found," Adam said. He walked over to us holding something small. It was about the size of a baseball.

"What is it?" I asked, as Baldwin and I moved closer to him.

"It's a golden bird."

Adam handed the bird to me and I knew right way what it was. It was heavy which indicated that it was made of solid gold. I passed it to Baldwin and he said, "Well this proves that some type of treasure was here."

I said, "This is the falcon Horus, an ancient god of the Egyptians."

"Yeah, I think you're right, Grandpa," Adam replied. "But why would this be here?" Baldwin handed the bird back to Adam who stuck it in his backpack.

"Maybe it was part of the treasure the Knights Templar brought here. Maybe it was part of an Egyptian treasure."

"Part of what treasure? If there was one, what happened to it?" Baldwin asked.

"Maybe someone took it. Someone worthy in God's eyes, whom he would let touch it. Maybe God took it to keep the nomads from stealing it."

Adam said, "Then why did God tell me in a dream to come here with the Sword of Jerusalem?"

"I don't know, Adam. I just don't know. The only thing I do know is that God works in mysterious ways."

Let's look around the cave some more," Baldwin said.

"Yeah, let's really check this cave out," I said.

We had the whole crew come in the cave to search, except for Eddie. After searching for another hour, we found a small golden disk with the Constellation of Orion engraved in it. It was clearly an Egyptian artifact. I stuck it in my pack for safe keeping. That was all we found.

I concluded that the yellow glow was being emitted by some type of bioluminescence in the stone. The yellow light was similar to the color of gold. It was a mystery for sure.

Disappointed, we went outside and sat on the ledge. We had some lunch and no one spoke as we refueled for the trip back down into the abyss.

My brain was racing. What happened to the Ark and treasure? We know it was here at one point in time. We found two artifacts proving that a treasure was here. How could it disappear into thin air? Maybe God did take the Ark out of the cave.

Then it occurred to me that if anyone took the treasure, it had to be after the nomads came here because of the charred bodies. So that would have happened right before we came here. If someone else was here, then why didn't we see anyone in the canyon? Why weren't they burned up by God's Fire?

My brain had all kinds of questions. Is the Ark still in the cave hidden somewhere? Did some people take the Ark and treasure? Did God take the Ark and treasure to keep it from man? What really caused the cave walls to be basked in a dim yellow light? We knew that a treasure was there, at one time, because we found two artifacts. Where is the rest of the treasure?

We may never know for sure what really happened. But I was not going to give up. We came all this way and I wasn't going to leave the Grand Canyon without an answer to these important questions. I had to solve this mystery, even if it killed me.

I sat there thinking about this weird mystery. I thought, *why were the nomads burned by the Fire of God if the Ark was not here? I concluded that since the nomads were killed by the Fire of God, then the Ark and treasure still had to be in the cave. Yes that's it! The Ark is still somewhere in the cave.*

After racking my brain for a few minutes, I asked Adam, "What did God exactly tell you, in that dream?"

"He told me to go into the cave and bring the Sword of Jerusalem to prove that I was the Keeper of the holy sword."

"Well, you had the sword but it was in its scabbard." After thinking about this for a while, I asked, "To prove you are the Keeper of the sword, wouldn't you have to show the blade to God? Wouldn't you have to pull it out of the scabbard to release its power?"

Adam thought for a minute. "Yeah, you're right because unless it's out of the scabbard the sword won't react to anything. That's a great point. What's your idea?"

I said, "You and I go back in the cave alone, because we're the only ones that have survived contact with the sword." I looked at Captain Baldwin. "George you stay here." He nodded.

"Ok, let's go, Grandpa."

As we walked back into the cavern, I had a plan. "Adam, when we are in front of the glowing pedestal, draw the sword and point it in the air."

"What do you think will happen?"

"I don't know for sure. Maybe the Ark and treasure will be revealed to us, or maybe not. We might even meet God or he could speak to us. The worst that could happen is God kills us, like the others."

"Why would he kill us? We believe in him."

"Like I said before, God works in mysterious ways."

We slowly approached the large pedestal. It was still glowing with the dim yellow light, as were the walls. Stopping in front of the large solid stone, I took hold of Adam's left hand, and gently squeezed it.

I asked him, "Are you ready?"

"Yes Sir, I am ready."

"Ok, draw the sword." I watched Adam's right hand wrap around the sword grip, as he pulled it out. He pointed it straight in the air and the sword started to give off the same yellow light. The yellow glow started changing to a white glow.

Something was happening, the yellow glowing pedestal changed to a white glowing light. Then unexpectedly, the top of the pedestal groaned. It startled us and we stepped back a little. Slowly it began to slide to one side, inch by inch, scraping along. I couldn't believe what I was seeing. It stopped when it was fully opened. Suddenly a bright blinding beam of white light shot straight up from inside the pedestal.

We were frozen in place watching the Ark of the Covenant rise ever so slowly from inside the pedestal, floating on layer of air. The Ark stopped moving when it was fully revealed and hovered there, with nothing supporting it. I was speechless. It was a beautiful glowing golden relic which you knew contained God's power. It's appearance was almost identical to the pictures I had seen in many books. I was astonished and mesmerized by its beauty.

Adam and I dropped to our knees showing respect for God. My eyes were glued to the Ark when I heard Adam speak. "Ok, I understand."

I glanced at him and asked, "What do you understand?" He didn't reply to me.

I could tell by his face that Adam was in another world. He was conversing with God. But I didn't hear God's voice at all. All I heard was a soft buzzing noise, similar to that of an electric current humming, emanating from the Ark.

Adam, staring wide-eyed at the Ark, said, "Yes, my Lord. We will obey, and keep your secret until the time is right." His conversation was over in a few seconds.

At a blazing speed, the Ark plunged back inside the pedestal. The large stone lid swiftly slammed back into place, with a thunderous boom, sealing the stone chamber.

The Ark was gone and so was the white light. The room and pedestal was once again bathed in a soft yellow glow, pulsating like a beating heart. I thought, *maybe it was duplicating the heartbeat of God.*

The sword stopped glowing as Adam put it back into the scabbard. I asked, "What did God say?"

"We must keep this place a secret and tell no one that we found the Ark. Not even our Templar Warriors. When the time is right, God will call on us again."

"When the time is right for what?"

Adam touched my arm. "Someday I will tell you, Grandfather. For now, we made a promise to God not to reveal where the Ark is hidden."

"Don't worry about me Adam. I still can't believe I saw the Ark. It's incredible ... simply incredible."

Adam replied, "Yes, it is," as he held my hand. "It's like a dream."

I took a quick look at the top of the pedestal. I couldn't see any seams or indications that there was a lid or that the pedestal had been opened. It was once again a solid block of stone.

As we slowly walked outside, Baldwin asked me, "Did you find the Ark?"

I shook my head and tried to appear disappointed. "No, George, we didn't. Let's go home before it gets dark. I had enough excitement for the day. I'm too old for this shit." By the look on his face, I didn't think Baldwin believed me.

Eddie said, "See, I told you there was no treasure." I didn't reply to his comment because we did find two relics, and the remaining treasure was probably hidden inside the pedestal.

My hands were still shaking after seeing the ancient instrument of God. It had been missing since 586 BC, more than 2,600 years. There was only one reason God let us find the Ark and that was because Adam was the Keeper of the Sword of Jerusalem. We had followed the clues etched in the blade to the Ark's location.

I wondered, *why would God choose a sinner like me to do his bidding? What does God have planned for us? Then I realized that maybe even God needs ruthless, but loyal men to cull the herd.*

*Signing off for now,*

*GOD BLESS AMERICA, LAND OF THE FREE, and HOME OF THE BRAVE!*

*Jack Gunn, a.k.a. Tocabaga Jack*

*If you have any idea what is going to happen next.* Email me at: THOMASHWARDBOOKS@GMAIL.COM.

I WILL REPLY.

# DRAMATIS PERSONAE
# LUCEM SANCTAM

**Adam de Molay** – A future Knights Templar leader. Sent to Jack Gunn, by God.

**Black Horse** – Medicine man for the Comanche Nation and father of Billy Bob.

**Billy Bob** – Lost son of Black Horse who lived in Indianola Mississippi.

**Canfield** – A Templar of the old order, who wanted to steal the Sword of Jerusalem.

**Captain George Baldwin** – A Templar Warrior commander, of the new order.

**Captain Sessions** – Combat officer, commands and controls combat operations in the field. Based at Tocabaga, Fort Desoto.

**Charlie Wilson** – Owner of the Dilkon City goods store on the Navajo Reservation.

**Christian de Molay** – Adam de Molay's uncle. A self-proclaimed Grand Master.

**Dan** – Navajo Police Captain.

**Eddie Moon** – A Havasupai Indian who helped find the treasure.

**Ed Seibert** – Police Chief of Flagstaff.

**Jeff** – Third in command of the new Templar Warriors.

**Jimmy Two Times** – A Navajo Indian school guard on the reservation.

**Maggie** – Amazon Warrior from Tocabaga.

**Pablo** – A bandit nomad that Maggie killed for kidnapping Adam.

**Pete** – Second in command, of the new Templar order.

**Quanah Iron Coat** – Chief of the Comanche Nation.

**Ragsdale** – A bad guy in Indianola, who runs a whore house. He claimed to be Billy Bob's father.

**Sergeant Smith** – A county Sheriff in Arizona.

**Stevens** – Police Officer in Flagstaff.

**White Feather** – A nomad bandit who claimed to be half Hopi Indian.

# APPENDIX A

## PICTURES

Isis Temple in Background

The Grand Canyon

Trails in the Canyon

Wupakti Ruins

Arizona Butte

Sunset Crater Volcano

# APPENDIX B
## REFERENCES

https://www.google.com/?gws_rd=ssl#q=isis+temple+treasure+grand+canyon&start=10

https://en.wikipedia.org/wiki/Isis_Temple

https://en.wikipedia.org/wiki/List_of_trails_in_Grand_Canyon_National_Park

http://www.onelight.com/hec/targets/grandcanyon/TempleofIsisintheGrandCanyon.pdf

http://www.cyberspaceorbit.com/0000tx09x.html

https://fourthdimensionalrecovery.wordpress.com/2013/03/12/proof-that-pyramids-exist-in-the-grand-canyon/

https://tjcoop3.wordpress.com/discovery-of-vast-prehistoric-works-built-by-giants/ancient-egyptian-treasures-in-the-grand-canyon/

http://www.nps.gov/grca/planyourvisit/havasupai.htm

http://www.americansouthwest.net/arizona/grand_canyon/havasu_canyon.html

http://www.spiritofmaat.com/Arkhive/nov2/gcegypt.htm

http://Arkhive.azcentral.com/arizonarepublic/viewpoints/articles/20111108grand-canyon-mystery.html

http://scribol.com/anthropology-and-history/did-the-ancient-egyptians-inhabit-the-grand-canyon

http://loveforlife.com.au/content/10/02/27/grand-canyon-finds-ancient-egyptian-treasures-grand-canyon-Arkheological-informatio

https://www.youtube.com/watch?v=VgsAunSO2E0

http://www.thelifeofadventure.com/the-aztec-treasure-cavern/

https://www.youtube.com/watch?v=WqsgpOVHBbM

http://www.nps.gov/pefo/index.htm

http://www.jewishencyclopedia.com/articles/1777-ark-of-the-covenant

https://en.wikipedia.org/wiki/Ark_of_the_Covenant

https://www.youtube.com/watch?v=G7Cf-hxz180

# ABOUT THE AUTHOR

Thomas H. Ward is a best-selling author of suspense thriller fiction and nonfiction works. He is best known for his ten-book series Tocabaga, and Templars Quest a three-book series, Critical Incidents, and Gun Talk, a nonfiction book about terrorism in the United States.

## Education and Experience

Born in Chicago in 1946 and raised in Cleveland he now resides in Tampa Florida. Ward, prior to becoming an Author, was a Metallurgical Engineer and Business Owner. He obtained an MBA in International Business. Having traveled extensively to thirteen different countries his favorite ones are China, Japan, and South Korea where he was based for a period of time. He has made 150 trips to Asian and Europe over a 20 year time period, becoming conversant in three different languages. Thomas is a student of World History and the Bible.

In his younger days, during the Cold War and Vietnam War, he was employed by a government subcontractor which required a Department of Defense (DOD) Secret Clearance and Atomic Energy Commission (AEC) Classified Clearance. Over the years he became an expert in security operations and the use of small arms.

He started writing technical manuals and business books years ago. Thomas turned to writing fictional stories when his publisher suggested he do so. "Thomas always had great stories to tell. His experience, travels, and imagination are a bonus for a fiction writer." Ward always places in his books the following quote which he composed:

*"In every truth there is non-truth;*
*in every fiction there is non-fiction."*

**—Thomas H. Ward**

**To Contact the Author:**

Visit Goodreads:

www.goodreads.com/author/
show/1803626.Thomas_H_Ward

Or by email:
THOMASHWARDBOOKS@GMAIL.COM.